W9-CFT-221

The Forsyte Saga

IN CHANCERY

The Forsyte Saga

IN CHANCERY

"Two households both alike in dignity . . .
From ancient grudge break to new mutiny."
—*Romeo and Juliet*

John Galsworthy

BOOK-OF-THE-MONTH CLUB
NEW YORK

AUTHOR'S NOTE

In Chancery is sequel to *The Man of Property* and to *Indian Summer of a Forsyte*, and continues *The Forsyte Saga*.

—J. G.

CONTENTS

PART I

CONTENTS

PART III

PART I

IN CHANCERY

CHAPTER I

AT TIMOTHY'S

THE possessive instinct never stands still. Through florescence and feud, frosts and fires, it followed the laws of progression even in the Forsyte family which had believed it fixed for ever. Nor can it be dissociated from environment any more than the quality of potato from the soil.

The historian of the English eighties and nineties will, in his good time, depict the somewhat rapid progression from self-contented and contained provincialism to still more self-contented if less contained imperialism — in other words, the ' possessive ' instinct of the nation on the move. And so, as if in conformity, was it with the Forsyte family. They were spreading not merely on the surface, but within.

When, in 1895, Susan Hayman, the married Forsyte sister, followed her husband at the ludicrously low age of seventy-four, and was cremated, it made strangely little stir among the six old Forsytes left. For this apathy there were three causes. First: the almost surreptitious burial of old Jolyon in 1892 down at Robin Hill — first of the Forsytes to desert the family grave at Highgate. That burial, coming

3

a year after Swithin's entirely proper funeral, had
occasioned a great deal of talk on Forsyte's 'Change,
the abode of Timothy Forsyte on the Bayswater
Road, London, which still collected and radiated
family gossip. Opinions ranged from the lamenta-
tion of Aunt Juley to the outspoken assertion of
Francie that it was ' a jolly good thing to stop all
that stuffy Highgate business.' Uncle Jolyon in his
later years — indeed, ever since the strange and
lamentable affair between his granddaughter June's
lover, young Bosinney, and Irene, his nephew Soames
Forsyte's wife — had noticeably rapped the family's
knuckles; and that way of his own which he had
always taken had begun to seem to them a little way-
ward. The philosophic vein in him, of course, had
always been too liable to crop out of the strata of
pure Forsyteism, so they were in a way prepared for
his interment in a strange spot. But the whole thing
was an odd business, and when the contents of his
Will became current coin on Forsyte 'Change, a
shiver had gone round the clan. Out of his estate
(£145,304 gross, with liabilities £35 7s. 4d.) he had
actually left £15,000 to ' whomever do you think,
my dear? To *Irene!*' that runaway wife of his
nephew Soames; Irene, a woman who had almost
disgraced the family, and — still more amazing —
was to him no blood relation. Not out and out, of
course; only a life interest — only the income from
it! Still, there it was; and old Jolyon's claim to be
the perfect Forsyte was ended once for all. That,
then, was the first reason why the burial of Susan
Hayman — at Woking — made little stir.

The second reason was altogether more expansive
and imperial. Besides the house on Campden Hill,
Susan had a place (left her by Hayman when he

died) just over the border in Hants, where the Hayman boys had learned to be such good shots and riders, as it was believed, which was of course nice for them and creditable to everybody; and the fact of owning something really countrified seemed somehow to excuse the dispersion of her remains — though what could have put cremation into her head they could not think! The usual invitations, however, had been issued, and Soames had gone down and young Nicholas, and the Will had been quite satisfactory so far as it went, for she had only had a life interest; and everything had gone quite smoothly to the children in equal shares.

The third reason why Susan's burial made little stir was the most expansive of all. It was summed up daringly by Euphemia, the pale, the thin: " Well, *I* think people have a right to their own bodies, even when they're dead." Coming from a daughter of Nicholas, a Liberal of the old school and most tyrannical, it was a startling remark — showing in a flash what a lot of water had run under the bridges since the death of Aunt Ann, just when the proprietorship of Soames over his wife's body was acquiring the uncertainty which had led to such disaster. Euphemia, of course, spoke like a child, and had no experience; for though well over thirty by now, her name was still Forsyte. But, making all allowances, her remark did undoubtedly show expansion of the principle of liberty, decentralisation and shift in the central point of possession from others to oneself. When Nicholas heard his daughter's remark from Aunt Hester he had rapped out: "Wives and daughters! There's no end to their liberty in these days. I knew that ' Jackson ' case would lead to things — lugging in Habeas Corpus like that!"

He had, of course, never really forgiven the Married Woman's Property Act, which would so have interfered with him if he had not mercifully married before it was passed. But, in truth, there was no denying the revolt among the younger Forsytes against being owned by others; that, as it were, Colonial disposition to own oneself, which is the paradoxical forerunner of Imperialism, was making progress all the time. They were all now married, except George, confirmed to the Turf and the Iseeum Club; Francie, pursuing her musical career in a studio off the King's Road, Chelsea, and still taking 'lovers' to dances; Euphemia, living at home and complaining of Nicholas; and those two Dromios, Giles and Jesse Hayman. Of the third generation there were not very many — young Jolyon had three, Winifred Dartie four, young Nicholas six already, young Roger had one, Marian Tweetyman one; St. John Hayman two. But the rest of the sixteen married — Soames, Rachel and Cicely of James's family; Eustace and Thomas of Roger's; Ernest, Archibald and Florence of Nicholas's; Augustus and Annabel Spender of the Hayman's — were going down the years unreproduced.

Thus, of the ten old Forsytes twenty-one young Forsytes had been born; but of the twenty-one young Forsytes there were as yet only seventeen descendants; and it already seemed unlikely that there would be more than a further unconsidered trifle or so. A student of statistics must have noticed that the birth rate had varied in accordance with the rate of interest for your money. Grandfather ' Superior Dosset ' Forsyte in the early nineteenth century had been getting ten per cent. for his, hence ten children. Those ten, leaving out the

four who had not married, and Juley, whose husband Septimus Small had, of course, died almost at
once, had averaged from four to five per cent. for
theirs, and produced accordingly. The twenty-one
whom they produced were now getting barely three
per cent. in the Consols to which their fathers had
mostly tied the Settlements they made to avoid death
duties, and the six of them who had been reproduced
had seventeen children, or just the proper two and
five-sixths per stem.

There were other reasons, too, for this mild re-
production. A distrust of their earning powers,
natural where a sufficiency is guaranteed, together
with the knowledge that their fathers did not die,
kept them cautious. If one had children and not
much income, the standard of taste and comfort
must of necessity go down; what was enough for
two was not enough for four, and so on — it would
be better to wait and see what Father did. Besides,
it was nice to be able to take holidays unhampered.
Sooner in fact than own children, they preferred to
concentrate on the ownership of themselves, conforming to the growing tendency — *fin de siècle,*
as it was called. In this way, little risk was run,
and one would be able to have a motor-car. Indeed,
Eustace already had one, but it had shaken him hor-
ribly, and broken one of his eye teeth; so that it
would be better to wait till they were a little safer.
In the meantime, no more children! Even young
Nicholas was drawing in his horns, and had made no
addition to his six for quite three years.

The corporate decay, however, of the Forsytes,
their dispersion rather, of which all this was symp-
tomatic, had not advanced so far as to prevent a
rally when Roger Forsyte died in 1899. It had been

a glorious summer, and after holidays abroad and at the sea they were practically all back in London, when Roger with a touch of his old originality had suddenly breathed his last at his own house in Princes Gardens. At Timothy's it was whispered sadly that poor Roger had always been eccentric about his digestion — had he not, for instance, preferred German mutton to all the other brands?

Be that as it may, his funeral at Highgate had been perfect, and coming away from it Soames Forsyte made almost mechanically for his Uncle Timothy's in the Bayswater Road. The 'Old Things' —Aunt Juley and Aunt Hester — would like to hear about it. His father —James — at eighty-eight had not felt up to the fatigue of the funeral; and Timothy himself, of course, had not gone; so that Nicholas had been the only brother present. Still, there had been a fair gathering; and it would cheer Aunts Juley and Hester up to know. The kindly thought was not unmixed with the inevitable longing to get something out of everything you do, which is the chief characteristic of the Forsytes, and indeed of the saner elements in every nation. In this practice of taking family matters to Timothy's in the Bayswater Road, Soames was but following in the footsteps of his father, who had been in the habit of going at least once a week to see his sisters at Timothy's and had only given it up when he lost his nerve at eighty-six, and could not go out without Emily. To go with Emily was of no use, for who could really talk to anyone in the presence of his own wife? Like James in the old days, Soames found time to go there nearly every Sunday, and sit in the little drawing-room into which, with his undoubted taste, he had intro-

duced a good deal of change and china not quite
up to his own fastidious mark, and at least two
rather doubtful Barbizon pictures, at Christmas-
tides. He himself, who had done extremely well
with the Barbizons, had for some years past moved
towards the Marises, Israels, and Mauve, and was
hoping to do better. In the riverside house which
he now inhabited near Mapledurham he had a gallery, beautifully hung and lighted, to which few
London dealers were strangers. It served, too, as
a Sunday afternoon attraction in those week-end
parties which his sisters, Winifred or Rachel, occa-
sionally organized for him. For though he was
but a taciturn showman, his quiet collected deter-
minism seldom failed to influence his guests, who
knew that his reputation was grounded not on mere
æsthetic fancy, but on his power of gauging the
future of market values. When he went to Timothy's he almost always had some little tale of triumph over a dealer to unfold, and dearly he loved
that coo of pride with which his Aunts would greet
it. This afternoon, however, he was differently ani-
mated, coming from Roger's funeral in his neat
dark clothes — not quite black, for after all an
uncle was but an uncle, and his soul abhorred ex-
cessive display of feeling. Leaning back in a marqueterie chair and gazing down his uplifted nose at
the sky-blue walls plastered with gold frames, he
was noticeably silent. Whether because he had
been to a funeral or not, the peculiar Forsyte build
of his face was seen to the best advantage this afternoon — a face concave and long, with a jaw which
divested of flesh would have seemed extravagant:
altogether a chinny face, though not at all ill-look-
ing. He was feeling more strongly than ever that

Timothy's was hopelessly ' rum-ti-too,' and the souls
of his aunts dismally mid-Victorian. The subject
on which alone he wanted to talk — his own undivorced position — was unspeakable. And yet it
occupied his mind to the exclusion of all else. It was
only since the Spring that this had been so, and a
new feeling grown up which was egging him
on towards what he knew might well be folly in a
Forsyte of forty-five. More and more of late he
had been conscious that he was ' getting on.' The
fortune, already considerable when he conceived the
house at Robin Hill which had finally wrecked his
marriage with Irene, had mounted with surprising
vigor in the twelve lonely years during which he
had devoted himself to little else. He was worth
to-day well over a hundred thousand pounds, and
had no one to leave it to — no real object for going
on with what was his religion. Even if he were to
relax his efforts, money made money, and he felt
that he would have a hundred and fifty thousand
before he knew where he was. There had always
been a strongly domestic, philoprogenitive side to
Soames; baulked and frustrated, it had hidden itself
away, but now had crept out again in this his ' prime
of life.' Concreted and focussed of late by the attraction of a girl's undoubted beauty, it had become
a veritable prepossession.

And this girl was French, not likely to lose her
head, or accept any unlegalised position. Moreover,
Soames himself disliked the thought of that. He
had tasted of the sordid side of sex during those
long years of forced celibacy, secretively, and always with disgust, for he was fastidious, and his
sense of law and order innate. He wanted no hole
and corner liaison. A marriage at the Embassy in

Paris, a few months' travel, and he could bring Annette back quite separated from a past which in truth was not too distinguished, for she only kept the accounts in her mother's Soho Restaurant; he could bring her back as something very new and chic with her French taste and self-possession, to reign at ' The Shelter ' near Mapledurham. On Forsyte 'Change and among his riverside friends it would be current that he had met a charming French girl on his travels and married her. There would be the flavour of romance, and a certain *cachet* about a French wife. No! He was not at all afraid of that; it was only this cursed undivorced condition of his, and — and the question whether Annette would take him, which he dared not put to the touch until he had a clear and even dazzling future to offer her.

In his aunts' drawing-room he heard with but muffled ears those usual questions: How was his dear father? Not going out, of course, now that the weather was turning chilly? Would Soames be sure to tell him that Hester had found boiled holly leaves most comforting for that pain in her side; a poultice every three hours, with red flannel afterwards? And could he relish just a little pot of their very best prune preserve — it was so delicious this year, and had such a wonderful effect? Oh! and about the Darties — *had* Soames heard that dear Winifred was having a most distressing time with Montagu? Timothy thought she really ought to have protection. It was said — but Soames mustn't take this for certain — that he had given some of Winifred's jewellery to a dreadful dancer. It was such a bad example for dear Val just as he was going to college. Soames had not heard? Oh, but

he must go and see his sister and look into it at
once! And did he think these Boers were really
going to resist? Timothy was in quite a stew about
it. The price of Consols was so high, and he had
such a lot of money in them. Did Soames think they
must go down if there was a war? Soames nodded.
But it would be over very quickly. It would be so
bad for Timothy if it wasn't. And of course
Soames' dear father would feel it very much at his
age. Luckily poor dear Roger had been spared this
dreadful anxiety. And Aunt Juley with a little
handkerchief wiped away the large tear trying to
climb the permanent pout on her now quite withered
left cheek; she was remembering dear Roger, and
all his originality, and how he used to stick pins
into her when they were little together. Aunt Hester, with her instinct for avoiding the unpleasant,
here chimed in: Did Soames think they would make
Mr. Chamberlain Prime Minister at once? He
would settle it all so quickly. She would like to see
that old Kruger sent to St. Helena. She could remember so well the news of Napoleon's death, and
what a relief it had been to his grandfather. Of
course she and Juley — "We were in pantalettes
then, my dear" — had not felt it much at the time.

Soames took a cup of tea from her, drank it
quickly, and ate three of those macaroons for which
Timothy's was famous. His faint, pale, supercilious smile had deepened just a little. Really, his
family remained hopelessly provincial, however
much of London they might possess between them.
In these go-ahead days their provincialism stared
out even more than it used to. Why, old Nicholas
was still a Free Trader, and a member of that ante-
diluvian home of Liberalism, the Remove Club —

though, to be sure, the members were pretty well all Conservative now, or he himself could not have joined; and Timothy, they said, still wore a night-cap. Aunt Juley spoke again. Dear Soames was looking so well, hardly a day older than he did when dear Ann died, and they were all there together, dear Jolyon, and dear Swithin, and dear Roger. She paused and caught the tear which had climbed the pout on her right cheek. Did he — did he ever hear anything of Irene nowadays? Aunt Hester visibly interposed her shoulder. Really, Juley was always saying something! The smile left Soames' face, and he put his cup down. Here was his subject broached for him, and for all his desire to expand, he could not take advantage.

Aunt Juley went on rather hastily:

"They say dear Jolyon first left her that fifteen thousand out and out; then of course he saw it would not be right, and made it for her life only."

Had Soames heard that?

Soames nodded.

"Your Cousin Jolyon is a widower now. He is her trustee; you knew that, of course?"

Soames shook his head. He did know, but wished to show no interest. Young Jolyon and he had not met since the day of Bosinney's death.

"He must be quite middle-aged by now," went on Aunt Juley dreamily. "Let me see, he was born when your dear uncle lived in Mount Street; long before they went to Stanhope Gate — in December '48, the year of the Commune. He must be fifty! Fancy that! Such a pretty baby, and we were all so proud of him; the very first of you all." Aunt Juley sighed, and a lock of not quite her own hair came loose and straggled, so that Aunt Hester gave a little shiver. Soames rose, he was experiencing a curious piece of self-discovery. That old wound to his pride and self-esteem was not yet closed. He had come thinking he could talk of it, even wanting to talk of his fettered condition, and — behold! he was shrinking away from this reminder by Aunt Juley, renowned for her Malapropisms.

Oh, Soames was not going already!

Soames smiled a little vindictively, and said:

"Yes. Good-bye. Remember me to Uncle Timothy!" And, leaving a cold kiss on each forehead, whose wrinkles seemed to try and cling to his lips as if longing to be kissed away, he left them looking brightly after him — dear Soames, it had been so good of him to come to-day, when they were not feeling very——!

With compunction tweaking at his chest Soames descended the stairs, where was always that rather pleasant smell of camphor and port wine, and house where draughts are not permitted. The poor old things — he had not meant to be unkind! And in the street he instantly forgot them, repossessed by the image of Annette and the thought of the cursed coil around him. Why had he not pushed the thing through and obtained divorce when that wretched Bosinney was run over, and there was evidence galore for the asking! And he turned towards his sister Winifred Dartie's residence in Green Street, Mayfair.

CHAPTER II

THAT a man of the world so subject to the vicissi-
tudes of fortune as Montagu Dartie should still be
living in a house he had inhabited twenty years at
least would have been more noticeable if the rent,
rates, taxes, and repairs of that house had not been
defrayed by his father-in-law. By that simple if
wholesale device James Forsyte had secured a certain stability in the lives of his daughter and his
grandchildren. After all, there is something in-
valuable about a safe roof over the head of a sportsman so dashing as Dartie. Until the events of the
last few days he had been almost supernaturally
steady all this year. The fact was he had acquired
a half share in a filly of George Forsyte's, who had
gone irreparably on the turf, to the horror of Roger,
now stilled by the grave. Sleeve-links, by Martyr,
out of Shirt-on-fire, by Suspender, was a bay filly,
three years old, who for a variety of reasons had
never shown her true form. With half ownership
of this hopeful animal, all the idealism latent somewhere in Dartie, as in every other man, had put up
its head, and kept him quietly ardent for months
past. When a man has something good to live for
it is astonishing how sober he becomes; and what
Dartie had was really good — a three to one chance

for an autumn handicap, publicly assessed at twenty-five to one. The old-fashioned heaven was a poor thing beside it, and his shirt was on the daughter of Shirt-on-fire. But how much more than his shirt depended on this granddaughter of Suspender! At that roving age of forty-five, trying to Forsytes — and, though perhaps less distinguishable from any other age, trying even to Darties — Montagu had fixed his current fancy on a dancer. It was no mean passion, but without money, and a good deal of it, likely to remain a love as airy as her skirts; and Dartie never had any money, subsisting miserably on what he could beg or borrow from Winifred — a woman of character, who kept him because he was the father of her children, and from a lingering admiration for those now-dying Wardour Street good looks which in their youth had fascinated her. She, together with anyone else who would lend him anything, and his losses at cards and on the turf, (extraordinary how some men make a good thing out of losses), were his whole means of subsistence; for James was now too old and nervous to approach, and Soames too formidably adamant. It is not too much to say that Dartie had been living on hope for months. He had never been fond of money for itself, had always despised the Forsytes with their investing habits, though careful to make such use of them as he could. What he liked about money was what it bought — personal sensation.

" No real sportsman cares for money," he would say, borrowing a ' pony ' if it was no use trying for a ' monkey.' There was something delicious about Montagu Dartie. He was, as George Forsyte said, a ' daisy.'

The morning of the Handicap dawned clear and bright, the last day of September, and Dartie, who had travelled to Newmarket the night before, arrayed himself in spotless checks and walked to an eminence to see his half of the filly take her final canter. If she won he would be a cool three thou. in pocket — a poor enough recompense for the sobriety and patience of these weeks of hope, while they had been nursing her for this race. But he had not been able to afford more. Should he 'lay it off' at the eight to one to which she had advanced? This was his single thought while the larks sang above him, and the grassy downs smelled sweet, and the pretty filly passed, tossing her head and glowing like satin. After all, if he lost it would not be he who paid, and to 'lay it off' would reduce his winnings to some fifteen hundred — hardly enough to purchase a dancer out and out. Even more potent was the itch in the blood of all the Darties for a real flutter. And turning to George he said: "She's a clipper. She'll win hands down; I shall go the whole hog." George, who had laid off every penny, and a few besides, and stood to win, however it came out, grinned down on him from his bulky height, with the words: "So ho, my wild one!" for after a chequered apprenticeship weathered with the money of a deeply complaining Roger, his Forsyte blood was beginning to stand him in good stead in the profession of owner.

There are moments of disillusionment in the lives of men from which the sensitive recorder shrinks. Suffice it to say that the good thing fell down. Sleeve-links finished in the ruck. Dartie's shirt was lost.

Between the passing of these things, and the day

when Soames turned his face towards Green Street, what had not happened!

When a man with the constitution of Montagu Dartie has exercised self-control for months from religious motives, and remains unrewarded, he does not curse God and die, he curses God and lives, to the distress of his family.

Winifred — a plucky woman, if a little too fashionable — who had borne the brunt of him for exactly twenty-one years, had never really believed that he would do what he now did. Like so many wives, she thought she knew the worst, but she had not yet known him in his forty-fifth year, when he, like other men, felt that it was now or never. Paying on the 2nd of October a visit of inspection to her jewel case, she was horrified to observe that her woman's crown and glory was gone — the pearls which Montagu had given her in '85, when Benedict was born, and which James had been compelled to pay for in the spring of '87, to save scandal. She consulted her husband at once. He ' pooh-poohed ' the matter. They would turn up! Nor till she said sharply: " Very well, then, Monty, I shall go down to Scotland Yard *myself,*" did he consent to take the matter in hand. Alas! that the steady and resolved continuity of design necessary to the accomplishment of sweeping operations should be liable to interruption by drink. That night Dartie returned home without a care in the world or a particle of reticence. Under normal conditions Winifred would merely have locked her door and let him sleep it off, but torturing suspense about her pearls had caused her to wait up for him. Taking a small revolver from his pocket and holding on to the dining table, he told her at once that

he did not care a cursh whether she lived s'long as
she was quiet; but he himself wash tired o' life.
Winifred, holding on to the other side of the dining
table, answered:

"Don't be a clown, Monty. Have you been to
Scotland Yard?"

Placing the revolver against his chest, Dartie
had pulled the trigger several times. It was not
loaded. Dropping it with an imprecation, he had
muttered: "For shake o' the children," and sank
into a chair. Winifred, having picked up the revolver, gave him some soda water. The liquor had
a magical effect. Life had ill-used him; Winifred
had never 'unshstood'm.' If he hadn't the right to
take the pearls he had given her himself, who had?
That Spanish filly had got'm. If Winifred had any
'jection he w'd cut — her — throat. What was the
matter with that? (Probably the first use of that
celebrated phrase — so obscure are the origins of
even the most classical language!)

Winifred, who had learned self-containment in a
hard school, looked up at him, and said: "Spanish
filly! Do you mean that girl we saw dancing in the
Pandemonium Ballet? Well, you are a thief and a
blackguard." It had been the last straw on a sorely
loaded consciousness; reaching up from his chair
Dartie seized his wife's arm, and recalling the
achievements of his boyhood, twisted it. Winifred
endured the agony with tears in her eyes, but no
murmur. Watching for a moment of weakness,
she wrenched it free; then placing the dining table
between them, said between her teeth: "You are the
limit, Monty." (Undoubtedly the inception of that
phrase — so is English formed under the stress of
circumstance.) Leaving Dartie with foam on his

dark moustache she went upstairs, and, after lock-
ing her door and bathing her arm in hot water, lay
awake all night, thinking of her pearls adorning
the neck of another, and of the consideration her
husband had presumably received therefor.

The man of the world awoke with a sense of
being lost to that world, and a dim recollection of
having been called a 'limit.' He sat for half an
hour in the dawn and the armchair where he had
slept — perhaps the unhappiest half-hour he had
ever spent, for even to a Dartie there is something
tragic about an end. And he knew that he had
reached it. Never again would he sleep in his dining-room and wake with the light filtering through
.those curtains bought by Winifred at Nickens and
Jarveys with the money of James. Never again
eat a devilled kidney at that rosewood table, after a
roll in the sheets and a hot bath. He took his note
case from his dress coat pocket. Four hundred
pounds, in fives and tens — the remainder of the
proceeds of his half of Sleeve-links, sold last night,
cash down, to George Forsyte, who, having won
over the race, had not conceived the sudden dislike
to the animal which he himself now felt. The ballet
was going to Buenos Aires the day after to-morrow
and he was going too. Full value for the pearls
had not yet been received; he was only at the soup.

He stole upstairs. Not daring to have a bath, or
shave (besides, the water would be cold), he
changed his clothes and packed stealthily all he
could. It was hard to leave so many shining boots,
but one must sacrifice something. Then, carrying
a valise in either hand, he stepped out on to the
landing. The house was very quiet — that house
where he had begotten his four children. It was a

curious moment, this, outside the room of his wife, once admired, if not perhaps loved, who had called him 'the limit.' He steeled himself with that phrase, and tiptoed on; but the next door was harder to pass. It was the room his daughters slept in. Maud was at school, but Imogen would be lying there; and moisture came into Dartie's early morning eyes. She was the most like him of the four, with her dark hair, and her luscious brown glance. Just coming out, a pretty thing! He set down the two valises. This almost formal abdication of fatherhood hurt him. The morning light fell on a face which worked with real emotion. Nothing so false as penitence moved him; but genuine paternal feeling, and that melancholy of 'never again.' He moistened his lips; and complete irresolution for a moment paralysed his legs in their check trousers. It was hard — hard to be thus compelled to leave his home! "D – n it!" he muttered, "I never thought it would come to this." Noises above warned him that the maids were beginning to get up. And grasping the two valises, he tiptoed on downstairs. His cheeks were wet, and the knowledge of that was comforting, as though it guaranteed the genuineness of his sacrifice. He lingered a little in the rooms below, to pack all the cigars he had, some papers, a crush hat, a silver cigarette box, a Ruff's Guide. Then, mixing himself a stiff whisky and soda, and lighting a cigarette, he stood hesitating before a photograph of his two girls, in a silver frame. It belonged to Winifred. 'Never mind,' he thought; 'she can get another taken, and I can't!' He slipped it into the valise. Then, putting on his hat and overcoat, he took two others, his best malacca cane, an umbrella, and opened the front door. Closing it softly behind him, he walked out, burdened as he had never been in all his life, and made his way round the corner to wait there for an early cab to come by. . . .

Thus had passed Montagu Dartie in the forty-fifth year of his age from the house which he had called his own. . . .

When Winifred came down, and realised that he was not in the house, her first feeling was one of dull anger that he should thus elude the reproaches she had carefully prepared in those long wakeful hours. He had gone off to Newmarket or Brighton, with that woman as likely as not. Disgusting! Forced to a complete reticence before Imogen and the servants, and aware that her father's nerves would never stand the disclosure, she had been unable to refrain from going to Timothy's that afternoon, and pouring out the story of the pearls to Aunts Juley and Hester in utter confidence. It was only on the following morning that she noticed the disappearance of that photograph. What did it mean? Careful examination of her husband's relics prompted the thought that he had gone for good. As that conclusion hardened she stood quite still in the middle of his dressing-room, with all the drawers pulled out, to try and realize what she was feeling. By no means easy! Though he was 'the limit' he was yet her property, and for the life of her she could not but feel the poorer. To be widowed yet not widowed at forty-two; with four children; made conspicuous, an object of commiseration! Gone to the arms of a Spanish jade! Memories, feelings, which she had thought quite dead, revived within her, painful, sullen, tenacious. Mechanically she closed drawer after drawer, went to her bed, lay on it, and buried her face in the pillows. She did not cry. What was the use of that? When she got off her bed to go down to lunch she felt as if only one thing could do her good, and that was to have Val home. He — her eldest boy — who was to go to Oxford next month at James' expense, was at Littlehampton taking his final gallops with his trainer for Smalls, as he would have phrased it following his father's diction. She caused a telegram to be sent to him.

" I must see about his clothes," she said to Imogen; " I can't have him going up to Oxford all anyhow. Those boys are so particular."

" Val's got heaps of things," Imogen answered.

" I know; but they want overhauling. I hope he'll come."

" He'll come like a shot, Mother. But he'll probably skew his Exam."

" I can't help that," said Winifred. " I want him."

With an innocent shrewd look at her mother's face, Imogen kept silence. It was father, of course! Val did come ' like a shot ' at six o'clock.

Imagine a cross between a pickle and a Forsyte and you have young Publius Valerius Dartie. A youth so named could hardly turn out otherwise. When he was born, Winifred, in the heyday of spirits, and the craving for distinction, had determined that her children should have names such as no others had ever had. (It was a mercy — she felt now — that she had just not named Imogen Thisbe.) But it was to George Forsyte, always a wag, that Val's christening was due. It so happened that Dartie dining with him, a week after the birth of his son and heir, had mentioned this aspiration of Winifred's.

"Call him Cato," said George, "it'll be damned piquant!" He had just won a tenner on a horse of that name.

"Cato!" Dartie had replied — they were a little ' on ' as the phrase was even in those days — " it's not a Christian name."

"Hallo you!" George called to a waiter in knee breeches. "Bring me the *Encyc'pedia Brit.* from the Library, letter C."

The waiter brought it.

"Here you are!" said George, pointing with his cigar: "Cato — Publius Valerius by Virgil out of Lydia. That's what you want. Publius Valerius is Christian enough."

Dartie, on arriving home, had informed Winifred. She had been charmed. It was so ' chic.' And Publius Valerius became the baby's name, though it afterwards transpired that they had got hold of the inferior Cato. In 1890, however, when little Publius was nearly ten, the word ' chic ' went out of fashion, and sobriety came in; Winifred began to have doubts. They were confirmed by little Publius himself who returned from his first term at school complaining that life was a burden to him — they called him Pubby. Winifred — a woman of real decision — promptly changed his school and his name to Val, the Publius being dropped even as an initial.

At nineteen he was a limber, freckled youth with a wide mouth, light eyes, long dark lashes, a rather charming smile, considerable knowledge of what he should not know, and no experience of what he ought to do. Few boys had more narrowly escaped being expelled — the engaging rascal. After kissing his mother and pinching Imogen, he ran upstairs three at a time, and came down four, dressed for dinner. He was awfully sorry, but his 'trainer,' who had come up too, had asked him to dine at the Oxford and Cambridge; it wouldn't do to miss — the old chap would be hurt. Winifred let him go with an unhapy pride. She had wanted him at home, but it was very nice to know that his tutor was so fond of him. He went out with a wink at Imogen, saying:

"I say, Mother, could I have two plover's eggs when I come in? — cook's got some. They top up so jolly well. Oh! and look here — have you any money? — I had to borrow a fiver from old Snobby."

Winifred, looking at him with fond shrewdness, answered:

"My dear, you *are* naughty about money. But you shouldn't pay him to-night, anyway; you're his guest." How nice and slim he looked in his white waistcoat, and his dark thick lashes!

"Oh, but we may go to the theatre, you see, Mother; and I think I ought to stand the tickets; he's always hard up, you know."

Winifred produced a five-pound note, saying:

"Well, perhaps you'd better pay him, but you mustn't stand the tickets too."

Val pocketed the fiver.

"If I do, I can't," he said. "Good-night, Mum!"

He went out with his head up and his hat cocked joyously, sniffing the air of Piccadilly like a young hound loosed into covert. Jolly good biz! After that mouldy old slow hole down there!

He found his 'tutor' not indeed at the Oxford and Cambridge, but at the Goat's Club. This 'tutor' was a year older than himself, a good-looking youth, with fine brown eyes, and smooth dark hair, a small mouth, an oval face, languid, immaculate, cool to a degree, one of those young men who without effort establish moral ascendancy over their companions. He had missed being expelled from school a year before Val, had spent that year at Oxford, and Val could almost see a halo round his head. His name was Crum, and no one could get through money quicker. It seemed to be his only aim in life — dazzling to young Val, in whom, however, the Forsyte would stand apart, now and then wondering where the value for that money was.

They dined quietly, in style and taste; left the Club smoking cigars, with just two bottles inside them, and dropped into stalls at the Liberty. For Val the sound of comic songs, the sight of lovely legs, were fogged and interrupted by haunting fears that he would never equal Crum's quiet dandyism. His idealism was roused; and when that is so, one is never quite at ease. Surely he had too wide a mouth, not the best cut of waistcoat, no braid on his trousers, and his lavender gloves had no thin black stitchings down the back. Besides, he laughed too much — Crum never laughed, he only smiled, with his regular dark brows raised a little so that they formed a gable over his just drooped lids. No! he would never be Crum's equal. All the same it was a jolly good show, and Cynthia Dark simply ripping. Between the acts Crum regaled him with particulars of Cynthia's private life, and the awful knowledge became Val's that, if he liked, Crum could go behind. He simply longed to say: " I say, take me! " but dared not, because of his deficiencies; and this made the last act or two almost miserable. On coming out Crum said: " It's half· an hour before they close; let's go on to the Pandemonium." They took a hansom to travel the hundred yards, and seats costing seven-and-six apiece because they were going to stand, and walked into the Promenade. It was in these little things, this utter negligence of money, that Crum had such engaging polish. The ballet was on its last legs and night, and the traffic of the Promenade was suffering for the moment. Men and women were crowded in three rows against the barrier. The whirl and dazzle on the stage, the half dark, the mingled tobacco fumes and women's scent, all that curious lure to promiscuity which belongs to Promenades, began to free young Val from his idealism. He looked admiringly in a young woman's face, saw she was not young, and quickly looked away. Shades of Cynthia Dark! The young woman's arm touched his unconsciously; there was a scent of musk and mignonette. Val looked round the corner of his lashes. Perhaps she *was* young, after all. Her foot trod on his; she begged his pardon. He said:

"Not at all; jolly good ballet, isn't it?"

"Oh, I'm tired of it; aren't you?"

Young Val smiled — his wide, rather charming smile. Beyond that he did not go — not yet convinced. The Forsyte in him stood out for greater certainty. And on the stage the ballet whirled its kaleidoscope of snow-white, salmon-pink, and emerald-green, and violet, and seemed suddenly to freeze into a stilly spangled pyramid. Applause broke out, and it was over! Maroon curtains had cut it off. The semi-circle of men and women round the barrier broke up, the young woman's arm pressed his. A little way off disturbance seemed centring round a man with a pink carnation; Val stole another glance at the young woman, who was looking towards it. Three men, unsteady, emerged, walking arm in arm. The one in the centre wore the pink carnation, a white waistcoat, a dark moustache; he reeled a little as he walked. Crum's voice said slow and level: "Look at that bounder, he's screwed!" Val turned to look. The 'bounder' had disengaged his arm, and was pointing straight at them. Crum's voice, level as ever, said:

"He seems to know you!" The 'bounder' spoke:

"H'llo!" he said. "You f'llows, look! There's my young rascal of a son!"

Val saw. It was his father! He could have sunk into the crimson carpet. It was not the meeting in ·this place, not even that his father was 'screwed'; it was Crum's word 'bounder,' which, as by heavenly revelation, he perceived at that moment to be true. Yes, his father looked a bounder with his dark good looks, and his pink carnation, and his square, self-assertive walk. And without a word he ducked behind the young woman and slipped out of the promenade. He heard the word, "Val!" behind him, and ran down deep-carpeted steps past the 'chuckers-out,' into the Square.

To be ashamed of his own father is perhaps the bitterest experience a young man can go through. It seemed to Val, hurrying away, that his career had ended before it had begun. How could he go up to Oxford now amongst all those chaps, those splendid friends of Crum's, who would know that his father was a 'bounder'! And suddenly he hated Crum. Who the devil was Crum, to say that? If Crum had been beside him at that moment, he would certainly have been jostled off the pavement. His own father — his own! A choke came up in his throat, and he dashed his hands down deep into

his overcoat pockets. Damn Crum! He conceived
the wild idea of running back and finding his father,
taking him by the arm and walking about with him
in front of Crum; but gave it up at once and pursued his way down Piccadilly. A young woman
planted herself before him. "Not so angry, darling!" He shied, dodged her, and suddenly became
quite cool. If Crum ever said a word, he would
jolly well punch his head, and there would be an
end of it. He walked a hundred yards or more,
contented with that thought, then lost its comfort
utterly. It wasn't simple like that! He remembered how, at school, when some parent came down
who did not pass the standard, it just clung to the
fellow afterwards. It was one of those things
nothing could remove. Why had his mother married his father, if he was a 'bounder'? It was
bitterly unfair — jolly low-down on a fellow to
give him a 'bounder' for father. The worst of it
was that now Crum had spoken the word, he realised that he had long known subconsciously that his
father was not 'the clean potato.' It was the beast-
liest thing that had ever happened to him —beast-
liest thing that had ever happened to any fellow! And, downhearted as he had never yet
been, he came to Green Street, and let himself in
with a smuggled latchkey. In the dining-room his
plover's eggs were set invitingly, with some cut
bread and butter, and a little whisky at the bottom
of a decanter — just enough, as Winifred had
thought, for him to feel himself a man. It made
him sick to look at them, and he went upstairs.

Winifred heard him pass, and thought: "The
dear boy's in. Thank goodness! If he takes after
his father I don't know what I shall do! But he
won't — he's like me. Dear Val!"

CHAPTER III

SOAMES PREPARES TO TAKE STEPS

WHEN Soames entered his sister's little Louis Quinze drawing-room, with its small balcony, always flowered with hanging geraniums in the summer, and now with pots of Lilium Auratum, he was struck by the immutability of human affairs. It looked just the same as on his first visit to the newly married Darties twenty-one years ago. He had chosen the furniture himself, and so completely that no subsequent purchase had ever been able to change the room's atmosphere. Yes, he had founded his sister well, and she had wanted it. Indeed, it said a great deal for Winifred that after all this time with Dartie she remained well-founded. From the first Soames had nosed out Dartie's nature from underneath the plausibility, *savoir faire,* and good looks which had dazzled Winifred, her mother, and even James, to the extent of permitting the fellow to marry his daughter without bringing anything into settlement — a fatal thing to do.

Winifred, whom he noticed next to the furniture, was sitting at her Buhl bureau with a letter in her hand. She rose and came towards him. Tall as himself, strong in the cheekbones, well tailored, something in her face disturbed Soames. She crumpled the letter in her hand, but seemed to change her mind and held it out to him. He was her lawyer as well as her brother.

Soames read, on Iseeum Club paper, these words:

"You will not get chance to insult in my own again. I am leaving country to-morrow. It's played out. I'm tired of being insulted by you. You've brought on yourself. No self-respecting man can stand it. I shall not ask you for anything again. Good-bye. I took the photograph of the two girls. Give them my love. I don't care what your family say. It's all their doing. I'm going to live new life.

"M. D."

This after-dinner note had a splotch on it not yet quite dry. He looked at Winifred — the splotch had clearly come from her; and he checked the words: "Good riddance!" Then it occurred to him that with this letter she was entering that very state which he himself so earnestly desired to quit — the state of a Forsyte who was not divorced.

Winifred had turned away, and was taking a long sniff from a little gold-topped bottle. A dull commiseration, together with a vague sense of injury, crept about Soames's heart. He had come to her to talk of his own position, and get sympathy, and here was she in the same position, wanting of course to talk of it, and get sympathy from him. It was always like that! Nobody ever seemed to think that he had troubles and interests of his own. He folded up the letter with the splotch inside, and said:

"What's it all about, now?"

Winifred recited the story of the pearls calmly.

"Do you think he's really gone, Soames? You see the state he was in when he wrote that."

Soames who, when he desired a thing, placated Providence by pretending that he did not think it likely to happen, answered:

"I shouldn't think so. I might find out at his Club."

"If George is there," said Winifred, "he would know."

"George?" said Soames; "I saw him at his father's funeral."

"Then he's sure to be there."

Soames, whose good sense applauded his sister's acumen, said grudgingly: "Well, I'll go round. Have you said anything in Park Lane?"

"I've told Emily," returned Winifred, who retained that 'chic' way of describing her mother. "Father would have a fit."

Indeed, anything untoward was now sedulously kept from James. With another look round at the furniture, as if to gauge his sister's exact position, Soames went out towards Piccadilly. The evening was drawing in — a touch of chill in the October haze. He walked quickly, with his close and concentrated air. He must get through, for he wished to dine in Soho. On hearing from the hall porter at the Iseeum that Mr. Dartie had not been in to-day, he looked at the trusty fellow and decided only to ask if Mr. George Forsyte was in the Club. He was. Soames, who always looked askance at his cousin George, as one inclined to jest at his expense, followed the page-boy slightly reassured by the thought that George had just lost his father. He must have come in for about thirty thousand, besides what he had under that settlement of

Roger's, which had avoided death duty.   He found
George in a bow-window, staring out across a half-
eaten plate of muffins.   His tall, bulky, black-
clothed figure loomed almost threatening, though
preserving still the supernatural neatness of the racing man.   With a faint grin on his fleshy face, he
said:

" Hallo, Soames!   Have a muffin? "

" No, thanks," murmured Soames; and, nursing
his hat, with the desire to say something suitable
and sympathetic, added:

" How's your mother? "

" Thanks," said George; " so-so.   Haven't seen
you for ages.   You never go racing.   How's the
City? "

Soames, scenting the approach of a jest, closed
up, and answered:

" I wanted to ask you about Dartie.   I hear
he's —— "

" Flitted, made a bolt for Buenos Aires with the
fair Lola.   Good for Winifred and the little Darties.   He's a treat."

Soames nodded.   Naturally inimical as these
cousins were, Dartie made them kin.

" Uncle James'll sleep in his bed now," resumed
George; " I suppose he's had a lot off you, too."

Soames smiled.

" Ah!   You saw him further," said George ami-
cably.   " He's a real rouser.   Young Val will want
a bit of looking after.   I was always sorry for
Winifred.   She's a plucky woman."

Again Soames nodded.   " I must be getting back
to her," he said; " she just wanted to know for certain.   We may have to take steps.   I suppose
there's no mistake? "

"It's quite O. K.," said George — it was he who invented so many of those quaint sayings which have been assigned to other sources. "He was drunk as a lord last night; but he went off all right this morning. His ship's the *Tuscarora;*" and, fishing out a card, he read mockingly:

"'Mr. Montagu Dartie. Poste Restante, Buenos Aires.' I should hurry up with the steps, if I were you. He fairly fed me up last night."

"Yes," said Soames; "but it's not always easy." Then, conscious from George's eyes that he had roused reminiscence of his own affair, he got up, and held out his hand. George rose too.

"Remember me to Winifred. You'll enter her for the Divorce Stakes straight off if you ask me."

Soames took a sidelong look back at him from the doorway. George had seated himself again and was staring before him; he looked big and lonely in those black clothes. Soames had never known him so subdued. 'I suppose he feels it in a way,' he thought. 'They must have about fifty thousand each, all told. They ought to keep the estate together. If there's a war, house property will go down. Uncle Roger was a good judge, though.' And the face of Annette rose before him in the darkening street; her brown hair and her blue eyes with their dark lashes, her fresh lips and cheeks, dewy and blooming in spite of London, her perfect French figure. 'Take steps!' he thought. Re-entering Winifred's house he encountered Val, and they went in together. An idea had occurred to Soames. His cousin Jolyon was Irene's trustee, the first step would be to go down and see him at Robin Hill. Robin Hill! The odd — the very odd feeling those words brought back! Robin Hill —

the house Bosinney had built for him and Irene —
the house they had never lived in — the fatal house!
And Jolyon lived there now! H'm! And suddenly he thought: 'They say he's got a boy at Oxford! Why not take young Val down and introduce them! It's an excuse! Less bald — very
much less bald!' So, as they went upstairs, he said
to Val:

"You've got a cousin at Oxford; you've never
met him. I should like to take you down with me
to-morrow to where he lives and introduce you.
You'll find it useful."

Val, receiving the idea with but moderate trans-
ports, Soames clinched it.

" I'll call for you after lunch. It's in the country
— not far; you'll enjoy it."

On the threshold of the drawing-room he recalled
with an effort that the steps he contemplated concerned Winifred at the moment, not himself.

Winifred was still sitting at her Buhl bureau.

" It's quite true," he said; " he's gone to Buenos
Aires, started this morning — we'd better have him
shadowed when he lands. I'll cable at once.
Otherwise we may have a lot of expense. The
sooner these things are done the better. I'm always regretting that I didn't —— " he stopped, and
looked sidelong at the silent Winifred. " By the
way," he went on, " can you prove cruelty? "

Winifred said in a dull voice:

" I don't know. What is cruelty? "

" Well, has he struck you, or anything? "

Winifred shook herself, and her jaw grew
square.

" He twisted my arm. Or would pointing a pistol count? Or being too drunk to undress himself,.
or —— No — I can't bring in the children."

"No," said Soames; "no. I wonder! Of course, there's legal separation — we can get that. But separation! Um!"

"What does it mean?" asked Winifred desolately.

"That he can't touch you, or you him; you're both of you married and unmarried." And again he grunted. What was it, in fact, but his own accursed position, legalised! No, he would not put her into that!

"It must be divorce," he said decisively; "failing cruelty, there's desertion. There's a way of shortening the two years, now. We get the Court to give us restitution of conjugal rights. Then if he doesn't obey, we can bring a suit for divorce in six months' time. Of course you don't want him back. But they won't know that. Still, there's the risk that he might come. I'd rather try cruelty."

Winifred shook her head. "It's so beastly."

"Well," Soames murmured, "perhaps there isn't much risk so long as he's infatuated and got money. Don't say anything to anybody, and don't pay any of his debts."

Winifred sighed. In spite of all she had been through, the sense of loss was heavy on her. And this idea of not paying his debts any more brought it home to her as nothing else yet had. Some richness seemed to have gone out of life. Without her husband, without her pearls, without that intimate sense that she made a brave show above the domestic whirlpool, she would now have to face the world. She felt bereaved indeed.

And into the chilly kiss he placed on her forehead, Soames put more than his usual warmth.

"I have to go down to Robin Hill to-morrow," he

said, " to see young Jolyon on business.   He's got a
boy at Oxford.   I'd like to take Val with me and
introduce him.   Come down to ' The Shelter ' for
the week-end and bring the children.   Oh! by the
way, no, that won't do; I've got some other people
coming."   So saying, he left her and turned towards Soho.

CHAPTER IV

SOHO

Of all quarters in the queer adventurous amal-
gam called London, Soho is perhaps least suited to
the Forsyte spirit. ' So-ho, my wild one!' George
would have said if he had seen his cousin going
there. Untidy, full of Greeks, Ishmaelites, cats,
Italians, tomatoes, restaurants, organs, coloured
stuffs, queer names, people looking out of upper
windows, it dwells remote from the British Body
Politic. Yet has it haphazard proprietory instincts
of its own, and a certain possessive prosperity which
keeps its rents up when those of other quarters go
down. For long years Soames' acquaintanceship
with Soho had been confined to its Western bastion,
Wardour Street. Many bargains had he picked up
there. Even during those seven years at Brighton
after Bosinney's death and Irene's flight, he had
bought treasures there sometimes, though he had no
place to put them; for when the conviction that his
wife had gone for good at last became firm within
him, he had caused a board to be put up in Montpelier Square:

FOR SALE

The Lease of this Desirable Residence

Enquire of Messrs. Lesson and Tukes, Court Street, Belgravia.

It had sold within a week — that desirable residence, in the shadow of whose perfection a man and a woman had eaten their hearts out.

Of a misty January evening, just before the board was taken down, Soames had gone there once more, and stood against the Square railings, looking at its unlighted windows, chewing the cud of possessive memories which had turned so bitter in the mouth. Why had she never loved him? Why? She had been given all she had wanted, and in return had given him, for three long years, all he had wanted — except, indeed, her heart. He had uttered a little involuntary groan, and a passing policeman had glanced suspiciously at him who no longer possessed the right to enter that green door with the carved brass knocker beneath the board 'For sale!' A choking sensation had attacked his throat, and he had hurried away into the mist. That evening he had gone to Brighton to live. . . .

Approaching Malta Street, Soho, and the Restaurant Bretagne, where Annette would be drooping her pretty shoulders over her accounts, Soames thought with wonder of those seven years at Brighton. How had he managed to go on so long in that town devoid of the scent of sweet-peas, where he had not even space to put his treasures? True, those had been years with no time at all for looking at them — years of almost passionate money-making, during which Forsyte, Bustard and Forsyte had become solicitors to more limited Companies than they could properly attend to. Up to the City of a morning in a Pullman car, down from the City of an evening in a Pullman car. Law papers again after dinner, then the sleep of the tired, and up again next morning. Saturday to Monday was spent at his Club in town — curious reversal of customary procedure, based on the deep and careful instinct that while working so hard he needed sea air to and from the station twice a day, and while resting must indulge his domestic affections. The Sunday visit to his family in Park Lane, to Timothy's, and to Green Street; the occasional visits elsewhere had seemed to him as necessary to health as sea air on weekdays. Even since his migration to Mapledurham he had maintained those habits until — he had known Annette. Whether Annette had produced the revolution in his outlook, or that outlook had produced Annette, he knew no more than we know where a circle begins. It was intricate and deeply involved with the growing consciousness that property without anyone to leave it to is the negation of true Forsyteism. To have an heir, some continuance of self, who would begin where he left off — ensure, in fact, that he would not leave off — had quite obsessed him for the last year and more. After buying a bit of Wedgwood one evening in April, he had dropped into Malta Street to look at a house of his father's which had been turned into a restaurant — a risky proceeding, and one not quite in accordance with the terms of the lease. He had stared for a little at the outside — painted a good cream colour, with two peacock-blue tubs containing little bay-trees in a recessed doorway — and at the words 'Restaurant Bretagne' above them in gold letters, rather favourably impressed. Entering, he had noticed that several people were already seated at little round green tables with little pots of fresh flowers on them and Brittany-ware plates, and had asked of a trim waitress to see the proprietor. They had shown him into a back room, where a girl was

sitting at a simple bureau covered with papers, and
a small round table was laid for two. The impression of cleanliness, order, and good taste was confirmed when the girl got up, saying, " You wish to
see *Maman, Monsieur*? " in a broken accent.

" Yes," Soames had answered, " I represent your
landlord ; in fact, I'm his son."

" Won't you sit down, sir, please?   Tell *Maman*
to come to this gentleman."

He was pleased that the girl seemed impressed,
because it showed business instinct ; and suddenly he
noticed that she was remarkably pretty — so remarkably pretty that his eyes found a difficulty in
leaving her face.   When she moved to put a chair
for him, she swayed in a curious subtle way, as if
she had been put together by someone with a special
secret skill; and her face and neck, which was a
little bared, looked as fresh as if they had been
sprayed with dew.   Probably at this moment
Soames decided that the lease had not been violated ;
though to himself and his father he based the decision on the efficiency of those illicit adaptations in
the building, on the signs of prosperity, and the obvious business capacity of Madame Lamotte.   He
did not, however, neglect to leave certain matters to
future consideration, which had necessitated further visits, so that the little back room had become
quite accustomed to his spare, not unsolid, but unob-
trusive figure, and his pale chinny face with clipped
moustache and dark hair not yet grizzling at the
sides.

' *Un Monsieur très distingué*,' Madame Lamotte
found him ; and presently, ' *Très amical, très gentil*,'
watching his eyes upon her daughter.

She was one of those generously built, fine-faced,

dark-haired Frenchwomen, whose every action and
tone of voice inspire perfect confidence in the thor-
oughness of their domestic tastes, their knowledge
of cooking, and the careful increase of their bank
balances.

After those visits to the Restaurant Bretagne began, other visits ceased — without, indeed, any definite decision, for Soames, like all Forsytes, and the
great majority of their countrymen, was a born
empiricist.   But it was this change in his mode of
life which had gradually made him so definitely conscious that he desired to alter his condition from
that of the unmarried married man to that of the
married man remarried.

Turning in to Malta Street on this evening of
early October, 1899, he bought a paper to see if
there were any after-development of the Dreyfus
case — a question which he had always found useful in making closer acquaintanceship with Madame Lamotte and her daughter, who were Catholic
and anti-Dreyfusard.

Scanning those columns, Soames found nothing
French, but noticed a general fall on the Stock Exchange and an ominous leader about the Transvaal.
He entered, thinking: 'War's a certainty.   I shall
sell my consols.'   Not that he had many personally,
the rate of interest was too wretched; but he should
advise his Companies — consols would assuredly go
down.   A look, as he passed the doorways of the
restaurant, assured him that business was good as
ever, and this, which in April would have pleased
him, now gave him a certain uneasiness.   If the
steps which he had to take ended in his marrying
Annette, he would rather see her mother safely back
in France, a move to which the prosperity of the

Restaurant Bretagne might become an obstacle. He would have to buy them out, of course, for French people only came to England to make money; and it would mean a higher price. And then that peculiar sweet sensation at the back of his throat, and a slight thumping about the heart, which he always experienced at the door of the little room, prevented his thinking how much it would cost.

Going in, he was conscious of an abundant black skirt vanishing through the door into the restaurant, and of Annette with her hands up to her hair. It was the attitude in which of all others he admired her — so beautifully straight and rounded and supple. And he said:

" I just came in to talk to your mother about pulling down that partition. No, don't call her."

" *Monsieur* will have supper with us? It will be ready in ten minutes." Soames, who still held her hand, was overcome by an impulse which surprised him.

" You look so pretty to-night," he said, " so very pretty. Do you know how pretty you look, Annette? "

Annette withdrew her hand, and blushed. " Monsieur is very good."

" Not a bit good," said Soames, and sat down gloomily.

Annette made a little expressive gesture with her hands; a smile was crinkling her red lips untouched by salve.

And, looking at those lips, Soames said:

" Are you happy over here, or do you want to go back to France? "

" Oh, I like London. Paris, of course. But London is better than Orleans, and the English country is so beautiful.   I have been to Richmond last Sunday."

Soames went through a moment of calculating struggle.   Mapledurham!   Dared he?   After all, dared he go so far as that, and show her what there was to look forward to!   Still!   Down there one could say things.   In this room it was impossible.

"I want you and your mother," he said suddenly, "to come for the afternoon next Sunday.   My house is on the river, it's not too late in this weather; and I can show you some good pictures.   What do you say?"

Annette clasped her hands.

"It will be lovelee.   The river is so beautiful."

"That's understood, then.   I'll ask Madame."

He need say no more to her this evening, and risk giving himself away.   But had he not already said *too* much?   Did one ask restaurant proprietors with pretty daughters down to one's country house without design?   Madame Lamotte would see, if Annette didn't.   Well! there was not much that Madame did not see.   Besides, this was the second time he had stayed to supper with them; he owed them hospitality. . . .

Walking home towards Park Lane — for he was staying at his father's — with the impression of Annette's soft clever hand within his own, his thoughts were pleasant, slightly sensual, rather puzzled. Take steps!   What steps?   How?   Dirty linen washed in public?   Pah!   With his reputation for sagacity, for far-sightedness and the clever extrication of others, he, who stood for proprietory interests, to become the plaything of that Law of which he was a pillar!   There was something revolting in the thought!   Winifred's affair was bad enough!

To have a double dose of publicity in the family!
Would not a liaison be better than that — a liaison,
and a son he could adopt? But dark, solid, watchful, Madame Lamotte blocked the avenue of that
vision. No! that would not work. It was not as if
Annette could have a real passion for him; one could
not expect that at his age. If her mother wished, if
the worldly advantage were manifestly great —
perhaps! If not, refusal would be certain. Besides, he thought: ' I am not a villain. I don't want
to hurt her; and I don't want anything underhand.
But I do want her, and I want a son! There's nothing for it but divorce — somehow — anyhow — divorce! ' Under the shadow of the plane-trees, in
the lamplight, he passed slowly along the railings of
the Green Park. Mist clung there among the bluish
tree shapes, beyond range of the lamps. How
many hundred times he had walked past those trees
from his father's house in Park Lane, when he was
quite a young man; or from his own house in Montpelier Square in those four years of married life!
And, to-night, making up his mind to free himself if
he could of that long useless marriage tie, he took a
fancy to walk on, in at Hyde Park Corner, out at
Knightsbridge Gate, just as he used to when going
home to Irene in the old days. What could she be
like now? — how had she passed the years since he
last saw her, twelve years in all, eight already since
Uncle Jolyon left her that money! Was she still
beautiful? Would he know her if he saw her?
' I've not changed much,' he thought; ' I expect she
has. She made me suffer.' He remembered suddenly one night, the first on which he went out to
dinner alone — an old Malburian dinner — the first
year of their marriage. With what eagerness he

had hurried back; and, entering softly as a cat, had heard her playing. Opening the drawing-room door noiselessly, he had stood watching the expression on her face, different from any he knew, so much more open, so confiding, as though to her music she was giving a heart he had never seen. And he remembered how she stopped and looked round, how her face changed back to that which he did know, and what an icy shiver had gone through him for all that the next moment he was fondling her shoulders. Yes, she had made him suffer! Divorce! It seemed ridiculous, after all these years of utter separation! But it would have to be. No other way! 'The question,' he thought with sudden realism, 'is — which of us? She or me? She deserted me. She ought to pay for it. There'll be someone, I suppose.' Involuntarily he uttered a little snarling sound, and, turning, made his way back to Park Lane.

CHAPTER V

JAMES SEES VISIONS

THE butler himself opened the door, and closing it softly, detained Soames on the inner mat.

" The master's poorly, sir," he murmured. " He wouldn't go to bed till you came in. He's still in the dining-room."

Soames responded in the hushed tone to which the house was now accustomed.

" What's matter with him, Warmson? "

" Nervous, sir, I think. Might be the funeral; might be Mrs. Dartie's comin' round this afternoon. I think he overheard something. I've took him in a negus. The mistress has just gone up."

Soames hung his hat on a mahogany stag's-horn.

" All right, Warmson, you can go to bed; I'll take him up myself." And he passed into the dining-room. . . .

James was sitting before the fire, in a big arm-chair, with a camel-hair shawl, very light and warm, over his frock-coated shoulders, on to which his long white whiskers drooped. His white hair, still fairly thick, glistened in the lamplight; a little moisture from his fixed, light grey eyes stained the cheeks, still quite well coloured, and the long deep

furrows running to the corners of the clean-shaven
lips, which moved as if mumbling thoughts. His
long legs, thin as a crow's, in shepherd's plaid
trousers, were bent at less than a right angle, and on
one knee a spindly hand moved continually, with
fingers wide apart and glistening tapered nails.
Beside him, on a low stool, stood a half-finished
glass of negus, bedewed with beads of heat. There
he had been sitting, with intervals for meals, all day.
At eighty-eight he was still organically sound, but
suffering terribly from the thought that no one ever
told him anything. It is, indeed, doubtful how he
had become aware that Roger was being buried that
day, for Emily had kept it from him. She was always keeping things from him. Emily was only
seventy! James had a grudge against his wife's
youth. He felt sometimes that he would never have
married her if he had known that she would have so
many years before her, when he had so few. It was
not natural. She would live fifteen or twenty years
after he was gone, and might spend a lot of money;
she had always had extravagant tastes. For all he
knew she might want to buy one of these motor-cars.
Cicely and Rachel and Imogen and all the young
people—they all rode those bicycles now, and went
off Goodness knew where. And now Roger was
gone. He didn't know — couldn't tell! The family was breaking up. Soames would know how
much his uncle had left. Curiously, he thought of
Roger as Soames' uncle, not as his own brother.
Soames! It was more and more the one solid spot
in a vanishing world. Soames was careful; he was
a warm man; but he had no one to leave his money
to. There it was! He didn't know! And there
was that fellow Chamberlain! For James' political

principles had been fixed between '70 and '85, when
' that rascally Radical ' had been the chief thorn in
the side of property, and he distrusted him to this
day, in spite of his conversion; he would get the
country into a mess, and make money go down before he had done with it. A stormy petrel of a
chap! Where was Soames? He had gone to the
funeral, of course, which they had tried to keep
from him. He knew that perfectly well; he had seen
his son's trousers. Roger! Roger in his coffin! He
remembered how, when they came up from school
together from the West, on the box seat of the old
Slowflyer in 1824, Roger had got into the ' boot '
and gone to sleep. James uttered a thin cackle. A
funny fellow — Roger — an original! He didn't
know! Younger than himself, and in his coffin!
The family was breaking up. There was Val going
to the university; he never came to see him now.
He would cost a pretty penny up there. It was an
extravagant age. And all the pretty pennies that
his four grandchildren would cost him danced before James' eyes. He did not grudge them the
money, but he grudged terribly the risk which the
spending of that money might bring on them; *he
grudged the diminution of security.* And now that
Cicely had married, she might be having children
too. He didn't know — couldn't tell! Nobody
thought of anything but spending money in these
days, and racing about, and having what they called
' a good time.' A motor-car went past the window.
Ugly great lumbering thing, making all that racket!
But there it was, the country rattling to the dogs!
People in such a hurry that they couldn't even care
for style — a neat turn-out like his barouche and
bays was worth all those new-fangled things. And

consols at 116! There must be a lot of money in the country. And now there was this old Kruger! They had tried to keep old Kruger from him. But he knew better; there would be a pretty kettle of fish out there! He had known how it would be when that fellow Gladstone — dead now, thank God! — made such a mess of it after that dreadful business at Majuba. He shouldn't wonder if the Empire split up and went to pot. And this vision of the Empire going to pot filled a full quarter of an hour with qualms of the most serious character. He had eaten a poor lunch because of them. But it was after lunch that the real disaster to his nerves occurred. He had been dozing when he became .aware of voices — low voices. Ah! they never told him anything! Winifred's and her mother's. " Monty! " That fellow Dartie — always that fellow Dartie! The voices had receded; and James had been left alone, with his ears standing up like a hare's, and fear creeping about his inwards. Why did they leave him alone? Why didn't they come and tell him? And an awful thought, which through long years had haunted him, concreted again swiftly in his brain. Dartie had gone bankrupt — fraudulently bankrupt, and to save Winifred and the children, he — James — would have to pay! Could he — could Soames turn him into a limited Company? No, he couldn't! There it was! With every minute before Emily came back the spectre fiercened. Why, it might be forgery! With eyes fixed on the doubted Turner in the centre of the wall, James suffered tortures. He saw Dartie in the dock, his grandchildren in the gutter, and himself in bed. He saw the doubted Turner being sold at Jobson's, and all the majestic edifice of prop-

erty in rags. He saw in fancy Winifred unfash-
ionably dressed, and heard in fancy Emily's voice
saying: " Now, don't fuss, James! " She was always saying: " Don't fuss! " She had no nerves;
he ought never to have married a woman eighteen
years younger than himself. Then Emily's real
voice said:

" Have you had a nice nap, James? "

Nap! He was in torment, and she asked him
that!

" What's this about Dartie? " he said, and his
eyes glared at her.

Emily's self-possession never deserted her.

" What have you been hearing? " she asked
blandly.

" What's this about Dartie? " repeated James.
" He's gone bankrupt."

" Fiddle! "

James made a great effort, and rose to the full
height of his stork-like figure.

" You never tell me anything," he said; " he's
gone bankrupt."

The destruction of that fixed idea seemed to
Emily all that mattered at the moment.

" He has not," she answered firmly. " He's gone
to Buenos Aires."

If she had said ' He's gone to Mars ' she could not
have dealt James a more stunning blow; his imagination, invested entirely in British securities, could
as little grasp one place as the other.

" What's he gone there for? " he said. " He's
got no money. What did he take? "

Agitated within by Winifred's news, and goaded
by the constant reiteration of this jeremiad, Emily
said calmly:

" He took Winifred's pearls and a dancer."

" What ! " said James, and sat down.

His sudden collapse alarmed her, and smoothing his forehead, she said:

" Now, don't fuss, James ! "

A dusky red had spread over James' cheeks and forehead.

" I paid for them," he said tremblingly; " he's a thief ! I — I knew how it would be. He'll be the death of me; he — " words failed him and he sat quite still. Emily, who thought she knew him so well, was alarmed, and went towards the sideboard where she kept some sal volatile. She could not see the tenacious Forsyte spirit working in that thin, tremulous shape against the extravagance of the emotion called up by this outrage on Forsyte principles — the Forsyte spirit deep in there, saying: ' You mustn't get into a fantod, it'll never do. You won't digest your lunch. You'll have a fit ! ' All unseen by her, it was doing better work in James than sal volatile.

" Drink this," she said.

James waved it aside.

" What was Winifred about," he said, " to let him take her pearls ? " Emily perceived the crisis past.

" She can have mine," she said comfortably. " I never wear them. She'd better get a divorce."

" There you go ! " said James. " Divorce ! We've never had a divorce in the family. Where's Soames ? "

" He'll be in directly."

" No, he won't," said James, almost fiercely; " he's at the funeral. You think I know nothing."

" Well," said Emily with calm, " you shouldn't get into such fusses when we tell you things." And

plumping up his cushions, and putting the sal volatile beside him, she left the room.

But James sat there seeing visions — of Winifred
in the Divorce Court, and the family name in the
papers; of the earth falling on Roger's coffin; of
Val taking after his father; of the pearls he had
paid for and would never see again; of money back
at four per cent., and the country going to the dogs;
and, as the afternoon wore into evening, and tea-
time passed, and dinner-time, those visions became
more and more mixed and menacing — of being
told nothing, till he had nothing left of all his
wealth, and they told him nothing of it. Where
was Soames? Why didn't he come in? . . . His
hand grasped the glass of negus, he raised it to
drink, and saw his son standing there looking at
him. A little sigh of relief escaped his lips, and putting the glass down, he said:

"There you are! Dartie's gone to Buenos
Aires!"

Soames nodded. "That's all right," he said;
" good riddance."

A wave of assuagement passed over James'
brain. Soames knew. Soames was the only one of
them all who had sense. Why couldn't he come and
live at home? He had no son of his own. And he
said plaintively:

"At my age I get nervous. I wish you were
more at home, my boy."

Again Soames nodded; the mask of his counte-
nance betrayed no understanding, but he went closer,
and as if by accident touched his father's shoulder.

"They sent their love to you at Timothy's," he
said. "It went off all right. I've been to see Winifred. I'm going to take steps." And he thought:
' Yes, and you mustn't hear of them.'

James looked up; his long white whiskers quivered, his thin throat between the points of his collar looked very gristly and naked.

" I've been very poorly all day," he said; " they never tell me anything."

Soames's heart twitched.

" Well, it's all right. There's nothing to worry about. Will you come up now? " and he put his hand under his father's arm.

James obediently and tremulously raised himself, and together they went slowly across the room, which had a rich look in the firelight, and out to the stairs. Very slowly they ascended.

" Good-night, my boy," said James at his bedroom door.

" Good-night, father," answered Soames. His hand stroked down the sleeve beneath the shawl; it seemed to have almost nothing in it, so thin was the arm. And, turning away from the light in the opening doorway, he went up the extra flight to his own bedroom.

' I want a son,' he thought, sitting on the edge of his bed; ' *I want a son.*'

CHAPTER VI

NO-LONGER-YOUNG JOLYON AT HOME

Trees take little account of Time, and the old oak on the upper lawn at Robin Hill looked no day older than when Bosinney sprawled under it and said to Soames: 'Forsyte, I've found the very place for your house.' Since then Swithin had dreamed, and old Jolyon died, beneath its branches. And now, close to the swing, no-longer-young Jolyon often painted there. Of all spots in the world it was perhaps the most sacred to him, for he had loved his father.

Contemplating its great girth — crinkled and a little mossed, but not yet hollow — he would speculate on the passage of time. That tree had seen, perhaps, all real English history; it dated, he shouldn't wonder, from the days of Elizabeth at least. His own fifty years were as nothing to its wood. When the house behind it, which he now owned, was three hundred years of age instead of twelve, that tree might still be standing there, vast and hollow — for who would commit such sacrilege as to cut it down? A Forsyte might perhaps still be living in that house, to guard it jealously. And Jolyon would wonder what the house would look like coated with such age. Wistaria was already

about its walls — the new look had gone. Would
it hold its own and keep the dignity Bosinney had bestowed on it, or would the giant London have lapped
it round and made it into an asylum in the midst of
a jerry-built wilderness? Often, within and without of it, he was persuaded that Bosinney had been
moved by the spirit when he built. He had put his
heart into that house, indeed! It might even become one of the 'homes of England' — a rare
achievement for a house in these degenerate days
of building. And the æsthetic spirit, moving hand
in hand with his Forsyte sense of possessive continuity, dwelt with pride and pleasure on his ownership thereof. There was the smack of reverence
and ancestor-worship (if only for one ancestor) in
his desire to hand this house down to his son and his
son's son. His father had loved the house, had
loved the view, the grounds, that tree; his last years
had been happy there, and no one had lived there before him. These last eleven years at Robin Hill
had formed in Jolyon's life, as a painter, the important period of success. He was now in the very van
of water-colour art, hanging on the line everywhere.
His drawings fetched high prices. Specialising in
that one medium with the tenacity of his breed, he
had 'arrived' — rather late, but not too late for a
member of the family which made a point of living
for ever. His art had really deepened and improved. In conformity with his position he had
grown a short fair beard, which was just beginning
to grizzle, and hid his Forsyte chin; his brown face
had lost the warped expression of his ostracised
period — he looked, if anything, younger. The
loss of his wife in 1894 had been one of those domestic tragedies which turn out in the end for the

good of all. He had, indeed, loved her to the last,
for his was an affectionate spirit, but she had become increasingly difficult: jealous of her step-daugh-
ter June, jealous even of her own little daughter
Holly, and making ceaseless plaint that he could not
love her, ill as she was, and ' useless to everyone,
and better dead.'   He had mourned her sincerely,
but his face had looked younger since she died.   If
she could only have believed that she made him
happy, how much happier would the twenty years of
their companionship have been!

June had never really got on well with her who
had reprehensibly taken her own mother's place;
and ever since old Jolyon died she had been established in a sort of studio in London.   But she had
come back to Robin Hill on her stepmother's death,
and gathered the reins there into her small decided
hands.   Jolly was then at Harrow; Holly still learning from Mademoiselle Beauce.   There had been
nothing to keep Jolyon at home, and he had removed
his grief and his paintbox abroad.   There he had
wandered, for the most part in Brittany, and at last
had fetched up in Paris.   He had stayed there several
months, and come back with the younger face and
the short fair beard.   Essentially a man who merely
lodged in any house, it had suited him perfectly that
June should reign at Robin Hill, so that he was free
to go off with his easel where and when he liked.
She was inclined, it is true, to regard the house
rather as an asylum for her *protégés;* but his own
outcast days had filled Jolyon for ever with sympathy towards an outcast, and June's ' lame ducks '
about the place did not annoy him.   By all means let
her have them down and feed them up; and though
his slightly cynical humour perceived that they min-

istered to his daughter's love of domination as well.
as moved her warm heart, he never ceased to admire
her for having so many ducks.　He fell, indeed, year
by year into a more and more detached and brotherly
attitude towards his own son and daughters, treating
them with a sort of whimsical equality.　When he
went down to Harrow to see Jolly, he never quite
knew which of them was the elder, and would sit
eating cherries with him out of one paper bag, with
an affectionate and ironical smile twisting up an eyebrow and curling his lips a little.　And he was always careful to have money in his pocket, and to be
modish in his dress, so that his son need not blush
for him.　They were perfect friends, but never
seemed to have occasion for verbal confidences, both
having the competitive self-consciousness of Forsytes.　They knew they would stand by each other
in scrapes, but there was no need to talk about it.
Jolyon had a perfect horror — partly original sin,
but partly the result of his early immorality — of
the moral attitude.　The most he could ever have
said to his son would have been:
　' Look here, old man, don't forget you're a gentleman;' and then have wondered whimsically whether
that was not a snobbish sentiment.　The great
cricket match was perhaps the most searching and
awkward time they annually went through together,
for Jolyon had been at Eton.　They would be particularly careful during that match, continually saying: ' Hooray!　Oh! hard luck, old man!' or ' Hooray!　Oh! bad luck, Dad!' to each other, when
some disaster at which their hearts bounded happened to the opposing school.　And Jolyon would
wear a grey top hat, instead of his usual soft one, to
save his son's feelings, for a black top hat he could

not stomach.   When Jolly went up tó Oxford, Jolyon went up with him, amused, humble, and a little
anxious not to discredit his boy amongst all these
youths who seemed so much more assured and old
than himself.   He often thought, ' Glad I'm a
painter '— for he had long dropped under-writing
at Lloyds — ' it's so innocuous.   You can't look
down on a painter — you can't take him seriously
enough.'   For Jolly, who had a sort of natural lordliness, had passed at once into a very small set, who
secretly amused his father.   The boy had fair hair
which curled a little, and his grandfather's deep-set
iron-grey eyes.   He was well-built and very upright, and always pleased Jolyon's æsthetic sense,
so that he was a tiny bit afraid of him, as artists
ever are of those of their own sex whom they admire
physically.   On that occasion, however, he actually
did screw up his courage to give his son advice, and
this was it:

"Look here, old man, you're bound to get into
debt; mind you come to me at once.   Of course, I'll
always pay them.   But you might remember that
one respects oneself more afterwards if one pays
one's own way.   And don't ever borrow, except
from me, will you? "

And Jolly had said:

"All right, Dad, I won't," and he never had.

"And there's just one other thing.   I don't know
much about morality and that, but there is this: It's
always worth while before you do anything to con-
sider whether it's going to hurt another person more
than is absolutely necessary."

Jolly had looked thoughtful, and nodded, and
presently had squeezed his father's hand.   And Jolyon had thought: ' I wonder if I had the right to say

that?' He always had a sort of dread of losing the
dumb confidence they had in each other; remembering how for long years he had lost his own father's,
so that there had been nothing between them but
love at a great distance. He under-estimated, no
doubt, the change in the spirit of the age since he
himself went up to Cambridge in '66; and perhaps
he under-estimated, too, his boy's power of understanding that he was tolerant to the very bone. It
was that tolerance of his, and possibly his scepticism,
which ever made his relations towards June so
queerly defensive. She was such a decided mortal;
knew her own mind so terribly well; wanted things
so inexorably until she got them — and then, indeed,
often dropped them like a hot potato. Her mother
had been like that, whence had come all those tears.
Not that his incompatibility with his daughter was
anything like what it had been with the first Mrs.
Young Jolyon. One could be amused where a
daughter was concerned; in a wife's case one could
not be amused. To see June set her heart and jaw
on a thing until she got it was all right, because it
was never anything which interfered fundamentally
with Jolyon's liberty — the one thing on which his
jaw was also absolutely rigid, a considerable jaw,
under that short grizzling beard. Nor was there
ever any necessity for real heart-to-heart encoun-
ters. One could break away into irony — as indeed
he often had to. But the real trouble with June was
that she had never appealed to his æsthetic sense,
though she might well have, with her red-gold hair
and her viking-coloured eyes, and that touch of the
Berserker in her spirit. It was very different with
Holly, soft and quiet, shy and affectionate, with a
playful imp in her somewhere. He watched this

younger daughter of his through the duckling stage with extraordinary interest. Would she come out a swan? With her sallow oval face and her grey wistful eyes and those long dark lashes, she might, or she might not. Only this last year had he been able to guess. Yes, she would be a swan — rather a dark one, always a shy one, but an authentic swan. She was eighteen now, and Mademoiselle Beauce was gone — the excellent lady had removed, after eleven years haunted by her continuous reminiscences of the 'well-brrred little Tayleurs,' to another family whose bosom would now be agitated by her reminiscences of the 'well-brrred little Forsytes.' She had taught Holly to speak French like herself.

Portraiture was not Jolyon's forte, but he had already drawn his younger daughter three times, and was drawing her a fourth, on the afternoon of October 4th, 1899, when a card was brought to him which caused his eyebrows to go up:

MR. SOAMES FORSYTE

THE SHELTER,   CONNOISSEURS' CLUB,
MAPLEDURHAM.   ST. JAMES'S

But here the Forsyte Saga must digress again. . . .

To return from a long travel in Spain to a darkened house, to a little daughter bewildered with tears, to the sight of a loved father lying peaceful in his last sleep, had never been, was never likely to be, forgotten by so impressionable and warm-hearted a man as Jolyon. A sense as of mystery, too, clung to that sad day, and about the end of one whose life had been so well-ordered, balanced, and above-board. It seemed incredible that his father could thus have vanished without, as it were, announcing his intention, without last words to his son, and due farewells. And those incoherent allusions of little Holly to 'the lady in grey,' of Mademoiselle Beauce to a Madame Errant (as it sounded) involved all things in a mist, lifted a little when he read his father's will and the codicil thereto. It had been his duty as executor of that will and codicil to inform Irene, wife of his cousin Soames, of her life interest in fifteen thousand pounds. He had called on her to explain that the existing investment in India Stock, ear-marked to meet the charge, would produce for her the interesting net sum of £430 odd a year, clear of Income Tax. This was but the third time he had seen his cousin Soames' wife — if indeed she was still his wife, of which he was not quite sure. He remembered having seen her sitting in the Botanical Gardens waiting for Bosinney — a passive, fascinating figure, reminding him of Titian's 'Heavenly Love,' and again, when, charged by his father, he had gone to Montpelier Square on the afternoon when Bosinney's death was known. He still recalled vividly her sudden appearance in the drawing-room doorway on that occasion — her beautiful face, passing from wild eagerness of hope to stony despair; remembered the compassion he had felt, Soames' snarling smile, his words, 'We are not at home,' and the slam of the front door.

This third time he saw a face and form more beautiful — freed from that warp of wild hope and despair. Looking at her, he thought: 'Yes, you are just what the dad would have admired!' And the strange story of his father's Indian summer became slowly clear to him. She spoke of old Jolyon with reverence and tears in her eyes. "He was so wonderfully kind to me; I don't know why. He looked so beautiful and peaceful sitting in that chair under the tree; it was I who first came on him sitting there, you know. Such a lovely day. I don't think an end could have been happier. We should all like to go out like that."

'Quite right!' he had thought. 'We should all like to go out in full summer with beauty stepping towards us across a lawn.'

And looking round the little, almost empty drawing-room, he had asked her what she was going to do now. "I am going to live again a little, Cousin Jolyon. It's wonderful to have money of one's own. I've never had any. I shall keep this flat, I think; I'm used to it; but I shall be able to go to Italy."

"Exactly!" Jolyon had murmured, looking at her faintly smiling lips; and he had gone away thinking: 'A fascinating woman! What a waste! I'm glad the dad left her that money. He had not seen her again, but every quarter he had signed her cheque, forwarding it to her bank, with a note to the Chelsea flat to say that he had done so; and always he had received a note in acknowledgment, generally from the flat, but sometimes from Italy; so that her personality had become embodied in slightly scented grey paper, an upright fine handwriting, and the words, 'Dear Cousin Jolyon.' Man of property that he now was, the slender cheque he signed often gave rise to the thought:

'Well, I suppose she just manages'; sliding into a
vague wonder how she was faring otherwise in a
world of men not wont to let beauty go unpossessed.
At first Holly had spoken of her sometimes, but
'ladies in grey' soon fade from children's memories; and the tightening of June's lips in those first
weeks after her grandfather's death whenever her
former friend's name was mentioned, had discour-
aged allusion.   Only once, indeed, had June spoken
definitely: "I've forgiven her. I'm frightfully
glad she's independent now.". . .

On receiving Soames' card, Jolyon said to the
maid — for he could not abide butlers — "Show
him into the study, please, and say I'll be there in a
minute"; and then he looked at Holly and asked:

"Do you remember 'the lady in grey,' who used
to give you music-lessons?"

"Oh, yes, why?   Has she come?"

Jolyon shook his head, and, changing his holland
blouse for a coat, was silent, perceiving suddenly
that such history was not for those young ears.
His face, in fact, became whimsical perplexity in-
carnate while he journeyed towards the study.

Standing by the french-window, looking out
across the terrace at the oak-tree, were two figures,
middle-aged and young, and he thought: 'Who's
that boy?   Surely they never had a child.'

The elder figure turned.   The meeting of those
two Forsytes of the second generation, so much
more sophisticated than the first, in the house built
for the one and owned and occupied by the other,
was marked by subtle defensiveness beneath distinct attempt at cordiality.   'Has he come about
his wife?' Jolyon was thinking; and Soames, 'How
shall I begin?' while Val, brought to break the ice,

stood negligently scrutinising this 'bearded pard' from under his dark, thick eyelashes.

"This is Val Dartie," said Soames, "my sister's son. He's just going up to Oxford. I thought I'd like him to know your boy."

"Ah! I'm sorry Jolly's away. What college?"

"B.N.C.," replied Val.

"Jolly's at the 'House,' but he'll be delighted to look you up."

"Thanks, awfully."

"Holly's in — if you could put up with a female relation, she'd show you round. You'll find her in the hall if you go through the curtains. I was just painting her."

With another " Thanks, awfully!" Val vanished, leaving the two cousins with the ice unbroken.

"I see you've some drawings at the 'Water Colours,'" said Soames.

Jolyon winced. He had been out of touch with the Forsyte family at large for twenty-six years, but they were connected in his mind with Frith's 'Derby Day' and Landseer prints. He had heard from June that Soames was a connoisseur, which made it worse. He had become aware, too, of a curious sensation of repugnance.

"I haven't seen you for a long time," he said.

"No," answered Soames between close lips, "not since — as a matter of fact, it's about that I've come. You're her trustee, I'm told."

Jolyon nodded.

"Twelve years is a long time," said Soames rapidly: "I — I'm tired of it."

Jolyon found no more appropriate answer than: "Won't you smoke?"

"No, thanks."

Jolyon himself lit a cigarette.

"I wish to be free," said Soames abruptly.

"I don't see her," murmured Jolyon through the fume of his cigarette.

"But you know where she lives, I suppose?"

Jolyon nodded. He did not mean to give her address without permission. Soames seemed to divine his thought.

"I don't want her address," he said; "I know it."

"What exactly do you want?"

"She deserted me. I want a divorce."

"Rather late in the day, isn't it?"

"Yes," said Soames. And there was a silence.

"I don't know much about these things — at least, I've forgotten," said Jolyon with a wry smile. He himself had had to wait for death to grant him a divorce from the first Mrs. Jolyon. "Do you wish me to see her about it?"

Soames raised his eyes to his cousin's face.

"I suppose there's someone," he said.

A shrug moved Jolyon's shoulders.

"I don't know at all. I imagine you may have both lived as if the other were dead. It's usual in these cases."

Soames turned to the window. A few early fallen oak-leaves strewed the terrace already, and were rolling round in the wind. Jolyon saw the figures of Holly and Val Dartie moving across the lawn towards the stables. 'I'm not going to run with the hare and hunt with the hounds,' he thought. 'I must act for her. The dad would have wished that.' And for a swift moment he seemed to see his father's figure in the old armchair, just beyond Soames, sitting with knees crossed, *The Times* in his hand. It vanished.

"My father was fond of her," he said quietly.

"Why he should have been I don't know," Soames answered without looking round. "She brought trouble to your daughter June; she brought trouble to everyone. I gave her all she wanted. I would have given her even — forgiveness — but she chose to leave me."

In Jolyon compassion was checked by the tone of that close voice. What was there in the fellow that made it so difficult to be sorry for him?

"I can go and see her, if you like," he said. "I suppose she might be glad of a divorce, but I know nothing."

Soames nodded.

"Yes, please go. As I say, I know her address; but I've no wish to see her." His tongue was busy with his lips, as if they were very dry.

"You'll have some tea?" said Jolyon, stifling the words: 'And see the house.' And he led the way into the hall. When he had rung the bell and ordered tea, he went to his easel to turn his drawing to the wall. He could not bear, somehow, that his work should be seen by Soames, who was standing there in the middle of the great room which had been designed expressly to afford wall space for his own pictures. In his cousin's face, with its unseizable family likeness to himself, and its chinny, narrow, concentrated look, Jolyon saw that which moved him to the thought: 'That chap could never forget anything — nor ever give himself away. He's pathetic!'

CHAPTER VII

THE COLT AND THE FILLY

WHEN young Val left the presence of the last generation he was thinking: 'This is jolly dull! Uncle Soames does take the bun. I wonder what this filly's like?' He anticipated no pleasure from her society; and suddenly he saw her standing there looking at him. Why, she was pretty! What luck!

" I'm afraid you don't know me," he said. " My name's Val Dartie —— I'm once removed, second cousin, something like that, you know. My mother's name was Forsyte."

Holly, whose slim brown hand remained in his because she was too shy to withdraw it, said:

" I don't know any of my relations. Are there many? "

" Tons. They're awful — most of them. At least, I don't know — some of them. One's relations always are, aren't they? "

" I expect they think one awful too," said Holly.

" I don't know why they should. No one could think *you* awful, of course."

Holly looked at him — the wistful candour in those grey eyes gave young Val a sudden feeling that he must protect her.

" I mean there are people and people," he added

68

astutely. "Your dad looks awfully decent, for instance."

"Oh yes!" said Holly fervently; "he is."

A flush mounted in Val's cheeks — that scene in the Pandemonium promenade — the dark man with the pink carnation developing into his own father! "But you know what the Forsytes are," he said almost viciously. "Oh! I forgot; you don't."

"What are they?"

"Oh! fearfully careful; not sportsmen a bit. Look at Uncle Soames!"

"I'd like to," said Holly.

Val resisted a desire to run his arm through hers. "Oh no," he said, "let's go out. You'll see him quite soon enough. What's your brother like?"

Holly led the way on to the terrace and down to the lawn without answering. How describe Jolly, who, ever since she remembered anything, had been her lord, master, and ideal?

"Does he sit on you?" said Val shrewdly. "I shall be knowing him at Oxford. Have you got any horses?"

Holly nodded. "Would you like to see the stables?"

"Rather!"

They passed under the oak-tree, through a thin shrubbery, into the stable-yard. There under a clock tower lay a fluffy brown-and-white dog, so old that he did not get up, but faintly waved the tail curled over his back.

"That's Balthasar," said Holly; "he's so old — awfully old, nearly as old as I am. Poor old boy! He's devoted to dad."

"Balthasar! That's a rum name. He isn't pure-bred, you know."

"No! but he's a darling," and she bent down to stroke the dog. Gentle and supple, with dark uncovered head and slim browned neck and hands, she seemed to Val strange and sweet, like a thing slipped between him and all previous knowledge.

"When grandfather died," she said, "he wouldn't eat for two days. He saw him die, you know."

"Was that old Uncle Jolyon? Mother always says he was a topper."

"He was," said Holly simply, and opened the stable door.

In a loose-box stood a silver roan of about fifteen hands, with a long black tail and mane. "This is mine — Fairy."

"Ah!" said Val, "she's a jolly palfrey. But you ought to bang her tail. She'd look much smarter." Then catching her wondering look, he thought suddenly: 'I don't know — anything she likes!' And he took a long sniff of the stable air. "Horses are ripping, aren't they? My dad — " he stopped.

"Yes?" said Holly.

An impulse to unbosom himself almost overcame him — but not quite. "Oh! I don't know — he's often gone a mucker over them. I'm jolly keen on them too — riding and hunting. I like racing awfully, as well; I should like to be a gentleman rider." And oblivious of the fact that he had but one more day in town, with two engagements, he plumped out:

"I say, if I hire a gee to-morrow, will you come a ride in Richmond Park?"

Holly clasped her hands.

"Oh yes! I simply love riding. But there's

Jolly's horse; why don't you ride him? Here he is. We could go after tea."

Val looked doubtfully at his trousered legs. He had imagined them immaculate before her eyes in high brown boots and Bedford cords.

" I don't much like riding his horse," he said. " He mightn't like it. Besides, Uncle Soames wants to get back, I expect. Not that I believe in buckling under to him, you know. You haven't got an uncle, have you? This is rather a good beast," he added, scrutinising Jolly's horse, a dark brown, which was showing the whites of its eyes. " You haven't got any hunting here, I suppose? "

" No; I don't know that I want to hunt. It must be awfully exciting, of course; but it's cruel, isn't it? June says so."

" Cruel? " ejaculated Val. " Oh! that's all rot. Who's June? "

" My sister — my half-sister, you know — much older than me." She had put her hands up to both cheeks of Jolly's horse, and was rubbing her nose against its nose with a gentle snuffling noise which seemed to have an hypnotic effect on the animal. Val contemplated her cheek resting against the horse's nose, and her eyes gleaming round at him. ' She's really a duck,' he thought.

They returned to the house less talkative, followed this time by the dog Balthasar, walking more slowly than anything on earth, and clearly expecting them not to exceed his speed limit.

" This is a ripping place," said Val from under the oak-tree, where they had paused to allow the dog Balthasar to come up.

" Yes," said Holly, and sighed. " Of course I want to go everywhere. I wish I were a gipsy."

"Yes, gipsies are jolly," replied Val, with a conviction which had just come to him; "you're rather like one, you know."

Holly's face shone suddenly and deeply, like dark leaves gilded by the sun.

"To go mad-rabbiting everywhere and see everything, and live in the open — oh! wouldn't it be fun?"

"Let's do it," said Val.

"Oh yes, let's!"

"It'd be grand sport, just you and I."

Then Holly perceived the quaintness and flushed.

"Well, we've got to do it," said Val obstinately, but reddening too. "I believe in doing things you want to do. What's down there?"

"The kitchen-garden, and the pond and the coppice, and the farm."

"Let's go down!"

Holly glanced back at the house.

"It's tea-time, I expect; there's dad beckoning."

Val, uttering a growly sound, followed her towards the house.

When they re-entered the hall gallery the sight of two middle-aged Forsytes drinking tea together had its magical effect, and they became quite silent. It was, indeed, an impressive spectacle. The two were seated side by side on an arrangement in marqueterie which looked like three silvery pink chairs made one, with a low tea-table in front of them. They seemed to have taken up that position, as far apart as the seat would permit, so that they need not look at each other too much; and they were eating and drinking rather than talking — Soames with his air of despising the tea-cake as it disappeared, Jolyon of finding himself slightly amusing.

To the casual eye neither would have seemed greedy, but both were getting through a good deal of sustenance. The two young ones having been supplied with food, the process went on silent and absorbative, till, with the advent of cigarettes, Jolyon said to Soames:

" And how's Uncle James? "

" Thanks, very shaky."

" We're a wonderful family, aren't we? The other day I was calculating the average age of the ten old Forsytes from my father's family Bible. I make it eighty-four already, and five still living. They ought to beat the record;" and looking whimsically at Soames, he added: " We aren't the men they were, you know."

Soames smiled. ' Do you really think I shall admit that I'm not their equal,' he seemed to be saying, ' or that I've got to give up anything, especially life? '

" We may live to their age, perhaps," pursued Jolyon, " but self-consciousness is a handicap, you know, and that's the difference between us. We've conviction. How and when self-consciousness was born I never can make out. My father had a little, but I don't believe any other of the old Forsytes ever had a scrap. Never to see yourself as others see you, it's a wonderful preservative. The whole history of the last century is in the difference between us. And between us and you," he added, gazing through a ring of smoke at Val and Holly, uncomfortable under his quizzical regard, " there'll be — another difference. I wonder what."

Soames took out his watch.

" We must go," he said, " if we're to catch our train."

"Uncle Soames never misses a train," muttered Val, with his mouth full.

"Why should I?" Soames answered simply.

"Oh! I don't know," grumbled Val, "other people do."

At the front door he gave Holly's slim brown hand a long and surreptitious squeeze.

"Look out for me to-morrow," he whispered; "three o'clock. I'll wait for you in the road; it'll save time. We'll have a ripping ride." He gazed back at her from the lodge gate, and, but for the principles of a man about town, would have waved his hand. He felt in no mood to tolerate his uncle's conversation. But he was not in danger. Soames preserved a perfect muteness, busy with far-away thoughts.

The yellow leaves came down about those two walking the mile and a half which Soames had traversed so often in those long-ago days when he came down to watch with secret pride the building of the house — that house which was to have been the home of him and her from whom he was now going to seek release. He looked back once, up that endless vista of autumn lane between the yellowing hedges. What an age ago! 'I don't want to see her,' he had said to Jolyon. Was that true? 'I may have to,' he thought; and he shivered, seized by one of those queer shudderings that they say mean footsteps on one's grave. A chilly world! A queer world! And glancing sidelong at his nephew, he thought: 'Wish I were his age! I wonder what she's like now!'

CHAPTER VIII

JOLYON PROSECUTES TRUSTEESHIP

WHEN those two were gone Jolyon did not return to his painting, for daylight was failing, but went to the study, craving unconsciously a revival of that momentary vision of his father sitting in the old brown leather chair with his knees crossed and his straight eyes gazing up from under the dome of his massive brow. Often in this little room, cosiest in the house, Jolyon would catch a moment of communion with his father. Not, indeed, that he had definitely any faith in the persistence of the human spirit — the feeling was not so logical — it was, rather, an atmospheric impact, like a scent, or one of those strong animistic impressions from forms, or effects of light, to which those with the artist's eye are especially prone. Here only — in this little unchanged room where his father had spent the most of his waking hours — could be retrieved the feeling that he was not quite gone, that the steady counsel of that old spirit and the warmth of his masterful lovability endured.

What would his father be advising now, in this sudden recrudescence of an old tragedy — what would he say to this menace against her to whom he had taken such a fancy in the last weeks of his life?

' I must do my best for her,' thought Jolyon; ' he
left her to me in his will.   But what *is* the best ? '

And as if seeking to regain the sapience, the balance and shrewd common sense of that old Forsyte,
he sat down in the ancient chair and crossed his
knees.   But he felt a mere shadow sitting there;
nor did any inspiration come, while the fingers of
the wind tapped on the darkening panes of the
french-window.

' Go and see her ? ' he thought, ' or ask her to come
down here?   What's her life been?   What is it
now, I wonder?   Beastly to rake up things at this
time of day.'   Again the figure of his cousin standing with a hand on a front door of a fine olive-green
leaped out, vivid, like one of those figures from old-
fashioned clocks when the hour strikes; and his
words sounded in Jolyon's ears clearer than any
chime: ' I manage my own affairs.   I've told you
once, I tell you again: We are not at home.'   The
repugnance he had then felt for Soames — for his
flat-cheeked, shaven face full of spiritual bull-dog-
gedness, for his spare, square, sleek figure slightly
crouched as it were over the bone he could not digest — came now again, fresh as ever, nay, with an
odd increase.   ' I dislike him,' he thought, ' I dislike him to the very roots of me.   And that's lucky;
it'll make it easier for me to back his wife.'   Half-
artist and half-Forsyte, Jolyon was constitutionally
averse from what he termed ' ructions '; unless an-
gered, he conformed deeply to that classic descrip-
tion of the she-dog, ' Er'd ruther run than fight.'
A little smile became settled in his beard.   Ironical
that Soames should come down here — to this
house, built for himself!   How he had gazed and
gaped at this ruin of his past intention; furtively

nosing at the walls and stairway, appraising everything!   And intuitively Jolyon thought: ' I believe
the fellow even now would like to be living here.
He could never leave off longing for what he once
owned!   Well, I must act, somehow or other; but
it's a bore — a great bore.'

Late that evening he wrote to the Chelsea flat,
asking if Irene would see him.

The old century which had seen the plant of individualism flower so wonderfully was setting in a
sky orange with coming storms.   Rumours of war
added to the briskness of a London turbulent at the
close of the summer holidays.   And the streets to
Jolyon, who was not often up in town, had a feverish look, due to these new motor-cars and cabs, of
which he disapproved æsthetically.   He counted
these vehicles from his hansom, and made the pro-
portion of them one in twenty.   ' They were one in
thirty about a year ago,' he thought; ' they've come
to stay.   Just so much more rattling round of
wheels and general stink' — for he was one of those
rather rare Liberals who object to anything new
when it takes a material form; and he instructed
his driver to get down to the river quickly, out of
the traffic, desiring to look at the water through the
mellowing screen of plane-trees.   At the little block
of flats which stood back some fifty yards from the
Embankment, he told the cabman to wait, and went
up to the first floor.

Yes, Mrs. Heron was at home!

The effect of a settled if very modest income was
at once apparent to him remembering the threadbare
refinement in that tiny flat eight years ago when he
announced her good fortune.   Everything was now
fresh, dainty, and smelled of flowers.   The general

effect was silvery with touches of black, hydrangea colour, and gold. ' A woman of great taste,' he thought. Time had dealt gently with Jolyon, for he was a Forsyte. But with Irene Time hardly seemed to deal at all — or such was his impression. She appeared to him not a day older, standing there in mole-coloured velvet corduroy, with soft dark eyes and dark gold hair, with outstretched hand and a little smile.

" Won't you sit down? "

He had probably never occupied a chair with a fuller sense of embarrassment.

" You look absolutely unchanged," he said.

" And you look younger, Cousin Jolyon."

Jolyon ran his hands through his hair, whose thickness was still a comfort to him.

" I'm ancient, but I don't feel it. That's one thing about painting, it keeps you young. Titian lived to ninety-nine, and had to have plague to kill him off. Do you know, the first time I ever saw you I thought of a picture by him? "

" When did you see me for the first time? "

" In the Botanical Gardens."

" How did you know me, if you'd never seen me before? "

" By someone who came up to you." He was looking at her hardily, but her face did not change; and she said quietly:

" Yes; many lives ago."

" What is *your* recipe for youth, Irene? "

" People who don't *live* are wonderfully preserved."

What a bitter little saying! People who don't live! It was an opening, and he took it. " You remember my Cousin Soames? "

He saw her smile faintly at that whimsicality, and at once went on: " He came to see me the day before yesterday! He wants a divorce. Do you? "

" I? " The word seemed startled out of her. " After twelve years? It's rather late. Won't it be difficult? "

Jolyon looked hard into her face. " Unless — " he said.

" Unless I have a lover now. But I have never had one since."

What did he feel at the simplicity and candour of those words? Relief, surprise, pity! Venus for twelve years without a lover!

" And yet," he said, " I suppose you would give a good deal to be free, too? "

" I don't know. What does it matter, now? "

" But if you were to love again? "

" I should love." In that simple answer she seemed to sum up the whole philosophy of one on whom the world had turned its back.

" Well! Is there anything you would like me to say to him? "

" Only that I'm sorry he's not free. He had his chance once. I don't know why he didn't take it."

" Because he was a Forsyte; we never part with things, you know, unless we want something in their place; and not always then."

Irene smiled. " Don't you, Cousin Jolyon? — I think you do."

" Of course, I'm a bit of a mongrel — not quite a pure Forsyte. I never take the halfpennies off my cheques, I put them on," said Jolyon uneasily.

" Well, what does Soames want in place of me now? "

" I don't know; perhaps children."

She was silent for a little, looking down.

"Yes," she murmured; "it's hard.   I would help him to be free if I could."

Jolyon gazed into his hat, his embarrassment was increasing fast; so was his admiration, his wonder, and his pity.   She was so lovely, and so lonely; and altogether it was such a coil!

"Well," he said, "I shall have to see Soames.   If there's anything I can do for you I'm always at your service.   You must think of me as a wretched substitute for my father.   At all events I'll let you know what happens when I speak to Soames.   He may supply the material himself."

She shook her head.

"You see, he has a lot to lose; and I have nothing. I should like him to be free; but I don't see what I can do."

"Nor I at the moment," said Jolyon, and soon after took his leave.   He went down to his hansom. Half-past three!   Soames would be at his office still.

"To the Poultry," he called through the trap. In front of the Houses of Parliament and White-hall, newsvendors were calling, 'Grave situation in the Transvaal!' but the cries hardly roused him, absorbed in recollection of that very beautiful fig-ure, of her soft dark glance, and the words: 'I have never had one since.'   What on earth did such a woman do with her life, backwatered like this? Solitary, unprotected, with every man's hand against her or rather — reaching out to grasp her at the least sign.   And year after year she went on like that!

The word 'Poultry' above the passing citizens brought him back to reality.

'Forsyte, Bustard and Forsyte,' in black letters
on a ground the colour of peasoup, spurred him to a
sort of vigour, and he went up the stone stairs mut-
tering: "Fusty musty ownerships! Well, we
couldn't do without them!"

"I want Mr. Soames Forsyte," he said to the boy
who opened the door.

"What name?"

"Mr. Jolyon Forsyte."

The youth looked at him curiously, never having
seen a Forsyte with a beard, and vanished.

The offices of 'Forsyte, Bustard and Forsyte'
had slowly absorbed the offices of 'Tooting and
Bowles,' and occupied the whole of the first floor.
The firm consisted now of nothing but Soames and
a number of managing and articled clerks. The
complete retirement of James some six years ago
had accelerated business, to which the final touch of
speed had been imparted when Bustard dropped off,
worn out, as many believed, by the suit of 'Fryer
versus Forsyte,' more in Chancery than ever and
less likely to benefit its beneficiaries. Soames, with
his saner grasp of actualities, had never permitted it
to worry him; on the contrary, he had long perceived that Providence had presented him therein
with £200 a year nett in perpetuity, and — why not?

When Jolyon entered, his cousin was drawing out
a list of holdings in consols, which in view of the
rumours of war he was going to advise his companies
to put on the market at once, before other companies
did the same. He looked round, sidelong, and said:

"How are you? Just one minute. Sit down,
won't you?" And having entered three amounts,
and set a ruler to keep his place, he turned towards
Jolyon, biting the side of his flat fore-finger.

" Yes? " he said.

" I have seen her."

Soames frowned.

" Well? "

" She has remained faithful to memory."

Having said that Jolyon was ashamed. His
cousin had flushed a dusky yellowish red. What had
made him tease the poor brute! " I was to tell you
she is sorry you are not free. Twelve years is a
long time. You know your law better than I do,
and what chance it gives you." Soames uttered a
curious little grunt, and the two remained a full
minute without speaking. ' Like wax!' thought Jolyon, watching that close face, where the flush was
fast subsiding. ' He'll never give me a sign of what
he's thinking, or going to do. Like wax!' And he
transferred his gaze to a plan of that flourishing
town, ' By-Street on Sea,' the future existence of
which lay exposed on the wall to the possessive instincts of the firm's clients. The whimsical thought
flashed through him: ' I wonder if I shall get a bill
of costs for this — " To attending Mr. Jolyon Forsyte in the matter of my divorce, to receiving his account of his visit to my wife, and to advising him to
go and see her again, sixteen and eightpence."'

Suddenly Soames said: " I can't go on like this.
I tell you, I can't go on like this." His eyes were
shifting from side to side, like an animal's when it
looks for way of escape. ' He really suffers,'
thought Jolyon; ' I've no business to forget that,
just because I don't like him.'

" Surely," he said gently, " it lies with yourself.
A man can always put these things through if he'll
take it on himself."

Soames turned square to him, with a sound which
seemed to come from somewhere very deep.

" Why should I suffer more than I've suffered already? Why should I? "

Jolyon could only shrug his shoulders. His reason agreed, his instinct rebelled; he could not have said why.

" Your father," went on Soames, " took an interest in her — why, goodness knows! And I suppose you do too? " he gave Jolyon a sharp look. " It seems to me that one only has to do another person a wrong to get all the sympathy. I don't know in what way I was to blame — I've never known. I always treated her well. I gave her everything she could wish for. I wanted her."

Again Jolyon's reason nodded; again his instinct shook its head. ' What is it? ' he thought; ' there must be something wrong in me. Yet if there is, I'd rather be wrong than right.'

" After all," said Soames with a sort of glum fierceness, " she was my wife."

In a flash the thought went through his listener: ' There it is! Ownerships! Well, we all own things. But — human beings! Pah! '

" You have to look at facts," he said drily, " or rather the want of them."

Soames gave him another quick suspicious look.

" The want of them? " he said. " Yes, but I am not so sure."

" I beg your pardon," replied Jolyon; " I've told you what she said. It was explicit."

" My experience has not been one to promote blind confidence in her word. We shall see."

Jolyon got up.

" Good-bye," he said curtly.

" Good-bye," returned Soames; and Jolyon went out trying to understand the look, half-startled, half-menacing, on his cousin's face. He sought Waterloo Station in a disturbed frame of mind, as though the skin of his moral being had been scraped; and all the way down in the train he thought of Irene in her lonely flat, and of Soames in his lonely office, and of the strange paralysis of life that lay on them both. 'In chancery!' he thought. 'Both their necks in chancery — and hers so pretty!'

CHAPTER IX

THE keeping of engagements had not as yet been a
conspicuous feature in the life of young Val Dartie,
so that when he broke two and kept one, it was the
latter event which caused him, if anything, the
greater surprise, while jogging back to town from
Robin Hill after his ride with Holly. She had been
even prettier than he had thought her yesterday, on
her silver-roan, long-tailed ' palfrey '; and it seemed
to him, self-critical in the brumous October gloam-
ing and the outskirts of London, that only his boots
had shone throughout their two-hour companionship. He took out his new gold ' hunter ' — present from James — and looked not at the time, but at
sections of his face in the glittering back of its
opened case. He had a temporary spot over one
eyebrow, and it displeased him, for it must have displeased her. Crum never had any spots. Together
with Crum rose the scene in the promenade of the
Pandemonium. To-day he had not had the faintest desire to unbosom himself to Holly about his
father. His father lacked poetry, the stirrings of
which he was feeling for the first time in his nineteen years. The Liberty, with Cynthia Dark, that
almost mythical embodiment of rapture; the Pande-

monium, with the woman of uncertain age — both seemed to Val completely ' off,' fresh from communion with this new, shy, dark-haired young cousin of his. She rode ' jolly well,' too, so that it had been all the more flattering that she had let him lead her where he would in the long gallops of Richmond Park, though she knew them so much better than he did. Looking back on it all, he was mystified by the barrenness of his speech; he felt that he could say ' an awful lot of fetching things ' if he had but the chance again, and the thought that he must go back to Littlehampton on the morrow, and to Oxford on the twelfth — ' to that beastly exam,' too — without the faintest chance of first seeing her again, caused darkness to settle on his spirit even more quickly than on the evening. He should write to her, however, and she had promised to answer. Perhaps, too, she would come up to Oxford to see her brother. That thought was like the first star, which came out as he rode into Padwick's livery stables in the purlieus of Sloane Square. He got off and stretched himself luxuriously, for he had ridden some twenty-five good miles. The Dartie within him made him chaffer for five minutes with young Padwick concerning the favourite for the Cambridgeshire; then with the words, " Put the gee down to my account," he walked away, a little wide at the knees, and flipping his boots with his knotty little cane. ' I don't feel a bit inclined to go out,' he thought. ' I wonder if mother will stand fizz for my last night ! ' With ' fizz ' and recollection, he could well pass a domestic evening.

When he came down, speckless after his bath, he found his mother scrupulous in a low evening dress, and, to his annoyance, his Uncle Soames. They

stopped talking when he came in; then his uncle
said:

"He'd better be told."

At those words, which meant something about
his father, of course, Val's first thought was of
Holly. Was it anything beastly? His mother began speaking.

"Your father," she said in her fashionably ap-
pointed voice, while her fingers plucked rather pitifully at sea-green brocade, "your father, my dear
boy, has — is not at New-market; he's on his way
to South America. He — he's left us."

Val looked from her to Soames. Left them!
Was he sorry? Was he fond of his father? It
seemed to him that he did not know. Then, suddenly — as at a whiff of gardenias and cigars — his
heart twitched within him, and he *was* sorry. One's
father belonged to one, could not go off in this fashion — it was not done! Nor had he always been
the 'bounder' of the Pandemonium promenade.
There were precious memories of tailors' shops and
horses, tips at school, and general lavish kindness,
when in luck.

"But why?" he said. Then, as a sportsman
himself, was sorry he had asked. The mask of his
mother's face was all disturbed; and he burst out:

"All right, Mother, don't tell me! Only, what
does it mean? "

" A divorce, Val, I'm afraid."

Val uttered a queer little grunt, and looked
quickly at his uncle — that uncle whom he had been
taught to look on as a guarantee against the consequences of having a father, even against the Dartie
blood in his own veins. The flat-cheeked visage
seemed to wince, and this upset him.

" It won't be public, will it? "

So vividly before him had come recollection of his
own eyes glued to the unsavoury details of many a
divorce suit in the public Press.

" Can't it be done quietly somehow?   It's so disgusting for — for mother, and — and everybody."

" Everything will be done as quietly as it can, you
may be sure."

" Yes — but, why is it necessary at all?   Mother
doesn't want to marry again."

Himself, the girls, their name tarnished in the
sight of his schoolfellows and of Crum, of the men
at Oxford, of — Holly! Unbearable! What was
to be gained by it?

" Do you, Mother? " he said sharply.

Thus brought face to face with so much of her
own feeling by the one she loved best in the world,
Winifred rose from the Empire chair in which she
had been sitting.   She saw that her son would be
against her unless he was told everything; and, yet,
how could she tell him?   Thus, still plucking at the
green brocade, she stared at Soames.   Val, too,
stared at Soames.   Surely this embodiment of respectability and the sense of property could not wish
to bring such a slur on his own sister!

Soames slowly passed a little inlaid paper-knife
over the smooth surface of a marqueterie table;
then, without looking at his nephew, he began:

" You don't understand what your mother has
had to put up with these twenty years.   This is only
the last straw, Val."   And glancing up sideways at
Winifred, he added:

" Shall I tell him? "

Winifred was silent.   If he were not told, he
would be against her! Yet, how dreadful to be told

such things of his own father! Clenching her lips, she nodded.

Soames spoke in a rapid, even voice:

"He has always been a burden round your mother's neck. She has paid his debts over and over again; he has often been drunk, abused and threatened her; and now he is gone to Buenos Aires with a dancer." And, as if distrusting the efficacy of those words on the boy, he went on quickly:

"He took your mother's pearls to give to her."

Val jerked up his hand then. At that signal of distress Winifred cried out:

"That'll do, Soames — stop!"

In the boy, the Dartie and the Forsyte were struggling. For debts, drink, dancers, he had a certain sympathy; but the pearls — no! That was too much! And suddenly he found his mother's hand squeezing his.

"You see," he heard Soames say, "we can't have it all begin over again. There's a limit; we must strike while the iron's hot."

Val freed his hand.

"But — you're — never going to bring out that about the pearls! I couldn't stand that — I simply couldn't!"

Winifred cried out:

"No, no, Val — oh no! That's only to show you how impossible your father is!" And his uncle nodded. Somewhat assuaged, Val took out a cigarette. His father had bought him that thin curved case. Oh! it was unbearable — just as he was going up to Oxford!

"Can't mother be protected without?" he said. "I could look after her. It could always be done later if it was really necessary."

A smile played for a moment round Soames's lips, and became bitter.

"You don't know what you're talking of; nothing's so fatal as delay in such matters."

"Why?"

"I tell you, boy, nothing's so fatal. I know from experience."

His voice had the ring of exasperation. Val regarded him round-eyed, never having known his uncle express any sort of feeling. Oh! Yes — he remembered now — there had been an Aunt Irene, and something had happened — something which people kept dark; he had heard his father once use an unmentionable word of her.

· "I don't want to speak ill of your father," Soames went on doggedly, "but I know him well enough to be sure that he'll be back on your mother's hands before a year's over. You can imagine what that will mean to her and to all of you after this. The only thing is to cut the knot for good."

In spite of himself, Val was impressed; and, happening to look at his mother's face, he got what was perhaps his first real insight into the fact that his own feelings were not always what mattered most.

"All right, mother," he said, "we'll back you up. Only I'd like to know when it'll be. It's my first term, you know. I don't want to be up there when it comes off."

"Oh! my dear boy," murmured Winifred, "it *is* a bore for you." So, by habit, she phrased what, from the expression of her face, was the most poignant regret. "When will it be, Soames?"

"Can't tell — not for months. We must get restitution first."

'What the deuce is that?' thought Val. 'What

silly brutes lawyers are! Not for months! I know one thing: I'm not going to dine in!' And he said: "Awfully sorry, mother, I've got to go out to dinner now."

Though it was his last night, Winifred nodded almost gratefully; they both felt that they had gone quite far enough in the expression of feeling.

Val sought the misty freedom of Green Street, reckless and depressed. And not till he reached Piccadilly did he discover that he had only eighteen-pence. One couldn't dine off eighteen-pence, and he was very hungry. He looked longingly at the windows of the Iseeum Club, where he had often eaten of the best with his father! Those pearls! There was no getting over them! But the more he brooded and the further he walked the hungrier he naturally became. Short of trailing home, there were only two places where he could go — his grandfather's in Park Lane, and Timothy's in the Bayswater Road. Which was the less deplorable? At his grandfather's he would probably get a better dinner on the spur of the moment. At Timothy's they gave you a jolly good feed when they expected you, not otherwise. He decided on Park Lane, not unmoved by the thought that to go up to Oxford without affording his grandfather a chance to tip him was hardly fair to either of them. His mother would hear he had been there, of course, and might think it funny; but he couldn't help that. He rang the bell.

"Hullo, Warmson, any dinner for me, d'you think?"

"They're just going in, Master Val. Mr. Forsyte will be very glad to see you. He was saying at lunch that he never saw you nowadays."

Val grinned:

" Well, here I am.   Kill the fatted calf, Warmson, let's have fizz."

Warmson smiled faintly — in his opinion Val was
a young limb.

" I will ask Mrs. Forsyte, Master Val."

" I say," Val grumbled, taking off his overcoat,
" I'm not at school any more, you know."

Warmson, not without a sense of humour, opened
the door beyond the stags-horn coatstand, with the
words:

" Mr. Valerus, ma'am."

" Confound him! " thought Val, entering.

A warm embrace, and a " Well, Val! " from
Emily; a rather quavery, " So there you are at
last! " from James, restored his sense of dignity.

" Why didn't you let us know?   There's only
saddle of mutton.   Champagne, Warmson," said
Emily.   And they went in.

At the great dining-table, shortened to its utmost,
under which so many fashionable legs had rested,
James sat at one end, Emily at the other, Val halfway between them; and something of the loneliness
of his grandparents, now that all their four children
were flown, reached the boy's spirit.   ' I hope I shall
kick the bucket long before I'm as old as grandfather,' he thought.   ' Poor old chap, he's as thin as
a rail! '   And lowering his voice while his grandfather and Warmson were in discussion about sugar
in the soup, he said to Emily:

" It's pretty brutal at home, Granny.   I suppose
you know."

" Yes, dear boy."

" Uncle Soames was there when I left.   I say,
isn't there anything to be done to prevent a divorce?
Why is he so beastly keen on it ? "

" Hush, my dear ! " murmured Emily; " we're keeping it from your grandfather."

James' voice sounded from the other end.

" What's that ? What are you talking about ? "

" About Val's college," returned Emily. " Young Pariser was there, James; you remember — he nearly broke the Bank at Monte Carlo afterwards."

James muttered that he did not know — Val must look after himself up there, or he'd get into bad ways. And he looked at his grandson with gloom, out of which affection distrustfully glimmered.

" What I'm afraid of," said Val to his plate, " is of being hard up, you know."

By instinct he knew that the weak spot in that old man was fear of insecurity for his grandchildren.

" Well," said James, and the soup in his spoon dribbled over, " you'll have a good allowance; but you must keep within it."

" Of course," murmured Val; " if it is good. How much will it be, Grandfather ? "

" Three hundred and fifty; it's too much. I had next to nothing at your age."

Val sighed. He had hoped for four, and been afraid of three. " I don't know what your young cousin has," said James; " he's up there. His father's a rich man."

" Aren't you ? " asked Val hardily.

" I ? " replied James, flustered. " I've got so many expenses. Your father — " and he was silent.

" Cousin Jolyon's got an awfully jolly place. I went down there with Uncle Soames — ripping stables."

" Ah ! " murmured James profoundly. " That house — I knew how it would be ! " And he lapsed into gloomy meditation over his fishbones. His son's tragedy, and the deep cleavage it had caused in the Forsyte family, had still the power to draw him down into a whirlpool of doubts and misgivings. Val, who hankered to talk of Robin Hill, because Robin Hill meant Holly, turned to Emily and said:

"Was that the house built for Uncle Soames?" And, receiving her nod, went on: " I wish you'd tell me about him, Granny. What became of Aunt Irene? Is she still going? He seems awfully worked-up about something to-night."

Emily laid her finger on her lips, but the word Irene had caught James' ear.

" What's that? " he said, staying a piece of mutton close to his lips. " Who's been seeing her? I knew we hadn't heard the last of that."

" Now, James," said Emily, " eat your dinner. Nobody's been seeing anybody."

James put down his fork.

" There you go," he said. " I might die before you'd tell me of it. Is Soames getting a divorce? "

" Nonsense," said Emily with incomparable aplomb; " Soames is much too sensible."

James had sought his own throat, gathering the long white whiskers together on the skin and bone of it.

" She — she was always ——— " he said, and with that enigmatic remark the conversation lapsed, for Warmson had returned. But later, when the saddle of mutton had been succeeded by sweet, savoury, and dessert, and Val had received a cheque for twenty pounds and his grandfather's kiss — like no other kiss in the world, from lips pushed out with a sort of fearful suddenness, as if yielding to weakness — he returned to the charge in the hall.

"Tell us about Uncle Soames, Granny. Why is he so keen on mother's getting a divorce?"

"Your Uncle Soames," said Emily, and her voice had in it an exaggerated assurance, "is a lawyer, my dear boy. He's sure to know best."

"Is he?" muttered Val. "But what did become of Aunt Irene? I remember she was jolly good-looking."

"She — er — " said Emily, "behaved very badly. We don't talk about it."

"Well, I don't want everybody at Oxford to know about our affairs," ejaculated Val; "it's a brutal idea. Why couldn't father be prevented without its being made public?"

Emily sighed. She had always lived rather in an atmosphere of divorce, owing to her fashionable proclivities — so many of those whose legs had been under her table having gained a certain notoriety. When, however, it touched her own family, she liked it no better than other people. But she was eminently practical, and a woman of courage, who never pursued a shadow in preference to its substance.

"Your mother," she said, "will be happier if she's quite free, Val. Good-night, my dear boy; and don't wear loud waistcoats up at Oxford, they're not the thing just now. Here's a little present."

With another five pounds in his hand, and a little warmth in his heart, for he was fond of his grandmother, he went out into Park Lane. A wind had cleared the mist, the autumn leaves were rustling, and the stars were shining. With all that money in his pocket an impulse to 'see life' beset him; but he had not gone forty yards in the direction of Piccadilly when Holly's shy face, and her eyes with an imp dancing in their gravity, came up before him, and his hand seemed to be tingling again from the pressure of her warm gloved hand. ' No, dash it! he thought, ' I'm going home! '

CHAPTER X

IT was full late for the river, but the weather was lovely, and summer lingered below the yellowing leaves. Soames took many looks at the day from his riverside garden near Mapledurham that Sunday morning. With his own hands he put flowers about his little house-boat, and equipped the punt, in which, after lunch, he proposed to take them on the river. Placing those Chinese-looking cushions, he could not tell whether or no he wished to take Annette alone. She was so very pretty — could he trust himself not to say irrevocable words, passing beyond the limits of discretion? Roses on the veranda were still in bloom, and the hedges evergreen, so that there was almost nothing of middle-aged autumn to chill the mood; yet was he nervous, fidgety, strangely distrustful of his powers to steer just the right course. This visit had been planned to produce in Annette and her mother a due sense of his possessions, so that they should be ready to receive with respect any overture he might later be disposed to make. He dressed with great care, making himself neither too young nor too old, very thankful that his hair was still thick and smooth and had no grey in it. Three times he went up to

97

his picture-gallery. If they had any knowledge at all, they must see at once that his collection alone was worth at least thirty thousand pounds. He minutely inspected, too, the pretty bedroom overlooking the river where they would take off their hats. It would be her bedroom if — if the matter went through, and she became his wife. Going up to the dressing-table he passed his hand over the lilac-coloured pincushion, into which were stuck all kind of pins; a bowl of pot-pourri exhaled a scent that made his head turn just a little. His wife! If only the whole thing could be settled out of hand, and there was not the nightmare of this divorce to be gone through first; and with gloom puckered on his forehead, he looked out at the river shining beyond the roses and the lawn. Madame Lamotte would never resist this prospect for her child; Annette would never resist her mother. If only he were free! He drove to the station to meet them. What taste Frenchwomen had! Madame Lamotte was in black with touches of lilac colour, Annette in greyish lilac linen, with cream coloured gloves and hat. Rather pale she looked and Londony; and her blue eyes were demure. Waiting for them to come down to lunch, Soames stood in the open french-window of the dining-room moved by that sensuous delight in sunshine and flowers and trees which only came to the full when youth and beauty were there to share it with one. He had ordered the lunch with intense consideration; the wine was a very special Sauterne, the whole appointments of the meal perfect, the coffee served on the veranda super-excellent. Madame Lamotte accepted crème de menthe; Annette refused. Her manners were charming, with just a suspicion of 'the con-

scious beauty' creeping into them. 'Yes,' thought
Soames, 'another year of London and that sort of
life, and she'll be spoiled.'

Madame was in sedate French raptures. *"Adorable! Le soleil est si bon!* How everything is *chic,*
is it not, Annette? Monseiur is a real Monte
Cristo." Annette murmured assent, with a look up
at Soames which he could not read. He proposed
a turn on the river. But to punt two persons when
one of them looked so ravishing on those Chinese
cushions was merely to suffer from a sense of lost
opportunity; so they went but a short way towards
Pangbourne, drifting slowly back, with every now
and then an autumn leaf dropping on Annette or on
her mother's black amplitude. And Soames was
not happy, worried by the thought: 'How — when
— where — can I say — what?' They did not
yet even know that he was married. To tell them he
was married might jeopardize his every chance;
yet, if he did not definitely make them understand that he wished for Annette's hand, it
would be dropping into some other clutch before he
was free to claim it.

At tea, which they both took with lemon, Soames
spoke of the Transvaal.

"There'll be war," he said.

Madame Lamotte lamented.

"Ces pauvres gens bergers!" Could they not
be left to themselves?

Soames smiled — the question seemed to him absurd.

Surely as a woman of business she understood
that the British could not abandon their legitimate
commercial interests.

"Ah! that!" But Madame Lamotte found that

the English were a little hypocrite. They were talking of justice and the Uitlanders, not of business. Monsieur was the first who had spoken to her of that.

"The Boers are only half-civilised," remarked Soames; "they stand in the way of progress. It will never do to let our suzerainty go."

"What does that mean to say? Suzerainty! What a strange word!" Soames became eloquent, roused by these threats to the principle of possession, and stimulated by Annette's eyes fixed on him. He was delighted when presently she said:

"I think Monsieur is right. They should be taught a lesson." She was sensible

"Of course," he said, "we must act with moderation. I'm no jingo. We must be firm without bullying. Will you come up and see my pictures?" Moving from one to another of these treasures, he soon perceived that they knew nothing. They passed his last Mauve, that remarkable study of a ' Hay-cart going Home,' as if it were a lithograph. He waited almost with awe to see how they would view the jewel of his collection — an Israels whose price he had watched ascending till he was now almost certain it had reached top value, and would be better on the market again. They did not view it at all. This was a shock; and yet to have in Annette a virgin taste to form would be better than to have the silly, half-baked predilections of the English middle-class to deal with. At the end of the gallery was a Meissonier of which he was rather ashamed — Meissonier was so steadily going down. Madame Lamotte stopped before it.

"Meissonier! Ah! What a jewel!' She had heard the name; Soames took advantage of that moment. Very gently touching Annette's arm, he said:

" How do you like my place, Annette? "

She did not shrink, did not respond; she looked at him full, looked down, and murmured:

" Who would not like it? It is so beautiful! "

" Perhaps some day —— " Soames said, and stopped.

So pretty she was, so self-possessed — she frightened him. Those cornflower-blue eyes, the turn of that creamy neck, her delicate curves — she was a standing temptation to indiscretion! No! No! One must be sure of one's ground — much surer! ' If I hold off,' he thought, ' it will tantalise her.' And he crossed over to Madame Lamotte, who was still in front of the Meissonier.

" Yes, that's quite a good example of his later work. You must come again, madame, and see them lighted up. You must both come and spend a night."

Enchanted, would it not be beautiful to see them lighted? By moonlight too, the river must be ravishing!

Annette murmured:

" Thou art sentimental, *Maman!* "

Sentimental! That black-robed, comely, substantial Frenchwoman of the world! And suddenly he was certain as he could be that there was no sentiment in either of them. All the better. Of what use sentiment! And yet —— !

He drove to the station with them, and saw them into the train. To the tightened pressure of his hand it seemed that Annette's fingers responded just a little; her face smiled at him through the dark.

He went back to the carriage, brooding. " Go on home, Jordan," he said to the coachman; " I'll walk." And he strode out into the darkening lanes, caution and the desire of possession playing see-saw within him. *" Bon soir, monsieur!"* How softly she had said it. To know what was in her mind! The French — they were like cats — one could tell nothing! But — how pretty! What a perfect young thing to hold in one's arms! What a mother for his heir! And he thought, with a smile, of his family and their surprise at a French wife, and their curiosity, and of the way he would play with it and buffet it — confound them! The poplars sighed in the darkness; an owl hooted. Shadows deepened in the water. ' I will and must be free,' he thought. ' I won't hang about any longer. I'll go and see Irene. If you want things done, do them yourself. I must live again — live and move and have my being.' And in echo to that queer biblicality church-bells chimed the call to evening prayer.

CHAPTER XI

AND VISITS THE PAST

On a Tuesday evening after dining at his Club Soames set out to do what required more courage and perhaps less delicacy than anything he had yet undertaken in his life — save perhaps his birth, and one other action. He chose the evening, indeed, partly because Irene was more likely to be in, but mainly because he had failed to find sufficient resolution by daylight, had needed wine to give him extra daring.

He left his hansom on the Embankment, and walked up to the Old Church, uncertain of the block of flats where he knew she lived. He found it hiding behind a much larger mansion; and having read the name, ' Mrs. Irene Heron ' — Heron, forsooth! Her maiden name: so she used that again, did she? — he stepped back into the road to look up at the windows of the first floor. Light was coming through in the corner flat, and he could hear a piano being played. He had never had a love of music, had secretly borne it a grudge in the old days when so often she had turned to her piano, making of it a refuge place into which she knew he could not enter. Repulse! The long repulse, at first strained and

secret, at last open! Bitter memory came with that
sound. It must be she playing, and thus almost assured of seeing her, he stood more undecided than
ever. Shivers of anticipation ran through him; his
tongue felt dry, his heart beat fast. '*I* have no
cause to be afraid,' he thought. And then the lawyer stirred within him. Was he doing a foolish
thing? Ought he not to have arranged a formal
meeting in the presence of her trustee? No! Not
before that fellow Jolyon, who sympathized with
her! Never! He crossed back into the doorway,
and, slowly, to keep down the beating of his heart,
mounted the single flight of stairs and rang the bell.
When the door was opened to him his sensations
were regulated by the scent which came — that perfume — from away back in the past, bringing muffled remembrance: fragrance of a drawing-room he
used to enter, of a house he used to own — perfume
of dried rose-leaves and honey!

"Say Mr. Forsyte," he said, "your mistress will
see me, I know." He had thought this out; she
would think it was Jolyon!

When the maid was gone and he was alone in the
tiny hall, where the light was dim from one pearly-
shaded sconce, and walls, carpet, everything was silvery, making the walled-in space all ghostly, he
could only think ridiculously: ' Shall I go in with my
overcoat on, or take it off? ' The music ceased, the
maid said from the doorway:

"Will you walk in, sir? "

Soames walked in. He noted mechanically that
all was still silvery, and that the upright piano was
of satinwood. She had risen and stood recoiled
against it; her hand, placed on the keys as if groping
for support, had struck a sudden discord, held for

a moment, and released. The light from the shaded piano-candle fell on her neck, leaving her face rather in shadow. She was in a black evening dress, with a sort of mantilla over her shoulders — he did not remember ever having seen her in black, and the thought passed through him: 'She dresses even when she's alone.'

" You! " he heard her whisper.

Many times Soames had rehearsed this scene in fancy. Rehearsal served him not at all. He simply could not speak. He had never thought that the sight of this woman whom he had once so passionately desired, so completely owned, and whom he had not seen for twelve years, could affect him in this way. He had imagined himself speaking and acting, half as man of business, half as judge. And now it was as if he were in the presence not of a mere woman and erring wife, but of some force, subtle and elusive as atmosphere itself, within him and outside. A kind of defensive irony welled up in him.

" Yes, it's a queer visit! I hope you're well."

" Thank you. Will you sit down? "

She had moved away from the piano, and gone over to a window-seat, sinking on to it, with her hands clasped in her lap. Light fell on her there, so that Soames could see her face, eyes, hair, strangely as he remembered them, strangely beautiful.

He sat down on the edge of a satin-wood chair, upholstered with silver-coloured stuff, close to where he was standing.

" You have not changed," he said.

" No? What have you come for? "

" To discuss things."

" I have heard what you want from your cousin."

" Well? "

" I am willing. I have always been."

The sound of her voice, reserved and close, the sight of her figure watchfully poised, defensive, was helping him now. A thousand memories of her, ever on the watch against him, stirred, and he said bitterly:

" Perhaps you will be good enough, then, to give me information on which I can act. The law must be complied with."

" I have none to give you that you don't know of."

" Twelve years! Do you suppose I can believe that? "

" I don't suppose you will believe anything I say; but it's the truth."

Soames looked at her hard. He had said that she had not changed; now he perceived that she had. Not in face, except that it was more beautiful; not in form, except that it was a little fuller — no! She had changed spiritually. There was more of her, as it were, something of activity and daring, where there had been sheer passive resistance. 'Ah!' he thought, ' that's her independent income! Confound Uncle Jolyon!'

" I suppose you're comfortably off now? " he said.

" Thank you, yes."

" Why didn't you let me provide for you? I would have, in spite of everything."

A faint smile came on her lips; but she did not answer.

" You are still my wife," said Soames. Why he said that, what he meant by it, he knew neither when he spoke nor after. It was a truism almost preposterous, but its effect was startling. She rose from the window-seat, and stood for a moment perfectly still, looking at him. He could see her bosom heaving. Then she turned to the window and threw it open.

" Why do that? " he said sharply. " You'll catch cold in that dress. I'm not dangerous." And he uttered a little sad laugh.

She echoed it — faintly, bitterly.

" It was — habit."

" Rather odd habit," said Soames as bitterly. " Shut the window! "

She shut it and sat down again. She had developed power, this woman — this — wife of his! He felt it issuing from her as she sat there, in a sort of armour. And almost unconsciously he rose and moved nearer; he wanted to see the expression on her face. Her eyes met his unflinching. Heavens! how clear they were, and what a dark brown against that white skin, and that burnt-amber hair! And how white her shoulders! Funny sensation this! He ought to hate her.

" You had better tell me," he said; " it's to your advantage to be free as well as to mine. That old matter is too old."

" I *have* told you."

" Do you mean to tell me there has been nothing — nobody? "

" Nobody. You must go to your own life."

Stung by that retort, Soames moved towards the piano and back to the hearth, to and fro, as he had been wont in the old days in their drawing-room when his feelings were too much for him.

" That won't do," he said. " You deserted me. In common justice it's for you —— "

He saw her shrug those white shoulders, heard her murmur:

"Yes. Why didn't you divorce me then? Should I have cared?"

He stopped, and looked at her intently with a sort of curiosity. What on earth did she do with herself, if she really lived quite alone? And why had he not divorced her? The old feeling that she had never understood him, never done him justice, bit him while he stared at her.

"Why couldn't you have made me a good wife?" he said.

"Yes; it was a crime to marry you. I have paid for it. You will find some way perhaps. You needn't mind my name, I have none to lose. Now I think you had better go."

A sense of defeat — of being defrauded of his self-justification, and of something else beyond power of explanation to himself, beset Soames like the breath of a cold fog. Mechanically he reached up, took from the mantel-shelf a little china bowl, reversed it, and said:

"Lowestoft. Where did you get this? I bought its fellow at Jobson's." And, visited by the sudden memory of how, those many years ago, he and she had bought china together, he remained staring at the little bowl, as if it contained all the past. Her voice roused him.

"Take it. I don't want it."

Soames put it back on the shelf.

"Will you shake hands?" he said.

A faint smile curved her lips. She held out her hand. It was cold to his rather feverish touch. 'She's made of ice,' he thought — 'she was always made of ice!' But even as that thought darted through him, his senses were assailed by the perfume of her dress and body, as though the warmth

within her, which had never been for him, were
struggling to show its presence. And he turned on
his heel. He walked out and away, as if someone
with a whip were after him, not even looking for
a cab, glad of the empty Embankment and the cold
river, and the thick-strewn shadows of the plane-
tree leaves — confused, flurried, sore at heart, and
vaguely disturbed, as though he had made some
deep mistake whose consequences he could not foresee. And the fantastic thought suddenly assailed
him: If instead of: ' I think you had better go,' she
had said, ' I think you had better stay!' What
should he have felt, what would he have done? That
cursed attraction of her was there for him even
now, after all these years of estrangement and bitter thoughts. It was there, ready to mount to his
head at a sign, a touch. "I was a fool to go!" he
muttered. "I've advanced nothing. Who could
imagine? I never thought ——!" Memory, flown
back to the first years of his marriage, played him
torturing tricks. She had not deserved to keep her
beauty — the beauty he had owned and known so
well. And a kind of bitterness at the tenacity of
his own admiration welled up in him. Most men
would have hated the sight of her, as she had deserved. She had spoiled his life, wounded his pride
to death, defrauded him of a son. And yet the mere
sight of her, cold and resisting as ever, had this
power to upset him utterly! It was some damned
magnetism she had! And no wonder if, as she as-
serted, she had lived untouched these last twelve
years. So Bosinney — cursed be his memory! —
had lived on all this time with her! Soames could
not tell whether he was glad of that knowledge
or no.

Nearing his Club at last he stopped to buy a paper. A headline ran: 'Boers reported to repudiate suzerainty!' Suzerainty! 'Just like her!' he thought: 'she always did. Suzerainty! I still have it by rights. She must be awfully lonely in that wretched little flat!'

CHAPTER XII

ON FORSYTE 'CHANGE

SOAMES belonged to two Clubs, ' The Connoisseurs,' which he put on his cards and seldom visited, and ' The Remove,' which he did not put on his cards and frequented. He had joined this Liberal institution five years ago, having made sure that its members were now nearly all sound Conservatives in heart and pocket, if not in principle. Uncle Nicholas had put him up. The fine reading-room was decorated in the Adam style.

On entering that evening he glanced at the tape for any news about the Transvaal, and noted that Consols were down seven-sixteenths since the morning. He was turning away to seek the reading-room when a voice behind him said:

" Well, Soames, that went off all right."

It was Uncle Nicholas, in a frock-coat and his special cut-away collar, with a black tie passed through a ring. Heavens! How young and dapper he looked at eighty-three!

" I think Roger'd have been pleased," his uncle went on. " The thing was very well done. Blackley's? I'll make a note of them. Buxton's done me no good. These Boers are upsetting me — that fellow Chamberlain's driving the country into war. What do you think? "

" Bound to come," murmured Soames.

Nicholas passed his hand over his thin, clean-shaven cheeks, very rosy after his summer cure; a slight pout had gathered on his lips. This business had revived all his Liberal principles.

" I mistrust that chap; he's a stormy petrel. House-property will go down if there's war. You'll have trouble with Roger's estate. I often told him he ought to get out of some of his houses. He was an opinionated beggar."

'There was a pair of you!' thought Soames. But he never argued with an uncle, in that way preserving their opinion of him as ' a long-headed chap,' and the legal care of their property.

" They tell me at Timothy's," said Nicholas, lowering his voice, " that Dartie has gone off at last. That'll be a relief to your father. He was a rotten egg."

Again Soames nodded. If there was a subject on which the Forsytes really agreed, it was the character of Montagu Dartie.

" You take care," said Nicholas, " or he'll turn up again. Winifred had better have the tooth out, I should say. No use preserving what's gone bad."

Soames looked at him sideways. His nerves, exacerbated by the interview he had just come through, disposed him to see a personal allusion in those words.

" I'm advising her," he said shortly.

" Well," said Nicholas, " the brougham's waiting; I must get home. I'm very poorly. Remember me to your father."

And having thus reconsecrated the ties of blood, he passed down the steps at his youthful gait and was wrapped into his fur coat by the junior porter.

'I've never known Uncle Nicholas other than
"very poorly,"' mused Soames, 'or seen him look
other than everlasting. What a family! Judging
by him, I've got thirty-eight years of health before
me. Well, I'm not going to waste them.' And going over to a mirror he stood looking at his face.
Except for a line or two, and three or four grey
hairs in his little dark moustache, had he aged any
more than Irene? The prime of life — he and she
in the very prime of life! And a fantastic thought
shot into his mind. Absurd! Idiotic! But again
it came. And genuinely alarmed by the recurrence,
as one is by the second fit of shivering which pres-
ages a feverish cold, he sat down on the weighing
machine. Eleven stone! He had not varied two
pounds in twenty years. What age was she?
Nearly thirty-seven — not too old to have a child
— not at all! Thirty-seven on the ninth of next
month. He remembered her birthday well — he
had always observed it religiously, even that last
birthday so soon before she left him, when he was
almost certain she was faithless. Four birthdays
in his house. He had looked forward to them, because his gifts had meant a semblance of gratitude,
a certain attempt at warmth. Except, indeed, that
last birthday — which had tempted him to be too
religious! And he shied away in thought. Memory
heaps dead leaves on corpse-like deeds, from under
which they do but vaguely offend the sense. And
then he thought suddenly: 'I could send her a present for her birthday. After all, we're Christians!
Couldn't I — couldn't we join up again!' And he
uttered a deep sigh sitting there. Annette! Ah!
but between him and Annette was the need for that
wretched divorce suit! And how?

"A man can always work these things, if he'll take it on himself," Jolyon had said.

But why should he take the scandal on himself with his whole career as a pillar of the law at stake? It was not fair! It was quixotic! Twelve years' separation in which he had taken no steps to free himself put out of court the possibility of using her conduct with Bosinney as a ground for divorcing her. By doing nothing to secure relief he had acquiesced, even if the evidence could now be gathered, which was more than doubtful. Besides, his own pride would never let him use that old incident, he had suffered from it too much. No! Nothing but fresh misconduct on her part — but she had denied it; and — almost — he had believed her. Hung up! Utterly hung up!

He rose from the scooped-out red velvet seat with a feeling of constriction about his vitals. He would never sleep with this going on in him! And, taking coat and hat again, he went out, moving eastward. In Trafalgar Square he became aware of some special commotion travelling towards him out of the mouth of the Strand. It materialised in newspaper men calling out so loudly that no words whatever could be heard. He stopped to listen, and one came by.

"Payper! Special! Ultimatium by Krooger! Declaration of war!" Soames bought the paper. There it was in the stop press! His first thought was: 'The Boers are committing suicide.' His second: 'Is there anything still I ought to sell?' If so he had missed the chance — there would certainly be a slump in the City to-morrow. He swallowed this thought with a nod of defiance. That ultimatum was insolent — sooner than let it pass he was prepared to lose money. They wanted a lesson, and they would get it; but it would take three months at least to bring them to heel. There weren't the troops out there; always behind time, the Government! Confound those newspaper rats! What was the use of waking everybody up? Breakfast to-morrow was quite soon enough. And he thought with alarm of his father. They would cry it down Park Lane. Hailing a hansom, he got in and told the man to drive there.

James and Emily had just gone up to bed, and after communicating the news to Warmson, Soames prepared to follow. He paused by after-thought to say:

"What do you think of it, Warmson?"

The butler ceased passing a hat brush over the silk hat Soames had taken off, and, inclining his face a little forward, said in a low voice:

"Well, sir, they 'aven't a chance, of course; but I'm told they're very good shots. I've got a son in the Inniskillings."

"You, Warmson? Why, I didn't know you were married."

"No, sir. I don't talk of it. I expect he'll be going out."

The slighter shock Soames had felt on discovering that he knew so little of one whom he thought he knew so well was lost in the slight shock of discovering that the war might touch one personally. Born in the year of the Crimean War, he had only come to consciousness by the time the Indian Mutiny was over; since then the many little wars of the British Empire had been entirely professional, quite unconnected with the Forsytes and all they stood for in the body politic. This war would surely be no exception. But his mind ran hastily over his family. Two of the Haymans, he had heard, were in some Yeomanry or other — it had always been a pleasant thought, there was a certain distinction about the Yeomanry; they wore, or used to wear, a blue uniform with silver about it, and rode horses. And Archibald, he remembered, had once on a time joined the Militia, but had given it up because his father, Nicholas, had made such a fuss about his 'wasting his time peacocking about in a uniform.' Recently he had heard somewhere that young Nicholas's eldest, very young Nicholas, had become a Volunteer. 'No,' thought Soames, mounting the stairs slowly, 'there's nothing in that!'

. He stood on the landing outside his parents' bed and dressing rooms, debating whether or not to put his nose in and say a reassuring word. Opening the landing window, he listened. The rumble from Piccadilly was all the sound he heard, and with the thought, 'If these motor-cars increase, it'll affect house property,' he was about to pass on up to the room always kept ready for him when he heard, distant as yet, the hoarse rushing call of a news-vendor. There it was, and coming past the house! He knocked on his mother's door and went in.

His father was sitting up in bed, with his ears pricked under the white hair which Emily kept so beautifully cut. He looked pink, and extraordinarily clean, in his setting of white sheet and pillow, out of which the points of his high, thin, night-gowned shoulders emerged in small peaks. His eyes alone, grey and distrustful under their withered lids, were moving from the window to Emily, who in a wrapper was walking up and down, squeezing a rubber ball attached to a scent bottle. The room reeked faintly of the eau-de-Cologne she was spraying.

"All right!" said Soames, "it's not a fire. The Boers have declared war — that's all."

Emily stopped her spraying.

"Oh!" was all she said, and looked at James.

Soames, too, looked at his father. He was taking it differently from their expectation, as if some thought, strange to them, were working in him.

"H'm!" he muttered suddenly, "I shan't live to see the end of this."

"Nonsense, James! It'll be over by Christmas."

"What do you know about it?" James answered her with asperity. "It's a pretty mess — at this time of night, too!" He lapsed into silence, and his wife and son, as if hypnotised, waited for him to say: 'I can't tell — I don't know; I knew how it would be!' But he did not. The grey eyes shifted, evidently seeing nothing in the room; then movement occurred under the bedclothes, and the knees were drawn up suddenly to a great height.

"They ought to send out Roberts. It all comes from that fellow Gladstone and his Majuba."

The two listeners noted something beyond the usual in his voice, something of real anxiety. It was as if he had said: 'I shall never see the old country peaceful and safe again. I shall have to die before I know she's won.' And in spite of the feeling that James must not be encouraged to be fussy, they were touched. Soames went up to the bedside and stroked his father's hand which had emerged from under the bedclothes, long and wrinkled with veins.

"Mark my words!" said James, "consols will go to par. For all I know, Val may go and enlist."

"Oh, come, James!" cried Emily, "you talk as if there were danger."

Her comfortable voice seemed to soothe James for once.

"Well," he muttered, "I told you how it would be. I don't know, I'm sure — nobody tells me anything. Are you sleeping here, my boy?"

The crisis was past, he would now compose himself to his normal degree of anxiety; and, assuring his father that he was sleeping in the house, Soames pressed his hand, and went up to his room.

The following afternoon witnessed the greatest crowd Timothy's had known for many a year. On national occasions, such as this, it was, indeed, almost impossible to avoid going there. Not that there was any danger, or rather, only just enough to make it necessary to assure each other that there was none.

Nicholas was there early. He had seen Soames the night before — Soames had said it was bound to come. This old Kruger was in his dotage — why, he must be seventy-five if he is a day! (Nicholas was eighty-three.) What had Timothy said? He had had a fit after Majuba. These Boers were a grasping lot! The dark-haired Francie, who had arrived on his heels, with the contradictious touch which became the free spirit of a daughter of Roger, chimed in:

"Kettle and pot! Uncle Nicholas. What price the Uitlanders?" What price, indeed! A new expression, and believed to be due to her brother George.

Aunt Juley thought Francie ought not to say such a thing. Dear Mrs. MacAnder's boy, Charlie MacAnder, was one, and no one could call him grasping. At this Francie uttered one of her *mots*, scandalising, and so frequently repeated:

"Well, his father's a Scotchman, and his mother's a cat."

Aunt Juley covered her ears, too late, but Aunt Hester smiled; as for Nicholas, he pouted — witticism of which he was not the author was hardly to his taste. Just then Marian Tweetyman arrived, followed almost immediately by young Nicholas. On seeing his son, Nicholas rose.

"Well, I must be going," he said, "Nick here will tell you what'll win the race." And with this hit at his eldest, who, as a pillar of accountancy, and director of an insurance company, was no more addicted to sport than his father had ever been, he departed. Dear Nicholas! What race was that? Or was it only one of his jokes? He was a wonderful man for his age! How many lumps would dear Marian take? And how were Giles and Jesse? Aunt Juley supposed their Yeomanry would be very busy now guarding the coast, though of course the Boers had no ships. But one never knew what the French might do if they had the chance, especially since that dreadful Fashoda scare, which had upset Timothy so terribly that he had made no investments for months afterwards. It was the ingratitude of the Boers that was so dreadful, after everything had been done for them — Dr. Jameson imprisoned, and he was so nice, Mrs. MacAnder had always said. And Sir Alfred Milner sent out to talk to them — such a clever man! She didn't know what they wanted.

But at this moment occurred one of those sensations — so precious at Timothy's — which great occasions sometimes bring forth:

"Miss June Forsyte."

Aunts Juley and Hester were on their feet at

once, trembling from smothered resentment, and old affection bubbling up, and pride at the return of a prodigal June! Well, this *was* a surprise! Dear June — after all these years! And how well she was looking! Not changed at all! It was almost on their lips to add, 'And how is your dear grandfather?' forgetting in that giddy moment that poor dear Jolyon had been in his grave for seven years now.

Ever the most courageous and downright of all the Forsytes, June, with her decided chin and her spirited eyes and her hair like flames, sat down, slight and short, on a gilt chair with a bead-worked seat, for all the world as if ten years had not elapsed since she had been to see them — ten years of travel and independence and devotion to lame ducks. Those ducks of late had been all definitely painters, etchers, or sculptors, so that her impatience with the Forsytes and their hopelessly inartistic outlook had become intense. Indeed, she had almost ceased to believe that her family existed, and looked around her now with a sort of challenging directness which brought exquisite discomfort to the roomful. She had not expected to meet any of them but 'the poor old things'; and why she had come to see *them* she hardly knew, except that, while on her way from Oxford Street to a studio in Latimer Road, she had suddenly remembered them with compunction as two long-neglected old lame ducks.

Aunt Juley broke the hush again: "We've just been saying, dear, how dreadful it is about these Boers! And what an impudent thing of that old Kruger!"

"Impudent!" said June. "I think he's quite right. What business have we to meddle with them? If he turned out all those wretched Uitlanders it would serve them right. They're only after money."

The silence of sensation was broken by Francie saying:

"What? Are you a pro-Boer?" (undoubtedly the first use of that expression).

"Well! Why can't we leave them alone?" said June, just as, in the open doorway, the maid said: "Mr. Soames Forsyte." Sensation on sensation! Greeting was almost held up by curiosity to see how June and he would take this encounter, for it was shrewdly suspected, if not quite known, that they had not met since that old and lamentable affair of her fiancé Bosinney with Soames' wife. They were seen to just touch each other's hands, and look each at the other's left eye only. Aunt Juley came at once to the rescue:

"Dear June is so original. Fancy, Soames, she thinks the Boers are not to blame."

"They only want their independence," said June; "and why shouldn't they have it?"

"Because," answered Soames, with his smile a little on one side, "they happen to have agreed to our suzerainty."

"Suzerainty!" repeated June scornfully; "we shouldn't like anyone's suzerainty over us."

"They got advantages in payment," replied Soames; "a contract is a contract."

"Contracts are not always just," flamed June, "and when they're not, they ought to be broken. The Boers are much the weaker. We could afford to be generous."

Soames sniffed. "That's mere sentiment," he said.

Aunt Hester, to whom nothing was more awful than any kind of disagreement, here leaned forward and remarked decisively:

"What lovely weather it has been for the time of year?"

But June was not to be diverted.

"I don't know why sentiment should be sneered at. It's the best thing in the world. She looked defiantly round, and Aunt Juley had to intervene again:

"Have you bought any pictures lately, Soames?"

Her incomparable instinct for the wrong subject had not failed her. Soames flushed. To disclose the name of his latest purchases would be like walking into the jaws of disdain. For somehow they all knew of June's predilection for 'genius' not yet on its legs, and her contempt for 'success' unless she had had a finger in securing.

"One or two," he muttered.

But June's face had changed; the Forsyte within her was seeing its chance. Why should not Soames buy some of the pictures of Eric Cobbley — her last lame duck? And she promptly opened her attack: Did Soames know his work? It was so wonderful. He was the coming man.

Oh yes, Soames knew his work. It was in his view 'splashy' and would never get hold of the public.

June blazed up.

"Of course it won't; that's the last thing one would wish for. I thought you were a connoisseur, not a picture-dealer."

"Of course Soames is a connoisseur," Aunt Juley said hastily; "he has wonderful taste — he can always tell beforehand what's going to be successful."

"Oh!" gasped June, and sprang up from the bead-covered chair. "I hate that standard of success. Why can't people buy things because they like them?"

"You mean," said Francie, "because *you* like them."

And in the slight pause young Nicholas was heard saying gently that Violet (his third) was taking lessons in pastel, he didn't know if they were any use.

"Well, good-bye, Auntie," said June; "I must get on," and kissing her aunts, she looked defiantly round the room, said "Good-bye" again, and went. A breeze seemed to pass out with her, as if everyone had sighed.

The third sensation came before anyone had time to speak:

"Mr. James Forsyte."

James came in using a stick slightly and wrapped in a fur coat which gave him a fictitious bulk.

Everyone stood up. James was so old; and he had not been at Timothy's for nearly two years.

"It's hot in here," he said.

Soames divested him of his coat, and as he did so could not help admiring the glossy way his father was turned out. James sat down, all knees, elbows, frock-coat, and long white whiskers.

"What's the meaning of that?" he said.

Though there was no apparent sense in his words, they all knew that he was referring to June. His eyes searched his son's face.

"I thought I'd come and see for myself. What have they answered Kruger?"

Soames took out an evening paper, and read the headline.

"'Instant action by our Government — state of war existing!'"

"Ah!" said James, and sighed. "I was afraid they'd cut and run like old Gladstone. We shall finish with them this time."

All stared at him. James! Always fussy, nervous, anxious! James with his continual, 'I told you it would be!' and his pessimism, and his cautious investments. There was something uncanny about such resolution in this the oldest living Forsyte.

"Where's Timothy?" said James. "He ought to pay attention to this."

Aunt Juley said she didn't know; Timothy had not said much at lunch to-day. Aunt Hester rose and threaded her way out of the room, and Francie said rather maliciously:

"The Boers are a hard nut to crack, Uncle James."

"H'm!" muttered James. "Where do you get your information? Nobody tells me."

Young Nicholas remarked in his mild voice that Nick (his eldest) was now going to drill regularly.

"Ah!" muttered James, and stared before him — his thoughts were on Val. "He's got to look after his mother," he said, "he's got no time for drilling and that, with that father of his." This cryptic saying produced silence, until he spoke again.

"What did June want here?" And his eyes rested with suspicion on all of them in turn. "Her father's a rich man now." The conversation turned on Jolyon, and when he had been seen last. It was supposed that he went abroad and saw all sorts of people now that his wife was dead; his water-colours were on the line, and he was a successful man. Francie went so far as to say:

" I should like to see him again; he was rather a dear."

Aunt Juley recalled how he had gone to sleep on the sofa one day, where James was sitting. He had always been very amiable; what did Soames think?

Knowing that Jolyon was Irene's trustee, all felt the delicacy of this question, and looked at Soames with interest. A faint pink had come up in his cheeks.

" He's going grey," he said.

Indeed! Had Soames seen him? Soames nodded, and the pink vanished.

James said suddenly: " Well — I don't know, I can't tell."

It so exactly expressed the sentiment of everybody present that there was something behind everything, that nobody responded. But at this moment Aunt Hester returned.

" Timothy," she said in a low voice, " Timothy has bought a map, and he's put in — he's put in three flags."

Timothy had ——! A sigh went round the company.

If Timothy had indeed put in three flags already, well! — it showed what the nation could do when it was roused. The war was as good as over.

CHAPTER XIII

JOLYON FINDS OUT WHERE HE IS

JOLYON stood at the window in Holly's old night nursery, converted into a studio, not because it had a north light, but for its view over the prospect away to the Grand Stand at Epsom. He shifted to the side window which overlooked the stableyard, and whistled down to the dog Balthasar who lay for ever under the clock tower. The old dog looked up and wagged his tail. 'Poor old boy!' thought Jolyon, shifting back to the other window.

He had been restless all this week, since his attempt to prosecute trusteeship, uneasy in his conscience which was ever acute, disturbed in his sense of compassion which was easily excited, and with a queer sensation as if his feeling for beauty had received some definite embodiment. Autumn was getting hold of the old oak-tree, its leaves were browning. Sunshine had been plentiful and hot this summer. As with trees, so with men's lives! '*I* ought to live long,' thought Jolyon; ' I'm getting mildewed for want of heat. If I can't work, I shall be off to Paris.' But memory of Paris gave him no pleasure. Besides, how could he go? He must stay and see what Soames was going to do. 'I'm her trustee. I can't leave her unprotected,' he

thought. It had been striking him as curious how
very clearly he could still see Irene in her little
drawing-room which he had only twice entered.
Her beauty must have a sort of poignant harmony!
No literal portrait would ever do her justice; the
essence of her was — ah! yes, what? . . . The
noise of hoofs called him back to the other window.
Holly was riding into the yard on her long-tailed
' palfrey.'   She looked up and he waved to her.
She had been rather silent lately; getting old, he
supposed, beginning to want her future, as they all
did —youngsters! Time was certainly the devil!
And with the feeling that to waste this swift-travel-
ling commodity was unforgivable folly, he took up
his brush. But it was no use; he could not concentrate his eye — besides, the light was going. ' I'll
go up to town,' he thought. In the hall a servant
met him.

"A lady to see you, sir; Mrs. Heron."

Extraordinary coincidence! Passing into the
picture-gallery, as it was still called, he saw Irene
standing over by the window.

She came towards him saying:

"I've been trespassing; I came up through the
coppice and garden. I always used to come that
way to see Uncle Jolyon."

"You couldn't trespass here," replied Jolyon;
"history makes that impossible. I was just thinking of you."

Irene smiled. And it was as if something shone
through; not mere spirituality — serener, completer,
more alluring.

"History!" she murmured. "I once told Uncle
Jolyon that love was for ever. Well, it isn't. Only
aversion lasts."

Jolyon stared at her.   Had she got over Bosinney at last?

"Yes!" he said, "aversion's deeper than love or hate because it's a natural product of the nerves, and we don't change them."

"I came to tell you that Soames has been to see me.   He said a thing that frightened me.   He said: 'You are still my wife!'"

"What!" ejaculated Jolyon.   "You ought not to live alone."   And he continued to stare at her, afflicted by the thought that where Beauty was, nothing ever ran quite straight, which, no doubt, was why so many people looked on it as immoral.

"What more?"

"He asked me to shake hands."

"Did you?"

"Yes.   When he came in I'm sure he didn't want to; he changed while he was there."

"Ah! you certainly ought not to go on living there alone."

"I know no woman I could ask; and I can't take a lover to order, Cousin Jolyon."

"Heaven forbid!" said Jolyon.   "What a damnable position!   Will you stay to dinner?   No? Well, let me see you back to town; I wanted to go up this evening."

"Truly?"

"Truly.   I'll be ready in five minutes."

On that walk to the station they talked of pictures and music, contrasting the English and French characters and the difference in their attitude to Art.   But to Jolyon the colours in the hedges of the long straight lane, the twittering of chaffinches who kept pace with them, the perfume of weeds being already burned, the turn of her neck, the fascination

of those dark eyes bent on him now and then, the
lure of her whole figure, made a deeper impression
than the remarks they exchanged. Unconsciously
he held himself straighter, walked with a more elas-
tic step.

In the train he put her through a sort of catechism
as to what she did with her days.

Made her dresses, shopped, visited a hospital,
played her piano, translated from the French.   She
had regular work from a publisher, it seemed, which
supplemented her income a little.   She seldom went
out in the evening.   " I've been living alone so long,
you see, that I don't mind it a bit.   I believe I'm
naturally solitary."

" I. don't believe that," said Jolyon.   " Do you
know many people? "

" Very few."

At Waterloo they took a hansom, and he drove
with her to the door of her mansions.   Squeezing
her hand at parting, he said:

" You know, you could always come to us at
Robin Hill; you must let me know everything that
happens.   Good-bye, Irene."

" Good-bye," she answered softly.

Jolyon climbed back into his cab, wondering why
he had not asked her to dine and go to the theatre
with him.   Solitary, starved, hung-up life that she
had!   " Hotch Potch Club," he said through the
trap-door.   As his hansom debouched on to the Embankment, a man in top-hat and overcoat passed,
walking quickly, so close to the wall that he seemed
to be scraping it.

' By Jove!' thought Jolyon; ' Soames himself!
What's *he* up to now? '   And, stopping the cab
round the corner he got out and retraced his steps to

where he could see the entrance to the mansions. Soames had halted in front of them, and was looking up at the light in her windows. 'If he goes in,' thought Jolyon, 'what shall I do? What have I the right to do?' What the fellow had said was true. She was still his wife, absolutely without protection from annoyance! 'Well, if he goes in,' he thought, 'I follow.' And he began moving towards the mansions. Again Soames advanced; he was in the very entrance now. But suddenly he stopped, spun round on his heel, and came back towards the river. 'What now?' thought Jolyon. 'In a dozen steps he'll recognise me.' And he turned tail. His cousin's footsteps kept pace with his own. But he reached his cab, and got in before Soames had turned the corner. "Go on!" he said through the trap. Soames' figure ranged up alongside.

"Hansom!" he said. "Engaged? Hallo!"

"Hallo!" answered Jolyon. "You?"

The quick suspicion on his cousin's face, white in the lamplight, decided him.

"I can give you a lift," he said, "if you're going West."

"Thanks," answered Soames, and got in.

"I've been seeing Irene," said Jolyon when the cab had started.

"Indeed!"

"You went to see her yesterday yourself, I understand."

"I did," said Soames; "she's my wife, you know."

The tone, the half-lifted sneering lip, roused sudden anger in Jolyon; but he subdued it.

"You ought to know best," he said, "but if you want a divorce it's not very wise to go seeing her, is it? One can't run with the hare and hunt with the hounds."

"You're very good to warn me," said Soames, " but I have not made up my mind."

"*She* has," said Jolyon, looking straight before him; "you can't take things up, you know, as they were twelve years ago."

"That remains to be seen."

"Look here!" said Jolyon, "she's in a damnable position, and I am the only person with any legal say in her affairs."

"Except myself," retorted Soames, "who am also in a damnable position. Hers is what she made for herself; mine what she made for me. I am not at all sure that in her own interests I shan't require her to return to me."

"What!" exclaimed Jolyon; and a shiver went through his whole body.

"I don't know what you may mean by ' what,' " answered Soames coldly; "your say in her affairs is confined to paying out her income; please bear that in mind. In choosing not to disgrace her by a divorce, I retained my rights, and, as I say, I am not at all sure that I shan't require to exercise them."

"My God!" ejaculated Jolyon, and he uttered a short laugh.

"Yes," said Soames, and there was a deadly quality in his voice. "I've not forgotten the nickname your father gave me, ' The man of property! ' I'm not called names for nothing."

"This is fantastic," murmured Jolyon. Well, the fellow couldn't force his wife to live with him. Those days were past, anyway! And he looked round at Soames with the thought: ' Is he real, this man?' But Soames looked very real, sitting square

yet almost elegant with the clipped moustache on his
pale face, and a tooth showing where a lip was lifted
in a fixed smile.   There was a long silence, while
Jolyon thought: ' Instead of helping her, I've made
things worse.'   Suddenly Soames said:
   " It would be the best thing that could happen to
her in many ways."
   At those words such a turmoil began taking place
in Jolyon that he could barely sit still in the cab.   It
was as if he were boxed up with hundreds of thou-
sands of his countrymen, boxed up with that something in the national character which had always
been to him revolting, something which he knew to
be extremely natural and yet which seemed to him
inexplicable — their intense belief in contracts and
vested rights, their complacent sense of virtue in the
exaction of those rights.   Here beside him in the
cab was the very embodiment, the corporeal sum as
it were, of the possessive instinct — his own kins-
man, too!   It was uncanny and intolerable!   ' But
there's something more in it than that!' he thought
with a sick feeling.   ' The dog, they say, returns to
his vomit!   The sight of her has reawakened something.   Beauty!   The devil's in it!'
   "As I say," said Soames, " I have not made up
my mind.   I shall be obliged if you will kindly leave
her quite alone."
   Jolyon bit his lips; he who had always hated rows
almost welcomed the thought of one now.
   " I can give you no such promise," he said shortly.
   " Very well," said Soames, " then we know where
we are.'   I'll get down here."   And stopping the
cab he got out without word or sign of farewell.
Jolyon travelled on to his Club.
   The first news of the war was being called in the

streets, but he paid no attention. What could he do to help her? If only his father were alive! *He* could have done so much! But why could he not do all that his father could have done? Was he not old enough? — turned fifty and twice married, with grown-up daughters and a son. 'Queer,' he thought. ' If she were plain I shouldn't be thinking twice about it. Beauty is the devil, when you're sensitive to it!' And into the Club reading-room he went with a disturbed heart. In that very room he and Bosinney had talked one summer afternoon; he well remembered even now the disguised and secret lecture he had given that young man in the interests of June, the diagnosis of the Forsytes he had hazarded; and how he had wondered what sort of woman it was he was warning him against. And now! He was almost in want of a warning himself. 'It's deuced funny!' he thought, ' really deuced funny!'

CHAPTER XIV

SOAMES DISCOVERS WHAT HE WANTS

IT is so much easier to say, " Then we know where we are," than to mean anything particular by the words. And in saying them Soames did but vent the jealous rankling of his instincts. He got out of the cab in a state of wary anger — with himself for not having seen Irene, with Jolyon for having seen her; and now with his inability to tell exactly what he wanted.

He had abandoned the cab because he could not bear to remain seated beside his cousin, and walking briskly eastwards he thought: ' I wouldn't trust that fellow Jolyon a yard. Once outcast, always outcast!' The chap had a natural sympathy with — with — laxity (he had shied at the word sin, because it was too melodramatic for use by a Forsyte).

Indecision in desire was to him a new feeling. He was like a child between a promised toy and an old one which had been taken away from him; and he was astonished at himself. Only last Sunday desire had seemed simple — just his freedom and Annette. ' I'll go and dine there,' he thought. To see her might bring back his singleness of intention, calm his exasperation, clear his mind.

The restaurant was fairly full — a good many

foreigners and folk whom, from their appearance, he took to be literary or artistic. Scraps of conversation came his way through the clatter of plates and glasses. He distinctly heard the Boers sympathised with, the British Government blamed. 'Don't think much of their clientèle,' he thought. He went stolidly through his dinner and special coffee without making his presence known, and when at last he had finished, was careful not to be seen going towards the sanctum of Madame Lamotte. They were, as he expected, having supper — such a much nicer-looking supper than the dinner he had eaten that he felt a kind of grief — and they greeted him with a surprise so seemingly genuine that he thought with sudden suspicion: 'I believe they knew I was here all the time.' He gave Annette a look furtive and searching. So pretty, seemingly so candid; could she be angling for him? He turned to Madame Lamotte and said:

"I've been dining here."

Really! If she had only known! There were dishes she could have recommended; what a pity! Soames was confirmed in his suspicion. 'I must look out what I'm doing!' he thought sharply.

"Another little cup of very special coffee, *monsieur;* a liqueur, Grand Marnier?" and Madame Lamotte rose to order these delicacies.

Alone with Annette, Soames said, "Well, Annette?" with a defensive little smile about his lips.

The girl blushed. This, which last Sunday would have set his nerves tingling, now gave him much the same feeling a man has when a dog that he owns wriggles and looks at him. He had a curious sense of power, as if he could have said to her, 'Come and kiss me,' and she would have come. And yet — it was strange — but there seemed another face and form in the room too; and the itch in his nerves, was it for that — or for this? He jerked his head toward the restaurant and said: "You have some queer customers. Do you like this life?"

Annette looked up at him for a moment, looked down, and played with her fork.

"No," she said, "I do not like it."

'I've got her,' thought Soames, 'if I want her. But do I want her?' She was graceful, she was pretty — very pretty; she was fresh, she had taste of a kind. His eyes travelled round the little room; but the eyes of his mind went another journey — a half-light, and silvery walls, a satinwood piano, a woman standing against it, reined back as it were from him — a woman with white shoulders that he knew, and dark eyes that he had sought to know, and hair like dull dark amber. And as in an artist who strives for the unrealisable and is ever thirsty, so there rose in him at that moment the thirst of the old passion he had never satisfied.

"Well," he said calmly, "you're young. There's everything before *you*."

Annette shook her head.

"I think sometimes there is nothing before me but hard work. I am not so in love with work as mother."

"Your mother is a wonder," said Soames, faintly mocking; "she will never let failure lodge in her house."

Annette sighed. "It must be wonderful to be rich."

"Oh! You'll be rich some day," answered Soames, still with that faint mockery; "don't be afraid."

Annette shrugged her shoulders. " *Monsieur* is very kind." And between her pouting lips she put a chocolate.

' Yes, my dear,' thought Soames, ' they're very pretty.'

Madame Lamotte, with coffee and liqueur, put an end to that colloquy. Soames did not stay long.

Outside in the streets of Soho, which always gave him such a feeling of property improperly owned, he mused. If only Irene had given him a son, he wouldn't now be squirming after women! The thought had jumped out of its little dark sentry-box in his inner consciousness. A son — something to look forward to, something to make the rest of life worth while, something to leave himself to, some perpetuity of self. ' If I had a son,' he thought bitterly, ' a proper legal son, I could make shift to go on as I used. One woman's much the same as another, after all.' But as he walked he shook his head. No! One woman was not the same as another. Many a time had he tried to think that in the old days of his thwarted married life; and he had always failed. He was failing now. He was trying to think Annette the same as that other. But she was not, she had not the lure of that old passion. ' And Irene's my wife,' he thought, ' my legal wife. I have done nothing to put her away from me. Why shouldn't she come back to me? It's the right thing, the lawful thing. It makes no scandal, no disturbance. If it's disagreeable to her — but why *should* it be? I'm not a leper, and she — she's no longer in love!' Why should he be put to the shifts and the sordid disgraces and the lurking defeats of the Divorce Court, when there she was like an empty house only waiting to be retaken into use and pos-

session by him who legally owned her? To one so
secretive as Soames the thought of re-entry into
quiet possession of his own property with nothing
given away to the world was intensely alluring.
' No,' he mused, ' I'm glad I went to see that girl.
I know now what I want most. If only Irene will
come back I'll be as considerate as she wishes; she
could give her own life; but perhaps — perhaps she
would come round to me.' There was a lump in his
throat. And doggedly along by the railings of the
Green Park, towards his father's house, he went,
trying to tread on his shadow walking before him in
the brilliant moonlight.

PART II

CHAPTER I

THE THIRD GENERATION

JOLLY FORSYTE was strolling down High Street, Oxford, on a November afternoon; Val Dartie was strolling up. Jolly had just changed out of boating flannels and was on his way to the ' Frying-pan,' to which he had recently been elected. Val had just changed out of riding clothes and was on his way to the fire — a bookmaker's in Cornmarket.

" Hallo! " said Jolly.

" Hallo! " replied Val.

The cousins had met but twice, Jolly, the second-year man, having invited the freshman to breakfast; and last evening they had seen each other again under somewhat exotic circumstances.

Over a tailor's in the Cornmarket resided one of those privileged young beings called minors, whose inheritances are large, whose parents are dead, whose guardians are remote, and whose instincts are vicious. At nineteen he had commenced one of those careers attractive and inexplicable to ordinary mortals for whom a single bankruptcy is good as a feast. Already famous for having the only roulette table then to be found in Oxford, he was anticipating his expectations at a dazzling rate. He out-crummed Crum, though of a sanguine and rather

beefy type which lacked the latter's fascinating lan-
guor. For Val it had been in the nature of baptism
to be taken there to play roulette; in the nature of
confirmation to get back into college, after hours,
through a window whose bars were deceptive.
Once, during that evening of delight, glancing up
from the seductive green before him, he had caught
sight, through a cloud of smoke, of his cousin standing opposite. ' *Rouge gagne, impair, et manque!* '
He had not seen him again.

" Come in to the Frying-pan and have tea," said
Jolly, and they went in.

A stranger, seeing them together, would have noticed an unseizable resemblance between these second cousins of the third generation of Forsytes; the
same bone formation in face, though Jolly's eyes
were darker grey, his hair lighter and more wavy.

" Tea and buttered buns, waiter, please," said
Jolly.

" Have one of my cigarettes?" said Val.   " I
saw you last night.   How did you do?"

" I didn't play."

" I won fifteen quid."

Though desirous of repeating a whimsical com-
ment on gambling he had once heard his father make
—' When you're fleeced you're sick, and when you
fleece you're sorry ' — Jolly contented himself with:

" Rotten game, I think; I was at school with that
chap.   He's an awful fool."

"Oh! I don't know," said Val, as one might
speak in defence of a disparaged god; "he's a pretty
good sport."

They exchanged whiffs in silence.

" You met my people, didn't you?" said Jolly.
" They're coming up to-morrow."

Val grew a little red.

"Really! I can give you a rare good tip for the Manchester November handicap."

"Thanks, I only take interest in the classic races."

"You can't make any money over them," said Val.

"I hate the ring," said Jolly; "there's such a row and stink. I like the paddock."

"I like to back my judgment," answered Val.

Jolly smiled; his smile was like his father's. "I haven't got any. I always lose money if I bet."

"You have to buy experience, of course."

"Yes, but it's all messed up with doing people in the eye."

"Of course, or they'll do you — that's the excitement."

Jolly looked a little scornful.

"What do you do with yourself? Row?"

"No — ride, and drive about. I'm going to play polo next term, if I can get my granddad to stump up."

"That's old Uncle James, isn't it? What's he like?"

"Older than forty hills," said Val, "and always thinking he's going to be ruined."

"I suppose my grandad and he were brothers."

"I don't believe any of that old lot were sportsmen," said Val; "they must have worshipped money."

"Mine didn't!" said Jolly warmly.

Val flipped the ash off his cigarette.

"Money's only fit to spend," he said; "I wish the deuce I had more."

Jolly gave him that direct upward look of judg-

ment which he had inherited from old Jolyon: One
didn't talk about money! And again there was silence, while they drank tea and ate the buttered
buns.

"Where are your people going to stay?" asked
Val, elaborately casual.

"'Rainbow.' What do you think of the war?"

"Rotten, so far. The Boers aren't sports a bit.
Why don't they come out into the open?"

"Why should they? They've got everything
against them except their way of fighting. I rather
admire them."

"They can ride and shoot," admitted Val, "but
they're a lousy lot. Do you know Crum?"

"Of Merton? Only by sight. He's in that fast
set too, isn't he? Rather La-di-da and Brumma-
gem."

Val said fixedly: "He's a friend of mine."

"Oh! Sorry!" And they sat awkwardly staring past each other, having pitched on their pet
points of snobbery. For Jolly was forming himself
unconsciously on a set whose motto was: 'We defy
you to bore us. Life isn't half long enough, and
we're going to talk faster and more crisply, do more
and know more, and dwell less on any subject than
you can possibly imagine. We are 'the best' —
made of wire and whipcord.' And Val was unconsciously forming himself on a set whose motto was:
'We defy you to interest or excite us. We have
had every sensation, or if we haven't, we pretend
we have. We are so exhausted with living that no
hours are too small for us. We will lose our shirts
with equanimity. We have flown fast and are past
everything. All is cigarette smoke. Bismillah!'
Competitive spirit, bone-deep in the English, was

obliging those two young Forsytes to have ideals; and at the close of a century ideals are mixed. The aristocracy had already in the main adopted the 'jumping-jesus' principle; though here and there one like Crum — who was an honourable — stood starkly languid for that gambler's Nirvana which had been the *summum bonum* of the old 'dandies' and of 'the mashers' in the eighties. And round Crum were still gathered a forlorn hope of blue-bloods with a plutocratic following.

But there was between the cousins another far less obvious antipathy — coming from the unseizable family resemblance, which each perhaps resented; or from some half-consciousness of that old feud persisting still between their branches of the clan, formed within them by odd words or half-hints dropped by their elders. And Jolly, tinkling his teaspoon, was musing: 'His tie-pin and his waistcoat and his drawl and his betting — good Lord!'

And Val, finishing his bun, was thinking: 'He's rather a young beast!'

"I suppose you'll be meeting your people?" he said, getting up. "I wish you'd tell them I should like to show them over B.N.C. — not that there's anything much there — if they'd care to come."

"Thanks, I'll ask them."

"Would they lunch? I've got rather a decent scout."

Jolly doubted if they would have time.

"You'll ask them, though?"

"Very good of you," said Jolly, fully meaning that they should not go; but, instinctively polite, he added: "You'd better come and have dinner with us to-morrow."

"Rather. What time?"

" Seven-thirty."

" Dress? "

" No." And they parted, a subtle antagonism alive within them.

Holly and her father arrived by a midday train. It was her first visit to the city of spires and dreams, and she was very silent, looking almost shyly at the brother who was part of this wonderful place. After lunch she wandered, examining his household gods with intense curiosity. Jolly's sitting-room was panelled, and Art represented by a set of Bartolozzi prints which had belonged to old Jolyon, and by college photographs — of young men, live young men, a little heroic, and to be compared with her memories of Val. Jolyon also scrutinised with care that evidence of his boy's character and tastes.

Jolly was anxious that they should see him rowing, so they set forth to the river. Holly, between her brother and her father, felt elated when heads were turned and eyes rested on her. That they might see him to the best advantage they left him at the Barge and crossed the river to the towing-path. Slight in build — for of all the Forsytes only old Swithin and George were beefy — Jolly was rowing ' Two ' in a trial eight. He looked very earnest and strenuous. With pride Jolyon thought him the best-looking boy of the lot; Holly, as became a sister, was more struck by one or two of the others, but would not have said so for the world. The river was bright that afternoon, the meadows lush, the trees still beautiful with colour. Distinguished peace clung around the old city; Jolyon promised himself a day's sketching if the weather held. The Eight passed a second time, spurting home along the Barges — Jolly's face was very set, so as not to

show that he was blown.   They returned across the
river and waited for him.

"Oh!" said Jolly in the Christ Church meadows,
"I had to ask that chap Val Dartie to dine with us
to-night.   He wanted to give you lunch and show
you B.N.C., so I thought I'd better; then you needn't
go.   I don't like him much."

Holly's rather sallow face had become suffused
with pink.

"Why not?"

"Oh! I don't know.   He seems to me rather
showy and bad form.   What are his people like,
Dad?   He's only a second cousin, isn't he?"

Jolyon took refuge in a smile.

"Ask Holly," he said; "she saw his uncle."

"I *liked* Val," Holly answered, staring at the
ground before her; "his uncle looked — awfully
different."   She stole a glance at Jolly from under
her lashes.

"Did you ever," said Jolyon with whimsical intention, "hear our family history, my dears?   It's
quite a fairy tale.   The first Jolyon Forsyte — at all
events the first we know anything of, and that would
be your great-great-grandfather — dwelt in the
land of Dorset on the edge of the sea, being by pro-
'fession an 'agriculturalist,' as your great-aunt put
it, and the son of an agriculturist — farmers, in
fact; your grandfather used to call them, 'Very
small beer.'"   He looked at Jolly to see how his
lordliness was standing it, and with the other eye
noted Holly's malicious pleasure in the slight drop
of her brother's face.

"We may suppose him thick and sturdy, standing
for England as it was before the Industrial Era began.   The second Jolyon Forsyte — your great-

grandfather, Jolly; better known as Superior Dosset Forsyte — built houses, so the chronicle runs, begat ten children, and migrated to London town. It is known that he drank sherry. We may suppose him representing the England of Napoleon's wars, and general unrest. The eldest of his six sons was the third Jolyon, your grandfather, my dears — tea merchant and chairman of companies, one of the soundest Englishmen who ever lived — and to me the dearest." Jolyon's voice had lost its irony, and his son and daughter gazed at him solemnly. "He was just and tenacious, tender and young at heart. You remember him, and I remember him. Pass to the others! Your great-uncle James, that's young Val's grandfather, had a son called Soames — whereby hangs a tale of no love lost, and I don't think I'll tell it you. James and the other eight children of 'Superior Dosset,' of whom there are still five alive, may be said to have represented Victorian England, with its principles of trade and individualism at five per cent. and your money back — if you know what that means. At all events they've turned thirty thousand pounds into a cool million between them in the course of their long lives. They never did a wild thing — unless it was your great-uncle Swithin, who I believe was once swindled at thimble-rig, and was called 'Four-in-hand Forsyte' because he drove a pair. Their day is passing, and their type, not altogether for the advantage of the country. They were pedestrian, but they too were sound. I am the fourth Jolyon Forsyte — a poor holder of the name — "

"No, Dad," said Jolly, and Holly squeezed his hand.

"Yes," repeated Jolyon, "a poor specimen, representing, I'm afraid, nothing but the end of the century, unearned income, amateurism, and individual liberty — a different thing from individualism, Jolly. You are the fifth Jolyon Forsyte, old man, and you open the ball of the new century."

As he spoke they turned in through the college gates, and Holly said: " It's fascinating, Dad."

None of them quite knew what she meant. Jolly was grave.

The Rainbow, distinguished, as only an Oxford hostel can be, for lack of modernity, provided one small oak-panelled private sitting-room, in which Holly sat to receive, white-frocked, shy, and alone, when the only guest arrived.

Rather as one would touch a moth, Val took her hand. And wouldn't she wear this ' measly flower '? It would look ripping in her hair. He removed a gardenia from his coat.

" Oh! No, thank you — I couldn't!" But she took it and pinned it at her neck, having suddenly remembered that word ' showy '! Val's buttonhole would give offence; and she so much wanted Jolly to like him. Did she realise that Val was at his best and quietest in her presence, and was that, perhaps, half the secret of his attraction for her?

" I never said anything about our ride, Val."

" Rather not! It's just between us."

By the uneasiness of his hands and the fidgeting of his feet he was giving her a sense of power very delicious; a soft feeling too — the wish to make him happy.

" Do tell me about Oxford. It must be ever so lovely."

Val admitted that it was frightfully decent to do what you liked; the lectures were nothing; and there

were some very good chaps. "Only," he added,
"of course I wish I was in town, and could come
down and see you."

Holly moved one hand shyly on her knee, and her
glance dropped.

"You haven't forgotten," he said, suddenly gathering courage, "that we're going madrabbiting together?"

Holly smiled.

"Oh! That was only make-believe. One can't
do that sort of thing after one's grown up, you
know."

"Dash it! cousins can," said Val. "Next Long
Vac — it begins in June, you know, and goes on for
ever — we'll watch our chance."

But, though the thrill of conspiracy ran through
her veins, Holly shook her head. "It won't come
off," she murmured.

"Won't it!" said Val fervently; "who's going to
stop it? Not your father or your brother."

At this moment Jolyon and Jolly came in; and romance fled into Val's patent leather and Holly's
white satin toes, where it itched and tingled during an evening not conspicuous for open-hearted-
ness.

Sensitive to atmosphere, Jolyon soon felt the latent antagonism between the boys, and was puzzled
by Holly; so he became unconsciously ironical,
which is fatal to the expansiveness of youth. A
letter, handed to him after dinner, reduced him to a
silence hardly broken till Jolly and Val rose to go.
He went out with them, smoking his cigar, and
walked with his son to the gates of Christ Church.
Turning back, he took out the letter and read it
again beneath a lamp.

" DEAR JOLYON,

" Soames came again to-night — my thirty-seventh birthday. You were right, I mustn't stay here. I'm going to-morrow to the Piedmont Hotel, but I won't go abroad without seeing you. I feel lonely and down-hearted.

"Yours affectionately,
"IRENE."

He folded the letter back into his pocket and walked on, astonished at the violence of his feelings. What had the fellow said or done?

He turned into High Street, down the Turl, and on among a maze of spires and domes and long college fronts and walls, bright or dark-shadowed in the strong moonlight.   In this very heart of England's gentility it was difficult to realise that a lonely woman could be importuned or hunted, but what else could her letter mean?   Soames must have been pressing her to go back to him again, with public opinion and the Law on his side, too!   ' Eighteen-ninety-nine! ' he thought, gazing at the broken glass shining on the top of a villa garden wall; ' but when it comes to property we're still a heathen people! I'll go up to-morrow morning.   I dare say it'll be best for her to go abroad.'   Yet the thought displeased him.   Why should Soames hunt her out of England!   Besides, he might follow, and out there she would be still more helpless against the attentions of her own husband! ' I must tread warily,' he thought; ' that fellow could make himself very nasty.   I didn't like his manner in the cab the other night.' His thoughts turned to his daughter June.   Could she help?   Once on a time Irene had been her greatest friend, and now she was a ' lame duck,' such as must appeal to June's nature! He determined to wire to his daughter to meet him at Paddington Station. Retracing his steps toward the Rainbow he questioned his own sensations. Would he be upsetting himself over every woman in like case? No! he would not. The candour of this conclusion discomfited him; and, finding that Holly had gone up to bed, he sought his own room. But he could not sleep, and sat for a long time at his window, huddled in an overcoat, watching the moonlight on the roofs.

Next door Holly too was awake, thinking of the lashes above and below Val's eyes, especially below; and of what she could do to make Jolly like him better. The scent of the gardenia was strong in her little bedroom, and pleasant to her.

And Val, leaning out of his first-floor window in B.N.C., was gazing at a moonlit quadrangle without seeing it at all, seeing instead Holly, slim and white-frocked, as she sat beside the fire when he first went in.

But Jolly, in his bedroom narrow as a ghost, lay with a hand beneath his cheek and dreamed he was with Val in one boat, rowing a race against him, while his father was calling from the towpath: 'Two! Get your hands away there, bless you!'

CHAPTER II

SOAMES PUTS IT TO THE TOUCH

OF all those radiant firms which emblazon with their windows the West End of London, Gaves and Cortegal were considered by Soames the most ' attractive '— word just coming into fashion. He had never had his Uncle Swithin's taste in precious stones, and the abandonment by Irene when she left his house in 1889 of all the glittering things he had given her had disgusted him with this form of investment. But he still knew a diamond when he saw one, and during the week before her birthday he had taken occasion, on his way into the Poultry or his way out therefrom, to dally a little before the greater jewellers where one got, if not one's money's worth, at least a certain cachet with the goods.

Constant cogitation since his cab drive with Jolyon had convinced him more and more of the supreme importance of this moment in his life, the supreme need for taking steps and those not wrong. And, alongside the dry and reasoned sense that it was now or never with his self-preservation, now or never if he were to range himself and found a family, went the secret urge of his senses roused by the sight of her who had once been a passionately desired wife, and the conviction that it was a sin

against common sense and the decent secrecy of
Forsytes to waste the wife he had.

In an opinion on Winifred's case, Dreamer, Q.C.
— he would much have preferred Waterbuck, but
they had made him a judge (so late in the day as to
rouse the usual suspicion of a political job) — had
advised that they should go forward and obtain restitution of conjugal rights, a point which to Soames
had never been in doubt.   When they had obtained
a decree to that effect they must wait to see if it was
obeyed.   If not, it would constitute legal desertion,
and they should obtain evidence of misconduct and
file their petition for divorce.   All of which Soames
knew perfectly well.   They had marked him ten
.and one.   This simplicity in his sister's case only
made him the more desperate about the difficulty in
his own.   Everything, in fact, was driving him towards the simple solution of Irene's return.   If it
were still against the grain with her, had *he* not
feelings to subdue, injury to forgive, pain to forget?
He at least had never injured her, and this was a
world of compromise!   He could offer her so much
more than she had now.   He would be prepared to
make a liberal settlement on her which would not
be upset.   He often scrutinised his image in these
days.   He had never been a peacock like that fellow
Dartie, or fancied himself a woman's man, but he
had a certain belief in his own appearance — not un-
justly, for it was well-coupled and preserved, neat,
healthy, pale, unblemished by drink or excess of any
kind.   The Forsyte jaw and the concentration of
his face were, in his eyes, virtues.   So far as he
could tell there was no feature of him which need
inspire dislike.

Thoughts and yearnings, with which one lives

daily, become natural, even if far-fetched in their inception. If he could only give tangible proof enough of his determination to let bygones be bygones, and to do all in his power to please her, why should she not come back to him?

He entered Gaves and Cortegal's therefore, on the morning of November the 9th, to buy a certain diamond brooch. "Four twenty-five and dirt cheap, sir, at the money. It's a lady's brooch." There was that in his mood which made him accept without demur. And he went on into the Poultry with the flat green morocco case in his breast pocket. Several times that day he opened it to look at the seven soft shining stones in their velvet oval nest.

". If the lady doesn't like it, sir, happy to exchange it any time. But there's no fear of that." If only there were not! He got through a vast amount of work, only soother of the nerves he knew. A cable came in while he was in the office with details from the agent in Buenos Aires, and the name and address of a stewardess who would be prepared to swear to what was necessary. It was a timely spur to Soames' intense and rooted distaste for the washing of dirty linen in public. And when he set forth by Underground to Victoria Station he received a fresh impetus towards the renewal of his married life from the account in his evening paper of a fashionable divorce suit. The homing instinct of all true Forsytes in anxiety and trouble, the corporate tendency which kept them strong and solid, made him choose to dine at Park Lane. He neither could nor would breathe a word to his people of his intention — too reticent and proud — but the thought that at least they would be glad if they knew, and wish him luck, was heartening.

James was in lugubrious mood, for the fire which the impudence of Kruger's ultimatum had lit in him had been cold-watered by the poor success of the last month, and the exhortations to effort in *The Times*. He didn't know where it would end. Soames sought to cheer him by the continual use of the word Buller. But James couldn't tell! There was Colley — and he got stuck on that hill, and this Ladysmith was down in a hollow, and altogether it looked to him a 'pretty kettle of fish'; he thought they ought to be sending the sailors —they were the chaps, they did a lot of good in the Crimea. Soames shifted the ground of consolation. Winifred had heard from Val that there had been a 'rag' and a bonfire on Guy Fawkes Day at Oxford, and that he had escaped detection by blacking his face.

"Ah!" James muttered, "he's a clever little chap." But he shook his head shortly afterwards, and remarked that he didn't know what would become of him, and looking wistfully at his son, murmured on that Soames had never had a boy. He would have liked a grandson of his own name. And now — well, there it was!

Soames flinched. He had not expected such a challenge to disclose the secret in his heart. And Emily, who saw him wince, said:

"Nonsense, James; don't talk like that!"

But James, not looking anyone in the face, muttered on. There were Roger and Nicholas and Jolyon; they all had grandsons. And Swithin and Timothy had never married. He had done his best; but he would soon be gone now. And, as though he had uttered words of profound consolation, he was silent, eating brains with a fork and a piece of bread, and swallowing the bread.

Soames excused himself directly after dinner. It was not really cold, but he put on his fur coat, which served to fortify him against the fits of nervous shivering he had been subject to all day. Subconsciously, he knew that he looked better thus than in an ordinary black overcoat. Then, feeling the morocco case flat against his heart, he sallied forth. He was no smoker, but he lit a cigarette, and smoked it gingerly as he walked along. He moved slowly down the Row towards Knightsbridge, timing himself to get to Chelsea at nine-fifteen. What did she do with herself evening after evening in that little hole? How mysterious women were! One lived alongside and knew nothing of them. What could she have seen in that fellow Bosinney to send her mad? For there was madness after all in what she had done — crazy moonstruck madness, in which all sense of values had been lost, and her life and his life ruined! And for a moment he was filled with a sort of exaltation, as though he were a man read of in a story who, possessed by the Christian spirit, would restore to her all the prizes of existence, forgiving and forgetting, and becoming the good fairy of her future. Under a tree opposite Knightsbridge Barracks, where the moonlight struck down clear and white, he took out once more the morocco case, and let the beams draw colour from those stones. Yes, they were of the first water! But, at the hard-closing snap of the case, another cold shiver ran through his nerves; and he walked on faster, clenching his gloved hands in the pockets of his coat, almost hoping she would not be in. The thought of how mysterious she was again beset him. Dining alone there night after night — in an evening dress, too, as if she were making believe to be in

society! Playing the piano — to herself! Not
even a dog or cat, so far as he had seen. And that
reminded him suddenly of the mare he kept for station work at Mapledurham. If ever he went to the
stable, there she was quite alone, half asleep, and
yet, on her home journeys going more freely than on
her way out, as if longing to be back and lonely in
her stable! 'I would treat her well,' he thought in-
coherently. 'I would be very careful.' And all
that capacity for home life of which a mocking Fate
seemed for ever to deprive him swelled suddenly in
Soames, so that he dreamed dreams opposite South
Kensington Station. In the King's Road a man
came slithering out of a public house playing a con-
certina. Soames watched him for a moment dance
crazily on the pavement to his own drawling jagged
sounds, then crossed over to avoid contact with this
piece of drunken foolery. A night in the lock-up!
What asses people were! But the man had noticed
his movement of avoidance, and streams of genial
blasphemy followed him across the street. 'I hope
they'll run him in,' thought Soames viciously. 'To
have ruffians like that about, with women out
alone!' A woman's figure in front had induced this
thought. Her walk seemed oddly familiar, and
when she turned the corner for which he was bound,
his heart began to beat. He hastened on to the corner to make certain. Yes! It was Irene; he could
not mistake her walk in that little drab street. She
threaded two more turnings, and from the last corner he saw her enter her block of flats. To make
sure of her now, he ran those few paces, hurried up
the stairs, and caught her standing at her door. He
heard the latch-key in the lock, and reached her side
just as she turned round, startled, in the open doorway.

" Don't be alarmed," he said, breathless, " I happened to see you.   Let me come in a minute."

She had put her hand up to her breast, her face was colourless, her eyes widened by alarm.   Then seeming to master herself, she inclined her head, and said: " Very well."

Soames closed the door.   He, too, had need to recover, and when she had passed into the sitting-room, waited a full minute, taking deep breaths to still the beating of his heart.   At this moment, so fraught with the future, to take out that morocco case seemed crude.   Yet, not to take it out left him there before her with no preliminary excuse for coming.   And in his dilemma he was seized with impatience at all this paraphernalia of excuse and justification.   This was a scene — it could be nothing else, and he must face it!   He heard her voice, uncomfortably, pathetically soft:

" Why have you come again?   Didn't you understand that I would rather you did not? "

He noticed her clothes — a dark brown velvet corduroy, a sable boa, a small round toque of the same.   They suited her admirably.   She had money to spare for dress, evidently!   He said abruptly:

" It's your birthday.   I brought you this," and he held out to her the green morocco case.

" Oh!   No — no! "

Soames pressed the clasp; the seven stones gleamed out on the pale grey velvet.

" Why not? " he said.   " Just as a sign that you don't bear me ill-feeling any longer."

" I couldn't."

Soames took it out of the case.

" Let me just see how it looks."

She shrank back.

He followed, thrusting his hand with the brooch in it against the front of her dress. She shrank again.

Soames dropped his hand.

" Irene," he said, " let bygones be bygones. If *I* can, surely you might. Let's begin again, as if nothing had been. Won't you? " His voice was wistful, and his eyes, resting on her face, had in them a sort of supplication.

She, who was standing literally with her back against the wall, gave a little gulp, and that was all her answer. Soames went on:

" Can you really want to live all your days half-dead in this little hole? Come back to me, and I'll give you all you want. You shall live your own life; I swear it."

He saw her face quiver ironically.

" Yes," he repeated, " but I mean it this time. I'll only ask one thing. I just want — I just want a son. Don't look like that! I want one. It's hard." His voice had grown hurried, so that he hardly knew it for his own, and twice he jerked his head back as if struggling for breath. It was the sight of her eyes fixed on him, dark with a sort of fascinated fright, which pulled him together and changed that painful incoherence to anger.

" Is it so very unnatural? " he said between his teeth. " Is it unnatural to want a child from one's own wife? You wrecked our life and put this blight on everything. We go on only half alive, and without any future. Is it so very unflattering to you that in spite of everything I — I still want you for my wife? Speak, for Goodness' sake! do speak."

Irene seemed to try, but did not succeed.

" I don't want to frighten you," said Soames more gently. " Heaven knows. I only want you to see that I can't go on like this. I want you back. I want you."

Irene raised one hand and covered the lower part of her face, but her eyes never moved from his, as though she trusted in them to keep him at bay. And all those years, barren and bitter, since — ah! when? — almost since he had first known her, surged up in one great wave of recollection in Soames; and a spasm that for his life he could not control constricted his face.

" It's not too late," he said; " it's not — if you'll only believe it."

Irene uncovered her lips, and both her hands made a writhing gesture in front of her breast. Soames seized them.

" Don't! " she said under her breath. But he stood holding on to them, trying to stare into her eyes which did not waver. Then she said quietly:

" I am alone here. You won't behave again as you once behaved."

Dropping her hands as though they had been hot irons, he turned away. Was it possible that there could be such relentless unforgiveness! Could that one act of violent possession be still alive within her? Did it bar him thus utterly? And doggedly he said, without looking up:

" I am not going till you've answered me. I am offering what few men would bring themselves to offer, I want a — a reasonable answer."

And almost with surprise he heard her say:

" You can't have a reasonable answer. Reason has nothing to do with it. You can only have the brutal truth: I would rather die."

Soames stared at her.

"Oh!" he said. And there intervened in him a sort of paralysis of speech and movement, the kind of quivering which comes when a man has received a deadly insult, and does not yet know how he is going to take it, or rather what it is going to do with him.

"Oh!" he said again, "as bad as that? Indeed! You would rather die. That's pretty!"

"I am sorry. You wanted me to answer. I can't help the truth, can I?"

At that queer spiritual appeal Soames turned for relief to actuality. He snapped the brooch back into its case and put it in his pocket.

"The truth!" he said; "there's no such thing with women. It's nerves — nerves."

He heard the whisper:

"Yes; nerves don't lie. Haven't you discovered that?" He was silent, obsessed by the thought: 'I *will* hate this woman. I *will* hate her.' That was the trouble! If only he could! He shot a glance at her who stood unmoving against the wall with her head up and her hands clasped, for all the world as if she were going to be shot. And he said quickly:

"I don't believe a word of it. You have a lover. If you hadn't, you wouldn't be such a — such a little idiot." He was conscious, before the expression in her eyes, that he had uttered something of a non-sequitur and dropped back too abruptly into the verbal freedom of his connubial days. He turned away to the door. But he could not go out. Something within him — that most deep and secret Forsyte quality, the impossibility of letting go, the impossibility of seeing the fantastic and forlorn nature of his own tenacity — prevented him. He turned

about again, and there stood, with his back against
the door, as hers was against the wall opposite,
quite unconscious of anything ridiculous in this
separation by the whole width of the room.

"Do you ever think of anybody but yourself?"
he said.

Irene's lips quivered; then she answered slowly:
"Do you ever think that I found out my mistake
— my hopeless, terrible mistake — the very first
week of our marriage; that I went on trying three
years — you know I went on trying? Was it for
myself?"

Soames gritted his teeth. "God knows what it
was. I've never understood you; I shall never understand you. You had everything you wanted;
and you can have it again, and more. What's the
matter with me? I ask you a plain question: What
is it?" Unconscious of the pathos in that enquiry,
he went on passionately: "I'm not lame, I'm not
loathsome, I'm not a boor, I'm not a fool. What is
it? What's the mystery about me?"

Her answer was a long sigh.

He clasped his hands with a gesture that for him
was strangely full of expression. "When I came
here to-night I was — I hoped — I meant everything that I could to do away with the past, and start
fair again. And you meet me with 'nerves,' and silence, and sighs. There's nothing tangible. It's
like — it's like a spider's web."

"Yes."

That whisper from across the room maddened
Soames afresh.

"Well, I don't choose to be in a spider's web. I'll
cut it." He walked straight up to her. "Now!"
What he had gone up to her to do he really did not

know.   But when he was close, the old familiar
scent of her clothes suddenly affected him.   He put
his hands on her shoulders and bent forward to kiss
her.   He kissed not her lips, but a little hard line
where the lips had been drawn in; then his face was
pressed away by her hands; he heard her say: " Oh!
No! "   Shame, compunction, sense of futility
flooded his whole being, he turned on his heel and
went straight out.

CHAPTER III

JOLYON found June waiting on the platform at Paddington. She had received his telegram while at
breakfast. Her abode — a studio and two bed-
rooms in a St. John's Wood garden — had been se-
lected by her for the complete independence which it
guaranteed. Unwatched by Mrs. Grundy, unhin-
dered by permanent domestics, she could receive
lame ducks at any hour of day or night, and not seldom had a duck without studio of its own made use
of June's. She enjoyed her freedom, and possessed
herself with a sort of virginal passion; the warmth
which she would have lavished on Bosinney, and of
which — given her Forsyte tenacity — he must
surely have tired, she now expended in champion-
ship of the underdogs and budding ' geniuses ' of
the artistic world. She lived, in fact, to turn ducks
into the swans she believed they were. The very
fervour of her protections warped her judgments.
But she was loyal and liberal; her small eager hand
was ever against the oppressions of academic and
commercial opinion, and though her income was
considerable, her bank balance was often a minus
quantity.
    She had come to Paddington Station heated in

her soul by a visit to Eric Cobbley. A miserable
Gallery had refused to let that straight-haired genius have his one-man show after all. Its impudent
manager, after visiting his studio, had expressed
the opinion that it would only be a ' one-horse show
from the selling point of view.' This crowning example of commercial cowardice towards her favourite lame duck — and he so hard up, with a wife and
two children, that he had caused her account to be
overdrawn — was still making the blood glow in
her small, resolute face, and her red-gold hair to
shine more than ever. She gave her father a hug,
and got into a cab with him, having as many fish to
fry with him as he with her. It became at once a
question which would fry them first.

Jolyon had reached the words: " My dear, I want
you to come with me," when, glancing at her face,
he perceived by her blue eyes moving from side to
side — like the tail of a preoccupied cat — that she
was not attending.

" Dad, is it true that I absolutely can't get at any
of my money? "

" Only the income, fortunately, my love."

" How perfectly beastly! Can't it be done somehow? There must be a way. I know I could buy
a small Gallery for ten thousand pounds."

" A small Gallery," murmured Jolyon, " seems a
modest desire. But your grandfather foresaw it."

" I think," cried June vigorously, " that all this
care about money is awful, when there's so much
genius in the world simply crushed out for want of
a little. I shall never marry and have children; why
shouldn't I be able to do some good instead of having
it all tied up in case of things which will never come
off? "

" Our name is Forsyte, my dear," replied Jolyon in the ironical voice to which his impetuous daughter had never quite grown accustomed; " and Forsytes, you know, are people who so settle their property that their grandchildren, in case they should die before their parents, have to make wills leaving the property that will only come to themselves when their parents die. Do you follow that? Nor do I, but it's a fact, anyway; we live by the principle that so long as there is a possibility of keeping wealth in the family it must not go out; if you die unmarried, your money goes to Jolly and Holly and their children if they marry. Isn't it pleasant to know that whatever you do you can none of you be destitute? "

" But can't I borrow the money? "

Jolyon shook his head. " Without power of anticipation. You could rent a Gallery, no doubt, if you could manage it out of your income."

June uttered a contemptuous sound.

" Yes; and have no income left to help anybody with."

" My dear child," murmured Jolyon, " wouldn't it come to the same thing? "

" No," said June shrewdly, " I could buy for ten thousand; that would only be four hundred a year. But I should have to pay a thousand a year rent, and that would only leave me five hundred. If I had that Gallery, Dad, think what I could do. I could make Eric Cobbley's name in no time, and ever so many others."

" Names worth making make themselves in time."

" When they're dead."

" Did you ever know anybody living, my dear, improved by having his name made? "

" Yes, you," said June, pressing his arm.

Jolyon started. 'I?' he thought. 'Oh! Ah! Now she's going to ask me to do something. We take it out, we Forsytes, each in our different ways.'

June came closer to him in the cab.

"Darling," she said, "*you* buy the Gallery, and I'll pay you four hundred a year for it. Then neither of us will be any the worse off. Besides, it's a splendid investment."

Jolyon wriggled. "Don't you think," he said, "that for an artist to buy a Gallery is a bit dubious? Besides, ten thousand pounds is a lump, and I'm not a commercial character."

June looked at him with admiring appraisement.

"Of course you're not, but you're awfully businesslike. And I'm sure we could make it pay. It'll be a perfect way of scoring off those wretched dealers and people." And again she squeezed her father's arm.

Jolyon's face expressed quizzical despair.

"Where is this desirable Gallery? Splendidly situated, I suppose?"

"Just off Cork Street."

'Ah!' thought Jolyon, 'I knew it was just off somewhere. Now for what I want out of *her!*'

"Well, I'll think of it, but not just now. You remember Irene? I want you to come with me and see her. Soames is after her again. She might be safer if we could give her asylum somewhere."

The word asylum, which he had used by chance, was of all most calculated to rouse June's interest.

"Irene! I haven't seen her since ——! Of course! I'd love to help her."

It was Jolyon's turn to squeeze her arm, in warm admiration for this spirited, generous-hearted little creature of his begetting.

" Irene is proud," he said, with a sidelong glance, in sudden doubt of June's discretion; " she's difficult to help. We must tread gently. This is the place. I wired her to expect us. Let's send up our cards."

" I can't bear Soames," said June as she got out; " he sneers at everything that isn't successful."

Irene was in what was called the ' Ladies drawing-room ' of the Piedmont Hotel.

Nothing if not morally courageous, June walked straight up to her former friend, kissed her cheek, and the two settled down on a sofa never sat on since the hotel's foundation. Jolyon could see that Irene was deeply affected by this simple forgiveness.

" So Soames has been worrying you? " he said.

" I had a visit from him last night; he wants me to go back to him."

" You're not, of course? " cried June.

Irene smiled faintly and shook her head. " But his position is horrible," she murmured.

" It's his own fault; he ought to have divorced you when he could."

Jolyon remembered how fervently in the old days June had hoped that no divorce would smirch her dead and faithless lover's name.

" Let us hear what Irene *is* going to do," he said.

Irene's lips quivered, but she spoke calmly.

" I'd better give him fresh excuse to get rid of me."

" How horrible! " cried June.

" What else can I do? "

" Out of the question," said Jolyon very quietly, " *sans amour.*"

He thought she was going to cry; but, getting up quickly, she half turned her back on them, and stood regaining control of herself.

June said suddenly:

" Well, I shall go to Soames and tell him he must leave you alone. What does he want at his age?"

" A child. It's not unnatural."

" A child!" cried June scornfully. " Of course! To leave his money to. If he wants one badly enough let him take somebody and have one; then you can divorce him, and he can marry her."

Jolyon perceived suddenly that he had made a mistake to bring June — her violent partizanship was fighting Soames' battle.

" It would be best for Irene to come quietly to us at Robin Hill, and see how things shape."

" Of course," said June; " only ——"

Irene looked full at Jolyon — in all his many attempts afterwards to analyze that glance he never could succeed.

" No! I should only bring trouble on you all. I will go abroad."

He knew from her voice that this was final. The irrelevant thought flashed through him: ' Well, I could see her there.' But he said:

" Don't you think you would be more helpless abroad, in case he followed?"

" I don't know. I can but try."

June sprang up and paced the room. " It's all horrible," she said. " Why should people be tortured and kept miserable and helpless year after year by this disgusting sanctimonious law?" But someone had come into the room, and June came to a standstill. Jolyon went up to Irene:

" Do you want money?"

" No."

" And would you like me to let your flat?"

" Yes, Jolyon, please."

" When shall you be going? "

" To-morrow."

" You won't go back there in the meantime, will you? " This he said with an anxiety strange to himself.

" No; I've got all I want here."

" You'll send me your address? "

She put out her hand to him. " I feel you're a rock."

" Built on sand," answered Jolyon, pressing her hand hard; " but it's a pleasure to do anything, at any time, remember that. And if you change your mind —— ! Come along, June; say good-bye."

June came from the window and flung her arms round Irene.

" Don't think of him," she said under her breath; " enjoy yourself, and bless you! "

With a memory of tears in Irene's eyes, and of a smile on her lips, they went away extremely silent, passing the lady who had interrupted the interview and was turning over the papers on the table.

Opposite the National Gallery June exclaimed:

" Of all undignified beasts and horrible laws! "

But Jolyon did not respond. He had something of his father's balance, and could see things impartially even when his emotions were roused. Irene was right; Soames' position was as bad or worse than her own. As for the law — it catered for a human nature of which it took a naturally low view. And, feeling that if he stayed in his daughter's company he would in one way or another commit an indiscretion, he told her he must catch his train back to Oxford; and hailing a cab, left her to Turner's water-colours, with the promise that he would think over that Gallery.

But he thought over Irene instead. Pity, they said, was akin to love! If so he was certainly in danger of loving her, for he pitied her profoundly. To think of her drifting about Europe so handicapped and lonely! 'I hope to goodness she'll keep her head!' he thought; 'she might easily grow desperate.' In fact, now that she had cut loose from her poor threads of occupation, he couldn't imagine how she would go on — so beautiful a creature, hopeless, and fair game for anyone! In his exasperation was more than a little fear and jealousy. Women did strange things when they were driven into corners. 'I wonder what Soames will do now!' he thought. 'A rotten, idiotic state of things! And I suppose they would say it was her own fault.' Very preoccupied and sore at heart, he got into his train, mislaid his ticket, and on the platform at Oxford took his hat off to a lady whose face he seemed to remember without being able to put a name to her, not even when he saw her having tea at the Rainbow.

CHAPTER IV

WHERE FORSYTES FEAR TO TREAD

QUIVERING from the defeat of his hopes, with the green morocco case still flat against his heart, Soames revolved thoughts bitter as death. A spider's web! Walking fast, and noting nothing in the moonlight, he brooded over the scene he had been through, over the memory of her figure rigid in his grasp. And the more he brooded, the more certain he became that she had a lover — her words, ' I would sooner die! ' were ridiculous if she had not. Even if she had never loved him, she had made no fuss until Bosinney came on the scene. No; she was in love again, or she would not have made that melodramatic answer to his proposal, which in all the circumstances was reasonable! Very well! That simplified matters.

' I'll take steps to know where I am,' he thought; ' I'll go to Polteed's the first thing to-morrow morning.'

But even in forming that resolution he knew he would have trouble with himself. He had employed Polteed's agency several times in the routine of his profession, even quite lately over Dartie's case, but he had never thought it possible to employ them to watch his own wife.

It was too insulting to himself!

He slept over that project and his wounded pride — or rather, kept vigil. Only while shaving did he suddenly remember that she called herself by her maiden name of Heron. Polteed would not know, at first at all events, whose wife she was, would not look at him obsequiously and leer behind his back. She would just be the wife of one of his clients. And that would be true — for was he not his own solicitor?

He was literally afraid not to put his design into execution at the first possible moment, lest, after all, he might fail himself. And making Warmson bring him an early cup of coffee, he stole out of the house before the hour of breakfast. He walked rapidly to one of those small West End streets where Polteed's and other firms ministered to the virtues of the wealthier classes. Hitherto he had always had Polteed to see him in the Poultry; but he well knew their address, and reached it at the opening hour. In the outer office, a room furnished so cosily that it might have been a moneylender's, he was attended by a lady who might have been a schoolmistress.

" I wish to see Mr. Claud Polteed. He knows me — never mind my name."

To keep everybody from knowing that he, Soames Forsyte, was reduced to having his wife spied on, was the overpowering consideration.

Mr. Claud Polteed — so different from Mr. Lewis Polteed — was one of those men with dark hair, slightly curved noses, and quick brown eyes, who might be taken for Jews but are really Phœnicians; he received Soames in a room hushed by thickness of carpet and curtains. It was, in fact, confiden-

tially furnished, without trace of document anywhere to be seen.

Greeting Soames deferentially, he turned the key
in the only door with a certain ostentation.

' If a client sends for me,' he was in the habit of
saying, ' he takes what precaution he likes.   If he
comes here, we convince him that we have no leak-
ages.   I may safely say we lead in security, if in
nothing else. . . .'   " Now, sir, what can I do for
you? "

Soames' gorge had risen so that he could hardly
speak.   It was absolutely necessary to hide from
this man that he had any but professional interest in
the matter; and, mechanically, his face assumed its
sideway smile.

" I've come to you early like this because there's
not an hour to lose "— if he lost an hour he might
fail himself yet!   " Have you a really trustworthy
woman free? "

Mr. Polteed unlocked a drawer, produced a mem-
orandum, ran his eyes over it, and locked the drawer
up again.

" Yes," he said; " the very woman."

Soames had seated himself and crossed his legs —
nothing but a faint flush, which might have been his
normal complexion, betrayed him.

" Send her off at once, then, to watch a Mrs. Irene
Heron of Flat D, Truro Mansions, Chelsea, till further notice."

" Precisely," said Mr. Polteed; " divorce, I pre-
sume? " and he blew into a speaking-tube.   " Mrs.
Blanch in?   I shall want to speak to her in ten minutes."

" Deal with any reports yourself," resumed
Soames, " and send them to me personally, marked

confidential, sealed and registered. My client exacts the utmost secrecy."

Mr. Polteed smiled, as though saying, ' You are teaching your grandmother, my dear sir '; and his eyes slid over Soames' face for one unprofessional instant.

"Make his mind perfectly easy," he said. " Do you smoke? "

" No," said Soames. " Understand me: Nothing may come of this. If a name gets out, or the watching is suspected, it may have very serious consequences."

Mr. Polteed nodded. " I can put it into the cipher category. Under that system a name is never mentioned; we work by numbers."

He unlocked another drawer and took out two slips of paper, wrote on them, and handed one to Soames.

"Keep that, sir; it's your key. I retain this duplicate. The case we'll call 7x. The party watched will be 17; the watcher 19; the Mansions 25; yourself — I should say, your firm — 31; my firm 32, myself 2. In case you should have to mention your client in writing I have called him 43; any person we suspect will be 47; a second person 51. Any special hint or instruction while we're about it? "

" No," said Soames; "that is — every consideration compatible."

Again Mr. Polteed nodded. " Expense? "

Soames shrugged. " In reason," he answered curtly, and got up. " Keep it entirely in your own hands."

" Entirely," said Mr. Polteed, appearing suddenly between him and the door. " I shall be seeing you

in that other case before long.   Good-morning, sir."
His eyes slid unprofessionally over Soames once
more, and he unlocked the door.
" Good-morning," said Soames, looking neither to
right nor left.

Out in the street he swore deeply, quietly, to himself.   A spider's web, and to cut it he must use this
spidery, secret, unclean method, so utterly repug-
nant to one who regarded his private life as his most
sacred piece of property.   But the die was cast, he
could not go back.   And he went on into the Poultry, and locked away the green morocco case and
the key to that cipher destined to make crystal-clear
his domestic bankruptcy.

Odd that one whose life was spent in bringing to
the public eye all the private coils of property, the
domestic disagreements of others, should dread so
utterly the public eye turned on his own; and yet not
odd, for who should know so well as he the whole un-
feeling process of legal regulation?

He worked hard all day.   Winifred was due at
four o'clock; he was to take her down to a conference in the Temple with Dreamer Q.C., and waiting
for her he re-read the letter he had caused her to
write the day of Dartie's departure, requiring him
to return.

" Dear Montagu,

" I have received your letter with the news that
you have left me for ever and are on your way to
Buenos Aires.   It has naturally been a great shock.
I am taking this earliest opportunity of writing to
tell you that I am prepared to let bygones be bygones
if you will return to me at once.   I beg you to do so.
I am very much upset, and will not say any more

now. I am sending this letter registered to the address you left at your Club. Please cable to me.

"Your still affectionate wife,

"WINIFRED DARTIE."

Ugh! What bitter humbug! He remembered leaning over Winifred while she copied what he had pencilled, and how she had said, laying down her pen, "Suppose he comes, Soames!" in such a strange tone of voice, as if she did not know her own mind. "He won't come," he had answered, "till he's spent his money. That's why we must act at once." Annexed to the copy of that letter was the original of Dartie's drunken scrawl from the Iseeum Club. Soames could have wished it had not been so manifestly penned in liquor. Just the sort of thing the Court would pitch on. He seemed to hear the Judge's voice say: "You took this seriously! Seriously enough to write him as you did? Do you think he meant it?" Never mind! The fact was clear that Dartie had sailed and had not returned. Annexed also was his cabled answer: 'Impossible return. Dartie.' Soames shook his head. If the whole thing were not disposed of within the next few months the fellow would turn up again like a bad penny. It saved a thousand a year at least to get rid of him, besides all the worry to Winifred and his father. 'I must stiffen Dreamer's back,' he thought; 'we must push it on.'

Winifred, who had adopted a kind of half-mourning which became her fair hair and tall figure very well, arrived in James' barouche drawn by James' pair. Soames had not seen it in the City since his father retired from business five years ago, and its incongruity gave him a shock. 'Times are changing,' he thought; 'one doesn't know what'll go next!' Top hats even were scarcer.   He enquired after Val.   Val, said Winifred, wrote that he was going to play polo next term.   She thought he was in a very good set.   She added with fashionably disguised anxiety: "Will there be much publicity about my affair, Soames?   *Must* it be in the papers? It's so bad for him, and the girls."

With his own calamity all raw within him, Soames answered:

"The papers are a pushing lot; it's very difficult to keep things out.   They pretend to be guarding the public's morals, and they corrupt them with their beastly reports.   But we haven't got to that yet. We're only seeing Dreamer to-day on the restitution question.   Of course he understands that it's to lead to a divorce; but you must seem genuinely anxious to get Dartie back — you might practice that attitude to-day."

Winifred sighed.

"Oh!   What a clown Monty's been!" she said.

Soames gave her a sharp look.   It was clear to him that she could not take her Dartie seriously, and would go back on the whole thing if given half a chance.   His own instinct had been firm in this matter from the first.   To save a little scandal now would only bring on his sister and her children real disgrace and perhaps ruin later on if Dartie were allowed to hang on to them, going down-hill and spending the money James would leave his daughter.   Though it *was* all tied up, that fellow would milk the settlements somehow, and make his family pay through the nose to keep him out of bankruptcy or even perhaps gaol!   They left the shining carriage, with the shining horses and the shining-hatted servants on the Embankment, and walked up to Dreamer Q.C.'s Chambers in Crown Office Row.

"Mr. Bellby is here, sir," said the clerk; "Mr. Dreamer will be ten minutes."

Mr. Bellby, the junior — not as junior as he might have been, for Soames only employed barristers of established reputation; it was, indeed, something of a mystery to him how barristers ever managed to establish that which made him employ them — Mr. Bellby was seated, taking a final glance through his papers. He had come from Court, and was in wig and gown, which suited a nose jutting out like the handle of a tiny pump, his small shrewd blue eyes, and rather protruding lower lip — no better man to supplement and stiffen Dreamer.

The introduction to Winifred accomplished, they leaped the weather and spoke of the war. Soames interjected suddenly:

"If he doesn't comply we can't bring proceedings for six months. I want to get on with the matter, Bellby."

Mr. Bellby, who had the ghost of an Irish brogue, smiled at Winifred and murmured: "The Law's delays, Mrs. Dartie."

"Six months!" repeated Soames; "it'll drive it up to June! We shan't get the suit on till after the long vacation. We must put the screw on, Bellby" — he would have all his work cut out to keep Winifred up to the scratch.

"Mr. Dreamer will see you now, sir."

They filed in, Mr. Bellby going first, and Soames escorting Winifred after an interval of one minute by his watch.

Dreamer Q.C., in a gown but divested of wig, was

standing before the fire, as if this conference were
in the nature of a treat; he had the leathery, rather
oily complexion which goes with great learning, a
considerable nose with glasses perched on it, and
little greyish whiskers; he luxuriated in the perpetual cocking of one eye, and the concealment of
his lower with his upper lip, which gave a smothered
turn to his speech.   He had a way, too, of coming
suddenly round the corner on the person he was
talking to; this, with a disconcerting tone of voice,
and a habit of growling before he began to speak —
had secured a reputation second in Probate and Divorce to very few.   Having listened, eye cocked, to
Mr. Bellby's breezy recapitulation of the facts, he
growled, and said:

" I know all that;" and coming round the corner
at Winifred, smothered the words:

" We want to get back, don't we, Mrs. Dartie? "

Soames interposed sharply:

" My sister's position, of course, is intolerable."

Dreamer growled.   " Exactly.   Now, can we
rely on the cable refusal, or must we wait till after
Christmas to give him a chance to have written —
that's the point, isn't it? "

" The sooner —— " Soames began.

" What do you say, Bellby? " said Dreamer, coming round his corner.

Mr. Bellby seemed to sniff the air like a hound.

" We won't be on till the middle of December.
We've no need to give um more rope than that."

" No," said Soames, " why should my sister be in-
commoded by his choosing to go —— "

" To Jericho! " said Dreamer, again coming
round his corner; " quite so.   People oughtn't to go
to Jericho, ought they, Mrs. Dartie? "   And he

raised his gown into a sort of fantail. "I agree.
We can go forward. Is there anything more?"

"Nothing at present," said Soames meaningly;
"I wanted you to see my sister."

Dreamer growled softly: "Delighted. Good-
evening!" And let fall the protection of his gown.

They filed out. Winifred went down the stairs.
Soames lingered. In spite of himself he was impressed by Dreamer.

"The evidence is all right, I think," he said to
Bellby. "Between ourselves, if we don't get the
thing through quick, we never may. D'you think
he understands that?"

"I'll make um," said Bellby. "Good man though
— good man."

Soames nodded and hastened after his sister. He
found her in a draught, biting her lips behind her
veil, and at once said:

"The evidence of the stewardess will be very
complete."

Winifred's face hardened; she drew herself up,
and they walked to the carriage. And, all through
that silent drive back to Green Street, the souls of
both of them revolved a single thought: 'Why, oh!
why should I have to expose my misfortune to the
public like this? Why have to employ spies to peer
into my private troubles? They were not of my
making.'

CHAPTER V

THE possessive instinct, which, so determinedly balked, was animating two members of the Forsyte family towards riddance of what they could no longer possess, was hardening daily in the British body politic.   Nicholas, originally so doubtful concerning a war which must affect property, had been heard to say that these Boers were a pig-headed lot; they were causing a lot of expense, and the sooner they had their lesson the better.   *He* would send out Wolseley!   Seeing always a little further than other people — whence the most considerable fortune of all the Forsytes — he had perceived already that Buller was not the man — 'a bull of a chap, who just went butting, and if they didn't look out Ladysmith would fall.'   This was early in December, so that when Black Week came, he was enabled to say to everybody: 'I told you so.'   During that week of gloom such as no Forsyte could remember, very young Nicholas attended so many drills in his corps, 'The Devil's Own,' that young Nicholas consulted the family physician about his son's health and was alarmed to find that he was perfectly sound.   The boy had only just eaten his dinners and been called to the bar, at some expense, and it

183

was in a way a nightmare to his father and mother
that he should be playing with military efficiency at
a time when military efficiency in the civilian popu-
lation might conceivably be wanted.   His grandfather, of course, pooh-poohed the notion, too thoroughly educated in the feeling that no British war
could be other than little and professional, and profoundly distrustful of Imperial commitments, by
which, moreover, he stood to lose, for he owned De
Beers, now going down fast, more than a sufficient
sacrifice on the part of his grandson.

At Oxford, however, rather different sentiments
prevailed.   The inherent effervescence of conglom-
erate youth had, during the two months of the term
before Black Week, been gradually crystallising out
into vivid oppositions.   Normal adolescence, ever
in England of a conservative tendency, though not
taking things too seriously, was vehement for a
fight to a finish and a good licking for the Boers.
Of this larger faction Val Dartie was naturally a
member.   Radical youth, on the other hand, a small
but perhaps more vocal body, was for stopping the
war and giving the Boers autonomy.   Until Black
Week, however, the groups were amorphous, without sharp edges, and argument remained but academic.   Jolly was one of those who knew not where
he stood.   A streak of his grandfather old Jolyon's
love of justice prevented him from seeing one side
only.   Moreover, in his set of 'the best' there was a
'jumping-jesus' of extremely advanced opinions
and some personal magnetism.   Jolly wavered.   His
father, too, seemed doubtful in his views.   And
though, as was proper at the age of twenty, he kept
a sharp eye on his father, watchful for defects
which might still be remedied, still that father had

an ' air ' which gave a sort of glamour to his creed
of ironic tolerance. Artists, of course, were notori-
ously Hamlet-like, and to this extent one must dis-
count for one's father, even if one loved him. But
Jolyon's original view, that to ' put your nose in
where you aren't wanted ' (as the Uitlanders had
done) ' and then work the oracle till you get on
top is not being quite the clean potato,' had, whether
founded in fact or no, a certain attraction for his
son, who thought a deal about gentility. On the
other hand Jolly could not abide such as his set
called ' cranks,' and Val's set called ' smugs,' so
that he was still balancing when the clock of Black
Week struck.   One — two — three, came those
ominous repulses at Stormberg, Magersfontein,
Colenso. The sturdy English soul reacting after
the first cried, ' Ah! but Methuen!' after the second: ' Ah! but Buller!' then, in inspissated gloom,
hardened. And Jolly said to himself: " No, damn
it! We've got to lick the beggars now; I don't care
whether we're right or wrong."   And, if he had
known it, his father was thinking the same thought.

That next Sunday, last of the term, Jolly was
bidden to wine with ' one of the best.' After the
second toast, ' Buller and damnation to the Boers,'
drunk — no heel taps — in the college Burgundy,
he noticed that Val Dartie, also a guest, was looking at him with a grin and saying something to his
neighbour. He was sure it was disparaging. The
last boy in the world to make himself conspicuous
or cause public disturbance, Jolly grew rather red
and shut his lips. The queer hostility he had always felt towards his second-cousin was strongly
and suddenly reinforced. " All right!" he said to
himself; " you wait, my friend!"   More wine than

was good for him, as the custom was, helped him to remember, when they all trooped forth to a secluded spot, to touch Val on the arm.

" What did you say about me in there? "

" Mayn't I say what I like? "

" No."

" Well, I said you were a pro-Boer — and so you are!"

" You're a liar!"

" D'you want a row? "

" Of course, but not here; in the garden."

" All right. Come on."

They went, eyeing each other askance, unsteady, and unflinching; they climbed the garden railings. The spikes on the top slightly ripped Val's sleeve, and occupied his mind. Jolly's mind was occupied by the thought that they were going to fight in the precincts of a college foreign to them both. It was not the thing, but never mind — the young beast!

They passed over the grass into very nearly darkness, and took off their coats.

" You're not screwed, are you? " said Jolly suddenly. " I can't fight you if you're screwed."

" No more than you."

" All right then."

Without shaking hands, they put themselves at once into postures of defence. They had drunk too much for science, and so were especially careful to assume correct attitudes, until Jolly smote Val almost accidentally on the nose. After that it was all a dark and ugly scrimmage in the deep shadow of the old trees, with no one to call 'time,' till, battered and blown, they unclinched and staggered back from each other, as a voice said:

" Your names, young gentlemen? "

At this bland query spoken from under the lamp at the garden gate, like some demand of a god, their nerves gave way, and snatching up their coats, they ran at the railings, shinned up them, and made for the secluded spot whence they had issued to the fight. Here, in dim light, they mopped their faces, and without a word walked, ten paces apart, to the college gate. They went out silently, Val going towards the Broad along the Brewery, Jolly down the lane towards the High. His head, still fumed, was busy with regret that he had not displayed more science, passing in review the counters and knock-out blows which he had not delivered. His mind strayed on to an imagined combat, infinitely unlike that which he had just been through, infinitely gallant, with sash and sword, with thrust and parry, as if he were in the pages of his beloved Dumas. He fancied himself La Mole, and Aramis, Bussy, Chicot, and D'Artagnan rolled into one, but he quite failed to envisage Val as Coconnas, Brissac, or Rochefort. The fellow was just a confounded cousin who didn't come up to Cocker. Never mind! He had given him one or two. 'Pro-Boer!' The word still rankled, and thoughts of enlisting jostled his aching head; of riding over the veldt, firing gallantly, while the Boers rolled over like rabbits. And, turning up his smarting eyes, he saw the stars shining between the house-tops of the High, and himself lying out on the Karoo (whatever that was) rolled in a blanket, with his rifle ready and his gaze fixed on a glittering heaven.

He had a fearful 'head' next morning, which he doctored, as became one of 'the best,' by soaking it in cold water, brewing strong coffee which he could not drink, and only sipping a little Hock at lunch.

The legend that ' some fool ' had run into him round a corner accounted for a bruise on his cheek. He would on no account have mentioned the fight, for, on second thoughts, it fell far short of his standards.

The next day he went 'down,' and travelled through to Robin Hill. Nobody was there but June and Holly, for his father had gone to Paris. He spent a restless and unsettled Vacation, quite out of touch with either of his sisters. June, indeed, was occupied with lame ducks, whom, as a rule, Jolly could not stand, especially that Eric Cobbley and his family, ' hopeless outsiders,' who were always littering up the house in the Vacation. And be-tween Holly and himself there was a strange division, as if she were beginning to have opinions of her own, which was so — unnecessary. He punched viciously at a ball, rode furiously but alone in Richmond Park, making a point of jumping the stiff, high hurdles put up to close certain worn avenues of grass —keeping his nerve in, he called it. Jolly was more afraid of being afraid than most boys. He bought a rifle, too, and put a range up in the home field, shooting across the pond into the kitchen-garden wall, to the peril of gardeners, with the thought that some day, perhaps, he would enlist and save South Africa for his country. In fact, now that they were appealing for Yeomanry recruits the boy was thoroughly upset. Ought he to go? None of 'the best,' so far as he knew — and he was in correspondence with several — were thinking of joining. If they *had* been making a move he would have gone at once — very competitive, and with a strong sense of form, he could not bear to be left behind in anything — but to do it off his own bat might look like 'swagger'; because of course it wasn't really necessary. Besides, he did not want to go, for the other side of this young Forsyte recoiled from leaping before he looked. It was altogether mixed pickles within him, hot and sickly pickles, and he became quite unlike his serene and rather lordly self.

And then one day he saw that which moved him to uneasy wrath — two riders, in a glade of the Park close to the Ham Gate, of whom she on the left-hand was most assuredly Holly on her silver roan, and he on the right-hand as assuredly that 'squirt' Val Dartie. His first impulse was to urge on his own horse and demand the meaning of this portent, tell the fellow to 'bunk,' and take Holly home. His second — to feel that he would look a fool if they refused. He reined his horse in behind a tree, then perceived that it was equally impossible to spy on them. Nothing for it but to go home and await her coming! Sneaking out with that young bounder! He could not consult with June, because she had gone up that morning in the train of Eric Cobbley and his lot. And his father was still in 'that rotten Paris.' He felt that this was emphatically one of those moments for which he had trained himself, assiduously, at school, where he and a boy called Brent had frequently set fire to newspapers and placed them in the centre of their studies to accustom them to coolness in moments of danger. He did not feel at all cool waiting in the stable-yard, idly stroking the dog Balthasar, who, queasy as an old fat monk, and sad in the absence of his master, turned up his face, panting with gratitude for this attention. It was half an hour before Holly came, flushed and ever so much prettier than she had any right to look. He saw her look at him quickly — guiltily of course — then followed her in, and, taking her arm, conducted her into what had been their grandfather's study. The room, not much used now, was still vaguely haunted for them both by a presence with which they associated tenderness, large drooping white moustaches, the scent of cigar smoke, and laughter. Here Jolly, in the prime of his youth, before he went to school at all, had been wont to wrestle with his grandfather, who even at eighty had an irresistible habit of crooking his leg. Here Holly, perched on the arm of the great leather chair, had stroked hair curving silvery over an ear into which she would whisper secrets. Through that window they had all three sallied times without number to cricket on the lawn, and a mysterious game called ' Wopsy-doozle ' not to be understood by outsiders, which made old Jolyon very hot. Here once on a warm night Holly had appeared in her ' nighty,' having had a bad dream, to have the clutch of it released. And here Jolly, having begun the day badly by introducing fizzy magnesia into Mademoiselle Beauce's new-laid egg, and gone on to worse, had been sent down (in the absence of his father) to the ensuing dialogue:

" Now, my boy, you mustn't go on like this."

" Well, she boxed my ears, Gran, so I only boxed hers, and then she boxed mine again."

" Strike a lady? That'll never do! Have you begged her pardon?"

" Not yet."

" Then you must go and do it at once. Come along."

" But she began it, Gran; and she had two to my one."

" My dear, it was an outrageous thing to do."

" Well, she lost her temper; and I didn't lose mine."

" Come along."

" You come too, then, Gran."

" Well — this time only."

And they had gone hand in hand.

Here — where the Waverley novels and Byron's works and Gibbon's *Roman Empire* and Humboldt's *Cosmos*, and the bronzes on the mantelpiece and that masterpiece of the oily school, ' Dutch Fishing-Boats at Sunset,' were fixed as fate, and for all sign of change old Jolyon might have been sitting there still, with legs crossed, in the armchair, and domed forehead and deep eyes grave above *The Times* — here they came, those two grandchildren.   And Jolly said:

" I saw you and that fellow in the Park."

The sight of blood rushing into her cheeks gave him some satisfaction; she *ought* to be ashamed!

" Well?" she said.

Jolly was surprised; he had expected more, or less.

" Do you know," he said weightily, " that he called me a pro-Boer last term?   And I had to fight him."

" Who won? "

Jolly wished to answer: ' I should have,' but it seemed beneath him.

" Look here! " he said, " what's the meaning of it?   Without telling anybody! "

" Why should I?   Dad isn't here; why shouldn't I ride with him? "

" You've got me to ride with.   I think he's an awful young rotter."

Holly went pale with anger.

" He isn't, it's your own fault for not liking him."

And slipping past her brother she went out, leaving him staring at the bronze Venus sitting on a tortoise, which had been shielded from him so far by his sister's dark head under her soft felt riding hat. He felt queerly disturbed, shaken to his young foundations. A lifelong domination lay shattered round his feet. He went up to the Venus and mechanically inspected the tortoise. Why didn't he like Val Dartie? He could not tell. Ignorant of family history, barely aware of that vague feud which had started thirteen years before with Bosinney's defection from June in favour of Soames' wife, knowing really almost nothing about Val, he was at sea. He just did dislike him. The question, however, was: What should he do? Val Dartie, it was true, was a second-cousin, but it was not the thing for Holly to go about with him. And yet to ' tell ' of what he had chanced on was against his creed. In this dilemma he went and sat in the old leather chair and crossed his legs. It grew dark while he sat there staring out through the long window at the old oak-tree, ample yet bare of leaves, becoming slowly just a shape of deeper dark printed on the dusk.

' Grandfather ! ' he thought without sequence, and took out his watch. He could not see the hands, but he set the repeater going. ' Five o'clock !' His grandfather's first gold hunter watch, butter-smoothed with age — all the milling worn from it, and dented with the mark of many a fall. The chime was like a little voice from out of that golden age, when they first came from St. John's Wood, London, to this house — came driving with grandfather in his carriage, and almost instantly took to the trees. Trees to climb, and grandfather watering the geranium-beds below! What was to be done? Tell Dad he must come home? Confide in June? — only she was so — so sudden! Do nothing and trust to luck? After all, the Vac. would soon be over. Go up and see Val and warn him off? But how get his address? Holly wouldn't give it him! A maze of paths, a cloud of possibilities! He lit a cigarette. When he had smoked it halfway through his brow relaxed, almost as if some thin old hand had been passed gently over it; and in his ear something seemed to whisper: 'Do nothing; be nice to Holly, be nice to her, my dear!' And Jolly heaved a sigh of contentment, blowing smoke through his nostrils. . . .

But up in her room, divested of her habit, Holly was still frowning. 'He is *not* — he is *not!*' were the words which kept forming on her lips.

CHAPTER VI

JOLYON IN TWO MINDS

A LITTLE private hotel over a well-known restaurant near the Gare St. Lazare was Jolyon's haunt in Paris. He hated his fellow Forsytes abroad — vapid as fish out of water in their well-trodden runs the Opera, Rue de Rivoli, and Moulin Rouge. Their air of having come because they wanted to be somewhere else as soon as possible annoyed him. But no other Forsyte came near this haunt, where he had a wood fire in his bedroom and the coffee was excellent. Paris was always to him more attractive in winter. The acrid savour from woodsmoke and chestnut-roasting braziers, the sharpness of the wintry sunshine on bright days, the open cafés defying keen-aired winter, the self-contained brisk boulevard crowds, all informed him that in winter Paris possessed a soul which, like a migrant bird, in high summer flew away.

He spoke French well, had some friends, knew little places where pleasant dishes could be met with, queer types observed. He felt philosophic in Paris, the edge of irony sharpened; life took on a subtle, purposeless meaning, became a bunch of flavours tasted, a darkness shot with shifting gleams of light.

When in the first week of December he decided to go to Paris, he was far from admitting that

Irene's presence was influencing him. He had not been there two days before he owned that the wish to see her had been more than half the reason. In England one did not admit what was natural. He had thought it might be well to speak to her about the letting of her flat and other matters, but in Paris he at once knew better. There was a glamour over the city. On the third day he wrote to her, and received an answer which procured him a pleasurable shiver of the nerves:

"My dear Jolyon,
        "It will be a happiness for me to see you.
                                        "Irene."

He took his way to her hotel on a bright day with a feeling such as he had often had going to visit an adored picture. No woman, so far as he remembered, had ever inspired in him this special sensuous and yet impersonal sensation. He was going to sit and feast his eyes, and come away knowing her no better, but ready to go and feast his eyes again to-morrow. Such was his feeling, when in the tarnished and ornate little lounge of a quiet hotel near the river she came to him preceded by a small page-boy who uttered the word, "*Madame,*" and vanished. Her face, her smile, the poise of her figure, were just as he had pictured, and the expression of her face said plainly: 'A friend!'

"Well," he said, "what news, poor exile?"
"None."
"Nothing from Soames?"
"Nothing."
"I have let the flat for you, and like a good steward I bring you some money. How do you like Paris?"

While he put her through this catechism, it seemed to him that he had never seen lips so fine and sensitive, the lower lip curving just a little upwards, the upper touched at one corner by the least conceivable dimple. It was like discovering a woman in what had hitherto been a sort of soft and breathed-on statue, almost impersonally admired. She owned that to be alone in Paris was a little difficult; and yet, Paris was so full of its own life that it was often, she confessed, as innocuous as a desert. Besides, the English were not liked just now!

"That will hardly be your case," said Jolyon; "you should appeal to the French."

"It has its disadvantages."

Jolyon nodded.

"Well, you must let *me* take you about while I'm here. We'll start to-morrow. Come and dine at my pet restaurant; and we'll go to the Opéra-Comique."

It was the beginning of daily meetings.

Jolyon soon found that for those who desired a static condition of the affections, Paris was at once the first and last place in which to be friendly with a pretty woman. Revelation was alighting like a bird in his heart, singing: '*Elle est ton rêve! Elle est ton rêve!*' Sometimes this seemed natural, sometimes ludicrous — a bad case of elderly rapture. Having once been ostracised by Society, he had never since had any real regard for conventional morality; but the idea of a love which she could never return — and how could she at his age? — hardly mounted beyond his subconscious mind. He was full, too, of resentment, at the waste and loneliness of her life. Aware of being some comfort to her, and of the pleasure she clearly took in

their many little outings, he was amiably desirous
of doing and saying nothing to destroy that pleasure. It was like watching a starved plant draw up
water, to see her drink-in his companionship. So
far as they could tell, no one knew her address except himself; she was unknown in Paris, and he but
little known, so that discretion seemed unnecessary
in those walks, talks, visits to concerts, picture-gal-
leries, theatres, little dinners, expeditions to Ver-
sailles, St. Cloud, even Fontainebleau. And time
fled — one of those full months without past to it
or future. What in his youth would certainly have
been headlong passion, was now perhaps as deep a
feeling, but far gentler, tempered to protective companionship by admiration, hopelessness, and a sense
of chivalry — arrested in his veins at least so long
as she was there, smiling and happy in their friend-
ship, and always to him more beautiful and spiritually responsive: for her philosophy of life
seemed to march in admirable step with his own,
conditioned by emotion more than by reason, ironically mistrustful, susceptible to beauty, almost passionately humane and tolerant, yet subject to instinctive rigidities of which as a mere man he was
less capable. And during all this companionable
month he never quite lost that feeling with which
he had set out on the first day as if to visit an
adored work of art, a wellnigh impersonal desire.
The future — inexorable pendant to the present —
he took care not to face, for fear of breaking up
his untroubled manner; but he made plans to renew
this time in places still more delightful, where the
sun was hot and there were strange things to see
and paint. The end came swiftly on the 20th of
January with a telegram:

" Have enlisted in Imperial Yeomanry.—JOLLY."

Jolyon received it just as he was setting out to meet her at the Louvre. It brought him up with a round turn. While he was lotus-eating here, his boy, whose philosopher and guide he ought to be, had taken this great step towards danger, hardship, perhaps even death. He felt disturbed to the soul, realising suddenly how Irene had twined herself round the roots of his being. Thus threatened with severance, the tie between them — for it had become a kind of tie — no longer had impersonal quality. The tranquil enjoyment of things in common, Jolyon perceived, was gone for ever. He saw his feeling as it was, in the nature of an infatuation. Ridiculous, perhaps, but so real that sooner or later it must disclose itself. And now, as it seemed to him, he could not, must not, make any such disclosure. The news of Jolly stood inexorably in the way. He was proud of this enlistment; proud of his boy for going off to fight for the country; for on Jolyon's pro-Boerism, too, Black Week had left its mark. And so the end was reached before the beginning! Well, luckily he had never made a sign!

When he came into the Gallery she was standing before the 'Virgin of the Rocks,' graceful, absorbed, smiling and unconscious. 'Have I to give up seeing *that?*' he thought. 'It's unnatural, so long as she's willing that I should see her.' He stood, unnoticed, watching her, storing up the image of her figure, envying the picture on which she was bending that long scrutiny. Twice she turned her head towards the entrance, and he thought: 'That's for me!' At last he went forward.

" Look! " he said.

She read the telegram, and he heard her sigh.

That sigh, too, was for him! His position was really cruel! To be loyal to his son he must just shake her hand and go. To be loyal to the feeling in his heart he must at least tell her what that feeling was. Could she, would she understand the silence in which he was gazing at that picture?

" I'm afraid I must go home at once," he said at last. " I shall miss all this awfully."

" So shall I; but, of course, you must go."

" Well! " said Jolyon holding out his hand.

Meeting her eyes, a flood of feeling nearly mastered him.

" Such is life! " he said. " Take care of yourself, my dear! "

He had a stumbling sensation in his legs and feet, as if his brain refused to steer him away from her. From the doorway, he saw her lift her hand and touch its fingers with her lips. He raised his hat solemnly, and did not look back again.

CHAPTER VII

DARTIE VERSUS DARTIE

THE suit — Dartie *versus* Dartie — for restitution of those conjugal rights concerning which Winifred was at heart so deeply undecided, followed the laws of subtraction towards day of judgment. This was not reached before the Courts rose for Christmas, but the case was third on the list when they sat again. Winifred spent the Christmas holidays a thought more fashionably than usual, with the matter locked up in her low-cut bosom. James was particularly liberal to her that Christmas, expressing thereby his sympathy, and relief, at the approaching dissolution of her marriage with that 'precious rascal,' which his old heart felt but his old lips could not utter.

The disappearance of Dartie made the fall in Consols a comparatively small matter; and as to the scandal — the real animus he felt against that fellow, and the increasing lead which property was attaining over reputation in a true Forsyte about to leave this world, served to drug a mind from which all allusions to the matter (except his own) were studiously kept. What worried him as a lawyer and a parent was the fear that Dartie might suddenly turn up and obey the Order of the Court when made. That would be a pretty how-de-do! The

fear preyed on him in fact so much that, in present-
ing Winifred with a large Christmas cheque, he
said: " It's chiefly for that chap out there; to keep
him from coming back." It was, of course, to pitch
away good money, but all in the nature of insurance
against that bankruptcy which would no longer
hang over him if only the divorce went through;
and he questioned Winifred rigorously until she
could assure him that the money had been sent.
Poor woman! — it cost her many a pang to send
what must find its way into the vanity-bag of ' that
creature!' Soames, hearing of it, shook his head.
They were not dealing with a Forsyte, reasonably
tenacious of his purpose. It was very risky without knowing how the land lay out there. Still, it
would look well with the Court; and he would see
that Dreamer brought it out. " I wonder," he said
suddenly, " where that ballet goes after the Argen-
tine "; never omitting a chance of reminder; for
he knew that Winifred still had a weakness, if not
for Dartie, at least for not laundering him in public. Though not good at showing admiration, he
admitted that she was behaving extremely well,
with all her children at home gaping like young
birds for news of their father — Imogen just on
the point of coming out, and Val very restive about
the whole thing. He felt that Val was the real
heart of the matter to Winifred, who certainly
loved him beyond her other children. The boy could
spoke the wheel of this divorce yet if he set his
mind to it. And Soames was very careful to keep
the proximity of the preliminary proceedings from
his nephew's ears. He did more. He asked him to
dine at the Remove, and over Val's cigar introduced
the subject which he knew to be nearest to his heart.

"I hear," he said, "that you want to play polo up at Oxford."

Val became less recumbent in his chair.

"Rather!" he said.

"Well," continued Soames, "that's a very expensive business. Your grandfather isn't likely to consent to it unless he can make sure that he's not got any other drain on him." And he paused to see whether the boy understood his meaning.

Val's dark thick lashes concealed his eyes, but a slight grimace appeared on his wide mouth, and he muttered:

"I suppose you mean my dad!"

"Yes," said Soames; "I'm afraid it depends on whether he continues to be a drag or not;" and said no more, letting the boy dream it over.

But Val was also dreaming in those days of a silver-roan palfrey and a girl riding it. Though Crum was in town and an introduction to Cynthia Dark to be had for the asking, Val did not ask; indeed, he shunned Crum and lived a life strange even to himself, except in so far as accounts with tailor and livery stable were concerned. To his mother, his sisters, his young brother, he seemed to spend his Vacation in 'seeing fellows,' and his evenings sleepily at home. They could not propose anything in daylight that did not meet with the one response: "Sorry; I've got to see a fellow"; and he was put to extraordinary shifts to get in and out of the house unobserved in riding clothes; until, being made a member of the Goat's Club, he was able to transport them there, where he could change unregarded and slip off on his hack to Richmond Park. He kept his growing sentiment religiously to himself. Not for a world would he breathe to

the ' fellows,' whom he was not ' seeing,' anything
so ridiculous from the point of view of their creed
and his. But he could not help its destroying his
other appetites. It was coming between him and
the legitimate pleasures of youth at last on its own
in a way which must, he knew, make him a milk-
sop in the eyes of Crum. All he cared for was to
dress in his last-created riding togs, and steal away
to the Robin Hill Gate, where presently the silver
roan would come demurely sidling with its slim and
dark-haired rider, and in the glades bare of leaves
they would go off side by side, not talking very much,
riding races sometimes, and sometimes holding
hands. More than once of an evening, in a moment
of expansion, he had been tempted to tell his mother
how this shy sweet cousin had stolen in upon
him and wrecked his 'life.' But bitter experience,
that all persons above thirty-five were spoil-
sports, prevented him. After all, he supposed he
would have to go through with College, and she
would have to ' come out,' before they could be
married; so why complicate things, so long as he
could see her? Sisters were teasing and unsympa-
thetic beings, a brother worse, so there was no one
to confide in; besides, this beastly divorce business!
Ah! what a misfortune to have a name which other
people hadn't! If only he had been called Gordon
or Scott or Howard or something fairly common!
But Dartie — there wasn't another in the direc-
tory! One might as well have been named Morkin
for all the covert it afforded! So matters went on,
till one day in the middle of January the silver-
roan palfrey and its rider were missing at the tryst.
Lingering in the cold, he debated whether he should
ride on to the house. But Jolly might be there,

and the memory of their dark encounter was still
fresh within him. One could not be always fighting
with her brother! So he returned dismally to town
and spent an evening plunged in gloom. At breakfast next day he noticed that his mother had on an
unfamiliar dress and was wearing her hat. The
dress was black with a glimpse of peacock blue, the
hat black and large — she looked exceptionally well.
But when after breakfast she said to him, " Come
in here, Val," and led the way to the drawing-room,
he was at once beset by qualms. Winifred carefully shut the door and passed her handkerchief
over her lips; inhaling the violette de Parme with
which it had been soaked, Val thought: ' Has she
found out about Holly? '

Her voice interrupted:

" Are you going to be nice to me, dear boy? "

Val grinned doubtfully.

" Will you come with me this morning —— "

" I've got to see —— " began Val, but something
in her face stopped him. " I say," he said, " you
don't mean —— "

" Yes, I have to go to the Court this morning."

Already! — that d — d business which he had
almost succeeded in forgetting, since nobody ever
mentioned it. In self-commiseration he stood picking little bits of skin off his fingers. Then noticing
that his mother's lips were all awry, he said impul-
sively: " All right, mother; I'll come. The brutes! "
What brutes he did not know, but the expression
exactly summed up their joint feeling, and restored
a measure of equanimity.

" I suppose I'd better change into a ' shooter,' "
he muttered, escaping to his room. He put on the
' shooter,' a higher collar, a pearl pin, and his neatest

grey spats, to a somewhat blasphemous accompaniment. Looking at himself in the glass, he said, "Well, I'm damned if I'm going to show anything!" and went down. He found his grandfather's carriage at the door, and his mother in furs, with the appearance of one going to a Mansion House Assembly. They seated themselves side by side in the closed barouche, and all the way to the Courts of Justice Val made but one allusion to the business in hand. "There'll be nothing about those pearls, will there?"

The little tufted white tails of Winifred's muff began to shiver.

"Oh no," she said, "it'll be quite harmless today. Your grandmother wanted to come too, but I wouldn't let her. I thought you could take care of me. You look so nice, Val. Just pull your coat collar up a little more at the back — that's right."

"If they bully you ——" began Val.

"Oh! they won't. I shall be very cool. It's the only way."

"They won't want me to give evidence or anything?"

"No, dear; it's all arranged." And she patted his hand. The determined front she was putting on it stayed the turmoil in Val's chest, and he busied himself in drawing his gloves off and on. He had taken what he now saw was the wrong pair to go with his spats; they should have been grey, but were deerskin of a dark tan; whether to keep them on or not he could not decide. They arrived soon after ten. It was his first visit to the Law Courts, and the building struck him at once.

"By Jove!" he said as they passed into the hall, "this'd make four or five jolly good racket courts."

Soames was awaiting them at the foot of some stairs.

"Here you are!" he said, without shaking hands, as if the event had made them too familiar for such formalities. "It's Happerly Browne, Court I. We shall be on first."

A sensation such as he had known when going in to bat was playing now in the top of Val's chest, but he followed his mother and uncle doggedly, looking at no more than he could help, and thinking that the place smelled 'fuggy.' People seemed to be lurking everywhere, and he plucked Soames by the sleeve.

"I say, Uncle, you're not going to let those beastly papers in, are you?"

Soames gave him the sideway look which had reduced many to silence in its time.

"In here," he said. "You needn't take off your furs, Winifred."

Val entered behind them, nettled and with his head up. In this confounded hole everybody — and there were a good many of them — seemed sitting on everybody else's knee, though really divided from each other by pews; and Val had a feeling that they might all slip down together into the well. This, however, was but a momentary vision — of mahogany, and black gowns, and white blobs of wigs and faces and papers, all rather secret and whispery — before he was sitting next his mother in the front row, with his back to it all, glad of her violette de Parme, and taking off his gloves for the last time. His mother was looking at him; he was suddenly conscious that she had really wanted him there next to her, and that he counted for something in this business. All right! He would show them! Squaring his shoulders, he crossed his legs and gazed inscrutably at his spats. But just then an ' old Johnny ' in a gown and long wig, looking awfully like a funny raddled woman, came through a door into the high pew opposite, and he had to uncross his legs hastily, and stand up with everybody else.

' Dartie *versus* Dartie ! '

It semed to Val unspeakably disgusting to have one's name called out like this in public! And, suddenly conscious that someone nearly behind him had begun talking about his family, he screwed his face round to see an old be-wigged buffer, who spoke as if he were eating his own words — queer-looking old cuss, the sort of man he had seen once or twice dining at Park Lane and punishing the port; he knew now where they ' dug them up.' All the same he found the old buffer quite fascinating, and would have continued to stare if his mother had not touched his arm. Reduced to gazing before him, he fixed his eyes on the Judge's face instead. Why should that old 'sportsman' with his sarcastic mouth and his quick-moving eyes have the power to meddle with their private affairs — hadn't he affairs of his own, just as many, and probably just as nasty? And there moved in Val, like an illness, all the deep-seated individualism of his breed. The voice behind him droned along : " Differences about money matters — extravagance of the respondent " (What a word! Was that his father ?) — " strained situation — frequent absences on the part of Mr. Dartie. My client, very rightly, your Ludship will agree, was anxious to check a course — but lead to ruin — remonstrated — gambling at cards and on the racecourse——" ('That's

right!' thought Val, 'pile it on!') "Crisis early
in October, when the respondent wrote her this letter from his Club." Val sat up and his ears burned.
" I propose to read it with the emendations necessary to the epistle of a gentleman who has been —
shall we say dining, me Lud?"

'Old brute!' thought Val, flushing deeper;
'you're not paid to make jokes!'

"'You will not get the chance to insult me again
in my own house. I am leaving the country to-
morrow. It's played out' — an expression, your
Ludship, not unknown in the mouths of those who
have not met with conspicuous success."

'Sniggering owls!' thought Val, and his flush
deepened.

"'I am tired of being insulted by you.' My client
will tell your Ludship that these so-called insults
consisted in her calling him 'the limit' — a very
mild expression, I venture to suggest, in all the circumstances."

Val glanced sideways at his mother's impassive
face, it had a hunted look in the eyes. 'Poor
mother' he thought, and touched her arm with his
own. The voice behind droned on.

"'I am going to live a new life. — M. D.'

"And next day, me Lud, the respondent left
by the steamship *Tuscarora* for Buenos Aires.
Since then we have nothing from him but a cabled
refusal in answer to the letter which my client wrote
the following day in great distress, begging him to
return to her. With your Ludship's permission, I
shall now put Mrs. Dartie in the box."

When his mother rose, Val had a tremendous
impulse to rise too and say: 'Look here! I'm going
to see you jolly well treat her decently.' He sub-

dued it, however; heard her saying, ' the truth, the whole truth, and nothing but the truth,' and looked up. She made a rich figure of it, in her furs and large hat, with a slight flush on her cheek-bones, calm, matter-of-fact; and he felt proud of her thus confronting all these ' confounded lawyers.' The examination began. Knowing that this was only the preliminary to divorce, Val followed with a certain glee the questions framed so as to give the impression that she really wanted his father back. It seemed to him that they were ' foxing Old Bagwigs finely.' And he had a most unpleasant jar when the Judge said suddenly:

" Now, why did your husband leave you — not because you called him 'the limit,' you know?"

Val saw his uncle lift his eyes to the witness box, without moving his face; heard a shuffle of papers behind him; and instinct told him that the issue was in peril. Had Uncle Soames and the old buffer behind made a mess of it? His mother was speaking with a slight drawl.

" No, my lord, but it had gone on a long time."

" What had gone on? "

" Our differences about money."

" But you supplied the money. Do you suggest that he left you to better his position? "

' The brute! The old brute, and nothing but the brute!' thought Val suddenly. ' He smells a rat — he's trying to get at the pastry!' And his heart stood still. If — if he did, then, of course, he would know that his mother didn't really want his father back. His mother spoke again, a thought more fashionably.

" No, my Lord, but you see I had refused to give him any more money. It took him a long time to believe that, but he did at last — and when he did —— "

" I see, you had refused. But you've sent him some since."

" My Lord, I wanted him back."

" And you thought that would bring him? "

" I don't know, my Lord, I acted on my father's advice."

Something in the Judge's face, in the sound of the papers behind him, in the sudden crossing of his uncle's legs, told Val that she had made just the right answer. ' Crafty!' he thought; ' by Jove, what humbug it all is!'

The Judge was speaking:

" Just one more question, Mrs. Dartie. Are you still fond of your husband? "

Val's hands, slack behind him, became fists. What business had that Judge to make things human suddenly? To make his mother speak out of her heart, and say what, perhaps, she didn't know herself, before all these people! It wasn't decent. His mother answered, rather low: "Yes, my Lord." Val saw the Judge nod. ' Wish I could take a cock-shy at your head!' he thought irreverently, as his mother came back to her seat beside him. Witnesses to his father's departure and continued absence followed — one of their own maids even, which struck Val as particularly beastly; there was more talking, all humbug; and then the Judge pronounced the decree for restitution, and they got up to go. Val walked out behind his mother, chin squared, eyelids drooped, doing his level best to despise everybody. His mother's voice in the corridor roused him from an angry trance.

" You behaved beautifully, dear. It was such a

comfort to have you.   Your uncle and I are going
to lunch."

"All right," said Val; "I shall have time to go
and see that fellow."   And, parting from them
abruptly, he ran down the stairs and out into the
air.   He bolted into a hansom, and drove to the
Goat's Club.   His thoughts were on Holly and
what he must do before her brother showed her
this thing in tomorrow's paper.

*   *   *   *   *

When Val had left them Soames and Winifred
made their way to the Cheshire Cheese.   He had
suggested it as a meeting place with Mr. Bellby.
At that early hour of noon they would have it to
themselves, and Winifred had thought it would be
'amusing' to see this far-famed hostelry.   Having
ordered a light repast, to the consternation of the
waiter, they awaited its arrival together with that
of Mr. Bellby, in silent reaction after the hour and
a half's suspense on the tenterhooks of publicity.
Mr. Bellby entered presently, preceded by his nose,
as cheerful as they were glum.   Well! they had got
the decree of restitution, and what was the matter
with that!

"Quite," said Soames in a suitably low voice,
"but we shall have to begin again to get evidence.
He'll probably try the divorce — it will look fishy if
it comes out that we knew of misconduct from the
start.   His questions showed well enough that
he doesn't like this restitution dodge."

"Pho!" said Mr. Bellby cheerily, "he'll forget!
Why, man, he'll have tried a hundred cases between
now and then.   Besides, he's bound by precedent to
give ye your divorce, if the evidence is satisfactory.
We won't let um know that Mrs. Dartie had knowl-

edge of the facts.   Dreamer did it very nicely —
he's got a fatherly touch about um!'"

Soames nodded.

" And I compliment ye, Mrs. Dartie," went on
Mr. Bellby; "ye've a natural gift for giving evidence.   Steady as a rock."

Here the waiter arrived with three plates balanced on one arm, and the remark: "I 'urried up
the pudden, sir.   You'll find plenty o' lark in it to-
day."

Mr. Bellby applauded his forethought with a dip
of his nose.   But Soames and Winifred looked
with dismay at their light lunch of gravified brown
masses, touching them gingerly with their forks in
the hope of distinguishing the bodies of the tasty
little song-givers.   Having begun, however, they
found they were hungrier than they thought, and
finished the lot, with a glass of port apiece.   Conversation turned on the war.   Soames thought
Ladysmith would fall, and it might last a year.
Bellby thought it would be over by the summer.
Both agreed that they wanted more men.   There
was nothing for it but complete victory, since it
was now a question of prestige.   Winifred brought
things back to more solid ground by saying that she
did not want the divorce suit to come on till after
the summer holidays had begun at Oxford, then the
boys would have forgotten about it before Val had
to go up again; the London season too would be
over.   The lawyers reassured her, an interval of
six months was necessary — after that the earlier
the better.   People were now beginning to come in,
and they parted — Soames to the city, Bellby to
his chambers, Winifred in a hansom to Park Lane
to let her mother know how she had fared.   The

issue had been so satisfactory on the whole that it was considered advisable to tell James, who never failed to say day after day that he didn't know about Winifred's affair, he couldn't tell. As his sands ran out, the importance of mundane matters became increasingly grave to him, as if he were feeling: 'I must make the most of it, and worry well; I shall soon have nothing to worry about.'

He received the report grudgingly. It was a new-fangled way of going about things, and he didn't know! But he gave Winifred a cheque, saying:

"I expect you'll have a lot of expense. That's a new hat you've got on. Why doesn't Val come and see us?"

Winifred promised to bring him to dinner soon. And, going home, she sought her bedroom where she could be alone. Now that her husband had been ordered back into her custody with a view to putting him away from her for ever, she would try once more to find out from her sore and lonely heart what she really wanted.

CHAPTER VIII

THE CHALLENGE

THE morning had been misty, verging on frost, but the sun came out while Val was jogging towards the Roehampton Gate, whence he would canter on to the usual tryst. His spirits were rising rapidly. There had been nothing so very terrible in the morning's proceedings beyond the general disgrace of violated privacy. ' If we were engaged! ' he thought, ' what happens wouldn't matter.' He felt, indeed, like human society, which kicks and clamours at the results of matrimony, and hastens to get married. And he galloped over the winter-dried grass of Richmond Park, fearing to be late. But again he was alone at the trysting spot, and this second defection on the part of Holly upset him dreadfully. He could not go back without seeing her to-day! Emerging from the Park, he proceeded towards Robin Hill. He could not make up his mind for whom to ask. Suppose her father were back, or her sister or brother were in! He decided to gamble, and ask for them all first, so that if he were in luck and they were not there, it would be quite natural in the end to ask for Holly; while if any of them *were* in — an ' excuse for a ride ' must be his saving grace.

" Only Miss Holly is in, sir."

" Oh! thanks. Might I take my horse round to the stables? And would you say — her cousin, Mr. Val Dartie."

When he returned she was in the hall, very flushed and shy. She led him to the far end, and they sat down on a wide window-seat.

" I've been awfully anxious," said Val in a low voice. "What's the matter?"

" Jolly knows about our riding."

" Is he in?"

" No; but I expect he will be soon."

" Then ——!" cried Val, and diving forward, he seized her hand. She tried to withdraw it, failed, gave up the attempt, and looked at him wistfully.

" First of all," he said, " I want to tell you something about my family. My Dad, you know, isn't altogether — I mean, he's left my mother and they're trying to divorce him; so they've ordered him to come back, you see. You'll see that in the paper to-morrow."

Her eyes deepened in colour and fearful interest; her hand squeezed his. But the gambler in Val was roused now, and he hurried on:

" Of course there's nothing very much at present, but there will be, I expect, before it's over; divorce suits are beastly, you know. I wanted to tell you, because — because — you ought to know — if —" and he began to stammer, gazing at her troubled eyes, " if — if you're going to be a darling and love me, Holly. I love you — ever so; and I want to be engaged." He had done it in a manner so inadequate that he could have punched his own head; and, dropping on his knees, he tried to get nearer to that soft, troubled face. " You do love me — don't you?

If you don't, I ——" There was a moment of silence and suspense, so awful that he could hear the sound of a mowing-machine far out on the lawn pretending there was grass to cut. Then she swayed forward; her free hand touched his hair, and he gasped: " Oh, Holly! "

Her answer was very soft: " Oh, Val! "

He had dreamed of this moment, but always in an imperative mood, as the masterful young lover, and now he felt humble, touched, trembly. He was afraid to stir off his knees lest he should break the spell; lest, if he did, she should shrink and deny her own surrender — so tremulous was she in his grasp, with her eyelids closed and his lips nearing them. Her eyes opened, seemed to swim a little; he pressed his lips to hers. Suddenly he sprang up; there had been footsteps, a sort of startled grunt. He looked round. No one! But the long curtains which barred off the outer hall were quivering.

" My God! Who was that? "

Holly too was on her feet.

" Jolly, I expect," she whispered.

Val clenched fists and resolution.

" All right! " he said, " I don't care a bit now we're engaged," and striding towards the curtains, he drew them aside. There at the fireplace in the hall stood Jolly, with his back elaborately turned. Val went forward. Jolly faced round on him.

" I beg your pardon for hearing," he said.

With the best intentions in the world, Val could not help admiring him at that moment; his face was clear, his voice quiet, he looked somehow distinguished, as if acting up to principle.

" Well! " he said abruptly, " it's nothing to you."

" Oh! " said Jolly; " you come this way," and he

crossed the hall. Val followed. At the study door he felt a touch on his arm; Holly's voice said:

" I'm coming too."

" No," said Jolly.

" Yes," said Holly.

Jolly opened the door, and they all three went in. Once in the little room, they stood in a sort of triangle on three corners of the worn Turkey carpet; awkwardly upright, not looking at each other, quite incapable of seeing any humour in the situation.

Val broke the silence.

" Holly and I are engaged."

Jolly stepped back and leaned against the lintel of the window.

" This is our house," he said; " I'm not going to insult you in it. But my father's away. I'm in charge of my sister. You've taken advantage of me."

" I didn't mean to," said Val hotly.

" I think you did," said Jolly. " If you hadn't meant to, you'd have spoken to me, or waited for my father to come back."

" There were reasons," said Val.

" What reasons?"

" About my family — I've just told her. I wanted her to know before things happen."

Jolly suddenly became less distinguished.

" You're kids," he said, " and you know you are."

" I am *not* a kid," said Val.

" You are — you're not twenty."

" Well, what are you?"

" I *am* twenty," said Jolly.

" Only just; anyway, I'm as good a man as you."

Jolly's face crimsoned, then clouded. Some

struggle was evidently taking place in him; and Val
and Holly stared at him, so clearly was that struggle
marked; they could even hear him breathing. Then
his face cleared up and became oddly resolute.

" We'll see that," he said. " I dare you to do
what I'm going to do."

" Dare me? "

Jolly smiled. "Yes," he said, "dare you; and I
know very well you won't."

A stab of misgiving shot through Val; this was
riding very blind.

" I haven't forgotten that you're a fire-eater,"
said Jolly slowly, " and I think that's about all you
are; or that you called me a pro-Boer."

. Val heard a gasp above the sound of his own
hard breathing, and saw Holly's face poked a little
forward, very pale, with big eyes.

" Yes," went on Jolly with a sort of smile, " we
shall soon see. I'm going to join the Imperial Yeomanry; and I dare you to do the same, Mr. Val
Dartie. '

Val's head jerked on its stem. It was like a blow
between the eyes, so utterly unthought of, so extreme and ugly in the midst of his dreaming; and
he looked at Holly with eyes grown suddenly, touch-
ingly haggard.

"Sit down!" said Jolly. "Take your time!
Think it over well." And he himself sat down on
the arm of his grandfather's chair.

Val did not sit down; he stood with hands thrust
deep into his breeches' pockets — hands clenched
and quivering. The full awfulness of this decision
one way or the other knocked at his mind with
double knocks as of an angry postman. If he did
not take that 'dare' he was disgraced in Holly's

eyes, and in the eyes of that young enemy, her brute of a brother. Yet if he took it, ah! then all would vanish — her face, her eyes, her hair, her kisses just begun!

"Take your time," said Jolly again; "I don't want to be unfair."

And they both looked at Holly. She had re-coiled against the bookshelves reaching to the ceil-ing; her dark head leaned against Gibbon's *Roman Empire,* her eyes in a sort of soft grey agony were fixed on Val. And he, who had not much gift of insight, had suddenly a gleam of vision. She would be proud of her brother — that enemy! She would be ashamed of him! His hands came out of his pockets as if lifted by a spring.

"All right!" he said. "Done!"

Holly's face — oh! it was queer! He saw her flush, start forward. He had done the right thing — her face was shining with wistful admiration. Jolly stood up and made a little bow as who should say: 'You've passed.'

"To-morrow, then," he said, "we'll go to-gether."

Recovering from the impetus which had carried him to that decision, Val looked at him maliciously from under his lashes. 'All right,' he thought, ' one to you. I shall have to join — but I'll get back on you somehow.' And he said with dignity: " I shall be ready."

"We'll meet at the main Recruiting Office, then," said Jolly, "at twelve o'clock." And, opening the window, he went out on to the terrace, conforming to the creed which had made him retire when he surprised them in the hall.

The confusion in the mind of Val thus left alone

with her for whom he had paid this sudden price was extreme. The mood of 'showing-off' was still, however, uppermost. One must do the wretched thing with an air!

"We shall get plenty of riding and shooting, anyway," he said; "that's one comfort." And it gave him a sort of grim pleasure to hear the sigh which seemed to come from the bottom of her heart.

"Oh! the war'll soon be over," he said; "perhaps we shan't even have to go out. I don't care, except for you." He would be out of the way of that beastly divorce. It was an ill-wind! He felt her warm hand slip into his. Jolly thought he had stopped their loving each other, did he? He held her tightly round the waist, looking at her softly through his lashes, smiling to cheer her up, promising to come down and see her soon, feeling somehow six inches taller and much more in command of her than he had ever dared feel before. Many times he kissed her before he mounted and rode back to town. So, swiftly, on the least provocation, does the possessive instinct flourish and grow.

CHAPTER IX

DINNER AT JAMES'S

DINNER parties were not now given at James's in Park Lane — to every house the moment comes when Master or Mistress is no longer 'up to it'; no more can nine courses be served to twenty mouths above twenty fine white expanses; nor does the household cat any longer wonder why she is suddenly shut up.

So with something like excitement Emily — who at seventy would still have liked a little feast and fashion now and then — ordered dinner for six instead of two, herself wrote a number of foreign words on cards, and arranged the flowers — mimosa from the Riviera, and white Roman hyacinths not from Rome. There would only be, of course, James and herself, Soames, Winifred, Val, and Imogen — but she liked to pretend a little and dally in imagination with the glory of the past. She so dressed herself that James remarked:

"What are you putting on that thing for? You'll catch cold."

But Emily knew that the necks of women are protected by love of shining, unto fourscore years, and she only answered:

" Let me put you on one of those dickies I got you, James; then you'll only have to change your trousers, and put on your velvet coat, and there you'll be.   Val likes you to look nice."

" Dicky!" said James.   " You're always wasting your money on something."

But he suffered the change to be made till his neck also shone, murmuring vaguely:

"He's an extravagant chap, I'm afraid."

A little brighter in the eye, with rather more colour than usual in his cheeks, he took his seat in the drawing-room to wait for the sound of the front-door bell.

" I've made it a proper dinner party," Emily said comfortably; " I thought it would be good practice for Imogen — she must get used to it now she's coming out."

James uttered an indeterminate sound, thinking of Imogen as she used to climb about his knee or pull Christmas crackers with him.

" She'll be pretty," he muttered, " I shouldn't wonder."

" She *is* pretty," said Emily; " she ought to make a good match."

" There you go," murmured James; " she'd much better stay at home and look after her mother."   A second Dartie carrying off his pretty granddaughter would finish him!   He had never quite forgiven Emily for having been as much taken in by Montagu Dartie as he himself had been.

" Where's Warmson?" he said suddenly.   " I should like a glass of Madeira to-night."

" There's champagne, James."

James shook his head.   " No body," he said: " I can't get any good out of it."

Emily reached forward on her side of the fire and rang the bell.

"Your master would like a bottle of Madeira opened, Warmson."

"No, no!" said James, the tips of his ears quivering with vehemence, and his eyes fixed on an object seen by him alone. "Look here, Warmson, you go to the inner cellar, and on the middle shelf of the end bin on the left you'll see seven bottles; take the one in the centre, and don't shake it. It's the last of the Madeira I had from Mr. Jolyon when we came in here — never been moved; it ought to be in prime condition still; but I don't know, I can't tell."

"Very good, sir," responded the withdrawing Warmson.

"I was keeping it for our golden wedding," said James suddenly, "but I shan't live three years at my age."

"Nonsense, James," said Emily, "don't talk like that."

"I ought to have got it up myself," murmured James, "he'll shake it as likely as not." And he sank into silent recollection of long moments among the open gas-jets, the cobwebs, and the good smell of wine-soaked corks, which had been appetiser to so many feasts. In the wine from that cellar was written the history of the forty-seven years since he had come to the Park Lane house with his young bride, and of the many generations of friends and acquaintances who had passed into the unknown; its depleted bins preserved the record of family festivity — all the marriages, births, deaths of his kith and kin. And when he was gone there it would be, and he didn't know what would become of it. It'd be drunk or spoiled, he shouldn't wonder!

From that deep reverie the entrance of his son dragged him, followed very soon by that of Winifred and her two eldest.

They went down arm-in-arm — James with Imogen, the debutante, because his pretty grandchild cheered him; Soames with Winifred; Emily with Val, whose eyes lighting on the oysters brightened. This was to be a proper full 'blow-out' with 'fizz' and port! And he felt in need of it, after what he had done that day, as yet undivulged. After the first glass or two it became pleasant to have this bombshell up his sleeve, this piece of sensational patriotism, or example, rather, of personal daring, to display — for his pleasure in what he had done for his Queen and Country was so far entirely personal. He was now a 'blood,' indissolubly connected with guns and horses; he had a right to swagger — not, of course, that he was going to. He should just announce it quietly, when there was a pause. And, glancing down the menu, he determined on 'Bombe aux fraises' as the proper moment; there would be a certain solemnity while they were eating that. Once or twice before they reached that rosy summit of the dinner he was attacked by remembrance that his grandfather was never told anything! Still, the old boy was drinking Madeira, and looking jolly fit! Besides, he ought to be pleased at this set-off to the disgrace of the divorce. The sight of his uncle opposite, too, was a sharp incentive. He was so far from being a sportsman that it would be worth a lot to see his face. Besides, better to tell his mother in this way than privately, which might upset them both! He was sorry for her, but after all one couldn't be expected to feel much for others when one had to part from Holly.

His grandfather's voice travelled to him thinly.

"Val, try a little of the Madeira with your ice. You won't get that up at college."

Val watched the slow liquid filling his glass, the essential oil of the old wine glazing the surface; inhaled its aroma, and thought: 'Now for it!' It was a rich moment. He sipped, and a gentle glow spread in his veins, already heated. With a rapid look round, he said, "I joined the Imperial Yeomanry to-day, Granny," and emptied his glass as though drinking the health of his own act.

"What!" It was his mother's desolate little word.

"Young Jolly Forsyte and I went down there together."

"You didn't sign?" from Uncle Soames.

"Rather! We go into camp on Monday."

"I *say!*" cried Imogen.

All looked at James. He was leaning forward with his hand behind his ear.

"What's that?" he said. "What's he saying? I can't hear."

Emily reached forward to pat Val's hand.

"It's only that Val has joined the Yeomanry, James; it's very nice for him. He'll look his best in uniform."

"Joined the — rubbish!" came from James, tremulously loud. "You can't see two yards before your nose. He — he'll have to go out there. Why! he'll be fighting before he knows where he is."

Val saw Imogen's eyes admiring him, and his mother still and fashionable with her handkerchief before her lips.

Suddenly his uncle spoke.

" You're under age."

" I thought of that," smiled Val; " I gave my age as twenty-one."

He heard his grandmother's admiring, " Well, Val, that *was* plucky of you"; was conscious of Warmson deferentially filling his champagne glass; and of his grandfather's voice moaning: "*I* don't know what'll become of you if you go on like this."

Imogen was patting his shoulder, his uncle looking at him sidelong; only his mother sat unmoving, till, affected by her stillness, Val said:

" It's all right, you know; we shall soon have them on the run. I only hope I shall come in for something."

He felt elated, sorry, tremendously important all at once. This would show Uncle Soames, and all the Forsytes, how to be a sportsman. He had certainly done something heroic and exceptional in giving his age as twenty-one.

Emily's voice brought him back to earth.

" You mustn't have a second glass, James. Warmson!"

" Won't they be astonished at Timothy's!" burst out Imogen. " I'd give anything to see their faces. Do you have a sword, Val, or only a popgun?"

"What made you?"

His uncle's voice produced a slight chill in the pit of Val's stomach. Made him? How answer that? He was grateful for his grandmother's comfortable:

" Well, I think it's very plucky of Val. I'm sure he'll make a splendid soldier; he's just the figure for it. We shall all be proud of him."

" What had young Jolly Forsyte to do with it? Why did you go together?" pursued Soames, uncannily relentless. "I thought you weren't friendly with him?"

"I'm not," mumbled Val, "but I wasn't going to be beaten by *him*." He saw his uncle look at him quite differently, as if approving. His grandfather was nodding too, his grandmother tossing her head. They all approved of his not being beaten by that cousin of his. There must be a reason! Val was dimly conscious of some disturbing point outside his range of vision; as it might be, the unlocated centre of a cyclone. And, staring at his uncle's face, he had a quite unaccountable vision of a woman with dark eyes, gold hair, and a white neck, who smelt nice, and had pretty silken clothes which he had liked feeling when he was quite small. By Jove, yes. Aunt Irene! She used to kiss him, and he had bitten her arm once, playfully, because he liked it — so soft. His grandfather was speaking:

"What's his father doing?"

"He's away in Paris," Val said, staring at the very queer expression on his uncle's face, like — like that of a snarling dog.

"Artists!" said James. The word, coming from the very bottom of his soul, broke up the dinner.

Opposite his mother in the cab going home, Val tasted the after-fruits of heroism, like medlars over-ripe.

She only said, indeed, that he must go to his tailor's at once and have his uniform properly made, and not just put up with what they gave him. But he could feel that she was very much upset. It was on his lips to console her with the spoken thought that he would be out of the way of that beastly divorce, but the presence of Imogen, and the knowledge that his mother would *not* be out of the way, restrained him. He felt aggrieved that she did not seem more proud of him. When Imogen had gone to bed, he risked the emotional.

"I'm awfully sorry to have to leave you, Mother."

"Well, I must make the best of it. We must try and get you a commission as soon as we can; then you won't have to rough it so. Do you know any drill, Val?"

"Not a scrap."

"I hope they won't worry you much. I must take you about to get the things to-morrow. Goodnight; kiss me."

With that kiss, soft and hot, between his eyes, and those words, 'I hope they won't worry you much,' in his ears, he sat down to a cigarette, before a dying fire. The heat was out of him — the glow of cutting a dash. It was all a damned heartaching bore. 'I'll be even with that chap Jolly,' he thought, trailing up the stairs, past the room where his mother was biting her pillow to smother a sense of desolation which was trying to make her sob.

And soon only one of the diners at James' was awake — Soames, in his bedroom above his father's.

So that fellow Jolyon was in Paris — what was he doing there? Hanging round Irene! The last report from Polteed had hinted that there might be something soon. Could it be this? That fellow, with his beard and his cursed amused way of speaking — son of the old man who had given him the nickname 'Man of Property,' and bought the fatal house from him. Soames had ever resented having had to sell the house at Robin Hill; never forgiven his uncle for having bought it, or his cousin for living in it.

Reckless of the cold, he threw his window up and gazed out across the Park. Bleak and dark the January night; little sound of traffic; a frost coming; bare trees; a star or two. 'I'll see Polteed to-morrow,' he thought. 'By God! I'm mad, I think, to want her still. That fellow! If ——? Um! No!'

CHAPTER X

DEATH OF THE DOG BALTHASAR

JOLYON, who had crossed from Calais by night, arrived at Robin Hill on Sunday morning. He had sent no word beforehand, so walked up from the station, entering his domain by the coppice gate. Coming to the log seat fashioned out of an old fallen trunk, he sat down, first laying his overcoat on it. 'Lumbago!' he thought; 'that's what love ends in at my time of life!' And suddenly Irene seemed very near, just as she had been that day of rambling at Fontainebleau when they sat on a log to eat their lunch. Hauntingly near! Odour drawn out of fallen leaves by the pale filtering sunlight soaked his nostrils. 'I'm glad it isn't spring,' he thought. With the scent of sap, and the song of birds, and the bursting of the blossoms, it would have been unbearable! 'I hope I shall be over it by then, old fool that I am!' and picking up his coat, he walked on into the field. He passed the pond and mounted the hill slowly. Near the top a hoarse barking greeted him. Up on the lawn above the fernery he could see his old dog Balthasar. The animal, whose dim eyes took his master for a stranger, was warning the world against him. Jolyon gave his special whistle. Even at that distance of a hundred yards and more he could see the dawning recognition in the obese brown-white body. The old dog got off his haunches, and his tail, close-curled over his back began a feeble, excited fluttering; he came waddling forward, gathered momentum, and disappeared over the edge of the fernery. Jolyon expected to meet him at the wicker gate, but Balthasar was not there, and, rather alarmed, he turned into the fernery. On his fat side, looking up with eyes already glazing, the old dog lay.

"What is it, my poor old man?" cried Jolyon. Balthasar's curled and fluffy tail just moved; his filming eyes seemed saying: "I can't get up, master, but I'm glad to see you."

Jolyon knelt down; his eyes, very dimmed, could hardly see the slowly ceasing heave of the dog's side. He raised the head a little— very heavy.

"What is it, dear man? Where are you hurt?" The tail fluttered once; the eyes lost the look of life. Jolyon passed his hands all over the inert warm bulk. There was nothing — the heart had simply failed in that obese body from the emotion of his master's return. Jolyon could feel the muzzle, where a few whitish bristles grew, cooling already against his lips. He stayed for some minutes kneeling, with his hand beneath the stiffening head. The body was very heavy when he bore it to the top of the field; leaves had drifted there, and he strewed it with a covering of them; there was no wind, and they would keep him from curious eyes until the afternoon. 'I'll bury him myself,' he thought. Eighteen years had gone since he first went into the St. John's Wood house with that tiny puppy in his pocket. Strange that the old dog should die just now! Was it an omen? He turned at the gate to look back at that russet mound, then went slowly towards the house, very choky in the throat.

June was at home; she had come down hot-foot on hearing the news of Jolly's enlistment. His patriotism had conquered her feeling for the Boers. The atmosphere of his house was strange and pockety when Jolyon came in and told them of the dog Balthasar's death. The news had a unifying effect. A link with the past had snapped — the dog Balthasar! Two of them could remember nothing before his day; to June he represented the last years of her grandfather; to Jolyon that life of domestic stress and aesthetic struggle before he came again into the kingdom of his father's love and wealth! And he was gone!

In the afternoon he and Jolly took picks and spades and went out to the field. They chose a spot close to the russet mound, so that they need not carry him far, and, carefully cutting off the surface turf, began to dig. They dug in silence for ten minutes, and then rested.

"Well, old man," said Jolyon, "so you thought you ought?"

"Yes," answered Jolly; "I don't want to a bit, of course."

How exactly those words represented Jolyon's own state of mind!

"I admire you for it, old boy. I don't believe I should have done it at your age — too much of a Forsyte, I'm afraid. But I suppose the type gets thinner with each generation. Your son, if you have one, may be a pure altruist; who knows?"

"He won't be like me, then, Dad; I'm beastly selfish."

"No, my dear, that you clearly are not." Jolly shook his head, and they dug again.

"Strange life a dog's," said Jolyon suddenly; "the only four-footer with rudiments of altruism, and a sense of God!"

Jolly looked at his father.

"Do you believe in God, Dad? I've never known."

At so searching a question from one to whom it was impossible to make a light reply, Jolyon stood for a moment feeling his back tried by the digging.

"What do you mean by God?" he said; "there are two irreconcilable ideas of God. There's the unknowable Creative Principle — one believes in That. And there's the Sum of altruism in man — naturally one believes in That."

"I see. That leaves out Christ, doesn't it?"

Jolyon stared. Christ, the link between those two ideas! Out of the mouth of babes! Here was orthodoxy scientifically explained at last! The sublime poem of the Christ life was man's attempt to join those two irreconcilable conceptions of God. And since the Sum of human altruism was as much a part of the Unknowable Creative Principle as anything else in Nature and the Universe, a worse link might have been chosen after all! Funny — how one went through life without seeing it in that sort of way!

"What do *you* think, old man?" he said.

Jolly frowned. "Of course, my first year we talked a good bit about that sort of thing. But in the second year one gives it up; I don't know why — it's awfully interesting."

Jolyon remembered that he also had talked a good deal about it his first year at Cambridge, and given it up in his second.

" I suppose," said Jolly, " it's the second God, you mean, that old Balthasar had a sense of."

" Yes, or he would never have burst his poor old heart because of something outside himself."

"But wasn't that just selfish emotion, really?"

Jolyon shook his head. " No, dogs are not pure Forsytes, they love something outside themselves."

Jolly smiled.

" Well, I think I'm one," he said. " You know, I only enlisted because I dared Val Dartie to."

" But why? "

" We bar each other," said Jolly shortly.

"Ah! " muttered Jolyon. So the feud went on, unto the third generation — this modern feud which had no overt expression?

' Shall I tell the boy about it?' he thought. But to what end — if he had to stop short of his own part?

And Jolly thought: ' It's for Holly to let him know about that chap. If she doesn't, it means she doesn't want him told, and I should be sneaking. Anyway, I've stopped it. I'd better leave well alone!'

So they dug on in silence, till Jolyon said:

" Now, old man, I think it's big enough." And, resting on their spades, they gazed down into the hole where a few leaves had drifted already on a sunset wind.

"I can't bear this part of it," said Jolyon suddenly.

" Let me do it, Dad. He never cared much for me."

Jolyon shook his head.

" We'll lift him very gently, leaves and all. I'd rather not see him again. I'll take his head. Now! "

With extreme care they raised the old dog's body, whose faded tan and white showed here and there under the leaves stirred by the wind. They laid it, heavy, cold, and unresponsive, in the grave, and Jolly spread more leaves over it, while Jolyon, deeply afraid to show emotion before his son, began quickly shovelling the earth on to that still shape. There went the past! If only there were a joyful future to look forward to! It was like stamping down earth on one's own life. They replaced the turf carefully on the smooth little mound, and, grateful that they had spared each others' feelings, returned to the house arm-in-arm.

CHAPTER XI

On Forsyte 'Change news of the enlistment spread fast, together with the report that June, not to be outdone, was going to become a Red Cross nurse. These events were so extreme, so subversive of pure Forsyteism, as to have a binding effect upon the family, and Timothy's was thronged next Sunday afternoon by members trying to find out what they thought about it all, and exchange with each other a sense of family credit. Giles and Jesse Hayman would no longer defend the coast but go to South Africa quite soon; Jolly and Val would be following in April; as to June — well, you never knew what she would really do!

The retirement from Spion Kop and the absence of any good news from the seat of war imparted an air of reality to all this, clinched in startling fashion by Timothy. The youngest of the old Forsytes — scarcely eighty, in fact — popularly supposed to resemble their father, ' Superior Dosset,' even in his best-known characteristic of drinking sherry — had been invisible for so many years that he was almost mythical. A long generation had elapsed since the risks of a publisher's business had worked on his nerves at the age of forty, so that he had got out with a mere thirty-five thousand pounds in the world, and started to make his living by careful investment. Putting by every year, at compound interest, he had doubled his capital in forty years without having once known what it was like to shake in his shoes over money matters. He was now putting aside some two thousand a year, and with the care he was taking of himself expected, so Aunt Hester said, to double his capital again before he died. What he would do with it then, with his sisters dead and himself dead, was often mockingly queried by free spirits such as Francie, Euphemia, or young Nicholas' second, Christopher, whose spirit was so free that he had actually said he was going on the stage. All admitted, however, that this was best known to Timothy himself, and possibly to Soames, who never divulged a secret.

Those few Forsytes who had seen him reported a man of thick and robust appearance, not very tall, with a brown-red complexion, grey hair, and little of the refinement of feature with which most of the Forsytes had been endowed by 'Superior Dosset's' wife, a woman of some beauty and a gentle temperament. It was known that he had taken surprising interest in the war, sticking flags into a map ever since it began, and there was uneasiness as to what would happen if the English were driven into the sea, when it would be almost impossible for him to put the flags in the right places. As to his knowledge of family movements or his views about them, little was known, save that Aunt Hester was always declaring that he was very upset. It was, then, in the nature of a portent when Forsytes, arriving on the Sunday after the evacuation of Spion

Kop, became conscious, one after the other, of a
presence seated in the only really comfortable armchair, back to the light, concealing the lower part of
his face with a large hand, and were greeted by the
awed voice of Aunt Hester:

"Your Uncle Timothy, my dear."

Timothy's greeting to them all was somewhat
identical; and rather, as it were, passed over by him
than expressed:

"How de do? How de do? 'Xcuse me gettin'
up!"

Francie was present, and Eustace had come in his
car; Winifred had brought Imogen, breaking the
ice of the restitution proceedings with the warmth
of family appreciation at Val's enlistment; and
Marian Tweetyman with the last news of Gile and
Jesse. These with Aunts Juley and Hester, young
Nicholas, Euphemia, and — of all people! —
George, who had come with Eustace in the car,
constituted an assembly worthy of the family's
palmiest days. There was not one chair vacant in
the whole of the little drawing-room, and anxiety
was felt lest someone else should arrive.

The constraint caused by Timothy's presence
having worn off a little, conversation took a military turn. George asked Aunt Juley when she was
going out with the Red Cross, almost reducing her
to a state of gaiety; whereon he turned to Nicholas
and said:

"Young Nick's a warrior bold, isn't he?
When's he going to don the wild khaki?"

Young Nicholas, smiling with a sort of sweet
deprecation, intimated that of course his mother
was very anxious.

"The Dromios are off, I hear," said George,

turning to Marian Tweetyman; "we shall all be there soon. *En avant,* the Forsytes! Roll, bowl, or pitch! Who's for a cooler?"

Aunt Juley gurgled, George was *so* droll! Should Hester get Timothy's map! Then he could show them all where they were.

At a sound from Timothy, interpreted as assent, Aunt Hester left the room.

George pursued his image of the Forsyte advance, addressing Timothy as Field Marshal; and Imogen, whom he had noted at once for ' a pretty filly,'— as Vivandière; and holding his top-hat between his knees, he began to beat it with imaginary drumsticks. The reception accorded to his fantasy was mixed. All laughed — George was licensed; but all felt that the family was being ' rotted '; and this seemed to them unnatural, now that it was going to give five of its members to the service of the Queen. George might go too far; and there was relief when he got up, offered his arm to Aunt Juley, marched up to Timothy, saluted him, kissed his aunt with mock passion, said, "Oh! what a treat, dear papa! Come on, Eustace!" and walked out, followed by the grave and fastidious Eustace, who had never smiled. Aunt Juley's bewildered, "Fancy not waiting for the map! You mustn't mind him, Timothy. He's *so* droll!" broke the hush, and Timothy removed the hand from his mouth.

"I don't know what things are comin' to," he was heard to say. "What's all this about goin' out there? That's not the way to beat those Boers."

Francie alone had the hardihood to observe:

"What is, then, Uncle Timothy?"

"All this new-fangled volunteerin' and expense — lettin' money out of the country."

Just then Aunt Hester brought in the map, handling it like a baby with eruptions. With the assistance of Euphemia it was laid on the piano, a small Colwood grand, last played on, it was believed, the summer before Aunt Ann died, thirteen years ago. Timothy rose. He walked over to the piano, and stood looking at his map while they all gathered round.

"There you are," he said; "that's the position up to date; and very poor it is. H'm!"

"Yes," said Francie, greatly daring, "but how are you going to alter it, Uncle Timothy, without more men?"

"Men!" said Timothy; "you don't want men — wastin' the country's money. You want a Napoleon, he'd settle it in a month."

"But if you haven't got him, Uncle Timothy?"

"That's their business," replied Timothy. "What have we kept the Army up for — to eat their heads off in time of peace! They ought to be ashamed of themselves, comin' on the country to help them like this! Let every man stick to his business, and we shall get on."

And looking round him, he added almost angrily:

"Volunteerin', indeed! Throwin' good money after bad! We must save! Conserve energy — that's the only way." And with a prolonged sound, not quite a sniff and not quite a snort, he trod on Euphemia's toe, and went out, leaving a sensation and a faint scent of barley-sugar behind him.

The effect of something said with conviction by one who has evidently made a sacrifice to say it is ever considerable. And the eight Forsytes left behind, all women except young Nicholas, were silent for a moment round the map. Then Francie said:

" Really, I think he's right, you know. After all, what is the Army for? They ought to have known. It's only encouraging them."

" My dear!" cried Aunt Juley, " but they've been so progressive. Think of their giving up their scarlet. They were always so proud of it. And now they all look like convicts. Hester and I were saying only yesterday we were sure they must feel it very much. Fancy what the Iron Duke would have said!"

" The new colour's very smart," said Winifred; " Val looks quite nice in his."

Aunt Juley sighed.

" I do so wonder what Jolyon's boy is like. To think we've never seen him! His father must be so proud of him."

"His father's in Paris," said Winifred.

Aunt Hester's shoulder was seen to mount suddenly, as if to ward off her sister's next remark, for Juley's crumpled cheeks had flushed.

" We had dear little Mrs. MacAnder here yesterday, just back from Paris. And whom d'you think she saw there in the street? You'll never guess."

" We shan't try, Auntie," said Euphemia.

" Irene! Imagine! After all this time; walking with a fair beard —— "

" Auntie! you'll kill me! A fair beard —— "

" I was going to say," said Aunt Juley severely, " a fair-bearded gentleman. And not a day older; she was always so pretty," she added, with a sort of lingering apology.

" Oh! tell us about her, Auntie," cried Imogen; " I can just remember her. She's the skeleton in the family cupboard, isn't she? And they're such fun."

Aunt Hester sat down.   Really, Juley had done it now!

" She wasn't much of a skeleton as I remember her," murmured Euphemia, " extremely well-covered."

" My dear! " said Aunt Juley, " what a peculiar way of putting it — not very nice."

" No, but what *was* she like? " persisted Imogen.

" I'll tell you, my child," said Francie; " a kind of modern Venus, very well-dressed."

Euphemia said sharply: " Venus was never dressed, and she had blue eyes of melting sapphire."

At this juncture Nicholas took his leave.

" Mrs. Nick. is awfully strict," said Francie with .a laugh.

" She has six children," said Aunt Juley; "it's very proper she should be careful."

" Was Uncle Soames awfully fond of her? " pursued the inexorable Imogen, moving her dark luscious eyes from face to face.

Aunt Hester made a gesture of despair, just as Aunt Juley answered: " Yes, your Uncle Soames was very much attached to her."

" I suppose she ran off with someone? "

" No, certainly not; that is — not precisely."

" What did she do, then, Auntie? "

" Come along, Imogen," said Winifred, " we must be getting back."

But Aunt Juley interjected resolutely: " She — she didn't behave at all well."

" Oh, bother! " cried Imogen; " that's as far as I ever get."

" Well, my dear," said Francie, " she had a love affair which ended with the young man's death; and then she left your uncle. I always rather liked her."

"She used to give me chocolates," murmured Imogen, "and smell nice."

"Of course!" remarked Euphemia.

"Not of course at all!" replied Francie, who used a particularly expensive essence of gilly-flower herself.

"I can't think what we are about," said Aunt Juley, raising her hands, "talking of such things!"

"Was she divorced?" asked Imogen from the door.

"Certainly not," cried Aunt Juley; "that is — certainly not."

A sound was heard over by the far door. Timothy had re-entered the back drawing-room. "I've come for my map," he said. "Who's been divorced?"

"No one, Uncle," replied Francie with perfect truth.

Timothy took his map off the piano.

"Don't let's have anything of that sort in the family," he said. "All this enlistin's bad enough. The country's breakin' up; I don't know what we're comin' to." He shook a thick finger at the room: "Too many women nowadays, and they don't know what they want."

So saying, he grasped the map firmly with both hands, and went out as if afraid of being answered.

The seven women whom he had addressed broke into a subdued murmur, out of which emerged Francie's, "Really, the Forsytes ———!" and Aunt Juley's: "He must have his feet in mustard and hot water to-night, Hester; will you tell Jane? The blood has gone to his head again, I'm afraid.". . .

That evening, when she and Hester were sitting

alone after dinner, she dropped a stitch in her crochet, and looked up:

"Hester, I can't think where I've heard that dear Soames wants Irene to come back to him again. Who was it told us that George had made a funny drawing of him with the words, 'He won't be happy till he gets it'?"

"Eustace," answered Aunt Hester from behind *The Times*; "he had it in his pocket, but he wouldn't show it us."

Aunt Juley was silent, ruminating. The clock ticked, *The Times* crackled, the fire sent forth its rustling purr. Aunt Juley dropped another stitch.

"Hester," she said, "I have had such a dreadful thought."

"Then don't tell me," said Aunt Hester quickly.

"Oh! but I must. You can't think how dreadful!" Her voice sank to a whisper:

"Jolyon — Jolyon, they say, has a — has a fair beard, now."

CHAPTER XII

PROGRESS OF THE CHASE

Two days after the dinner at James's, Mr. Polteed provided Soames with food for thought.

"A gentleman," he said, consulting the key concealed in his left hand, " 47 as we say, has been paying marked attention to 17 during the last month in Paris. But at present there seems to have been nothing very conclusive. The meetings have all been in public places, without concealment — restaurants, the Opera, the Comique, the Louvre, Luxembourg Gardens, lounge of the hotel, and so forth. She has not yet been traced to his rooms, nor *vice versa*. They went to Fontainebleau — but nothing of value. In short, the situation is promising, but requires patience." And looking up suddenly, he added:

"One rather curious point — 47 has the same name as — er — 31 ! "

"The fellow knows I'm her husband," thought Soames.

"Christian name — an odd one — Jolyon," continued Mr. Polteed. "We know his address in Paris and his residence here. We don't wish, of course, to be running a wrong hare."

"Go on with it, but be careful," said Soames doggedly.

Instinctive certainty that this detective fellow had fathomed his secret made him all the more reticent.

"Excuse me," said Mr. Polteed, "I'll just see if there's anything fresh in."

He returned with some letters. Relocking the door, he glanced at the envelopes.

"Yes, here's a personal one from 19 to myself."

"Well?" said Soames.

"Um!" said Mr. Polteed, "she says: '47 left for England to-day. Address on his baggage: Robin Hill. Parted from 17 in Louvre Gallery at 3:30; nothing very striking. Thought it best to stay and continue observation of 17. You will deal with 47 in England if you think desirable, no doubt.'" And Mr. Polteed lifted an unprofessional glance on Soames, as though he might be storing material for a book on human nature after he had gone out of business. "Very intelligent woman, 19, and a wonderful make-up. Not cheap, but earns her money well. There's no suspicion of being shadowed so far. But after a time, as you know, sensitive people are liable to get the feeling of it, without anything definite to go on. I should rather advise letting-up on 17, and keeping an eye on 47. We can't get at correspondence without great risk. I hardly advise that at this stage. But you can tell your client that it's looking up very well." And again his narrowed eyes gleamed at his taciturn customer.

"No," said Soames suddenly, "I prefer that you should keep the watch going discreetly in Paris, and not concern yourself with this end."

"Very well," replied Mr. Polteed, "we can do it."

"What — what is the manner between them?"

"I'll read you what she says," said Mr. Polteed, unlocking a bureau drawer and taking out a file of papers; "she sums it up somewhere confidentially. Yes, here it is! ' 17 very attractive — conclude 47 longer in the tooth '(slang for age, you know) — ' distinctly gone — waiting his time — 17 perhaps holding off for terms, impossible to say without knowing more. But inclined to think on the whole — doesn't know her mind — likely to act on impulse some day. Both have style."

"What does that mean?" said Soames between close lips.

"Well," murmured Mr. Polteed with a smile, showing many white teeth, "an expression we use. In other words, it's not likely to be a week-end business — they'll come together seriously or not at all."

"H'm!" muttered Soames, "that's all, is it?"

"Yes," said Mr. Polteed, "but quite promising."

'Spider!' thought Soames. "Good-day!"

He walked into the Green Park that he might cross to Victoria Station and take the Underground into the City. For so late in January it was warm; sunlight, through the haze, sparkled on the frosty grass — an illumined cobweb of a day.

Little spiders — and great spiders! And the greatest spinner of all, his own tenacity, for ever wrapping its cocoon of threads round any clear way out. What was that fellow hanging round Irene for? Was it really as Polteed suggested? Or was Jolyon but taking compassion on her loneliness, as he would call it — sentimental radical chap that he had always been? If it were, indeed, as Polteed hinted! Soames stood still. It could not be! The fellow was six years older than himself, no better looking! No richer! What attraction had he?

'Besides, he's come back,' he thought; 'that doesn't look ——I'll go and see him!' and, taking out a card, he wrote:

"If you can spare half an hour some afternoon this week, I shall be at the Connoisseurs any day between 5.30 and 6, or I could come to the Hotch Potch if you prefer it. I want to see you. — S. F."

He walked up St. James's Street and confided it to the porter at the Hotch Potch.

"Give Mr. Jolyon Forsyte this as soon as he comes in," he said, and took one of the new motor cabs into the City. . . .

Jolyon received that card the same afternoon, and turned his face towards the Connoisseurs. What did Soames want now? Had he got wind of Paris? And stepping across St. James's Street, he determined to make no secret of his visit. 'But it won't do,' he thought, ' to let him know *she's* there, unless he knows already.' In this complicated state of mind he was conducted to where Soames was drinking tea in a small bay-window.

"No tea, thanks," said Jolyon, "but I'll go on smoking if I may."

The curtains were not yet drawn, though the lamps outside were lighted; the two cousins sat waiting on each other.

"You've been in Paris, I hear," said Soames at last.

"Yes; just back."

"Young Val told me; he and your boy are going off, then?"

Jolyon nodded.

"You didn't happen to see Irene, I suppose. It appears she's abroad somewhere."

Jolyon wreathed himself in smoke before he answered: "Yes, I saw her."

" How was she? "

" Very well."

There was another silence; then Soames roused himself in his chair.

" When I saw you last," he said, " I was in two minds. We talked, and you expressed your opinion. I don't wish to re-open that discussion. I only wanted to say this: My position with her is extremely difficult. I don't want you to go using your influence against me. What happened is a very long time ago. I'm going to ask her to let bygones be bygones."

" You have asked her, you know," murmured Jolyon.

" The idea was new to her then; it came as a shock. But the more she thinks of it, the more she must see that it's the only way out for both of us."

" That's not my impression of her state of mind," said Jolyon with particular calm. " And, forgive my saying, you misconceive the matter if you think reason comes into it at all."

He saw his cousin's pale face grow paler — he had used, without knowing it, Irene's own words.

" Thanks," muttered Soames, " but I see things perhaps more plainly than you think. I only want to be sure that you won't try to influence her against me."

" I don't know what makes you think I have any influence," said Jolyon; " but if I have I'm bound to use it in the direction of what I think is her happiness. I am what they call a ' feminist,' I believe."

" Feminist! " repeated Soames, as if seeking to gain time. " Does that mean that you're against me? "

" Bluntly," said Jolyon, " I'm against any woman

living with any man whom she definitely dislikes. It appears to me rotten."

"And I suppose each time you see her you put your opinions into her mind."

"I am not likely to be seeing her."

"Not going back to Paris?"

"Not so far as I know," said Jolyon, conscious of the intent watchfulness in Soames' face.

"Well, that's all I had to say. Anyone who comes between man and wife, you know, incurs heavy responsibility."

Jolyon rose and made him a slight bow.

"Good-bye," he said, and, without offering to shake hands, moved away, leaving Soames staring after him. 'We Forsytes,' thought Jolyon, hailing a cab, 'are very civilised. With simpler folk that might have come to a row. If it weren't for my boy going to the war ——" The war! A gust of his old doubt swept over him. A precious war! Domination of peoples or of women! Attempts to master and possess those who did not want you! The negation of gentle decency! Possession, vested rights; and anyone 'agin' 'em — outcast! 'Thank Heaven!' he thought, '*I always* felt 'agin' 'em, anyway!' Yes! Even before his first disastrous marriage he could remember fuming over the bludgeoning of Ireland, or the matrimonial suits of women trying to be free of men they loathed. Parsons would have it that freedom of soul and body were quite different things! Pernicious doctrine, that! Body and soul could not thus be separated. Free will was the strength of any tie, and not its weakness. 'I ought to have told Soames,' he thought, 'that I think him comic. Ah! but he's tragic, too!'

Was there anything indeed more tragic in the world than a man enslaved by his own possessive instinct, who couldn't see the sky for it, or even enter fully into what another person felt! ' I must write and warn her,' he thought; ' he's going to have another try.' And all the way home to Robin Hill he rebelled at the strength of that duty to his son which prevented him from posting back to Paris. . . .

But Soames sat long in his chair, the prey of a no less gnawing ache — a jealous ache, as if it had been revealed to him that this fellow held precedence of himself, and had spun fresh threads of resistance to his way out. 'Does that mean that you're against me?' he had got nothing out of that disingenuous question. Feminist! Phrasey fellow! ' I mustn't rush things,' he thought. ' I have some breathing space; he's not going back to Paris, unless he was lying. I'll let the spring come!' Though how the spring would serve him, save by adding to his ache, he could not tell. And gazing down into the street, where figures were passing from pool to pool of the light from the high lamps, he thought: ' Nothing seems any good — nothing seems worth while. I'm lonely — that's the trouble.'

He closed his eyes; and at once he seemed to see Irene, in a dark street below a church — passing, turning her neck so that he caught the gleam of her eyes and her white forehead under a little dark hat, which had gold spangles on it and a veil hanging down behind. He opened his eyes — so vividly he had seen her! A woman *was* passing below, but not she! Oh no, there was nothing there!

CHAPTER XIII

'HERE WE ARE AGAIN!'

IMOGEN'S frocks for her first season exercised the
judgment of her mother and the purse of her grandfather all through the month of March. With
Forsyte tenacity Winifred quested for perfection.
It took her mind off the slowly approaching rite
which would give her a freedom but doubtfully desired; took her mind, too, off her boy and his fast
approaching departure for a war from which the
news remained disquieting. Like bees busy on summer flowers, or bright gadflies hovering and darting
over spiky autumn blossoms, she and her 'little
daughter,' tall nearly as herself and with a bust
measurement not far inferior, hovered in the shops
of Regent Street, the establishments of Hanover
Square and of Bond Street, lost in consideration and
the feel of fabrics. Dozens of young women of
striking deportment and peculiar gait paraded before Winifred and Imogen, draped in 'creations.'
The models — 'Very new, modom; quite the latest
thing—' which those two reluctantly turned down
would have filled a museum; the models which they
were obliged to have nearly emptied James' bank.
It was no good doing things by halves, Winifred
felt, in view of the need for making this first and

sole untarnished season a conspicuous success. Their patience in trying the patience of those impersonal creatures who swam about before them could alone have been displayed by such as were moved by faith. It was for Winifred a long prostration before her dear goddess Fashion, fervent as a Catholic might make before the Virgin; for Imogen an experience by no means too unpleasant — she often looked so nice, and flattery was implicit everywhere: in a word it was 'amusing.'

On the afternoon of the 20th of March, having, as it were, gutted Skyward's, they had sought refreshment over the way at Caramel and Baker's, and, stored with chocolate frothed at the top with cream, turned homewards through Berkeley Square of an evening touched with spring. Opening the door — freshly painted a light olive-green; nothing neglected that year to give Imogen a good send-off — Winifred passed towards the silver basket to see if anyone had called, and suddenly her nostrils twitched. What was that scent?

Imogen had taken up a novel sent from the library, and stood absorbed. Rather sharply, because of the queer feeling in her breast, Winifred said:

"Take that up, dear, and have a rest before dinner."

Imogen, still reading, passed up the stairs. Winifred heard the door of her room slammed to, and drew a long savouring breath. Was it spring tickling her senses — whipping up nostalgia for her 'clown,' against all wisdom and outraged virtue? A male scent! A faint reek of cigars and lavender-water not smelt since that early autumn night six months ago, when she had called him 'the limit.' Whence came it, or was it ghost of scent — sheer emanation from memory? She looked round her. Nothing — not a thing, no tiniest disturbance of her hall, nor of the dining-room. A little day-dream of a scent — illusory, saddening, silly! In the silver basket were new cards, two with ' Mr. and Mrs. Polegate Thom,' and one with ' Mr. Polegate Thom ' thereon; she sniffed them, but they smelled severe. ' I must be tired,' she thought. ' I'll go and lie down.' Upstairs, the drawing-room was darkened, waiting for some hand to give it evening light; and she passed on up to her bed-room. This, too, was half-curtained and dim, for it was six o'clock. Winifred threw off her coat — that scent again! — then stood, as if shot, transfixed against the bed-rail. Something dark had risen from the sofa in the far corner. A word of — horror — in her family escaped her: " God! "

" It's I — Monty," said a voice.

Clutching the bed-rail, Winifred reached up and turned the switch of the light hanging above her dressing-table. He appeared just on the rim of the light's circumference, emblazoned from the absence of his watch-chain down to boots neat and sooty brown, but — yes! — split at the toe-cap. His chest and face were shadowy. Surely he was thin — or was it a trick of the light? He advanced, lighted now from toe-cap to the top of his dark head — surely a little grizzled! His complexion had darkened, sallowed; his black moustache had lost boldness, become sardonic; there were lines which she did not know about his face. There was no pin in his tie. His suit — ah! — she knew that — but how unpressed, and unglossy! She stared again at the toe-cap of his boot. Something big and relentless had been 'at him,' had turned and twisted, raked and scraped him. And she stayed, not speaking, motionless, staring at that crack across the toe.

"Well!" he said, "I got the letter. I'm back."

Winifred's bosom began to heave. The nostalgia for her husband which had rushed up with that scent was struggling with a deeper jealousy than any she had felt yet. There he was — a dark, and as if harried, shadow of his sleek and brazen self! What force had done this to him — squeezed him like an orange to its dry rind! That woman!

"I'm back," he said again. "I've had a beastly time. By God! I came steerage. I've got nothing but what I stand in, and that bag."

"And who has the rest?" cried Winifred, suddenly alive. "How dared you come? You knew it was just for divorce that you got that letter to come back. Don't touch me!"

They held each to the rail of the big bed where they had spent so many years of nights together. Many times, yes — many times she had wanted him back. But now that he had come she was filled with this cold and deadly resentment. He put his hand up to his moustache; but did not frizz and twist it in the old familiar way, he just pulled it downwards.

"Gad!" he said: "If you knew the time I've had!"

"I'm glad I don't!"

"Are the kids all right?"

Winifred nodded. "How did you get in?"

"With my key."

"Then the maids don't know. You can't stay here, Monty."

He uttered a little sardonic laugh.

" Where then? "

" Anywhere."

" Well, look at me! That — that damned ———— "

" If you mention *her*," cried Winifred, " I go straight out to Park Lane and I don't come back."

Suddenly he did a simple thing, but so uncharacteristic that it moved her. He shut his eyes. It was as if he had said: ' All right! I'm dead to the world!'

" You can have a room for the night," she said; " your things are still here. Only Imogen is at home."

He leaned back against the bed-rail. " Well, it's in your hands," and his own made a writhing movement. " I've been through it. You needn't hit too hard — it isn't worth while. I've been frightened; I've been frightened, Freddie."

That old pet name, disused for years and years, sent a shiver through Winifred.

' What am I to do with him?' she thought. ' What in God's name am I to do with him?'

" Got a cigarette? "

She gave him one from a little box she kept up there for when she couldn't sleep at night, and lighted it. With that action the matter-of-fact side of her nature came to life again.

" Go and have a hot bath. I'll put some clothes out for you in the dressing-room. We can talk later."

He nodded, and fixed his eyes on her — they looked half-dead, or was it that the folds in the lids had become heavier?

' He's not the same,' she thought. He would never be quite the same again! But what would he be?

"All right," he said, and went towards the door. He even moved differently, like a man who has lost illusion and doubts whether it is worth while to move at all.

When he was gone, and she heard the water in the bath running, she put out a complete set of garments on the bed in his dressing-room, then went downstairs and fetched up the biscuit box and whisky. Putting on her coat again, and listening a moment at the bathroom door, she went down and out. In the street she hesitated. Past seven o'clock! Would Soames be at his Club or at Park Lane? She turned towards the latter. Back! Soames had always feared it — she had sometimes hoped it. Back! So like him — clown that he was — with this: 'Here we are again!' to make fools of them all — of the Law, of Soames, of herself! Yet to have done with the Law, not to have that murky cloud hanging over her and the children! What a relief! Ah! but how to accept his return? That 'woman' had ravaged him, taken from him passion such as he had never bestowed on herself, such as she had not thought him capable of. There was the sting! That selfish, blatant 'clown' of hers, whom she herself had never really stirred, had been swept and ungarnished by another woman! Insulting! Too insulting! Not right, not decent to take him back! And yet she had asked for him; the Law perhaps would make her now! He was as much her husband as ever — she had put herself out of court! And all he wanted, no doubt, was money — to keep him in cigars and lavender-water! That scent! 'After all, I'm not old,' she thought, 'not old yet!' But that woman who had reduced him to those words: 'I've been through it. I've been frightened

— frightened, Freddie!' She neared her father's house, driven this way and that, while all the time the Forsyte undertow was drawing her to deep conclusion that after all he was her property, to be held against a robbing world. And so she came to James's.

"Mr. Soames? In his room? I'll go up; don't say I'm here."

Her brother was dressing. She found him before a mirror, tying a black bow with an air of despising its ends.

" Hullo! " he said, contemplating her in the glass; " what's wrong? "

" Monty! " said Winifred stonily.

Soames spun round. " What! "

" Back! "

" Hoist," muttered Soames, " with our own petard. Why the deuce didn't you let me try cruelty? I always knew it was too much risk this way."

" Oh! Don't talk about that! What shall I do? "

Soames answered, with a deep, deep sound.

" Well? " said Winifred impatiently.

" What has he to say for himself? "

" Nothing. One of his boots is split across the toe."

Soames stared at her.

" Ah! " he said, " of course! On his beam ends. So — it begins again! This'll about finish father."

" Can't we keep it from him? "

" Impossible. He has an uncanny flair for anything that's worrying."

And he brooded, with fingers hooked into his blue silk braces. " There ought to be some way in law," he muttered, " to make him safe."

" No," cried Winifred, " I won't be made a fool of again; I'd sooner put up with him."

The two stared at each other. Their hearts were full of feeling, but they could give it no expression — Forsytes that they were.

" Where did you leave him? "

" In the bath," and Winifred gave a little bitter laugh. " The only thing he's brought back is lavender-water."

" Steady! " said Soames; " you're thoroughly upset. I'll go back with you."

" What's the use? "

" We ought to make terms with him."

" Terms! It'll always be the same. When he recovers — cards and betting, drink and —— ! " She was silent, remembering the look on her husband's face. The burnt child — the burnt child! Perhaps ——!

" Recovers? " replied Soames: " Is he ill? "

" No; burnt out; that's all."

Soames took his waistcoat from a chair and put it on, he took his coat and got into it, he scented his handkerchief with eau-de-Cologne, threaded his watch-chain, and said: " We haven't any luck."

And in the midst of her own trouble Winifred was sorry for him, as if in that little saying he had revealed deep trouble of his own.

" I'd like to see mother," she said.

" She'll be with father in their room. Come down quietly to the study. I'll get her."

Winifred stole down to the little dark study, chiefly remarkable for a Canaletto too doubtful to be placed elsewhere, and a fine collection of Law Reports unopened for many years. Here she stood, with her back to maroon-coloured curtains closedrawn, staring at the empty grate, till her mother came in followed by Soames.

"Oh! my poor dear!" said Emily: "How miserable you look in here! This is too bad of him, really!"

As a family they had so guarded themselves from the expression of all unfashionable emotion that it was impossible to go up and give her daughter a good hug. But there was comfort in her cushioned voice, and her still dimpled shoulders under some rare black lace. Summoning pride and the desire not to distress her mother, Winifred said in her most off-hand voice:

"It's all right, Mother; no good fussing."

"I don't see," said Emily, looking at Soames, "why Winifred shouldn't tell him that she'll prosecute him if he doesn't keep off the premises. He took her pearls; and if he's not brought them back, that's quite enough."

Winifred smiled. They would all plunge about with suggestions of this and that, but she knew already what she would be doing, and that was — nothing. The feeling that, after all, she had won a sort of victory, retained her property, was every moment gaining ground in her. No! if she wanted to punish him, she could do it at home without the world knowing.

"Well," said Emily, "come into the dining-room comfortably — you must stay and have dinner with us. Leave it to me to tell your father." And, as Winifred moved towards the door, she turned out the light. Not till then did they see the disaster in the corridor.

There, attracted by light from a room never lighted, James was standing with his dun-coloured camel-hair shawl folded about him, so that his arms were not free and his silvered head looked cut off from his fashionably trousered legs as if by an expanse of desert. He stood, inimitably stork-like, with an expression as if he saw before him a frog too large to swallow.

"What's all this?" he said. "Tell your father? You never tell me anything."

The moment found Emily without reply. It was Winifred who went up to him, and, laying one hand on each of his swathed, helpless arms, said:

"Monty's not gone bankrupt, Father. He's only come back."

They all three expected something serious to happen, and were glad she had kept that grip of his arms, but they did not know the depth of root in that shadowy old Forsyte. Something wry occurred about his shaven mouth and chin, something scratchy between those long silvery whiskers. Then he said with a sort of dignity: "He'll be the death of me. I knew how it would be."

"You mustn't worry, Father," said Winifred calmly. "I mean to make him behave."

"Ah!" said James. "Here, take this thing off, I'm hot." They unwound the shawl. He turned, and walked firmly to the dining-room.

"I don't want any soup," he said to Warmson, and sat down in his chair. They all sat down too, Winifred still in her hat, while Warmson laid the fourth place. When he left the room, James said: "What's he brought back?"

"Nothing, Father."

James concentrated his eyes on his own image in a table-spoon. "Divorce!" he muttered; "rubbish! What was I about? I ought to have paid him an allowance to stay out of England. Soames! you go and propose it to him."

It seemed so right and simple a suggestion that even Winifred was surprised when she said: " No, I'll keep him now he's back; he must just behave — that's all."

They all looked at her. It had always been known that Winifred had pluck.

"Out there!" said James elliptically, " who knows what cut-throats! You look for his revolver! Don't go to bed without. You ought to have Warmson to sleep in the house. I'll see him myself to-morrow."

They were touched by this declaration, and Emily said comfortably: " That's right, James, we won't have any nonsense."

" Ah!" muttered James darkly, " I can't tell."

The advent of Warmson with fish diverted conversation.

When, directly after dinner, Winifred went over to kiss her father good-night, he looked up with eyes so full of question and distress that she put all the comfort she could into her voice.

" It's all right, Daddy, dear; don't worry. I shan't need anyone — he's quite bland. I shall only be upset if you worry. Good-night, bless you!"

James repeated the words, " Bless you!" as if he did not quite know what they meant, and his eyes followed her to the door.

She reached home before nine, and went straight upstairs.

Dartie was lying on the bed in his dressing-room, fully re-dressed in a blue serge suit and pumps; his arms were crossed behind his head, and an extinct cigarette drooped from his mouth.

Winifred remembered ridiculously the flowers in her window-boxes after a blazing summer day; the way they lay, or rather stood — parched, yet rested by the sun's retreat. It was as if a little dew had come already on her burnt-up husband.

He said apathetically: " I suppose you've been to Park Lane. How's the old man? "

Winifred could not help the bitter answer: " Not dead."

He winced, actually he winced.

" Understand, Monty," she said, " I will *not* have him worried. If you aren't going to behave yourself, you may go back, you may go anywhere. Have you had dinner? "

" No."

" Would you like some? "

He shrugged his shoulders.

" Imogen offered me some. I didn't want any."

Imogen! In the plenitude of emotion Winifred had forgotten her.

" So you've seen her? What did she say? "

" She gave me a kiss."

With mortification Winifred saw his dark sardonic face relaxed. ' Yes! ' she thought, ' he cares for her, not for me a bit.'

Dartie's eyes were moving from side to side.

" Does she know about me? " he said.

It flashed through Winifred that here was the weapon she needed. *He minded their knowing!*

" No. Val knows. The others don't; they only know you went away."

She heard him sigh with relief.

" But they *shall* know," she said firmly, " if you give me cause."

" All right! " he muttered, " hit me! I'm down! "

Winifred went up to the bed. " Look here, Monty! I don't want to hit you. I don't want to hurt you. I shan't allude to anything. I'm not going to worry.

What's the use?" She was silent a moment. "I can't stand any more, though, and I won't! You'd better know. You've made me suffer. But I used to be fond of you. For the sake of that —— " She met the heavy-lidded gaze of his brown eyes with the downward stare of her green-grey eyes; touched his hand suddenly, turned her back, and went into her room.

She sat there a long time before her glass, fingering her rings, thinking of this subdued dark man, almost a stranger to her, on the bed in the other room; resolutely not 'worrying', but gnawed by jealousy of what he had been through, and now and again just visited by pity.

CHAPTER XIV

OUTLANDISH NIGHT

SOAMES doggedly let the spring come — no easy task for one conscious that time was flying, his birds in the bush no nearer the hand, no issue from the web anywhere visible. Mr. Polteed reported nothing, except that his watch went on — costing a lot of money. Val and his cousin were gone to the war, whence came news more favourable; Dartie was behaving himself so far; James had retained his health; business prospered almost terribly — there was nothing to worry Soames except that he was ' held up,' could take no step in any direction.

He did not exactly avoid Soho, for he could not afford to let them think that he had ' piped off,' as James would have put it — he might want to ' pipe on ' again at any minute. But he had to be so restrained and cautious that he would often pass the door of the Restaurant Bretagne without going in, and wander out of the purlieus of that region which always gave him the feeling of having been possessively irregular.

He wandered thus one May night into Regent Street and the most amazing crowd he had ever seen: a shrieking, whistling, dancing, jostling, grotesque and formidably jovial crowd, with false noses

and mouth-organs, penny whistles and long feathers, every appanage of idiocy, as it seemed to him.
Mafeking! Of course, it had been relieved! Good!
But was that an excuse? Who were these people,
what were they, where had they come from into the
West End? His face was tickled, his ears whistled
into. Girls cried: ' Keep your hair on, stucco! ' A
youth so knocked off his top-hat that he recovered it
with difficulty. Crackers were exploding beneath
his nose, between his feet. He was bewildered, ex-
asperated, offended. This stream of people came
from every quarter, as if impulse had unlocked
flood-gates, let flow waters of whose existence he
had heard, perhaps, but believed in never. This,
then, was the populace, the innumerable living negation of gentility and Forsyteism. This was — egad!
— Democracy! It stank, yelled, was hideous! In
the East End, or even Soho, perhaps — but here in
Regent Street, in Piccadilly! What were the police
about! In 1900, Soames, with his Forsyte thou-
sands, had never seen the cauldron with the lid off;
and now looking into it, could hardly believe his
scorching eyes. The whole thing was unspeakable!
These people had no restraint, they seemed to think
him funny; such swarms of them, rude, coarse,
laughing — and what laughter! Nothing sacred to
them! He shouldn't be surprised if they began to
break windows. In Pall Mall, past those august
dwellings, to enter which people paid sixty pounds,
this shrieking, whistling, dancing dervish of a
crowd was swarming. From the Club windows his
own kind were looking out on them with regulated
amusement. They didn't realise! Why, this was
serious — might come to anything! The crowd was
cheerful, but some day they would come in differ-

ent mood! He remembered there had been a mob in the late eighties, when he was at Brighton; they had smashed things and made speeches. But more than dread, he felt a deep surprise. They were hysterical — it wasn't English! And all about the relief of a little town as big as — Watford, six thousand miles away. Restraint, reserve! Those qualities to him more dear almost than life, those indispensable attributes of property and culture, where were they? It wasn't English! No, it wasn't English! So Soames brooded, threading his way on. It was as if he had suddenly caught sight of someone cutting the covenant ' for quiet possession ' out of his legal documents; or of a monster lurking and stalking out in the future, casting its shadow before. Their want of stolidity, their want of reverence! It was like discovering that nine-tenths of the people of England were foreigners. And if that were so — then, anything might happen!

At Hyde Park Corner he ran into George Forsyte, very sunburnt from racing, holding a false nose in his hand.

" Hallo, Soames! " he said; " have a nose! "

Soames responded with a pale smile.

" Got this from one of these sportsmen," went on George, who had evidently been dining; " had to lay him out — for trying to bash my hat. I say, one of these days we shall have to fight these chaps, they're getting so damned cheeky — all radicals and socialists. They want our goods. You tell Uncle James that, it'll make him sleep."

' *In vino veritas*,' thought Soames, but he only nodded, and passed on up Hamilton place. There was but a trickle of roysterers in Park Lane, not very noisy. And looking up at the houses he thought: ' After all, we're the backbone of the country. They won't upset us easily. Possession's nine points of the law.'

But, as he closed the door of his father's house behind him, all that queer outlandish nightmare in the streets passed out of his mind almost as completely as if, having dreamed it, he had awakened in the warm clean morning comfort of his spring-mattressed bed.

Walking into the centre of the great empty drawing-room, he stood still.

A wife! Somebody to talk things over with. One had a right! Damn it! One had a right!

PART III

CHAPTER I

SOAMES IN PARIS

SOAMES had travelled little. Aged nineteen he had
made the 'petty tour' with his father, mother, and
Winifred — Brussels, the Rhine, Switzerland, and
home. by way of Paris. Aged twenty-seven, just
when he began to take interest in pictures, he had
spent five hot weeks in Italy, looking into the Ren-
aissance — not so much in it as he had been led to
expect — and a fortnight in Paris on his way back,
looking into himself, as became a Forsyte sur-
rounded by people so strongly self-centred and
'foreign' as the French. His knowledge of their
language being derived from his public school, he
did not understand them when they spoke. Silence
he had found better for all parties; one did not
make a fool of oneself. He had disliked the look
of the men's clothes, the closed-in cabs, the theatres
which looked like beehives, the Galleries which
smelled of beeswax. He was too cautious and too
shy to explore that side of Paris supposed by Forsytes to constitute its attraction under the rose; and
as for a collector's bargain — not one to be had!
As Nicholas might have put it — they were a grasping lot. He had come back uneasy, saying Paris
was overrated.

When, therefore, in June of 1900, he went to
Paris, it was but his third attempt on the centre of
civilization. This time, however, the mountain
was going to Mahomet; for he felt by now more
deeply civilised than Paris, and perhaps he really
was. Moreover, he had a definite objective. This
was no mere genuflection to a shrine of taste and
immorality, but the prosecution of his own legitimate affairs. He went, indeed, because things were
getting past a joke. The watch went on and on,
and — nothing — nothing! Jolyon had never returned to Paris, and no one else was ' suspect!'
Busy with new and very confidential matters, Soames
was realising more than ever how essential reputation is to a solicitor. But at night and in his leisure moments he was ravaged by the thought that
time was always flying and money flowing in, and
his own future as much ' in irons' as ever. Since
Mafeking night he had become aware that a ' young
fool of a doctor' was hanging round Annette.
Twice he had come across him — a cheerful young
fool, not more than thirty. Nothing annoyed
Soames so much as cheerfulness — an indecent,
extravagant sort of quality, which had no relation
to facts. The mixture of his desires and hopes
was, in a word, becoming torture; and lately the
thought had come to him that perhaps Irene
knew she was being shadowed. It was this which
finally decided him to go and see for himself;
to go and once more try to break down her
repugnance, her refusal to make her own and
his path comparatively smooth once more. If he
failed again — well, he would see what she did with
herself, anyway!

He went to an hotel in the Rue Caumartin, highly

recommended to Forsytes, where practically nobody spoke French. He had formed no plan. He
did not want to startle her; yet must contrive that
she had no chance to evade him by flight. And next
morning he set out in bright weather.

Paris had an air of gaiety, a sparkle over its star-
shape which almost annoyed Soames. He stepped
gravely, his nose lifted a little sideways in real curiosity. He desired now to understand things
French. Was not Annette French? There was
much to be got out of his visit, if he could only get
it. In this laudable mood and the Place de la Con-
corde he was nearly run down three times. He
came on the ' Cours la Reine,' where Irene's hotel
was situated, almost too suddenly, for he had not
yet fixed on his procedure. Crossing over to the
river side, he noted the building, white and cheerful-
looking, with green sunblinds, seen through a
screen of plane-tree leaves. And, conscious that it
would be far better to meet her casually in some
open place than to risk a call, he sat down on a
bench whence he could watch the entrance. It
was not quite eleven o'clock, and improbable that
she had yet gone out. Some pigeons were strutting
and preening their feathers in the pools of sunlight
between the shadows of the plane-trees. A work-
man in a blue blouse passed, and threw them crumbs
from the paper which contained his dinner. A
' bonne' coiffed with ribbon shepherded two little
girls with pigtails and frilled drawers. A cab
meandered by, whose cocher wore a blue coat and a
black-glazed hat. To Soames a kind of affectation
seemed to cling about it all, a sort of picturesque-
ness which was out of date. A theatrical people,
the French! He lit one of his rare cigarettes, with

a sense of injury that Fate should be casting his life
into outlandish waters. He shouldn't wonder if
Irene quite enjoyed this foreign life; she had never
been properly English — even to look at! And he
began considering which of those windows could be
hers under the green sunblinds. How could he
word what he had come to say so that it might
pierce the defence of her proud obstinacy? He
threw the fag-end of his cigarette at a pigeon, with
the thought: 'I can't stay here for ever twiddling
my thumbs. Better give it up and call on her in
the late afternoon.' But he still sat on, heard
twelve strike, and then half-past. 'I'll wait till
one,' he thought, 'while I'm about it.' But just
then he started up, and shrinkingly sat down again.
A woman had come out in a cream-coloured frock,
and was moving away under a fawn-coloured parasol. Irene herself! He waited till she was too
far away to recognise him, then set out after her.
She was strolling as though she had no particular
objective; moving, if he remembered rightly, toward the Bois de Boulogne. For half an hour at
least he kept his distance on the far side of the way
till she had passed into the Bois itself. Was she
going to meet someone after all? Some confounded Frenchman — one of those 'Bel Ami'
chaps, perhaps, who had nothing to do but hang
about women — for he had read that book with
difficulty and a sort of disgusted fascination. He
followed doggedly along a shady alley, losing sight
of her now and then when the path curved. And it
came back to him how, long ago, one night in Hyde
Park he had slid and sneaked from tree to tree,
from seat to seat, hunting blindly, ridiculously, in
burning jealousy for her and young Bosinney. The

path bent sharply, and, hurrying, he came on her
sitting in front of a small fountain — a little green-
bronze Niobe veiled in hair to her slender hips, gazing at the pool she had wept.   He came on her so
suddenly that he was past before he could turn and
take off his hat.   She did not start up.   She had
always had great self-command — it was one of the
things he most admired in her, one of his greatest
grievances against her, because he had never been
able to tell what she was thinking.   Had she realised that he was following?   Her self-possession
made him angry; and, disdaining to explain his
presence, he pointed to the mournful little Niobe,
and said:

"That's rather a good thing."

He could see, then, that she was struggling to
preserve her composure.

"I didn't want to startle you; is this one of your
haunts?"

"Yes."

"A little lonely."   As he spoke, a lady, strolling
by, paused to look at the fountain and passed on.

Irene's eyes followed her.

"No," she said, prodding the ground with her
parasol, "never lonely.   One has always one's
shadow."

Soames understood; and, looking at her hard, he
exclaimed:

"Well, it's your own fault.   You can be free of
it at any moment.   Irene, come back to me, and be
free."

Irene laughed.

"Don't!" cried Soames, stamping his foot; "it's
inhuman.   Listen!   Is there *any* condition I can
make which will bring you back to me?   If I prom-

ise you a separate house — and just a visit now and then?"

Irene rose, something wild suddenly in her face and figure.

"None! None! None! You may hunt me to the grave. I will not come."

Outraged and on edge, Soames recoiled.

"Don't make a scene!" he said sharply. And they both stood motionless, staring at the little Niobe, whose greenish flesh the sunlight was burnishing.

"That's your last word, then," muttered Soames, clenching his hands; "you condemn us both."

Irene bent her head. "I can't come back. Good-bye!"

A feeling of monstrous injustice flared up in Soames.

"Stop!" he said, "and listen to me a moment. You gave me a sacred vow — you came to me without a penny. You had all I could give you. You broke that vow without cause, you made me a by-word; you refused me a child; you've left me in prison; you — you still move me so that I want you — I want you. Well, what do you think of yourself?"

Irene turned, her face was deadly pale, her eyes burning dark.

"God made me as I am," she said; "wicked if you like — but not so wicked that I'll give myself again to a man I hate."

The sunlight gleamed on her hair as she moved away, and seemed to lay a caress all down her clinging cream-coloured frock.

Soames could neither speak nor move. That word 'hate' — so extreme, so primitive — made all

the Forsyte in him tremble.   With a deep imprecation he strode away from where she had vanished,
and ran almost into the arms of the lady sauntering
back — the fool, the shadowing fool!

He was soon dripping with perspiration, in the
depths of the Bois.

' Well,' he thought, ' I need have no consideration
for her now; she has not a grain of it for me.   I'll
show her this very day that she's my wife still.'

But on the way home to his hotel, he was forced
to the conclusion that he did not know what he
meant.   One could not make scenes in public, and
short of scenes in public what was there he could
do?   He almost cursed his own thin-skinnedness.
She might deserve no consideration; but he — alas!
deserved some at his own hands.   And sitting
lunchless in the hall of his hotel, with tourists passing every moment, Baedeker in hand, he was visited
by black dejection.   In irons!   His whole life, with
every natural instinct and every decent yearning
gagged and fettered, and all because Fate had
driven him seventeen years ago to set his heart
upon this woman — so utterly, that even now he
had no real heart to set on any other!   Cursed was
the day he had met her, and his eyes for seeing in
her anything but the cruel Venus she was!   And
yet, still seeing her with the sunlight on the clinging
China crêpe of her gown, he uttered a little groan,
so that a tourist who was passing, thought: ' Man in
pain!   Let's see! what did I have for lunch? '

Later, in front of a café near the Opera, over a
glass of cold tea with lemon and a straw in it, he
took the malicious resolution to go and dine at her
hotel.   If she were there, he would speak to her;
if she were not, he would leave a note.   He dressed
carefully, and wrote as follows:

"Your idyll with that fellow Jolyon Forsyte is known to me at all events.   If you pursue it, understand that I will leave no stone unturned to make things unbearable for him.

"S. F."

He sealed this note but did not address it, refusing to write the maiden name which she had impudently resumed, or to put the word Forsyte on the envelope lest she should tear it up unread.   Then he went out, and made his way though the glowing streets, abandoned to evening pleasure-seekers. Entering her hotel, he took his seat in a far corner of the dining-room whence he could see all entrances and exits.   She was not there.   He ate little, quickly, watchfully.   She did not come.   He lingered in the lounge over his coffee, drank two liqueurs of brandy.   But still she did not come.   He went over to the key board and examined the names. Number twelve, on the first floor!   And he determined to take the note up himself.   He mounted red-carpeted stairs, past a little salon; eight, ten, twelve!   Should he knock, push the note under, or ———?   He looked furtively round and turned the handle.   The door opened, but into a little space leading to another door; he knocked on that — no answer.   The door was locked.   It fitted very closely to the floor; the note would not go under. He thrust it back into his pocket, and stood a moment listening.   He felt somehow certain that she was not there.   And suddenly he came away, passing the little salon down the stairs.   He stopped at the bureau and said:

"Will you kindly see that Mrs. Heron has this note?"

"Madame Heron left to-day, Monsieur — sud-

denly, about three o'clock.   There was illness in
her family."

Soames compressed his lips.   " Oh! " he said;
" do you know her address? "

" *Non, Monsieur.*   England, I think."

Soames put the note back into his pocket and
went out.   He hailed an open horse-cab which was
passing.

" Drive me anywhere! "

The man, who, obviously, did not understand,
smiled, and waved his whip.   And Soames was
borne along in that little yellow-wheeled Victoria
all over star-shaped Paris, with here and there a
pause, and the question, " *C'est par ici, Monsieur?* "
" No, go on," till the man gave it up in despair, and
the yellow-wheeled chariot continued to roll between the tall, flat-fronted shuttered houses and
plane-tree avenues — a little Flying Dutchman of
a cab.

' Like my life,' thought Soames, ' without object,
on and on! '

CHAPTER II

IN THE WEB

SOAMES returned to England the following day, and on the third morning received a visit from Mr. Polteed, who wore a flower and carried a brown billycock hat. Soames motioned him to a seat.

" The news from the war is not so bad, is it? " said Mr. Polteed. " I hope I see you well, sir."

" Thanks! quite."

Mr. Polteed leaned forward, smiled, opened his hand, looked into it, and said softly:

" I think we've done your business for you at last."

" What? " ejaculated Soames.

" Nineteen reports quite suddenly what I think we shall be justified in calling conclusive evidence," and Mr. Polteed paused.

"Well? "

" On the 10th instant, after witnessing an interview between 17 and a party, earlier in the day, 19 can swear to having seen him coming out of her bedroom in the hotel about ten o'clock in the evening. With a little care in the giving of the evidence that will be enough, especially as 17 has left Paris — no doubt with the party in question. In fact, they both slipped off, and we haven't got on to them again, yet; but we shall — we shall. She's worked hard under very difficult circumstances, and I'm glad she's brought it off at last." Mr. Polteed took out a cigarette, tapped its end against the table, looked at Soames, and put it back. The expression on his client's face was not encouraging.

"Who is this new person?" said Soames abruptly.

" That we don't know. She'll swear to the fact, and she's got his appearance pat."

Mr. Polteed took out a letter, and began reading:

" ' Middle-aged, medium height, blue dittoes in afternoon, evening dress at night, pale, dark hair, small dark moustache, flat cheeks, good chin, grey eyes, small feet, guilty look —— ' "

Soames rose and went to the window. He stood there in sardonic fury. Congenital idiot — spidery congenital idiot! Seven months at fifteen pounds a week — to be tracked down as his own wife's lover! Guilty look! He threw the window open.

"It's hot," he said, and came back to his seat. Crossing his knees, he bent a supercilious glance on Mr. Polteed.

"I doubt if that's quite good enough," he said, drawling the words, "with no name or address. I think you may let that lady have a rest, and take up our friend 47 at this end." Whether Polteed had spotted him he could not tell; but he had a mental vision of him in the midst of his cronies dissolved in inextinguishable laughter. ' Guilty look! ' Damnation!

Mr. Polteed said in a tone of urgency, almost of pathos: " I assure you we have put it through sometimes on less than that. It's Paris, you know. Attractive woman living alone. Why not risk it, sir? We might screw it up a peg."

Soames had sudden insight. The fellow's professional zeal was stirred: 'Greatest triumph of my career; got a man his divorce through a visit to his own wife's bedroom! Something to talk of there, when I retire!' And for one wild moment he thought: 'Why not?' After all, hundreds of men of medium height had small feet and a guilty look!

"I'm not authorised to take any risk!" he said shortly.

Mr. Polteed looked up.

"Pity," he said, "quite a pity! That other affair seemed very costive."

Soames rose.

"Never mind that. Please watch 47, and take care not to find a mare's nest. Good-morning!"

Mr. Polteed's eye glinted at the words 'mare's nest!'

"Very good. You shall be kept informed."

And Soames was alone again. The spidery, dirty, ridiculous business! Laying his arms on the table, he leaned his forehead on them. Full ten minutes he rested thus, till a managing clerk roused him with the draft prospectus of a new issue of shares, very desirable, in Manifold and Topping's. That afternoon he left work early and made his way to the Restaurant Bretagne. Only Madame Lamotte was in. Would *Monsieur* have tea with her?

Soames bowed.

When they were seated at right angles to each other in the little room, he said abruptly:

"I want a talk with you, *Madame*."

The quick lift of her clear brown eyes told him that she had long expected such words.

" I have to ask you something first : That young doctor — what's his name? Is there anything between him and Annette? "

Her whole personality had become, as it were, like jet — clear-cut, black, hard, shining.

" Annette is young," she said ; " so is *monsieur le docteur*. Between young people things move quickly ; but Annette is a good daughter. Ah! what a jewel of a nature! "

The least little smile twisted Soames' lips.

" Nothing definite, then? "

" But definite — no, indeed! The young man is vereę nice, but — what would you? There is no money at present."

She raised her willow-patterned tea-cup ; Soames did the same. Their eyes met.

" I am a married man," he said, " living apart from my wife for many years. I am seeking to divorce her."

Madame Lamotte put down her cup. Indeed! What tragic things there were! The entire absence of sentiment in her inspired a queer species of contempt in Soames.

" I am a rich man," he added, fully conscious that the remark was not in good taste. " It is useless to say more at present, but I think you understand."

Madame's eyes, so open that the whites showed above them, looked at him very straight.

" *Ah! ça — mais nous avons le temps!* " was all she said. "Another little cup? " Soames refused, and, taking his leave, walked westward.

He had got that off his mind ; she would not let Annette commit herself with that cheerful young

ass until — !   But what chance of his ever being
able to say: ' I'm free.'   What chance?   The future had lost all semblance of reality.   He felt like
a fly, entangled in cobweb filaments, watching the
desirable freedom of the air with pitiful eyes.

He was short of exercise, and wandered on to
Kensington Gardens, and down Queen's Gate towards Chelsea.   Perhaps she had gone back to her
flat.   That at all events he could find out.   For
since that last and most ignominious repulse his
wounded self-respect had taken refuge again in the
feeling that she must have a lover.   He arrived
before the little Mansions at the dinner-hour.   No
need to enquire!   A grey-haired lady was watering
the flower-boxes in her window.   It was evidently
let.   And he walked slowly past again, along the
river — an evening of clear, quiet beauty, all harmony and comfort, except within his heart.

CHAPTER III

RICHMOND PARK

ON the afternoon that Soames crossed to France a cablegram was received by Jolyon at Robin Hill:

"Your son down with enteric no immediate danger will cable again."

It reached a household already agitated by the imminent departure of June, whose berth was booked for the following day. She was, indeed, in the act of confiding Eric Cobbley and his family to her father's care when the message arrived.

The resolution to become a Red Cross nurse, taken under stimulus of Jolly's enlistment, had been loyally fulfilled with the irritation and regret which all Forsytes feel at what curtails their individual liberties. Enthusiastic at first about the ' wonderfulness ' of the work, she had begun after a month to feel that she could train herself so much better than others could train her. And if Holly had not insisted on following her example, and being trained too, she must inevitably have 'cried off.' The departure of Jolly and Val with their troop in April had further stiffened her failing resolve. But now, on the point of departure, the thought of leaving Eric Cobbley, with a wife and two children, adrift in the cold waters of an unappreciative world weighed on her so that she was still in danger of backing out. The reading of that cablegram, with its disquieting reality, clinched the matter. She saw herself already nursing Jolly — for of course they would let her nurse her own brother! Jolyon — ever wide and doubtful — had no such hope. Poor June! Could any Forsyte of her generation grasp how rude and brutal life was? Ever since he knew of his boy's arrival at Cape Town the thought of him had been a kind of recurrent sickness in Jolyon. He could not get reconciled to the feeling that Jolly was in danger all the time. The cablegram, grave though it was, was almost a relief. He was now safe from bullets, anyway. And yet — this enteric was a virulent disease! *The Times* was full of deaths therefrom. Why could *he* not be lying out there in that up-country hospital, and his boy safe at home? The un-Forsytean self-sacrifice of his three children, indeed, had quite bewildered Jolyon. He would eagerly change places with Jolly, because he loved his boy; but no such personal motive was influencing *them*. He could only think that it marked the decline of the Forsyte type.

Late that afternoon Holly came out to him under the old oak-tree. She had grown up very much during these last months of hospital training away from home. And, seeing her approach, he thought: ' She has more sense than June, child though she is; more wisdom. Thank God *she* isn't going out.' She had seated herself in the swing, very silent and still. ' She feels this,' thought Jolyon, ' as much as I.' And, seeing her eyes fixed on him, he said: " Don't take it to heart too much, my child. If he weren't ill, he might be in much greater danger."

Holly got out of the swing.

" I want to tell you something, Dad. It was through me that Jolly enlisted and went out."

" How's that? "

" When you were away in Paris, Val Dartie and I fell in love. We used to ride in Richmond Park; we got engaged. Jolly found it out, and thought he ought to stop it; so he dared Val to enlist. It was all my fault, Dad; and I want to go out too. Because if anything happens to either of them I should feel awful. Besides, I'm just as much trained as June."

Jolyon gazed at her in a stupefaction that was tinged with irony. So this was the answer to the riddle he had been asking himself; and his three children were Forsytes after all. Surely Holly might have told him all this before! But he smothered the sarcastic sayings on his lips. Tenderness to the young was perhaps the most sacred article of his belief. He had got, no doubt, what he deserved. Engaged! So this was why he had so lost touch with her! And to young Val Dartie — nephew of Soames — in the other camp! It was all terribly distasteful. He closed his easel, and set his drawing against the tree.

" Have you told June? "

" Yes; she says she'll get me into her cabin somehow. It's a single cabin; but one of us could sleep on the floor. If you consent, she'll go up now and get permission."

"Consent? " thought Jolyon. ' Rather late in the day to ask for that! ' But again he checked himself.

" You're too young, my dear; they won't let you."

" June knows some people that she helped to go to Cape Town. If they won't let me nurse yet, I could stay with them and go on training there. Let me go, Dad! "

Jolyon smiled because he could have cried.

" I never stop anyone from doing anything," he said.

Holly flung her arms round his neck.

" Oh! Dad, you are the best in the world."

' That means the worst,' thought Jolyon. If he had ever doubted his creed of tolerance he did so then.

" I'm not friendly with Val's family," he said, " and I don't know Val, but Jolly didn't like him."

Holly looked at the distance, and said:

" I love him."

" That settles it," said Jolyon dryly, then catching the expression on her face, he kissed her, with the thought: ' Is anything more pathetic than the faith of the young?' Unless he actually forbade her going it was obvious that he must make the best of it, so he went up to town with June. Whether due to her persistence, or the fact that the official they saw was an old school friend of Jolyon's, they obtained permission for Holly to share the single cabin. He took them to Surbiton station the following evening, and they duly slid away from him, provided with money, invalid foods, and those letters of credit without which Forsytes do not travel.

He drove back to Robin Hill under a brilliant sky to his late dinner, served with an added care by servants trying to show him that they sympathised, eaten with an added scrupulousness to show them that he appreciated that sympathy. But it was a real relief to get to his cigar on the terrace of flagstones — cunningly chosen by young Bosinney for shape and colour — with night closing in around him, so beautiful a night, hardly whispering in the trees, and smelling so sweet that it made him ache. The grass was drenched with dew, and he kept to those flag-stones, up and down, till presently it began to seem to him that he was one of three, not wheeling, but turning right about at each end, so that his father was always nearest to the house, and his son always nearest to the terrace edge. Each had an arm lightly within his arm; he dared not lift his hand to his cigar lest he should disturb them. and it burned away, dripping ash on him, till it dropped from his lips, at last, which were getting hot. .They left him then, and his arms felt chilly. Three Jolyons in one Jolyon they had walked!

He stood still, counting the sounds — a carriage passing on the highroad, a distant train, the dog at Gage's farm, the whispering trees, the groom playing on his penny whistle. A multitude of stars up there — bright and silent, so far off! No moon as yet! Just enough light to show him the dark flags. and swords of the iris flowers along the terrace edge — his favourite flower that had the night's own colour on its curving crumpled petals. He turned round to the house. Big, unlighted, not a soul beside himself to live in all that part of it. Stark loneliness! He could not go on living here alone. And yet, so long as there was beauty, why should a man feel lonely? The answer — as to some idiot's riddle — was: Because he did. The greater the beauty, the greater the loneliness, for at the back of beauty was harmony, and at the back of harmony was — union. Beauty could not comfort if the soul were out of it. The night, maddeningly lovely, with bloom of grapes on it in star-shine, and the breath of grass and honey coming from it, he could not enjoy, while she who was to him the life of beauty, its embodiment and essence, was cut off from him, utterly cut off now, he felt, by honourable decency.

He made a poor fist of sleeping, striving too hard after that resignation which Forsytes find difficult to reach, bred to their own way and left so comfortably off by their fathers. But after dawn he dozed off, and soon was dreaming a strange dream.

He was on a stage with immensely high rich curtains — high as the very stars — stretching in a semi-circle from footlights to footlights. He himself was very small, a little black restless figure roaming up and down; and the odd thing was that he was not altogether himself, but Soames as well, so that he was not only experiencing but watching. This figure of himself and Soames was trying to find a way out through the curtains, which, heavy and dark, kept him in. Several times he had crossed in front of them before he saw with delight a sudden narrow rift — a tall chink of beauty the colour of iris flowers, like a glimpse of Paradise, remote, ineffable. Stepping quickly forward to pass into it, he found the curtains closing before him. Bitterly disappointed he — or was it Soames? — moved on, and there was the chink again through the parted curtains, which again closed too soon. This went on and on and he never got through till he woke with the word " Irene " on his lips. The dream disturbed him badly, especially that identification of himself with Soames.

Next morning, finding it impossible to work, he spent hours riding Jolly's horse in search of fatigue.

And on the second day he made up his mind to move to London and see if he could not get permission to follow his daughters to South Africa. He had just begun to pack the following morning when he received this letter:

> " GREEN HOTEL,
> " RICHMOND.
> "*June* 13.

" MY DEAR JOLYON,

" You will be surprised to see how near I am to you. Paris became impossible — and I have come here to be within reach of your advice. I would so love to see you again. Since you left Paris I don't think I have met anyone I could really talk to. Is all well with you and with your boy? No one knows, I think, that I am here at present.

> " Always your friend,
> " IRENE."

Irene within three miles of him! — and again in flight! He stood with a very queer smile on his lips. This was more than he had bargained for!

About noon he set out on foot across Richmond Park, and as he went along, he thought: ' Richmond Park! By Jove, it suits us Forsytes!' Not that Forsytes lived there — nobody lived there save royalty, rangers, and the deer — but in Richmond Park Nature was allowed to go so far and no further, putting up a brave show of being natural, seeming to say: ' Look at my instincts — they are almost passions, very nearly out of hand, but not quite, of course; the very hub of possession is to possess oneself.' Yes! Richmond Park possessed itself, even on that bright day of June, with arrowy cuckoos shifting the tree-points of their calls, and the wood doves announcing high summer.

The Green Hotel, which Jolyon entered at one o'clock, stood nearly opposite that more famous hostelry, the Crown and Sceptre; it was modest, highly respectable, never out of cold beef, gooseberry tart, and a dowager or two, so that a carriage and pair was almost always standing before the door.

In a room draped in chintz so slippery as to forbid all emotion, Irene was sitting on a piano stool covered with crewel work, playing 'Hansel and Gretel' out of an old score. Above her on a wall, not yet Morris-papered, was a print of the Queen on a pony, amongst deer-hounds, Scotch caps, and slain stags; beside her in a pot on the window-sill was a white and rosy fuchsia. The Victorianism of the room almost talked; and in her clinging frock Irene seemed to Jolyon like Venus emerging from the shell of the past century.

" If the proprietor had eyes," he said, " he would show you the door; you have broken through his decorations." Thus lightly he smothered up an emotional moment. Having eaten cold beef, pickled walnut, gooseberry-tart, and drunk stone-bottle ginger-beer, they walked into the Park, and light talk was succeeded by the silence Jolyon had dreaded.

" You haven't told me about Paris," he said at last.

" No. I've been shadowed for a long time; one gets used to that. But then Soames came. By the little Niobe — the same story; would I go back to him ? "

" Incredible ! "

She had spoken without raising her eyes, but she looked up now. Those dark eyes clinging to his said as no words could have: 'I have come to an end; if you want me, here I am.'

For sheer emotional intensity had he ever — old as he was — passed through such a moment?

The words: 'Irene, I adore you!' almost escaped him. Then, with a clearness of which he would not have believed mental vision capable, he saw Jolly lying with a white face turned to a white wall.

"My boy is very ill out there," he said quietly.

Irene slipped her arm through his.

"Let's walk on, I understand."

No miserable explanation to attempt! She had understood! And they walked on among the bracken, knee-high already, between the rabbit-holes and the oak-trees, talking of Jolly. He left her two hours later at the Richmond Hill Gate, and turned towards home.

'She knows of my feeling for her, then,' he thought. Of course! One could not keep knowledge of that from such a woman!

CHAPTER IV

JOLLY was tired to death of dreams. They had left him now too wan and weak to dream again; left him to lie torpid, faintly remembering far-off things; just able to turn his eyes and gaze through the window near his cot at the trickle of river running by in the sands, at the straggling milk-bush of the Karoo beyond. He knew what the Karoo was now, even if he had not seen a Boer roll over like a rabbit, or heard the whiffle of flying bullets. This pestilence had sneaked on him before he had smelled powder. A thirsty day and a rash drink, or perhaps a tainted fruit — who knew? Not he, who had not even strength left to grudge the evil thing its victory — just enough to know that there were many lying here with him, that he was sore with frenzied dreaming; just enough to watch that thread of river and be able to remember faintly those far-away things. . . .

The sun was nearly down. It would be cooler soon. He would have liked to know the time — to feel his old watch, so butter-smooth, to hear the repeater strike. It would have been friendly, home-like. He had not even strength to remember that the old watch was last wound the day he began to

lie here. The pulse of his brain beat so feebly that
faces which came and went, nurse's, doctor's, or-
derly's, were indistinguishable, just one indifferent
face; and the words spoken about him meant all the
same thing, and that almost nothing.   Those
things he used to do, though far and faint, were
more distinct — walking past the foot of the old
steps at Harrow 'bill' — 'Here, sir! Here, sir!'
— wrapping boots in the Westminster Gazette,
greenish paper, shining boots — grandfather coming from somewhere dark — a smell of earth — the
mushroom house! Robin Hill! Burying poor old
Balthasar in the leaves! Dad! Home.' . . .
Consciousness came again with noticing that the
river had no water in it — someone was speaking
too. Want anything? No. What could one
want? Too weak to want — only to hear his
watch strike. . . .
Holly! She wouldn't bowl properly. Oh!
Pitch them up! Not sneaks! . . . 'Back her,
Two and Bow!' He was Two! . . . Consciousness came once more with a sense of the violet dusk
outside, and a rising blood-red crescent moon. His
eyes rested on it fascinated; in the long minutes of
brain-nothingness it went moving up and up. . . .
"He's going, doctor!" Not pack boots again?
Never? 'Mind your form, Two!' Don't cry!
Go quietly — over the river — sleep! . . . Dark?
If somebody would — strike — his — watch! . . .

CHAPTER V

A SEALED letter in the handwriting of Mr. Polteed remained unopened in Soames' pocket throughout two hours of sustained attention to the affairs of the ' New Colliery Company,' which, declining almost from the moment of old Jolyon's retirement from the Chairmanship, had lately run down so fast that there was now nothing for it but a ' winding-up.' He took the letter out to lunch at his City Club, sacred to him for the meals he had eaten there with his father in the early seventies, when James used to like him to come and see for himself the nature of his future life.

Here in a remote corner before a plate of roast mutton and mashed potato, he read:

" DEAR SIR,
    " In accordance with your suggestion we have duly taken the matter up at the other end with gratifying results. Observation of 47 has enabled us to locate 17 at the Green Hotel, Richmond. The two have been observed to meet daily during the past week in Richmond Park. Nothing absolutely crucial has so far been notified. But in conjunction with what we had from Paris at the beginning of

296

the year, I am confident we could now satisfy the
Court. We shall, of course, continue to watch the
matter until we hear from you.
                    " Very faithfully yours,
                              " CLAUD POLTEED."

Soames read it through twice and beckoned to the
waiter.
" Take this away; it's cold."
" Shall I bring you some more, sir? "
" No. Get me some coffee in the other room."
And, paying for what he had not eaten, he went
out, passing two acquaintances without sign of recognition.
' Satisfy the Court! ' he thought, sitting at a little
round marble table with the coffee before him.
That fellow Jolyon! He poured out his coffee,
sweetened and drank it. He would disgrace him in
the eyes of his own children! And rising, with that
resolution hot within him, he found for the first time
the inconvenience of being his own solicitor. He
could not treat this scandalous matter in his own
office. He must commit the soul of his private dignity to a stranger, some other professional dealer in
family dishonour. Who was there he could go to?
Linkman and Laver in Budge Row, perhaps — re-
liable, not too conspicuous, only nodding acquaintances. But before he saw them he must see Polteed again. But at this thought Soames had a moment of sheer weakness. To part with his secret?
How find the words? How subject himself to contempt and secret laughter? Yet, after all, the fellow knew already — oh yes, he knew. And, feeling
that he must finish with it now, he took a cab into
the West End.

In this hot weather the window of Mr. Polteed's room was positively open, and the only precaution was a wire gauze, preventing the intrusion of flies. Two or three had tried to come in, and been caught, so that they seemed to be clinging there with the intention of being devoured presently. Mr. Polteed, following the direction of his client's eye, rose apologetically and closed the window.

'Posing ass!' thought Soames. Like all who fundamentally believe in themselves he was rising to the occasion, and, with his little sideway smile, he said: " I've had your letter. I'm going to act. I suppose you know who the lady you've been watching really is? "

Mr. Polteed's expression at that moment was a masterpiece. It so clearly said: ' Well, what do you think? But mere professional knowledge, I assure you — pray forgive it! ' He made a little half airy movement with his hand, as who should say: ' Such things — such things will happen to us! '

" Very well, then," said Soames, moistening his lips; " there's no need to say more. I'm instructing Linkman and Laver of Budge Row to act for me. I don't want to hear your evidence, but kindly make your report to them at five o'clock, and continue to observe the utmost secrecy."

Mr. Polteed half closed his eyes, as if to comply at once. " My dear sir," he said.

" Are you convinced," asked Soames with sudden energy, " that there is enough? "

The faintest movement occurred to Mr. Polteed's shoulders.

" You can risk it," he murmured; " with what we have, and human nature, you can risk it."

Soames rose. " You will ask for Mr. Linkman.

Thanks; don't get up." He could not bear Mr. Polteed to slide as usual between him and the door.
In the sunlight of Piccadilly he wiped his forehead.
This had been the worst of it — he could stand the
strangers better. And he went back into the City
to do what still lay before him.

That evening in Park Lane, watching his father
dine, he was overwhelmed by his old longing for a
son — a son, to watch *him* eat as he went down the
years, to be taken on *his* knee as James on a time
had been wont to take him; a son of his own begetting, who could understand him because he was the
same flesh and blood — understand, and comfort
him, and become more rich and cultured than himself because he would start even better off. To get
old — like that thin, grey, wiry-frail figure sitting
there — and quite alone with possessions heaping
up around him; to take no interest in anything because it had no future and must pass away from
him to hands and mouths and eyes for whom he
cared no jot! No! He would force it through now,
and be free to marry, and have a son to care for him
before he grew to be like the old old man his father,
wistfully watching now his sweetbread, now his son.

In that mood he went up to bed. But, lying warm
between those fine linen sheets of Emily's providing,
he was visited by memories and torture. Visions of
Irene, almost the solid feeling of her body, beset
him. Why had he ever been fool enough to see her
again, and let his flood back on him so that it was
pain to think of her with that fellow — that stealing
fellow!

CHAPTER VI

A SUMMER DAY

HIS boy was seldom absent from Jolyon's mind in the days which followed the first walk with Irene in Richmond Park. No further news had come; enquiries at the War Office elicited nothing; nor could he expect to hear from June and Holly for three weeks at least. In these days he felt how insufficient were his memories of Jolly, and what an amateur of a father he had been. There was not a single memory in which anger played a part; not one reconciliation, because there had never been a rupture; nor one heart-to-heart confidence, not even when Jolly's mother died. Nothing but half-ironical affection. He had been too afraid of committing himself in any direction, for fear of losing his liberty, or interfering with that of his boy.

Only in Irene's presence had he relief, highly complicated by the ever-growing perception of how divided he was between her and his son. With Jolly was bound up all that sense of continuity and social creed of which he had drunk deeply in his youth and again during his boy's public school and varsity life — all that sense of not going back on what father and son expected of each other. With Irene was bound up all his delight in beauty and in Nature. And he seemed to know less and less which was the stronger within him. From such sentimental paralysis he was rudely awakened, however, one afternoon, just as he was starting off to Richmond, by a young man with a bicycle and a face oddly familiar, who came forward faintly smiling.

"Mr. Jolyon Forsyte? Thank you!" Placing an envelope in Jolyon's hand he wheeled off the path and rode away. Bewildered, Jolyon opened it.

"Admiralty Probate and Divorce, Forsyte v. Forsyte and Forsyte!" A sensation of shame and disgust was followed by the instant reaction: 'Why! here's the very thing you want, and you don't like it!' But she must have had one too; and he must go to her at once. He turned things over as he went along. It was an ironical business. For, whatever the Scriptures said about the heart, it took more than mere longings to satisfy the law. They could perfectly well defend this suit, or at least in good faith try to. But the idea of doing so revolted Jolyon. If not her lover in deed he was in desire, and he knew that she was ready to come to him. Her face had told him so. Not that he exaggerated her feeling for him. She had had her grand passion, and he could not expect another from her at his age. But she had trust in him, affection for him; and must feel that he would be a refuge. Surely she would not ask him to defend the suit, knowing that he adored her! Thank Heaven she had not that maddening British conscientiousness which refused happiness for the sake of refusing! She must rejoice at this chance of being free — after seventeen years of death in life! As to publicity, the fat was in the fire! To defend the suit would not take away the slur. Jolyon had all the proper feeling of a

Forsyte whose privacy is threatened: If he was to
be hung by the Law, by all means let it be for a
sheep! Moreover the notion of standing in a witness box and swearing to the truth that no gesture,
not even a word of love had passed between them
seemed to him more degrading than to take the tacit
stigma of being an adulterer — more truly degrading, considering the feeling in his heart, and just as
bad and painful for his children. The thought of
explaining away, if he could, before a judge and
twelve average Englishmen, their meetings in Paris,
and the walks in Richmond Park, horrified him.
The brutality and hypocritical censoriousness of the
whole process; the probability that they would not
be believed — the mere vision of her, whom he
looked on as the embodiment of Nature and of
Beauty, standing there before all those suspicious,
gloating eyes was hideous to him. No, no! To defend a suit only made a London holiday, and sold
the newspapers. A thousand times better accept
what Soames and the gods had sent!

'Besides,' he thought honestly, 'who knows
whether, even for my boy's sake, I could have stood
this state of things much longer? Anyway, her
neck will be out of chancery at last!' Thus absorbed, he was hardly conscious of the heavy heat.
The sky had become overcast, purplish, with little
streaks of white. A heavy heat-drop plashed a little
star pattern in the dust of the road as he entered
the Park. 'Phew!' he thought, 'thunder! I hope
she's not come to meet me; there's a ducking up
there!' But at that very minute he saw Irene coming towards the Gate. 'We must scuttle back to
Robin Hill,' he thought.

     *   *   *   *   *   *

The storm had passed over the Poultry at four o'clock, bringing welcome distraction to the clerks in every office. Soames was drinking a cup of tea when a note was brought in to him:

"DEAR SIR,

Forsyte v. Forsyte and Forsyte

"In accordance with your instructions, we beg to inform you that we personally served the respondent and co-respondent in this suit to-day, at Richmond, and Robin Hill, respectively.

"Faithfully yours,
"LINKMAN AND LAVER."

For some minutes Soames stared at that note. Ever since he had given those instructions he had been tempted to annul them. It was so scandalous, such a general disgrace! The evidence, too, what he had heard of it, had never seemed to him conclusive; somehow, he believed less and less that those two had gone all lengths. But this, of course, would drive them to it; and he suffered from the thought. That fellow to have her love, where he had failed! Was it too late? Now that they had been brought up sharp by service of this petition, had he not a lever with which he could force them apart? 'But if I don't act at once,' he thought, 'it will be too late, now they've had this thing. I'll go and see him; I'll go down!'

And sick with nervous anxiety, he sent out for one of the 'new-fangled' motor-cabs. It might take a long time to run that fellow to ground, and Goodness knew what decision they might come to after such a shock! 'If I were a theatrical ass,' he thought, 'I suppose I should be taking a horse-whip

or a pistol or something!' He took instead a bundle
of papers in the case of 'Magentie versus Wake,'
intending to read them on the way down. He did
not even open them, but sat quite still, jolted and
jarred, unconscious of the draught down the back
of his neck, or the smell of petrol. He must be
guided by the fellow's attitude; the great thing was
to keep his head!

London had already begun to disgorge its work-
ers as he neared Putney Bridge; the ant-heap was
on the move outwards. What a lot of ants, all with
a living to get, holding on by their eyelids in the
great scramble! Perhaps for the first time in his
life Soames thought: '*I* could let go if I liked!
Nothing could touch me; I could snap my fingers,
live as I wished — enjoy myself!' No! One could
not live as he had and just drop it all — settle down
in Capua, to spend the money and reputation he had
made. A man's life was what he possessed and
sought to possess. Only fools thought otherwise
— fools, and socialists, and libertines!

The cab was passing villas now, going a great
pace. 'Fifteen miles an hour, I should think!' he
mused; 'this'll take people out of town to live!' and
he thought of its bearing on the portions of London
owned by his father — he himself had never taken
to that form of investment, the gambler in him having all the outlet needed in his pictures. And the
cab sped on, down the hill past Wimbledon Common. This interview! Surely a man of fifty-one
with grown-up children, and hung on the line,
would not be reckless. 'He won't want to disgrace
the family,' he thought; 'he was as fond of his
father as I am of mine, and they were brothers.
That woman brings destruction — what is it in her?'

I've never known.' The cab branched off, along
the side of a wood, and he heard a late cuckoo calling, almost the first he had heard that year. He
was now almost opposite the site he had originally
chosen for his house, and which had been so un-
ceremoniously rejected by Bosinney in favour of
his own choice. He began passing his handkerchief over his face and hands, taking deep breaths
to give him steadiness. 'Keep one's head,' he
thought, 'keep one's head!'

The cab turned in at the drive which might have
been his own, and the sound of music met him. He
had forgotten the fellow's daughters.

"I may be out again directly," he said to the
driver, "or I may be kept some time;" and he rang
the bell.

Following the maid through the curtains into the
inner hall, he felt relieved that the impact of this
meeting would be broken by June or Holly, which-
ever was playing in there, so that with complete
surprise he saw Irene at the piano, and Jolyon sitting in an armchair listening. They both stood up.
Blood surged into Soames' brain, and all his resolution to be guided by this or that left him utterly.
The look of his farmer forbears — dogged Forsytes down by the sea, from 'Superior Dosset'
back — grinned out of his face.

"Very pretty!" he said.

He heard the fellow murmur:

"This is hardly the place — we'll go to the study,
if you don't mind." And they both passed him
through the curtain opening. In the little room to
which he followed them, Irene stood by the open
window, and the 'fellow' close to her by a big
chair. Soames pulled the door to behind him with

a slam; the sound carried him back all those years to the day when he had shut out Jolyon — shut him out for meddling with his affairs.

"Well," he said, "what have you to say for yourselves?"

The fellow had the effrontery to smile.

"What we have received to-day has taken away your right to ask. I should imagine you will be glad to have your neck out of chancery."

"Oh!" said Soames; "you think so! I came to tell you that I'll divorce her with every circumstance of disgrace to you both, unless you swear to keep clear of each other from now on."

He was astonished at his fluency, because his mind was stammering and his hands twitching. Neither of them answered; but their faces seemed to him as if contemptuous.

"Well," he said; "you — Irene?"

Her lips moved, but Jolyon laid his hand on her arm.

"Let her alone!" said Soames furiously. "Irene, will you swear it?"

"No."

"Oh! and you?"

"Still less."

"So then you're guilty, are you?"

"Yes, guilty." It was Irene speaking in that serene voice, with that unreached air which had maddened him so often; and, carried beyond himself, he cried:

"*You* are a devil."

"Go out! Leave this house, or I'll do you an injury." That fellow to talk of injuries! Did he know how near his throat was to being scragged?

"A trustee," he said, "embezzling trust property! A thief, stealing his cousin's wife."

" Call me what you like. You have chosen your part, we have chosen ours. Go out! "

If he had brought a weapon Soames might have used it at that moment.

" I'll make you pay! " he said.

" I shall be very happy."

At that deadly turning of the meaning of his speech by the son of him who had nicknamed him ' the man of property,' Soames stood glaring. It was ridiculous!

There they were, kept from violence by some secret force. No blow possible, no words to meet the case. But he could not, did not know how to turn and go away. His eyes fastened on Irene's face — the last time he would ever see that fatal face — the last time, no doubt!

" You," he said suddenly, " I hope you'll treat him as you treated me — that's all."

He saw her wince, and with a sensation not quite triumph, not quite relief, he wrenched open the door, passed out through the hall, and got into his cab. He lolled against the cushion with his eyes shut. Never in his life had he been so near to murderous violence, never so thrown away the restraint which was his second nature. He had a stripped and naked feeling, as if all virtue had gone out of him — life meaningless, mind striking work. Sunlight streamed in on him, but he felt cold. The scene he had passed through had gone from him already, what was before him would not materialise, he could catch on to nothing; and he felt frightened, as if he had been hanging over the edge of a precipice, as if with another turn of the screw sanity would have failed him. 'I'm not fit for it,' he thought; ' I mustn't — I'm not fit for it.' The cab sped on, and in mechanical procession trees, houses, people passed, but had no significance. 'I feel very queer,' he thought; 'I'll take a Turkish bath. I — I've been very near to something. It won't do.' The cab whirred its way back over the bridge, up the Fulham Road, along the Park.

"To the Hammam," said Soames.

Curious that on so warm a summer day, heat should be so comforting! Crossing into the hot room he met George Forsyte coming out, red and glistening.

"Hallo!" said George; "what are you training for? You've not got much superfluous."

Buffoon! Soames passed him with his sideway smile. Lying back, rubbing his skin uneasily for the first signs of perspiration, he thought: 'Let them laugh! I *won't* feel anything! I can't stand violence! It's not good for me!'

CHAPTER VII

SOAMES left dead silence in the little study.

"Thank you for that good lie," said Jolyon suddenly. "Come out — the air in here is not what it was!"

In front of a long high southerly wall on which were trained peach-trees, the two walked up and down in silence. Old Jolyon had planted some cupressus-trees, at intervals, between this grassy terrace and the dipping meadow full of buttercups and ox-eyed daisies; for twelve years they had flourished, till their dark spiral shapes had quite a look of Italy. Birds fluttered softly in the wet shrubbery; the swallows swooped past, with a steel-blue sheen on their swift little bodies; the grass felt springy beneath the feet, its green refreshed; and butterflies chased each other. After that painful scene the quiet of Nature was wonderfully poignant. Under the sun-soaked wall ran a narrow strip of garden-bed full of mignonette and pansies, and from the bees came a low hum in which all other sounds were set — the mooing of a cow deprived of her calf, the calling of a cuckoo from an elm-tree at the bottom of the meadow. Who would have thought that behind them, within ten miles, London began — that London of the Forsytes, with its wealth, its misery; its dirt and noise; its jumbled stone isles of beauty, its grey sea of hideous brick and stucco? That London which had seen Irene's early tragedy, and Jolyon's own hard days; that web; that princely workhouse of the possessive instinct!

And while they walked Jolyon pondered those words: 'I hope you'll treat him as you treated me.' That would depend on himself. Could he trust himself? Did Nature permit a Forsyte not to make a slave of what he adored? Could beauty be confided to him? Or should she not be just a visitor, coming when she would, possessed for moments which passed, to return only at her own choosing? 'We are a breed of spoilers!' thought Jolyon, 'close and greedy; the bloom of life is not safe with us. Let her come to me as she will, when she will, not at all if she will not. Let me be just her stand-by, her perching-place; never — never her cage!'

She was the chink of beauty in his dream. Was he to pass through the curtains now and reach her? Was the rich stuff of many possessions, the close encircling fabric of the possessive instinct walling in that little black figure of himself, and Soames — was it to be rent so that he could pass through into his vision, find there something not out of the senses only? 'Let me,' he thought, 'ah! let me only know how not to grasp and destroy!'

But at dinner there were plans to be made. To-night she would go back to the hotel, but to-morrow he would take her up to London. He must instruct his solicitor — Jack Herring. Not a finger must be raised to hinder the process of the Law. Dam-

ages exemplary, judicial strictures, costs, what they
liked — let it go through at the first moment, so
that her neck might be out of chancery at last! To-
morrow he would see Herring — they would go
and see him together. And then — abroad, leaving
no doubt, no difficulty about evidence, making the
lie she had told into the truth. He looked round at
her; and it seemed to his adoring eyes that more
than a woman was sitting there. The spirit of universal beauty, deep, mysterious, which the old painters, Titian, Giorgione, Botticelli, had known how
to capture and transfer to the faces of their women
— this flying beauty seemed to him imprinted on
her brow, her hair, her lips, and in her eyes.

' And this is to be mine!' he thought. ' It fright-
ens me!'

After dinner they went out on to the terrace to
have coffee. They sat there long, the evening was
so lovely, watching the summer night come very
slowly on. It was still warm and the air smelled
of lime blossom — early this summer. Two bats
were flighting with the faint mysterious little noise
they make. He had placed the chairs in front of
the study window, and moths flew past to visit the
discreet light in there. There was no wind, and not
a whisper in the old oak-tree twenty yards away!
The moon rose from behind the copse, nearly full;
and the two lights struggled, till moonlight conquered, changing the colour and quality of all the
garden, stealing along the flagstones, reaching
their feet, climbing up, changing their faces.

" Well," said Jolyon at last, " you'll be so tired;
we'd better start. The maid will show you Holly's
room," and he rang the study bell. The maid who
came handed him a telegram. Watching her take

Irene away, he thought: ' This must have come an
hour or more ago, and she didn't bring it out to us!
That shows! Well, we'll be hung for a sheep soon!'
And, opening the telegram, he read:

"JOLYON FORSYTE, Robin Hill.— Your son passed
painlessly away on June 20th. Deep sympathy "
— some name unknown to him.

He dropped it, spun round, stood motionless.
The moon shone in on him; a moth flew in his face.
The first day of all that he had not thought almost
ceaselessly of Jolly. He went blindly towards the
window, struck against the old armchair — his
father's — and sank down on to the arm of it. He
sat there huddled forward, staring into the night.
Gone out like a candle flame; far from home, from
love, all by himself, in the dark! His boy! From
a little chap always so good to him — so friendly!
Twenty years old, and cut down like grass — to
have no life at all! ' I didn't really know him,' he
thought, ' and he didn't know me; but we loved
each other. It's only love that matters.'

To die out there — lonely — wanting them —
wanting home! This seemed to his Forsyte heart
more painful, more pitiful than death itself. No
shelter, no protection, no love at the last! And all
the deeply rooted clanship in him, the family feeling and essential clinging to his own flesh and blood
which had been so strong in old Jolyon — was so
strong in all the Forsytes — felt outraged, cut, and
torn by his boy's lonely passing. Better far if he
had died in battle, without time to long for them to
come to him, to call out for them, perhaps, in his
delirium!

The moon had passed behind the oak-tree now,
endowing it with uncanny life, so that it seemed

watching him— the oak-tree his boy had been so fond of climbing, out of which he had once fallen and hurt himself, and hadn't cried!

The door creaked. He saw Irene come in, pick up the telegram and read it. He heard the faint rustle of her dress. She sank on her knees close to him, and he forced himself to smile at her. She stretched up her arms and drew his head down on her shoulder. The perfume and warmth of her encircled him; her presence gained slowly his whole being.

CHAPTER VIII

SWEATED to serenity, Soames dined at the Remove and turned his face toward Park Lane. His father had been unwell lately. This would have to be kept from him! Never till that moment had he realised how much the dread of bringing James' grey hairs down with sorrow to the grave had counted with him; how intimately it was bound up with his own shrinking from scandal. His affection for his father, always deep, had increased of late years with the knowledge that James looked on him as the real prop of his decline. It seemed pitiful that one who had been so careful all his life and done so much for the family name — so that it was almost a byword for solid, wealthy respectability — should at his last gasp have to see it in all the newspapers. This was like lending a hand to Death, that final enemy of Forsytes. 'I must tell mother,' he thought, 'and when it comes on, we must keep the papers from him somehow. He sees hardly anyone.' Letting himself in with his latchkey, he was beginning to ascend the stairs when he became conscious of commotion on the second-floor landing. His mother's voice was saying:

" Now, James, you'll catch cold. Why can't you wait quietly? "

His father's answering:

" Wait? I'm always waiting. Why doesn't he come in? "

" You can speak to him to-morrow morning, instead of making a guy of yourself on the landing."

" He'll go up to bed, I shouldn't wonder. I shan't sleep."

" Now come back to bed, James."

" Um! I might die before to-morrow morning for all you can tell."

" You shan't have to wait till to-morrow morning; I'll go down and bring him up. Don't fuss! "

" There you go — always so cock-a-hoop. He mayn't come in at all."

" Well, if he doesn't come in you won't catch him by standing out here in your dressing-gown."

Soames rounded the last bend and came in sight of his father's tall figure wrapped in a brown silk quilted gown, stooping over the balustrade above. Light fell on his silvery hair and whiskers, investing his head with a sort of halo.

"Here he is! " he heard him say in a voice which sounded injured, and his mother's comfortable answer from the bed-room door:

" That's all right. Come in, and I'll brush your hair." James extended a thin, crooked finger, oddly like the beckoning of a skeleton, and passed through the doorway of his bedroom.

' What is it? ' thought Soames. ' What has he got hold of now? '

His father was sitting before the dressing-table sideways to the mirror, while Emily slowly passed two silver-backed brushes through and through his hair. She would do this several times a day, for it had on him something of the effect produced on a cat by scratching between its ears.

"There you are!" he said. " I've been waiting."

Soames stroked his shoulder, and, taking up a silver buttonhook, examined the mark on it.

" Well," he said, " you're looking better."

James shook his head.

" I want to say something. Your mother hasn't heard." He announced Emily's ignorance of what he hadn't told her, as if it were a grievance.

" Your father's been in a great state all the evening. I'm sure I don't know what about." The faint ' whish-whish ' of the brushes continued the soothing of her voice.

"No! *you* know nothing," said James. " Soames can tell me." And, fixing his grey eyes, in which there was a look of strain, uncomfortable to watch, on his son, he muttered:

" I'm getting on, Soames. At my age I can't tell. I might die any time. There'll be a lot of money. There's Rachel and Cicely got no children; and Val's out there — that chap his father will get hold of all he can. And somebody'll pick up Imogen, I shouldn't wonder."

Soames listened vaguely — he had heard all this before. Whish-whish! went the brushes.

" If that's all —— !" said Emily.

" All!" cried James; " it's nothing. I'm coming to that." And again his eyes strained pitifully at Soames.

" It's you, my boy," he said suddenly; " you ought to get a divorce."

That word, from those of all lips, was almost too much for Soames' composure. His eyes reconcentrated themselves quickly on the buttonhook, and as if in apology James hurried on:

" I don't know what's become of her — they say she's abroad. Your Uncle Swithin used to admire her — he was a funny fellow." (So he always alluded to his dead twin — ' The Stout and the Lean of it,' they had been called.) " She wouldn't be alone, I should say." And with that summing-up of the effect of beauty on human nature, he was silent, watching his son with eyes doubting as a bird's. Soames, too, was silent. Whish-whish! went the brushes.

" Come, James! Soames knows best. It's his business."

" Ah!" said James, and the word came from deep down; " but there's all my money, and there's his — who's it to go to? And when he dies the name goes out."

Soames replaced the buttonhook on the lace and pink silk of the dressing-table coverlet.

" The name?" said Emily, " there are all the other Forsytes."

" As if that helped *me*," muttered James. " I shall be in my grave, and there'll be nobody, unless he marries again."

" You 're quite right," said Soames quietly; " I 'm getting a divorce."

James' eyes almost started from his head.

" What?" he cried. " There! nobody tells me anything."

" Well," said Emily, " who would have imagined you wanted it? My dear boy, that *is* a surprise, after all these years."

" It'll be a scandal," muttered James, as if to himself; " but I can't help that. Don't brush so hard. When'll it come on?"

" Before the Long Vacation; it's not defended."

James' lips moved in secret calculation.   " I shan't live to see my grandson," he muttered.

Emily ceased brushing.   " Of course you will, James.   Soames will be as quick as he can."

There was a long silence, till James reached out his arm.

" Here! let's have the eau-de-Cologne," and, putting it to his nose, he moved his forehead in the direction of his son.   Soames bent over and kissed that brow just where the hair began.   A relaxing quiver passed over James' face, as though the wheels of anxiety within were running down.

" I'll get to bed," he said; " I shan't want to see the papers when that comes.   They're a morbid lot; but I can't pay attention to them, I'm too old."

Queerly affected, Soames went to the door; he heard his father say:

" Here, I'm tired.   I'll say a prayer in bed."

And his mother answering:

" That's right, James; it'll be ever so much more comfy."

CHAPTER IX

On Forsyte 'Change the announcement of Jolly's death, among a batch of troopers, caused mixed sensation. Strange to read that Jolyon Forsyte (fifth of the name in direct descent) had died of disease in the service of his country, and not be able to feel it personally. It revived the old grudge against his father for having estranged himself. For such was still the prestige of old Jolyon that the other Forsytes could never quite feel, as might have been expected, that it was they who had cut off his descendants for irregularity. The news increased, of course, the interest and anxiety about Val; but then Val's name was Dartie, and even if he were killed in battle or got the Victoria Cross, it would not be at all the same as if his name were Forsyte. Not even casualty or glory to the Haymans would be really satisfactory. Family pride felt defrauded.

How the rumour arose, then, that 'something very dreadful, my dear,' was pending, no one, least of all Soames, could tell, secret as he kept everything. Possibly some eye had seen 'Forsyte v. Forsyte and Forsyte' in the cause list; and had added it to 'Irene in Paris with a fair beard.' Possibly

some wall at Park Lane had ears.   The fact remained that it *was* known — whispered among the
old, discussed among the young — that family pride
must soon receive a blow.

Soames, paying one of his Sunday visits to Timothy's — paying it with the feeling that after the
suit came on he would be paying no more — felt
knowledge in the air as he came in.   Nobody, of
course, dared speak of it before him, but each of
the four other Forsytes present held their breath,
aware that nothing could prevent Aunt Juley from
making them all uncomfortable.   She looked so
piteously at Soames, she checked herself on the
point of speech so often, that Aunt Hester excused
herself and said she must go and bathe Timothy's
eye — he had a sty coming.   Soames, impassive,
slightly supercilious, did not stay long.   He went
out with a curse stifled behind his pale, just smiling
lips.

Fortunately for the peace of his mind, cruelly tortured by the coming scandal, he was kept busy day
and night with plans for his retirement — for he
had come to that grim conclusion.   To go on seeing
all those people who had known him as a 'long-
headed chap,' an astute adviser — after *that* — no!
The   fastidiousness   and   pride   which   was   so
strangely, so inextricably blended in him with possessive obtuseness, revolted against the thought.
He would retire, live privately, go on buying pictures, make a great name as a collector — after all,
his heart was more in that than it had ever been in
Law.   In pursuance of this now fixed resolve, he
had to get ready to amalgamate his business with
another firm without letting people know, for that
would excite curiosity and make humiliation cast

its shadow before.   He had pitched on the firm of
Cuthcott, Holliday, Kingson, two of whom were
dead.   The full name after the amalgamation would
therefore be Cuthcott, Holliday, Kingson, Forsyte,
Bustard and Forsyte.   But after debate as to which
of the dead still had any influence with the living,
it was decided to reduce the title to Cuthcott, Kingson and Forsyte, of whom Kingson would be the
active and Soames the sleeping partner.   For leaving his name, prestige, and clients behind him,
Soames would receive considerable value.

One night, as befitted a man who had arrived at
so important a stage of his career, he made a calculation of what he was worth, and after writing
off liberally for depreciation by the war, found his
value to be some hundred and thirty thousand
pounds.   At his father's death, which could not,
alas, be delayed much longer, he must come into at
least another fifty thousand, and his yearly expen-
diture at present just reached two.   Standing among
his pictures, he saw before him a future full of bargains earned by the trained faculty of knowing
better than other people.   Selling what was about
to decline, keeping what was still going up, and
exercising judicious insight into future taste, he
would make a unique collection, which at his death
would pass to the nation under the title 'Forsyte
Bequest.'

If the divorce went through, he had determined
on his line with Madame Lamotte.   She had, he
knew, but one real ambition — to live on her
'rentes' in Paris near her grandchildren.   He
would buy the goodwill of the Restaurant Bretagne
at a fancy price.   Madame would live like a Queen-
Mother in Paris on the interest, invested as she

would know how. (Incidentally Soames meant to put a capable manager in her place, and make the restaurant pay good interest on his money. There were great possibilities in Soho.) On Annette he would promise to settle fifteen thousand pounds (whether designedly or not), precisely the sum old Jolyon had settled on 'that woman.'

A letter from Jolyon's solicitor to his own had disclosed the fact that 'those two' were in Italy. And an opportunity had been duly given for noting that they had first stayed at a hotel in London. The matter was clear as daylight, and would be disposed of in half an hour or so; but during that half-hour he, Soames, would go down to hell; and after that half-hour all bearers of the Forsyte name would feel the bloom was off the rose. He had no illusions like Shakespeare that roses by any other name would smell as sweet. The name was a possession, a concrete, unstained piece of property, the value of which would be reduced some twenty per cent. at least. Unless it were Roger, who had once refused to stand for Parliament, and — oh, irony! — Jolyon, hung on the line, there had never been a distinguished Forsyte. But that very lack of distinction was the name's greatest asset. It was a private name, intensely individual, and his own property; it had never been exploited for good or evil by intrusive report. He and each member of his family owned it wholly, sanely, secretly, without any more interference from the public than had been necessitated by their births, their marriages, their deaths. And during these weeks of waiting and preparing to drop the Law, he conceived for that Law a bitter distaste, so deeply did he resent its coming violation of his name, forced on him by the need he felt to perpetuate that name in a lawful manner. The monstrous injustice of the whole thing excited in him a perpetual suppressed fury. He had asked no better than to live in spotless domesticity, and now he must go into the witness box, after all these futile, barren years, and proclaim his failure to keep his wife — incur the pity, the amusement, the contempt of his kind. It was all upside down. She and that fellow ought to be the sufferers, and they — were in Italy! In these weeks the Law he had served so faithfully, looked on so reverently as the guardian of all property, seemed to him quite pitiful. What could be more insane than to tell a man that he owned his wife,· and punish him when someone unlawfully took her away from him? Did the law not know that a man's name was to him the apple of his eye, that it was far harder to be regarded as cuckold than as seducer? He actually envied Jolyon the reputation of succeeding where he, Soames, had failed. The question of damages worried him, too. He wanted to make that fellow suffer, but he remembered his cousin's words, "I shall be very happy," with the uneasy feeling that to claim damages would make not Jolyon but himself suffer; he felt uncannily that Jolyon would rather like to pay them — the chap was so loose. Besides, to claim damages was not the thing to do. The claim, indeed, had been made almost mechanically; and as the hour drew near Soames saw in it just another dodge of this insensitive and topsy-turvy Law to ·make him ridiculous; so that people might sneer and say: "Oh yes, he got quite a good price for her!" And he gave instructions that his Counsel should state that the money would be given to a

Home for Fallen Women. He was a long time hitting off exactly the right charity; but, having pitched on it, he used to wake up in the night and think: ' It won't do, too lurid; it'll draw attention. Something quieter — better taste.' He did not care for dogs, or he would have named them; and it was in desperation at last — for his knowledge of charities was limited — that he decided on the blind. That could not be inappropriate, and it would make the Jury assess the damages high.

A good many suits were dropping out of the list, which happened to be exceptionally thin that summer, so that his case would be reached before August. As the day grew nearer, Winifred was his only comfort. She showed the fellow-feeling of one who had been through the mill, and was the ' feme-sole ' in whom he confided, well knowing that she would not let Dartie into her confidence. That ruffian would be only too rejoiced! At the end of July, on the afternoon before the case, he went in to see her. They had not yet been able to leave town, because Dartie had already spent their summer holiday, and Winifred dared not go to her father for more money while he was waiting not to be told anything about this affair of Soames.

Soames found her with a letter in her hand.

" That from Val? " he asked gloomily. " What does he say? "

" He says he's married," said Winifred.

" Whom to, for Goodness' sake? "

Winifred looked at him.

" To Holly Forsyte, Jolyon's daughter."

" What? "

" He got leave and did it. I didn't even know he knew her. Awkward, isn't it? "

Soames uttered a short laugh at that characteristic minimisation.

"Awkward! Well, I don't suppose they'll hear
about this till they come back. They'd better stay
out there. That fellow will give her money."

"But I want Val back," said Winifred almost
piteously; "I miss him; he helps me to get on."

"I know," murmured Soames. "How's Dartie
behaving now?"

"It might be worse; but it's always money.
Would you like me to come down to the Court to-
morrow, Soames?"

Soames stretched out his hand for hers. The
gesture so betrayed the loneliness in him that she
pressed it between her two.

"Never mind, old boy. You'll feel ever so much
better when it's all over."

"I don't know what I've done," said Soames
huskily; "I never have. It's all upside down. I
was fond of her; I've always been."

Winifred saw a drop of blood ooze out of his lip,
and the sight stirred her profoundly.

"Of course," she said, "it's been *too* bad of her
all along! But what shall I do about this marriage
of Val's, Soames? I don't know how to write to
him, with this coming on. You've seen that child.
Is she pretty?"

"Yes, she's pretty," said Soames. "Dark—
lady-like enough."

'That doesn't sound so bad,' thought Winifred.
'Jolyon had style.'

"It *is* a coil," she said. "What will father say?"

"Mustn't be told," said Soames. "The war'll
soon be over now, you'd better let Val take to farm-
ing out there."

It was tantamount to saying that his nephew was lost.

"I haven't told Monty," Winifred murmured desolately.

The case was reached before noon next day, and was over in little more than half an hour. Soames — pale, spruce, sad-eyed in the witness box — had suffered so much beforehand that he took it all like one dead. The moment the decree nisi was pronounced he left the Courts of Justice.

Four hours until he became public property! 'Solicitor's divorce suit!' A surly, dogged anger replaced that dead feeling within him. 'Damn them all!' he thought; 'I won't run away. I'll act as if nothing had happened.' And in the sweltering heat of Fleet Street and Ludgate Hill he walked all the way to his City Club, lunched, and went back to his office. He worked there stolidly throughout the afternoon.

On his way out he saw that his clerks knew, and answered their involuntary glances with a look so sardonic that they were immediately withdrawn. In front of St. Paul's, he stopped to buy the most gentlemanly of the evening papers. Yes! there he was! 'Well-known solicitor's divorce. Cousin co-respondent. Damages given to the blind' — so, they had got that in! At every other face, he thought: 'I wonder if you know!' And suddenly he felt queer, as if something were racing round in his head.

What was this? He was letting it get hold of him! He mustn't! He would be ill. He mustn't think! He would get down to the river and row about, and fish. 'I'm not going to be laid up,' he thought.

It flashed across him that he had something of
importance to do before he went out of town.
Madame Lamotte! He must explain the Law.
Another six months before he was really free!
Only he did not want to see Annette! And he
passed his hand over the top of his head — it was
very hot.

He branched off through Covent Garden. On
this sultry day of late July the garbage-tainted air
of the old market offended him, and Soho seemed
more than ever the disenchanted home of rapscal-
lionism. Alone, the Restaurant Bretagne, neat,
daintily painted, with its blue tubs and the dwarf
trees therein, retained an aloof and Frenchified
self-respect. It was the slack hour, and pale trim
waitresses were preparing the little tables for dinner. Soames went through into the private part.
To his discomfiture Annette answered his knock.
She, too, looked pale and dragged down by the heat.

" You are quite a stranger," she said languidly.
Soames smiled.

" I haven't wished to be ; I've been busy. Where's
your mother, Annette ? I've got some news for
her."

" Mother is not in."

It seemed to Soames that she looked at him in a
queer way. What did she know ? How much had
her mother told her ? The worry of trying to make
that out gave him an alarming feeling in his head.
He gripped the edge of the table, and dizzily saw
Annette come forward, her eyes clear with surprise. He shut his own and said :

" It's all right. I've had a touch of the sun, I
think." The sun! What he had was a touch of
darkness! Annette's voice, French and composed,
said :

"Sit down, it will pass, then." Her hand pressed his shoulder, and Soames sank into a chair. When the dark feeling dispersed, and he opened his eyes, she was looking down at him. What an inscrutable and odd expression for a girl of twenty!

"Do you feel better?"

"It's nothing," said Soames. Instinct told him that to be feeble before her was not helping him — age was enough handicap without that. Will-power was his fortune with Annette; he had lost ground these latter months from indecision — he could not afford to lose any more. He got up, and said:

"I'll write to your mother. I'm going down to my river house for a long holiday. I want you both to come there presently and stay. It's just at its best. You will, won't you?"

"It will be veree nice." A pretty little roll of that 'r,' but no enthusiasm. And rather sadly he added:

"You're feeling the heat, too, aren't you, Annette? It'll do you good to be on the river. Good-night." Annette swayed forward. There was a sort of compunction in the movement.

"Are you fit to go? Shall I give you some coffee?"

"No," said Soames firmly. "Give me your hand."

She held out her hand, and Soames raised it to his lips. When he looked up, her face wore again that strange expression. 'I can't tell' he thought as he went out; 'but I mustn't think — I mustn't worry.'

But worry he did, walking toward Pall Mall. English, not of her religion, middle-aged, scarred as it were by domestic tragedy, what had he to give her? Only wealth, social position, leisure, admiration! It was much, but was it enough for a beautiful girl of twenty? He felt so ignorant about Annette. He had, too, a curious fear of the French nature of her mother and herself. They knew so well what they wanted. They were almost Forsytes. They would never grasp a shadow and miss a substance!

The tremendous effort it was to write a simple note to Madame Lamotte when he reached his Club warned him still further that he was at the end of his tether.

"MY DEAR MADAME (he said),

"You will see by the enclosed newspaper cutting that I obtained my decree of divorce to-day. By the English Law I shall not, however, be free to marry again till the decree is confirmed six months hence. In the meanwhile I have the honour to ask to be considered a formal suitor for the hand of your daughter. I shall write again in a few days and beg you both to come and stay at my river house.

"I am, dear Madame,
"Sincerely yours,
"SOAMES FORSYTE."

Having sealed and posted this letter, he went into the dining-room. Three mouthfuls of soup convinced him that he could not eat; and, causing a cab to be summoned, he drove to Paddington Station and took the first train to Reading. He reached his house just as the sun went down, and wandered out on to the lawn. The air was drenched with the scent of pinks and picotees in his flower borders. A stealing coolness came off the river.

Rest — peace! Let a poor fellow rest! Let not worry and shame and anger chase like evil ' night-birds in his head! Like those doves perched half-sleeping on their dovecot, like the furry creatures in the woods on the far side, and the simple folk in their cottages, like the trees and the river itself, whitening fast in twilight, like the darkening corn-flower-blue sky where stars were coming up — let him cease *from himself,* and rest!

CHAPTER X

PASSING OF AN AGE

THE marriage of Soames with Annette took place in Paris on the last day of January, 1901, with such privacy that not even Emily was told until it was accomplished. The day after the wedding he brought her to one of those quiet hotels in London where greater expense can be incurred for less result than anywhere else under heaven. Her beauty in the best Parisian frocks was giving him more satisfaction than if he had collected a perfect bit of china, or a jewel of a picture; he looked forward to the moment when he would exhibit her in Park Lane, in Green Street, and at Timothy's.

If someone had asked him in those days, " In confidence — are you in love with this girl? " he would have replied: " In love? What is love? If you mean do I feel to her as I did towards Irene in those old days when I first met her and she would not have me; when I sighed and starved after her and couldn't rest a minute until she yielded — no! If you mean do I admire her youth and prettiness, do my senses ache a little when I see her moving about — yes! Do I think she will keep me straight, make me a creditable wife and a good mother for my children? — again yes! What more do I need?

and what more do three-quarters of the women
who are married get from the men who marry
them?" And if an enquirer had pursued his query,
"And do you think it was fair to have tempted this
girl to give herself to you for life unless you have
really touched her heart?" he would have answered: "The French see these things differently
from us. They look at marriage from the point
of view of establishments and children; and, from
my own experience, I am not at all sure that theirs
is not the sensible view. I shall not expect this time
more than I can get, or she can give. Years hence
I shouldn't be surprised if I have trouble with her;
but I shall be getting old, I shall have children by
then. I shall shut my eyes. I have my great passion; hers is perhaps to come — I don't suppose it
will be for me. I offer her a great deal, and I don't
expect much in return, except children, or at least
a son. But one thing I am sure of — she has very
good sense!"

And if, insatiate, the enquirer had gone on, "You
do not look, then, for spiritual union in this marriage?" Soames would have lifted his sideway
smile, and rejoined: "That's as it may be. If I get
satisfaction for my senses, perpetuation of myself,
good taste and good humour in the house, it is all
I can expect at my age. I am not likely to be going
out of my way towards any far-fetched sentimen-
talism." Whereon, the enquirer must in good taste
have ceased enquiry.

The Queen was dead, and the air of the greatest
city upon earth grey with unshed tears. Fur-
coated and top-hatted, with Annette beside him in
dark furs, Soames crossed Park Lane on the morning of the funeral procession, to the rails in Hyde

Park. Little moved though he ever was by public matters, this event, supremely symbolical, this summing-up of a long rich period, impressed his fancy. In '37, when she came to the throne, ' Superior Dosset ' was still building houses to make London hideous; and James, a stripling of twenty-six, just laying the foundations of his practice in the Law. Coaches still ran; men wore stocks, shaved their upper lips, ate oysters out of barrels; ' tigers ' swung behind cabriolets; women said, ' La! ' and owned no property; there were manners in the land, and pigsties for the poor; unhappy devils were hanged for little crimes, and Dickens had but just begun to write. Wellnigh two generations had slipped by — of steamboats, railways, telegraphs, bicycles, electric light, telephones, and now these motor cars — of such accumulated wealth, that eight per cent. had become three, and Forsytes were numbered by the thousand! Morals had changed, manners had changed, men had become monkeys twice-removed, God had become Mammon — Mammon so respectable as to deceive himself. Sixty-four years that favoured property, and had made the upper middle class; buttressed, chiselled, polished it, till it was almost indistinguishable in manners, morals, speech, appearance, habit, and soul from the nobility. An epoch which had gilded individual liberty so that if a man had money, he was free in law and fact. An era which had canonised hypocrisy, so that to seem to be respectable was to be. A great Age, whose transmuting influence nothing had escaped save the nature of man and the nature of the Universe.

And to witness the passing of this Age, London — its pet and fancy — was pouring forth her citizens through every gate into Hyde Park, hub of Victorianism, happy hunting-ground of Forsytes. Under the grey heavens, whose drizzle just kept off, the dark concourse gathered to see the show. The ' good old ' Queen, full of years and virtue, had emerged from her seclusion for the last time to make a London holiday. From Houndsditch, Acton, Ealing, Hampstead, Islington, and Bethnal Green; from Hackney, Hornsey, Leytonstone, Battersea, and Fulham; and from those green pastures where Forsytes flourish — Mayfair and Kensington, St. James' and Belgravia, Bayswater and Chelsea and the Regents Park, the people swarmed down on to the roads where death would presently pass with dusky pomp and pageantry. Never again would a Queen reign so long, or people have a chance to see much history buried for their money. A pity the war dragged on, and that the Wreath of Victory could not be laid upon her coffin! All else would be there to follow and commemorate — soldiers, sailors, foreign princes, half-masted bunting, tolling bells, and above all the surging, great, dark-coated crowd, with perhaps a simple sadness here and there deep in hearts beneath black clothes put on by regulation. After all, more than a Queen was going to her rest, a woman who had braved sorrow, lived well and wisely according to her lights.

Out in the crowd against the railings, with his arm hooked in Annette's, Soames waited. Yes! the Age was passing! What with this Trade-Unionism, and Labour fellows in the House of Commons, with continental fiction, and something in the general feel of everything, not to be expressed in words, things were very different; he recalled the crowd on Mafeking night, and George Forsyte saying:

" They're all socialists, they want our goods." Like
James, Soames didn't know, he couldn't tell — with
Edward on the throne! Things would never be as
safe again as under good old Viccy! Convulsively
he pressed his young wife's arm. There, at any
rate, was something substantially his own, domes-
tically certain again at last; something which made
property worth while — a real thing once more.
Pressed close against her and trying to ward others
off, Soames was content. The crowd swayed round
them, ate sandwiches and dropped crumbs; boys
who had climbed the plane-trees chattered above like
monkeys, threw twigs and orange-peel. It was past
time; they should be coming soon! And, suddenly,
a little behind them to the left, he saw a tallish
man with a soft hat and short grizzling beard, and
a tallish woman in a little round fur cap and veil.
Jolyon and Irene talking, smiling at each other,
close together like Annette and himself! They
had not seen him; and stealthily, with a very queer
feeling in his heart, Soames watched those two.
They looked happy! What had they come here for
— inherently illicit creatures, rebels from the Victorian ideal? What business had they in this
crowd? Each of them twice exiled by morality —
making a boast, as it were, of love and laxity! He
watched them fascinated; admitting grudgingly
even with his arm thrust through Annette's that
— that she — Irene —— No! he would *not* admit
it; and he turned his eyes away. He would *not*
see them, and let the old bitterness, the old longing
rise up within him! And then Annette turned to
him and said: " Those two people, Soames; they
know you, I am sure. Who are they? "
Soames nosed sideways.

" What people? "

" There, you see them; just turning away. They know you."

" No," Soames answered; " a mistake, my dear."

" A lovely face! And how she walk! *Elle est très distinguée!*"

Soames looked then. Into his life, out of his life she had walked like that — swaying and erect, remote, unseizable; ever eluding the contact of his soul! He turned abruptly from that receding vision of the past.

" You'd better attend," he said, " they're coming now!"

But while he stood, grasping her arm, seemingly intent on the head of the procession, he was quivering with the sense of always missing something, with instinctive regret that he had not got them both.

Slow came the music and the march, till, in silence, the long line wound in through the Park gate. He heard Annette whisper, " How sad it is and beautiful!" felt the clutch of her hand as she stood up on tiptoe; and the crowd's emotion gripped him. There it was — the bier of the Queen, coffin of the Age slow passing! And as it went by there came a murmuring groan from all the long line of those who watched, a sound such as Soames had never heard, so unconscious, primitive, deep and wild, that neither he nor any knew whether they had joined in uttering it. Strange sound, indeed! Tribute of an Age to its own death. . . . Ah! Ah! . . . The hold on life had slipped. That which had seemed eternal was gone! The Queen — God bless her!

It moved on with the bier, that travelling groan,

as a fire moves on over grass in a thin line; it kept
step, and marched alongside down the dense crowds
mile after mile. It was a human sound, and yet inhuman, pushed out by animal subconsciousness, by
intimate knowledge of universal death and change.
None of us — none of us can hold on for ever!

It left silence for a little — a very little time, till
tongues began, eager to retrieve interest in the show.
Soames lingered just long enough to gratify Annette, then took her out of the Park to lunch at his
father's in Park Lane. . . .

James had spent the morning gazing out of his
bedroom window. The last show he would see —
last of so many! So she was gone! Well, she was
getting an old woman. Swithin and he had seen her
crowned — slim slip of a girl, not so old as Imogen!
She had got very stout of late. Jolyon and he had
seen her married to that German chap, her husband
— he had turned out all right before he died, and
left her with that son of his. And he remembered
the many evenings he and his brothers and their
cronies had wagged their heads over their wine and
walnuts and that fellow in his salad days. And
now he had come to the throne. They said he had
steadied down — he didn't know — couldn't tell!
He'd make the money fly still, he shouldn't wonder.
What a lot of people out there! It didn't seem so
very long since he and Swithin stood in the crowd
outside Westminster Abbey when she was crowned,
and Swithin had taken him to Cremorne afterwards
— racketty chap, Swithin; no, it didn't seem much
longer ago than Jubilee Year, when he had joined
with Roger in renting a balcony in Piccadilly. Jolyon,
Swithin, Roger all gone, and he would be ninety in
August! And there was Soames married again to

a French girl. The French were a queer lot, but
they made good mothers, he had heard. Things
changed! They said this German Emperor was
here for the funeral, his telegram to old Kruger had
been in shocking taste. He shouldn't be surprised
if that chap made trouble some day. Change!
H'm! Well, they must look after themselves when
he was gone: he didn't know where he'd be! And
now Emily had asked Dartie to lunch, with Winifred and Imogen, to meet Soames' wife — she was
always doing something. And there was Irene living with that fellow Jolyon, they said. He'd marry
her now, he supposed.

'My brother Jolyon,' he thought, 'what would
he have said to it all?' And somehow the utter impossibility of knowing what his elder brother, once
so looked up to, would have said, so worried James
that he got up from his chair by the window, and
began slowly, feebly to pace the room.

'She was a pretty thing, too,' he thought; 'I was
fond of her. Perhaps Soames didn't suit her — I
don't know—I can't tell. We never had any trouble
with *our* wives.' Women had changed — everything had changed! And now the Queen was dead
— well, there it was! A movement in the crowd
brought him to a standstill at the window, his nose
touching the pane and whitening from the chill of it.
They had got her as far as Hyde Park Corner —
they were passing now! Why didn't Emily come up
here where she could see, instead of fussing about
lunch. He missed her at that moment — missed
her! Through the bare branches of the plane-trees
he could just see the procession, could see the hats
coming off the people's heads — a lot of them would
catch colds, he shouldn't wonder! A voice behind
him said:

" You've got a capital view here, James! "

" *There* you are! " muttered James; " why did n't you come before? You might have missed it! "

And he was silent, staring with all his might.

" What's that noise? " he asked suddenly.

" There's no noise," returned Emily; "what are you thinking of? — they wouldn't cheer."

" I can hear it."

" Nonsense, James! "

No sound came through those double panes; what James heard was the groaning in his own heart at the sight of his Age passing.

"Don't you ever tell me where I'm buried," he said suddenly. " I shan't want to know." And he turned from the window. There she went, the old Queen; she'd had a lot of anxiety — she'd be glad to be out of it, he should think!

Emily took up the hair-brushes.

" There'll be just time to brush your head," she said, " before they come. You must look your best, James."

" Ah! " muttered James; " they say she's pretty."

The meeting with his new daughter-in-law took place in the dining-room. James was seated by the fire when she was brought in. He placed his hands on the arms of the chair and slowly raised himself. Stooping and immaculate in his frock-coat, thin as a line in Euclid, he received Annette's hand in his; and the anxious eyes of his furrowed face, which had lost its colour now, doubted above her. A little warmth came into them and into his cheeks, refracted from her bloom.

" How are you? " he said. " You've been to see the Queen, I suppose? Did you have a good crossing?" In this way he greeted her from whom he hoped for a grandson of his name.

Gazing at him, so old, thin, white, and spotless, Annette murmured something in French which James did not understand.

"Yes, yes," he said, "you want your lunch, I expect. Soames, ring the bell; we won't wait for that chap Dartie." But just then they arrived. Dartie had refused to go out of his way to see 'the old girl.' With an early cock-tail beside him, he had taken a 'squint' from the smoking-room of the Iseeum, so that Winifred and Imogen had been obliged to come back from the Park to fetch him thence. His brown eyes rested on Annette with a stare of almost startled satisfaction. The second beauty that fellow Soames had picked up! What women could see in him! Well, she would play him the same trick as the other, no doubt; but in the meantime he was a lucky devil! And he brushed up his moustache, having in nine months of Green Street domesticity regained almost all his flesh and his assurance. Despite the comfortable efforts of Emily, Winifred's composure, Imogen's enquiring friendliness, Dartie's showing-off, and James' solicitude about her food, it was not, Soames felt, a successful lunch for his bride. He took her away very soon.

"That Monsieur Dartie," said Annette in the cab, " je n'amie pas ce type — lá!"

"No, by George!" said Soames.

"Your sister is veree amiable, and the girl is pretty. Your father is veree old. I think your mother has trouble with him; I should not like to be her."

Soames nodded at the shrewdness, the clear hard

judgment in his young wife; but it disquieted him a
little. The thought may have just flashed through
him, too: ' When I'm eighty she'll be fifty-five, having trouble with me! '

" There's just one other house of my relations I
must take you to," he said; " you'll find it funny,
but we must get it over; and then we'll dine and go
to the theatre."

In this way he prepared her for Timothy's. But
Timothy's was different. They were *delighted* to
see dear Soames after this long long time; and so
this was Annette!

" You are *so* pretty, my dear; almost too young
and pretty for dear Soames, aren't you? But he's
very attentive and careful — such a good hus-
b —— " Aunt Juley checked herself, and placed her
lips just under each of Annette's eyes — she afterwards described them to Francie, who dropped in,
as: " Cornflower-blue, so pretty, I quite wanted to
kiss them. I must say dear Soames is a perfect connoisseur. In her French way, and not so very
French either, I think she's as pretty — though not
so distinguished, not so alluring — as Irene. Because she *was* alluring, wasn't she? with that white
skin and those dark eyes, and that hair, *coleur de* —
what was it? I always forget."

" *Feuille morte,*" Francie prompted.

" Of course, dead leaves — so strange. I remember when I was a girl, before we came to London,
we had a foxhound puppy — to ' walk ' it was called
then; it had a tan top to its head and a white chest,
and beautiful dark brown eyes, and it was a lady."

" Yes, auntie," said Francie, " but I don't see the
connection."

" Oh! " replied Aunt Juley, rather flustered, " it

was so alluring, and her eyes and hair, you know —— " She was silent, as if surprised in some indelicacy. *"Feuille morte,"* she added suddenly; " Hester — do remember that! " . . .

Considerable debate took place between the two sisters whether Timothy should or should not be summoned to see Annette.

" Oh, don't bother! " said Soames.

" But it's no trouble, only of course Annette's being French might upset him a little. He was so scared about Fashoda. I think perhaps we had better not run the risk, Hester. It's nice to have her all to ourselves, isn't it? And how are you, Soames? Have you quite got over your —— "

Hester interposed hurriedly:

" What do you think of London, Annette? "

Soames, disquieted, awaited the reply. It came, sensible, composed: " Oh! I know London, I have visited before."

He had never ventured to speak to her on the subject of the restaurant. The French had different notions about gentility, and to shrink from connection with it might seem to her ridiculous; he had waited to be married before mentioning it; and now he wished he hadn't.

' And what part do you know best? " asked Aunt Juley.

" Soho," said Annette simply.

Soames snapped his jaw.

" Soho? " repeated Aunt Juley; " Soho? "

' That'll go round the family,' thought Soames.

" It's very French, and interesting," he said.

" Yes," murmured Aunt Juley, " your Uncle Roger had some houses there once; he was always having to turn the tenants out, I remember."

Soames changed the subject to Mapledurham.

" Of course," said Aunt Juley, " you will be going down there soon to settle in. We are all so looking forward to the time when Annette has a dear little —— "

" Juley! " cried Aunt Hester desperately, " ring for tea! "

Soames dared not wait for tea, and took Annette away.

" I shouldn't mention Soho if I were you," he said in the cab. " It's rather a shady part of London; and you're altogether above that restaurant business now; I mean," he added, " I want you to know nice people, and the English are fearful snobs."

Annette's clear eyes opened; a little smile came on her lips.

" Yes? " she said.

' H'm! ' thought Soames, ' that's meant for me! ' and he looked at her hard. ' She's got good business instincts,' he thought. ' I must make her grasp it once for all! '

" Look here, Annette! it's very simple, only it wants understanding. Our professional and leisured class still think themselves a cut above our business classes, except of course the very rich. It may be stupid, but there it is, you see. It isn't advisable in England to let people know that you ran a restaurant or kept a shop or were in any kind of trade. It may have been extremely creditable, but it puts a sort of label on you; you don't have such a good time, or meet such nice people — that's all."

" I see," said Annette; " it is the same in France."

" Oh! " murmured Soames, at once relieved and taken aback. " Of course, class is everything, really."

" Yes," said Annette; "*comme vous etes sage.*"

' That's all right,' thought Soames, watching her lips, ' only she's pretty cynical.' His knowledge of French was not yet such as to make him grieve that she had not said ' *tu.*' He slipped his arm round her, and murmured with an effort:

"*Et vous êtes ma belle femme.*"

Annette went off into a little fit of laughter.

"*Oh, non!*" she said. "*Oh, non! ne parlez pas Français*, Soames. What is that old lady, your aunt, looking forward to? "

Soames bit his lip. "God knows!" he said; " she's always saying something; " but he knew better than God.

CHAPTER XI

SUSPENDED ANIMATION

THE war dragged on. Nicholas had been heard to
say that it would cost three hundred millions if it
cost a penny before they'd done with it! The in-
come-tax was seriously threatened. Still, there
would be South Africa for their money, once for
all. And though the possessive instinct felt badly
shaken at three o'clock in the morning, it recovered
by breakfast-time with the recollection that one
gets nothing in this world without paying for it.
So, on the whole, people went about their business
much as if there were no war, no concentration
camps, no slippery de Wet, no feeling on the Con-
tinent, no anything unpleasant. Indeed, the attitude
of the nation was typified by Timothy's map, whose
animation was suspended — for Timothy no longer
moved the flags, and they could not move themselves, not even backwards and forwards as they
should have done.

Suspended animation went further; it invaded
Forsyte 'Change, and produced a general uncertainty as to what was going to happen next. The
announcement in the marriage column of *The
Times,* ' Jolyon Forsyte to Irene, only daughter of
the late Professor Heron,' had occasioned doubt

whether Irene had been justly described. And yet, on the whole, relief was felt that she had not been entered as, ' Irene, late the wife,' or ' the divorced wife,' ' of Soames Forsyte.' Altogether, there had been a kind of sublimity from the first about the way the family had taken that ' affair.' As James had phrased it, ' There it was.' No use to fuss! Nothing to be had out of admitting that it had been a ' nasty jar ' — in the phraseology of the day.

But what would happen now that both Soames and Jolyon were married again? That was very intriguing. George was known to have laid Eustace six to four on a little Jolyon before a little Soames. George was so droll! It was rumoured, too, that he and Dartie had a bet as to whether James would attain the age of ninety, though which of them had backed James no one knew.

At the end of May, Winifred came round to say that Val had been wounded in the leg by a spent bullet, and was to be discharged. His wife was nursing him. He would have a little limp — nothing to speak of. He wanted his grandfather to buy him a farm out there where he could breed horses. Her father was giving Holly eight hundred a year, so they could be quite comfortable, because his grandfather would give Val five, he had said; but as to the farm, he didn't know — couldn't tell: he didn't want Val to go throwing away his money.

" But, you know," said Winifred, " he must do something."

Aunt Hester thought that perhaps his dear grandfather was wise, because if he didn't buy a farm it couldn't turn out badly.

" But Val loves horses," said Winifred. " It'd be such an occupation for him."

Aunt Juley thought that horses were very uncertain, had not Montagu found them so?

"Val's different," said Winifred; "he takes after
me."

Aunt Juley was sure that dear Val was very
clever. "I always remember," she added, "how
he gave his bad penny to a beggar. His dear grandfather was so pleased. He thought it showed such
presence of mind. I remember his saying that he
ought to go into the Navy."

Aunt Hester chimed in: Did not Winifred think
that it was much better for the young people to be
secure and not run any risk at their age?

"Well," said Winifred, "if they were in London,
perhaps; in London it's amusing to do nothing. But
out there, of course, he'll simply get bored to death."

Aunt Hester thought that it would be nice for
him to work, if he were quite sure not to lose by it.
It was not as if they had no money. Timothy, of
course, had done so well by retiring. Aunt Juley
wanted to know what Montagu had said.

Winifred did not tell her, for Montagu had merely
remarked: "Wait till the old man dies."

At this moment Francie was announced. Her
eyes were brimming with a smile.

"Well," she said, "what do you think of it?"

"Of what, dear?"

"In *The Times* this morning."

"We haven't seen it, we always read it after
dinner; Timothy has it till then."

Francie rolled her eyes.

"Do you think you *ought* to tell us?" said Aunt
Juley. "What *was* it?"

"Irene's had a son at Robin Hill."

Aunt Juley drew in her breath. "But," she said,
"they were only married in March!"

" Yes, Auntie; isn't it interesting? "

" Well," said Winifred, " I'm glad. I was sorry for Jolyon losing his boy. It might have been Val."

Aunt Juley seemed to go into a sort of dream.

" I wonder," she murmured, " what dear Soames will think? He has so wanted to have a son himself. A little bird has always told me that."

" Well," said Winifred, " he's going to — bar accidents."

Gladness trickled out of Aunt Juley's eyes.

" How delightful! " she said. " When? "

" November."

Such a lucky month! But she did wish it could be sooner. It was a long time for James to wait, at his age!

To wait! They dreaded it for James, but they were used to it themselves. Indeed, it was their great distraction. To wait! For *The Times* to read; for one or other of their nieces or nephews to come in and cheer them up; for news of Nicholas's health; for that decision of Christopher's about going on the stage; for information concerning the mine of Mrs. MacAnder's nephew; for the doctor to come about Hester's inclination to wake up early in the morning; for books from the library which were always out; for Timothy to have a cold; for a nice quiet warm day, not too hot, when they could take a turn in Kensington Gardens. To wait, one on each side of the hearth in the drawing-room, for the clock between them to strike; their thin, veined, knuckled hands plying knitting-needles and crochet-hooks, their hair ordered to stop — like Canute's waves — from any further advance in colour. To wait in their black silks or satins for the Court to say that Hester might wear her dark green, and

Juley her darker maroon. To wait, slowly turning over and over in their old minds the little joys and sorrows, events and expectancies, of their little family world, as cows chew patient cuds in a familiar field. And this new event was so well worth waiting for. Soames had always been their pet, with his tendency to give them pictures, and his almost weekly visits which they missed so much, and his need for their sympathy evoked by the wreck of his first marriage. This new event — the birth of an heir to Soames — was so important for him, and for his dear father, too, that James might not have to die without some certainty about things. James did so dislike uncertainty; and with Montagu, of course, he could not feel really satisfied to leave no grandchildren but the young Darties. After all, one's own name did count! And as James' ninetieth birthday neared they wondered what precautions he was taking. He would be the first of the Forsytes to reach that age, and set, as it were, a new standard in holding on to life. That was so important, they felt, at their ages eighty-seven and eighty-five; though they did not want to think of themselves when they had Timothy, who was not yet eighty-two, to think of. There was, of course, a better world. 'In my Father's house are many mansions' was one of Aunt Juley's favourite sayings — it always comforted her, with its suggestion of house property, which had made the fortune of dear Roger. The Bible was, indeed, a great resource, and on *very* fine Sundays there was church in the morning; and sometimes Juley would steal into Timothy's study when she was sure he was out, and just put an open New Testament casually among the books on his little table — he was a great reader, of

course, having been a publisher. But she had noticed that Timothy was always cross at dinner afterwards. And Smither had told her more than
once that she had picked books off the floor in doing
the room. Still, with all that, they did feel that
heaven could not be quite so cosy as the rooms in
which they and Timothy had waited for so long.
Aunt Hester, especially, could not bear the thought
of the exertion. Any change, or rather the thought
of a change — for there never *was* any — always
upset her very much. Aunt Juley, who had more
spirit, sometimes thought it would be quite exciting;
she had so enjoyed that visit to Brighton the year
dear Susan died. But then Brighton one knew was
nice, and it was so difficult to tell what heaven would
be like, so on the whole she was more than content
to wait.

On the morning of James' birthday, August the
5th, they felt extraordinary animation, and little
notes passed between them by the hand of Smither
while they were having breakfast in their beds.
Smither must go round and take their love and little
presents and find out how Mr. James was, and
whether he had passed a good night with all the
excitement. And on the way back would Smither
call in at Green Street — it was a little out of her
way, but she could take the bus up Bond Street afterwards; it would be a nice little change for her —
and ask dear Mrs. Dartie to be sure and look in
before she went out of town.

All this Smither did — an undeniable servant
trained thirty years ago under Aunt Ann to a perfection not now procurable. Mr. James, so Mrs.
James said, had passed an excellent night, he sent
his love; Mrs. James had said he was very funny

and had complained that he didn't know what all
the fuss was about. Oh! and Mrs. Dartie sent her
love, and she would come to tea.

Aunts Juley and Hester, rather hurt that their
presents had not received special mention — they
forgot every year that James could not bear to receive presents, 'throwing away their money on
him,' as he always called it — were 'delighted';
it showed that James was in good spirits, and that
was so important for him. And they began to wait
for Winifred. She came at four, bringing Imogen,
and Maud, just back from school, and 'getting such
a pretty girl, too,' so that it was extremely difficult
to ask for news about Annette. Aunt Juley, however, summoned courage to enquire whether Winifred had heard anything, and if Soames was anxious.

"Uncle Soames is always anxious, Auntie," interrupted Imogen; "he can't be happy now he's
got it."

The words struck familiarly on Aunt Juley's ears.
Ah! yes; that funny drawing of George's, which
had *not* been shown them! But what did Imogen
mean? That her uncle always wanted more than he
could have? It was not at all nice to think like that.

Imogen's voice rose clear and clipped:

"Imagine! Annette's only two years older than
me; it must be awful for her, married to Uncle
Soames."

Aunt Juley lifted her hands in horror.

"My dear," she said, "you don't know what
you're talking about. Your Uncle Soames is a
match for anybody. He's a very clever man, and
good-looking and wealthy, and most considerate
and careful, and not at all old, considering everything."

Imogen, turning her luscious glance from one to other of the ' old dears,' only smiled.

" I hope," said Aunt Juley quite severely, " that *you* will marry as good a man."

" *I* shan't marry a good man, Auntie," murmured Imogen; " they're dull."

" If you go on like this," replied Aunt Juley, still very much upset, " you won't marry anybody. We'd better not pursue the subject; " and turning to Winifred, she said: " How is Montagu? "

That evening, while they were waiting for dinner, she murmured:

" I've told Smither to get up half a bottle of the sweet champagne, Hester. I think we ought to drink dear James' health, and — and the health of Soames' wife; only, let's keep that quite secret. I'll just say like this, ' And *you know,* Hester!' and then we'll drink. It might upset Timothy."

" It's more likely to upset us," said Aunt Hester. "But we must, I suppose; for such an occasion."

"Yes," said Aunt Juley rapturously, " it *is* an occasion! Only fancy if he has a dear little boy, to carry the family on! I do feel it so important, now that Irene has had a son. Winifred says George is calling Jolyon ' The Three-Decker,' because of his three families, you know! George *is* droll. And fancy! Irene is living after all in the house Soames had built for them both. It does seem hard on dear Soames; and he's always been so regular."

That night in bed, excited and a little flushed still by her glass of wine and the secrecy of the second toast, she lay with her prayer-book opened flat, and her eyes fixed on a ceiling yellowed by the light from her reading-lamp. Young things! It was so

nice for them all! And she would be so happy if
she could see dear Soames happy. But, of course,
he must be now, in spite of what Imogen had said.
He would have all that he wanted: property, and
wife, and children! And he would live to a green
old age, like his dear father, and forget all about
Irene and that dreadful case. If only she herself
could be here to buy his children their first rocking-
horse! Smither should choose it for her at the
stores, nice and dappled. Ah! how Roger used to
rock her until she fell off! Oh dear! that was a
long time ago! It *was!* 'In my Father's house
are many mansions ———' A little scrattling noise
caught her ear — 'but no mice!' she thought mechanically. The noise increased. There! it *was* a
mouse! How naughty of Smither to say there
wasn't. It would be eating through the wainscot
before they knew where they were, and they would
have to have the builders in. They were such de-
structive things! And she lay, with her eyes just
moving, following in her mind that little scrattling
sound, and waiting for sleep to release her from it.

CHAPTER XII

BIRTH OF A FORSYTE

SOAMES walked out of the garden door, crossed the lawn, stood on the path above the river, turned round and walked back to the garden door, without having realised that he had moved. The sound of wheels crunching the drive convinced him that time had passed, and the doctor gone. What, exactly, had he said?

" This is the position, Mr. Forsyte. I can make pretty certain of her life if I operate, but the baby will be born dead. If I don't operate, the baby will most probably be born alive, but it's a great risk for the mother — a great risk. In either case I don't think she can ever have another child. In her state she obviously can't decide for herself, and we can't wait for her mother. It's for you to make the decision, while I'm getting what's necessary. I shall be back within the hour."

The decision! What a decision! No time to get a specialist down! No time for anything!

The sound of wheels died away, but Soames still stood intent; then, suddenly covering his ears, he walked back to the river. To come before its time like this, with no chance to foresee anything, not even to get her mother here! It was for her mother

to make that decision, and she couldn't arrive from
Paris till to-night! If only he could have understood the doctor's jargon, the medical niceties, so
as to be sure he was weighing the chances properly;
but they were Greek to him — like a legal problem
to a layman. And yet he *must* decide! He
brought his hand away from his brow wet, though
the air was chilly. These sounds which came from
her room! To go back there would only make it
more difficult. He must be calm, clear. On the
one hand life, nearly certain, of his young wife,
death quite certain, of his child; and — no more
children afterwards! On the other, death, *perhaps*
of his wife, nearly certain life for the child; and —
no more children afterwards! Which to choose?
. . . It had rained this last fortnight — the river
was very full, and in the water, collected round the
little house-boat moored by his landing-stage, were
many leaves from the woods above, brought off by
a frost. Leaves fell, lives drifted down! Death!
To decide about death! And no one to give him a
hand. Life lost was lost for good. Let nothing
go that you could keep; for, if it went, you couldn't
get it back. It left you bare, like those trees when
they lost their leaves; barer and barer until you,
too, withered and came down. And, by a queer
somersault of thought, he seemed to see not Annette
lying up there behind that window-pane on which
the sun was shining, but Irene lying in their bedroom in Montpelier Square, as it might conceivably
have been her fate to lie, sixteen years ago. Would
he have hesitated then? Not a moment! Operate,
operate! Make certain of her life! No decision
— a mere instinctive cry for help, in spite of his
knowledge, even then, that she did not love him!

But this! Ah! there was nothing overmastering
in his feeling for Annette! Many times these last
months, especially since she had been growing
frightened, he had wondered. She had a will of
her own, was selfish in her French way. And yet
— so pretty! What would she wish — to take the
risk? 'I know she wants the child,' he thought.
'If it's born dead, and no more chance afterwards
— it'll upset her terribly. No more chance! All
for nothing! Married life with her for years and
years without a child. Nothing to steady her!
She's too young. Nothing to look forward to, for
her — for me! *For me!*' He stuck his hands
against his chest! Why couldn't he think without
bringing himself in — get out of himself and see
what he ought to do? The thought hurt him, then
lost edge, as if it had come in contact with a breast-
plate. Out of oneself! Impossible! Out into
soundless, scentless, touchless, sightless space!
The very idea was ghastly, futile! And touching
there the bedrock of reality, the bottom of his Forsyte spirit, Soames rested for a moment. When
one ceased, all ceased; it might go on, but there'd be
nothing in it!

He looked at his watch. In half an hour the doctor would be back. He *must* decide! If against
the operation and she died, how face her mother
and the doctor afterwards? How face his own
conscience? It was *his* child that she was having.
If for the operation — then he condemned them
both to childlessness. And for what else had he
married her but to have a lawful heir? And his
father — at death's door, waiting for the news!
'It's cruel!' he thought; 'I ought never to have
such a thing to settle! It's cruel!' He turned

towards the house. Some deep, simple way of deciding! He took out a coin, and put it back. If he spun it, he knew he would not abide by what came up! He went into the dining-room, furthest away from that room whence the sounds issued. The doctor had said there was a chance. In here that chance seemed greater; the river did not flow, nor the leaves fall. A fire was burning. Soames unlocked the tantalus. He hardly ever touched spirits, but now he poured himself out some whisky and drank it neat, craving a faster flow of blood. 'That fellow Jolyon,' he thought; 'he had children already. He has the woman I really loved; and now a son by her! And I — I'm asked to destroy my only child! Annette *can't* die; it's not possible. She's strong!'

He was still standing sullenly at the sideboard when he heard the doctor's carriage, and went out to him. He had to wait for him to come downstairs.

"Well, doctor?"

"The situation's the same. Have you decided?"

"Yes," said Soames; "don't operate!"

"Not? You understand — the risk's great?" In Soames' set face nothing moved but the lips.

"You said there was a chance?"

"A chance, yes; not much of one."

"You say the baby *must* be born dead if you do?"

"Yes."

"Do you still think that in any case she can't have another?"

"One can't be absolutely sure, but it's most unlikely."

" She's strong," said Soames; " we'll take the risk."

The doctor looked at him very gravely. " It's on your shoulders," he said; " with my own wife, I couldn't."

Soames' chin jerked up as if someone had hit him. " Am I of any use up there? " he asked.

" No; keep away."

" I shall be in my picture-gallery, then; you know where."

The doctor nodded, and went upstairs.

Soames continued to stand, listening. ' By this time to-morrow,' he thought, ' I may have her death on my hands.' No! it was unfair — monstrous, to put it that way! Sullenness dropped on him again, and he went up to the gallery. He stood at the window. The wind was in the north; it was cold, clear; very blue sky, heavy ragged white clouds chasing across; the river blue, too, through the screen of goldening trees; the woods all rich with colour, glowing, burnished — an early autumn. If it were his own life, would he be taking that risk? ' But *she'd* take the risk of losing me,' he thought, ' sooner than lose her child! She doesn't really love me!' What could one expect — a girl and French? The one thing really vital to them both, vital to their marriage and their futures, was a child! ' I've been through a lot for this,' he thought, 'I'll hold on — hold on. There's a chance of keeping both — a chance!' One kept till things were taken — one naturally kept! He began walking round the gallery. He had made one purchase lately which he knew was a fortune in itself, and he halted before it — a girl with dull gold hair which looked like filaments of metal gazing at a little

golden monster she was holding in her hand. Even
at this tortured moment he could just feel the extraordinary nature of the bargain he had made — admire the quality of the table, the floor, the chair,
the girl's figure, the absorbed expression on her
face, the dull gold filaments of her hair, the bright
gold of the little monster. Collecting pictures;
growing richer, richer! What use, if —— ! He
turned his back abruptly on the picture, and went
to the window. Some of his doves had flown up
from their perches round the dovecot, and were
stretching their wings in the wind. In the clear
sharp sunlight their whiteness almost flashed.
They flew far, making a flung-up hieroglyphic
against the sky. Annette fed the doves; it was
pretty to see her. They took it out of her hand;
they knew she was matter-of-fact. A choking sensation came into his throat. She would not —
could not die! She was too — too sensible; and
she was strong, really strong, like her mother, in
spite of her fair prettiness!

It was already growing dark when at last he
opened the door, and stood listening. Not a sound!
A milky twilight crept about the stairway and the
landings below. He had turned back when a sound
caught his ear. Peering down, he saw a black
shape moving, and his heart stood still. What was
it? Death? The shape of Death coming from
her door? No! only a maid without cap or apron.
She came to the foot of his flight of stairs and said
breathlessly:

" The doctor wants to see you, sir."

He ran down. She stood flat against the wall to
let him pass, and said:

" Oh, sir! it's over."

"Over?" said Soames, with a sort of menace; "what d'you mean?"

"It's born, sir."

He dashed up the four steps in front of him, and came suddenly on the doctor in the dim passage. The man was wiping his brow.

"Well?" he said; "quick!"

"Both living; it's all right, I think."

Soames stood quite still, covering his eyes.

"I congratulate you," he heard the doctor say; "it was touch and go."

Soames let fall the hand which was covering his face.

"Thanks," he said; "thanks very much. What is it?"

"Daughter — luckily; a son would have killed her — the head."

A daughter!

"The utmost care of both," he heard the doctor say, "and we shall do. When does the mother come?"

"To-night, between nine and ten, I hope."

"I'll stay till then. Do you want to see them?"

"Not now," said Soames; "before you go. I'll have dinner sent up to you." And he went downstairs.

Relief unspeakable, and yet — a daughter! It seemed to him unfair. To have taken that risk — to have been through this agony — and what agony! — for a daughter! He stood before the blazing fire of wood logs in the hall, touching it with his toe and trying to readjust himself. 'My father!' he thought. A bitter disappointment, no disguising it! One never got all one wanted in this life! And there was no other — at least, if there was, it was no use!

While he was standing there, a telegram was brought him.

" Come up at once, your father sinking fast. —
MOTHER."

He read it with a choking sensation.   One would have thought he couldn't feel anything after these last hours, but he felt this.   Half-past seven, a train from Reading at nine, and madame's train, if she had caught it, came in at eight-forty — he would meet that, and go on.   He ordered the carriage, ate some dinner mechanically, and went upstairs.   The doctor came out to him.

" They're sleeping."

" I won't go in," said Soames with relief.   " My father's dying; I have to go up.   Is it all right? "

The doctor's face expressed a kind of doubting admiration.   ' If they were all as unemotional! ' he might have been saying.

" Yes, I think you may go with an easy mind. You'll be down soon? "

" To-morrow," said Soames.   " Here's the address."

The doctor seemed to hover on the verge of sympathy.

" Good-night! " said Soames abruptly, and turned away.   He put on his fur coat.   Death!   It was a chilly business.   He smoked a cigarette in the carriage — one of his rare cigarettes.   The night was windy and flew on black wings; the carriage lights had to search out the way.   His father! That old, old man!   A comfortless night — to die!

The London train came in just as he reached the station, and Madame Lamotte, substantial, dark-clothed, very yellow in the lamplight, came towards the exit with a dressing-bag.

" This all you have? " asked Soames.

" But yes; I had not the time.   How is my little one? "

" Doing well — both.   A girl! "

" A girl!   What joy!   I had a frightful crossing! "

Her black bulk, solid, unreduced by the frightful crossing, climbed into the brougham.

" And you, *mon cher?* "

" My father's dying," said Soames between his teeth.   " I'm going up.   Give my love to Annette."

" *Tiens!* " murmured Madame Lamotte; " *quel malheur!* "

Soames took his hat off, and moved towards his train.   ' The French! ' he thought.

CHAPTER XIII

JAMES IS TOLD

A SIMPLE cold, caught in the room with double windows, where the air and the people who saw him were filtered, as it were, the room he had not left since the middle of September — and James was in deep waters. A little cold, passing his little strength and flying quickly to his lungs. "He mustn't catch cold," the doctor had declared, and he had gone and caught it. When he first felt it in his throat he had said to his nurse — for he had one now — "There, I knew how it would be, airing the room like that!" For a whole day he was highly nervous about himself and went in advance of all precautions and remedies; drawing every breath with extreme care and having his temperature taken every hour. Emily was not alarmed.

But next morning when she went in the nurse whispered: "He won't have his temperature taken."

Emily crossed to the side of the bed where he was lying, and said softly, "How do you feel, James?" holding the thermometer to his lips. James looked up at her.

"What's the good of that?" he murmured huskily; "I don't want to know."

Then she *was* alarmed. He breathed with difficulty, he looked terribly frail, white, with faint red discolorations. She had 'had trouble' with him, Goodness knew; but he was James, had been James for nearly fifty years; she couldn't remember or imagine life without James — James, behind all his fussiness, his pessimism, his crusty shell, deeply affectionate, really kind and generous to them all!

All that day and the next he hardly uttered a word, but there was in his eyes a noticing of everything done for him, a look on his face which told her he was fighting; and she did not lose hope. His very stillness, the way he conserved every little scrap of energy, showed the tenacity with which he was fighting. It touched her deeply; and though her face was composed and comfortable in the sick-room, tears ran down her cheeks when she was out of it.

About tea-time on the third day — she had just changed her dress, keeping her appearance so as not to alarm him, because he noticed everything — she saw a difference. 'It's no use; I'm tired,' was written plainly across that white face, and when she went up to him," he muttered: "Send for Soames."

"Yes, James," she said comfortably; "all right — at once." And she kissed his forehead. A tear dropped there, and as she wiped it off she saw that his eyes looked grateful. Much upset, and without hope now, she sent Soames the telegram.

When he entered out of the black windy night, the big house was still as a grave. Warmson's broad face looked almost narrow; he took the fur coat with a sort of added care, saying:

"Will you have a glass of wine, sir?"

Soames shook his head, and his eyebrows made enquiry.

Warmson's lips twitched. "He's asking for you, sir;" and suddenly he blew his nose. "It's a long time, sir," he said, "that I've been with Mr. Forsyte — a long time."

Soames left him folding the coat, and began to mount the stairs. This house, where he had been born and sheltered, had never seemed to him so warm, and rich, and cosy, as during this last pilgrimage to his father's room. It was not his taste; but in its own substantial, lincrusta way it was the acme of comfort and security. And the night was so dark and windy; the grave so cold and lonely!

He paused outside the door. No sound came from within. He turned the handle softly and was in the room before he was perceived. The light was shaded. His mother and Winifred were sitting on the far side of the bed; the nurse was moving away from the near side where was an empty chair. 'For me!' thought Soames. As he moved from the door his mother and sister rose, but he signed with his hand and they sat down again. He went up to the chair and stood looking at his father. James' breathing was as if strangled; his eyes were closed. And in Soames, looking on his father so worn and white and wasted, listening to his strangled breathing, there rose a passionate vehemence of anger against Nature, cruel, inexorable Nature, kneeling on the chest of that wisp of a body, slowly pressing out the breath, pressing out the life of the being who was dearest to him in the world. His father, of all men, had lived a careful life, moderate, abstemious, and this was his reward — to have life slowly, painfully squeezed out of him! And, without knowing that he spoke, he said: "It's cruel."

He saw his mother cover her eyes and Winifred bow her face towards the bed. Women! They put up with things so much better than men. He took a step nearer to his father. For three days James had not been shaved, and his lips and chin were covered with hair, hardly more snowy than his forehead. It softened his face, gave it a queer look already not of this world. His eyes opened. Soames went quite close and bent over. The lips moved.

"Here I am, Father."

"Um — what — what news? They never tell —— " the voice died, and a flood of emotion made Soames' face work so that he could not speak. Tell him? — yes. But what? He made a great effort, got his lips together, and said:

"Good news, dear, good — Annette, a son."

"Ah!" It was the queerest sound, ugly, relieved, pitiful, triumphant — like the noise a baby makes getting what it wants. The eyes closed, and that strangled sound of breathing began again. Soames recoiled to the chair and stonily sat down. The lie he had told, based, as it were, on some deep, temperamental instinct that after death James would not know the truth, had taken away all power of feeling for the moment. His arm brushed against something. It was his father's naked foot. In the struggle to breathe he had pushed it out from under the clothes. Soames took it in his hand, a cold foot, light and thin, white, very cold. What use to put it back, to wrap up that which must be colder soon! He warmed it mechanically with his hand, listening to his father's laboured breathing; while the power of feeling rose again within him. A little sob, quickly smothered, came from Winifred, but his mother sat unmoving, with her eyes fixed on James. Soames signed to the nurse.

" Where's the doctor? " he whispered.

" He's been sent for."

" Can't you do anything to ease his breathing? "

" Only an injection; and he can't stand it. The doctor said, while he was fighting —— "

" He's not fighting," whispered Soames, " he's being slowly smothered. It's awful."

James stirred uneasily, as if he knew what they were saying. Soames rose and bent over him. James feebly moved his two hands, and Soames took them.

" He wants to be pulled up," whispered the nurse.

Soames pulled. He thought he pulled gently, but a look almost of anger passed over James' face. The nurse plumped the pillows. Soames laid the hands down, and bending over kissed his father's forehead. As he was raising himself again, James' eyes bent on him a look which seemed to come from the very depths of what was left within. ' I'm done, my boy,' it seemed to say, ' take care of them, take care of yourself; take care — I leave it all to you.'

" Yes, yes," Soames whispered, " yes, yes."

Behind him the nurse did he knew not what, for his father made a tiny movement of repulsion as if resenting that interference; and almost at once his breathing eased away, became quiet; he lay very still. The strained expression on his face passed, a curious white tranquillity took its place. His eyelids quivered, rested; the whole face rested, at ease. Only by the faint puffing of his lips could they tell that he was breathing. Soames sank back on his chair, and fell to cherishing the foot again.

He heard the nurse quietly crying over there by the fire; curious that she, a stranger, should be the only one of them who cried! He heard the quiet lick and flutter of the fire flames. One more old Forsyte going to his long rest — wonderful, they were! — wonderful how he had held on! His mother and Winifred were leaning forward, hanging on the sight of James' lips. But Soames bent sideways over the feet, warming them both; they gave him comfort, colder and colder though they grew. Suddenly he started up; a sound, a dreadful sound such as he had never heard, was coming from his father's lips, as if an outraged heart had broken with a long moan. What a strong heart, to have uttered that farewell! It ceased. Soames looked into the face. No motion; no breath! Dead! He kissed the brow, turned round and went out of the room. He ran upstairs to the bedroom, his old bedroom, still kept for him, flung himself face down on the bed, and broke into sobs which he stifled with the pillow. . . .

A little later he went downstairs and passed into the room. James lay alone, wonderfully calm, free from shadow and anxiety, with the gravity on his ravaged face which underlies great age, the worn fine gravity of old coins.

Soames looked steadily at that face, at the fire, at all the room with windows thrown open to the London night.

" Good-bye! " he whispered, and went out.

CHAPTER XIV

HIS

HE had much to see to, that night and all next day.
A telegram at breakfast reassured him about Annette, and he only caught the last train back to
Reading, with Emily's kiss on his forehead and in
his ears her words:

" I don't know what I should have done without
you, my dear boy."

He reached his house at midnight. The weather
had changed, was mild again, as though, having
finished its work and sent a Forsyte to his last account, it could relax. A second telegram, received
at dinner-time, had confirmed the good news of Annette, and, instead of going in, Soames passed down
through the garden in the moonlight to his house-
boat. He could sleep there quite well. Bitterly
tired, he lay down on the sofa in his fur coat and
fell asleep. He woke soon after dawn and went on
deck. He stood against the rail, looking west
where the river swept round in a wide curve under
the woods. In Soames, appreciation of natural
beauty was curiously like that of his farmer ances-
tors, a sense of grievance if it wasn't there, sharpened, no doubt, and civilised, by his researches
among landscape painting. But dawn has power to
fertilise the most matter-of-fact vision, and he was

stirred. It was another world from the river he knew, under that remote cool light; a world into which man had not entered, an unreal world, like some strange shore sighted by discovery. Its colour was not the colour of convention, was hardly colour at all; its shapes were brooding yet distinct; its silence stunning; it had no scent. Why it should move him he could not tell, unless it were that he felt so alone in it, bare of all relationship and all possessions. Into such a world his father might be voyaging, for all resemblance it had to the world he had left. And Soames took refuge from it in wondering what painter could have done it justice. The white-grey water was like — like the belly of .a fish! Was it possible that this world on which he looked was all private property, except the water — and even that was tapped! No tree, no shrub, not a blade of grass, not a bird or beast, not even a fish that was not owned. And once on a time all this was jungle and marsh and water, and weird creatures roamed and sported without human cognizance to give them names; rotting luxuriance had rioted where those tall, carefully planted woods came down to the water, and marsh-misted reeds on that far side had covered all the pasture. Well! they had got it under, kennelled it all up, labelled it, and stowed it in lawyer's offices. And a good thing too! But once in a way, as now, the ghost of the past came out to haunt and brood and whisper to any human who chanced to be awake: ' Out of my unowned loneliness you all came, into it some day you will all return.'

And Soames, who felt the chill and the eeriness of that world — new to him and so very old: the world, unowned, visiting the scene of its past —

went down and made himself tea on a spirit-lamp. When he had drunk it, he took out writing materials and wrote two paragraphs:

" On the 20th instant at his residence in Park Lane, James Forsyte, in his ninety-first year. Funeral at noon on the 24th at Highgate. No flowers by request."

" On the 20th instant at The Shelter, Mapledurham, Annette, wife of Soames Forsyte, of a daughter." And underneath on the blotting-paper he traced the word " son."

It was eight o'clock in an ordinary autumn world when he went across to the house. Bushes across the river stood round and bright-coloured out of a milky haze; the wood-smoke went up blue and straight; and his doves cooed, preening their feathers in the sunlight.

He stole up to his dressing-room, bathed, shaved, put on fresh linen and dark clothes.

Madame Lamotte was beginning her breakfast when he went down.

She looked at his clothes, said, " Don't tell me! " and pressed his hand. " Annette is prettee well. But the doctor say she can never have no more children. You knew that? " Soames nodded. " It is a pity. *Mais la petite est adorable. Du café?* "

Soames got away from her as soon as he could. She offended him — solid, matter-of-fact, quick, clear — *French*. He could not bear her vowels, her ' r's '; he resented the way she had looked at him, as if it were his fault that Annette could never bear him a son! His fault! He even resented her cheap adoration of the daughter he had not yet seen.

Curious how he jibbed away from sight of his wife and child!

One would have thought he must have rushed up at the first moment. On the contrary, he had a sort of physical shrinking from it — fastidious possessor that he was. He was afraid of what Annette was thinking of him, author of her agonies, afraid of the look of the baby, afraid of showing his disappointment with the present and — the future.

He spent an hour walking up and down the drawing-room before he could screw his courage up to mount the stairs and knock on the door of their room.

Madame Lamotte opened it.

"Ah! At last you come! *Elle vous attend!*" She passed him, and Soames went in with his noiseless step, his jaw firmly set, his eyes furtive.

Annette was very pale and very pretty lying there. The baby was hidden away somewhere; he could not see it. He went up to the bed, and with sudden emotion bent and kissed her forehead.

"Here you are then, Soames," she said. "I am not so bad now. But I suffered terribly, terribly. I am glad I cannot have any more. Oh! how I suffered!"

Soames stood silent, stroking her hand; words of endearment, of sympathy, absolutely would not come; the thought passed through him: 'An English girl wouldn't have said that!' At this moment he knew with certainty that he would never be near to her in spirit and in truth, nor she to him. He had collected her — that was all! And Jolyon's words came rushing into his mind: " I should imagine you will be glad to have your neck out of chancery." Well, he had got it out! Had he got it in again?

"We must feed you up," he said, " you'll soon be strong."

" Don't you want to see baby, Soames? She is asleep."

" Of course," said Soames, " very much."

He passed round the foot of the bed to the other side and stood staring. For the first moment what he saw was much what he had expected to see — a baby. But as he stared and the baby breathed and made little sleeping movements with its tiny features, it seemed to assume an individual shape, grew to be like a picture, a thing he would know again; not repulsive, strangely bud-like and touching. It had dark hair. He touched it with his finger, he wanted to see its eyes. They opened, they were dark — whether blue or brown he could not tell. . The eyes winked, stared, they had a sort of sleepy depth in them. And suddenly his heart felt queer, warm, as if elated.

" *Ma petite fleur!* " Annette said softly.

" Fleur," repeated Soames: " Fleur! we'll call her that."

The sense of triumph and renewed possession swelled within him.

By God! this — this thing was *his!*